hardcore
hardboiled

hardcore hardboiled

Edited by Todd Robinson
Introduction by Otto Penzler

KENSINGTON BOOKS
http://www.kensingtonbooks.com

KENSINGTON BOOKS are published by

Kensington Publishing Corp.
850 Third Avenue
New York, NY 10022

CONTENTS

Introduction

Otto Penzler

Okay, let's be clear about this. You go to a Website named *Thuglit*, or you buy a book titled *Hardcore Hardboiled*, you are definitely not hoping to find a new Agatha Christie story about an old little spinster in a village. You do not expect stories about vicars, rose gardens, tea, clothes shopping, recipes, or cats (unless maybe the recipe's essential ingredient is a cat). I also hope you are not looking for subtlety.

Guy calls his friend to say he's been castrated. "Bleeding's . . . bad," he says. "Why are you calling me?" his pal replies. "Call 9-1-1."

Girl finds her boyfriend shot dead, gaping hole in the chest, lying in a pool of blood. "Shit," she shouts. "Somebody finally got the bastard. Calls for a drink."

Kid looks at a really hot number and she spots him. "You don't stop gawking," she tells him, "I'm gonna cut you up like a Chink's dog."

The contributors to this volume are mostly young (even conceding that nowadays *everybody* seems young to me), writing in a style as colorful as Elton John's laundry. It is mostly vulgar, nasty, obscene, violent, and sewer-mouthed. It is visceral, unadorned, and crueler than a puppy juggler. Lines that you could quote to your mother are harder to find than Amelia Earhart.

If these stories have no more soft, fuzzy charm than funnel spiders, they make up for it with plots that are stuffed tighter than ballpark sausages. You have to look hard to find two consecutive pages that don't deal with sex or violence, but why would you want to? The whole point is that Thuglit, represented by these stories, reflects (though thankfully in a seriously heightened way) contemporary society, which offers abundant evidence of increased sexuality (when I was a kid, pubescent girls in America did not have sex, unless they were the kind of girls you'll find in this book) and growing violence (Mickey Spillane, the toughest guy anybody knew back in the dark ages of the 1950s, seems like a weenie of the first rank compared to the guys—and, sweet Jesus, the dolls—in this collection).

If you are sensitive and easily offended, I'm guessing this collection is not for you. There are men here whose softest part is their teeth. And they come in second to the women, whose warmth and compassion is as rare as Siberian haute cuisine. If you're man enough, you'll love this book. If you're not, give it to your girlfriend. If she accepts it and enjoys it, never turn your back on her.

A Message from Big Daddy Thug

What is Thuglit?

A couple years back, some friends and I complained loudly about the market for short crime fiction. Where was the edge? Where had it gone? Was it ever there in the first place?

Try as we might, we couldn't find a place for storytellers in the twenty-first century—a place that at least had the same allowances as network television. A place with tolerance (dare I say, love?) of good old-fashioned sex, violence, and bad behavior.

All we found were journals dedicated to publishing the type of fiction that my Great Aunt Sadie would approve of as she sat back in her rocking chair and drank Herbal Essences or whatever the hell they call that fruity tea crap.

We decided to start up a website—Thuglit.com—devoted to the kind of storytelling where no deed (good or bad) goes unpunished. No love is pure and every heart is clogged with greed, lust, and malice.

But what is Thuglit, you ask?

Thuglit is the darkness inside us all. It's painful and ugly and smells like the monkey pit at the zoo. And not just the monkey pit on a normal day.

Oh no.

It's the day when that smartass kid threw his leftover chili nachos through the bars and the monkeys are suffering through some serious gastrointestinal distress.

Breathe deep, my friends. It's that kind of stink.

Recognize it?

That's because it's inside you too.

Collected on these pages clutched between your sweaty little knuckles is the best from our first year. You're holding award nominees, award winners, and some new fiction by some of the best names in the business.

These stories contain some of the hardest, craziest, funniest fiction that anyone has ever written. There's the cop who breaks more laws than he defends. The lesbian killer in fishnets. Moralistic (and not-so) mobsters. The heroin-addicted ape engaging in pit fights. The ghosts of Johnny Cash and Ol' Blue Eyes haunt the streets. The lesbian killer. The memory-addled thief. Vampires with bad teeth. The pubic-ly challenged. Did I mention the lesbian?

Dive in. Enjoy the stink.

And Aunt Sadie? My apologies . . .

—TODD ROBINSON (BIG DADDY THUG)
August 13, 2007

Ten Dimes

Mike Toomey

The guy sat down next to me. He laid a deck of smokes down on the bar. Camels. "Beer," he said when Philly came around.

"Jesus Christ," Philly said, more to me. "Beer. I got sixteen friggin' beers back here."

"Pick one," the guy told him and we both watched as Philly drew a mug of his most expensive foreign lager.

The guy extracted a butt from the pack and lit it with a gold lighter, which he conspicuously examined before sliding it back into the deck. "I'm looking for a fence," he said without looking at me. I didn't say anything; everybody thinks they got something to sell. Most people got dick. Most people think that just because they stole it, somebody wants to buy it.

"I'm looking for a fence," he repeated with a rehearsed casualness.

"I heard ya," I said. "Try a carpenter."

I didn't say anything, just moved to a different stool further away from him. I can't buy from every guy who walks in off the street claiming he's got something to move.

Philly glanced at me. I made a subtle move with my head

and that was it. He took the guy's half-finished beer and dumped it in the sink behind the bar.

"I wasn't finished with that," the guy said.

"You're done," Philly told him. "C'mon, now get on out 'fore I toss ya out. Be a good guy, huh?"

"Sure. Sure thing," the guy said. He stood up slowly, put his jacket on and picked up his smokes. He started to leave, then hesitated. He turned to face me; I didn't move to look at him.

"C'mon, pally, will ya?" Philly said.

The guy raised his index finger asking for one minute before Philly came out from behind the bar. "How much will you give me for ten dimes?" he asked.

"A dollar," I answered and the guy walked out the door.

The Ten Dimes is a myth. It don't exist, a rumor everybody forgot to ignore. They were supposed to be in the box when The Man went under; they were supposed to be in the right-hand pocket of his tuxedo pants like they'd been for the previous thirty years. It became a habit in the sixties when his kid got snatched-up (the boy kid, not the girls). He always carried ten dimes in his pocket in case he needed to make phone calls. This was back before cell phones, a long time ago, when a pay phone cost ten cents. The Man was a creature of habit, and so, for the rest of his life—long after Jr. was back safe and sound—he carried ten dimes in his pocket. He liked to jingle them while he sang. So when he went down a few years ago, the family decided that when they put him under, the ten dimes should go with him—along with a gold lighter, a watch, a toy train from *Von Ryan's Express*, and a bunch of other shit he toted around with him.

Now the rumor; the story every half-assed gangster from the Strip tells is that somebody got the dimes. Some friend of a friend of the mortician went to see the body and lifted the ten dimes when everyone turned away. Some guys tell it with The Man's dimes being replaced with an ordinary ten dimes; some people have him going under with empty pockets. Either way, it's a good story because—short of exhuming him—there's really no way to prove or disprove it. The story had been up and down the Strip. Everybody knew a guy who knew a guy—but this was the first time anybody tried to sell them to me.

Three days later the guy came back. Word had been that he'd been to every other fence on the Strip and no one was buying. He pulled the same act as the first time; sitting down, ordering a beer, talking without looking at me.

"I got these things," he said.

"I know," I told him. I'd been thinking about him and his ten dimes since he left.

"I need to sell them," he said.

"I know," I told him.

We both sat sipping our drinks, not looking at each other.

"How do I know they're legit?" I asked.

He pulled the gold lighter out of the deck of Camels, lit one, and slid the lighter down to me. It was gold, real gold—heavy. A weight in your hands. There was a monogram on it: The Man's initials. Still, this proved nothing. Everybody knows his initials; the guy could have had this made. Still.

The guy stood up. He took a pull on his beer and a last drag on his smoke. He put the lighter into the deck and the deck into his pocket. "Listen," he said, "either you're going to believe me or you aren't. Obviously you aren't, so I'm sorry for having bothered you."

He headed for the door.

"Hey," I said. "Sit down."

"What?" the guy asked.

"I said sit down."

The guy sat down, next to me this time. I motioned Philly to pour us a couple. We waited until the beers were set and Philly was gone. We each took the head off our mug.

"If you even . . ." I started.

"I know," the guy said.

I could feel him looking at me occasionally but didn't turn to see.

"What do you want for 'em?" I asked.

"Two large," he answered.

"For the lot?" I asked.

"The lot?" he repeated. "Shit, apiece. Two grand apiece."

"Twenty grand for ten dimes?" I asked.

The guy just nodded.

"No chance," I told him. "Ten large."

I probably would have gone as high as twelve hundred dollars apiece, but we both agreed ten large was a fair price for a buck in change.

"You want to do this thing right now?" I asked.

"Yeah," he said. " 'Cause I carry 'em around with me all day."

"Where, then?"

He told me a place.

"You know where it is?"

"Yeah, I know."

"Like nine tonight?" he asked.

"Yeah," I said. "Nine tonight."

And he left without paying for his drink.

I pulled into the place at ten to nine and he was waiting there, engine running. He had a big old American car, Buick or something. The kind of car a half-assed gangster drove because it bore some resemblance to a Cadillac. Some people might call it a poor man's Cadillac—a Lincoln's a poor man's Cadillac, a Buick's a Buick. I waited to see if he would come and sit in with me. When he didn't, I went over to his car. He had Dean Martin on the tape.

"Hey," he said without looking.

"Hey," I answered in the same way.

"Dino," he said after an awkward beat of two guys in a car listening to the radio. "He could sing. He was a talent—you ever see *Rio Bravo*?"

I didn't answer.

"He could act, he was funny. He was the real deal, not like this guy."

I thought of Dino drinking apple juice on stage. Faking it in the later years while The Man was still chasing sunrises. "Yeah," I said.

"*From Here to Eternity*?" The guy continued. "That's bullshit too, he never went to the war."

"He was 4-F," I said quietly.

The guy paused, as if noticing I was there for the first time.

"He's what?" He was too young to know what it was.

"Never mind," I said. "You got it?"

"Yeah," he said. "Yeah." He pulled out a pouch and made it jingle so I could hear the coins inside.

"You got the money?" he asked. I reached into my coat and handed him an envelope. He counted it. Then handed me the pouch, which I didn't examine. We sat there for a minute, he put the envelope inside his coat.

I turned so I was facing him. "These are them, right?"

"Yeah," he answered.

"I mean, these were his, right?"

"I told you they were."

"These were supposed to go under with him?"

"What I say?"

I said The Man's name, full, with the middle name. He repeated it, as confirmation.

"You took them from him?"

"Yes," he said and repeated the name.

I jammed a screwdriver into his ear.

I left the money; I'm a fence, not a thief. I didn't take the money. I paid fair market value for the dimes. The money was his. I didn't do it for the money. I got money.

I met him once. We were both from the same place.

We both ended up in the same place. I met him once, years ago, a lifetime ago, when we were both passing through Big Town. We had mutual friends. They vouched for him; said he was a good guy, stand-up. Said he went to bat for the Clipper once with that broad he married.

We were in this bar and a friend we had in common pointed out that we were from the same place. We spent the rest of the night talking about it. I bought him a drink; he drank half of it and left the rest on top of a urinal. That's what he did. That's what he always did.

We talked about people we'd both known and the places we'd grown up. I told him he should write a song about it—*A man, broken, from Hoboken*—or something like that. You know what he told me? He couldn't read music. Can you imagine?

He was a good man. He didn't deserve what that guy did to him. I took the dimes myself and laid nine of them on his grave. I kept one. I don't think he'd mind. It cost me ten grand.

I think he'll understand. We were from the same place.

Brant Bites Back

Ken Bruen

Roberts, his commanding officer, had just joined Brant in the canteen. He had a tea and a slice of Danish—he'd been looking forward to it all morning. The pastry was fresh from the oven and he wasn't too happy about the way Brant was eyeing it. He'd been telling Brant about a new case, a guy was attacking women, beating the living shit out of them and then . . .

Get this.

Sinking his teeth in their neck and apparently sucking deep.

Brant reached over, and using his large thick fingers, tore a chunk off the Danish, asked, "You don't mind Guv, but I missed breakfast?"

Roberts was appalled, all the years they'd worked together and all the shite Brant had pulled, he still managed to amaze.

Brant popped the chunk in his mouth, chewed noisily and—Roberts felt—deliberately, then said, "A vampire, give me a fucking break."

He was now staring at the shredded remains of the ruined pastry and Roberts sighed, pushed it across the table. He couldn't eat it after this, said, "Knock yourself out."

Brant grabbed it, said, "Why we love you, Guv."

Always the loaded tone, you knew he was fucking with you but you could never quite pin him down. Now the bastard was eyeing his tea, no fucking way. Roberts gulped half of it down and near gasped—it was steaming hot, and burned the roof of his mouth.

Brant asked, "Jesus, you got a thirst there Guv, on the beer were you?"

Roberts, his so-called breakfast destroyed, resigned himself, got back to the biz in hand, said, "Whatever he is, he's got Clapham Common scared, women are afraid to go there anymore."

Brant wiped the crumbs from his mouth, using the sleeve of his sergeant's uniform, said, "I enjoyed that, bit stale though, you shouldn't let them fob that second hand gear on you Guv, you being a ranking officer and all."

Most of the time, Roberts wanted to wallop the be-jaysus out of Brant and he felt the desire all over again.

Brant asked, "How many victims?"

Roberts' mouth hurt from the burn and he said, "Four, but that's only those who've come forward. There may be more, you know women are sometimes reluctant to come forward."

Brant, the demonic smile in full neon said, "Why, we're not going to bite them?"

It was exactly the sort of comment that ensured Brant would never rise above his present rank.

The brass had been trying for years to get rid of him but whatever else, Brant was the ultimate survivor. Brown, their Super, never stopped trying to find some devious means of destroying Brant, even used a young cop named McDonald to try and bring Brant down.

Big mistake, especially for McDonald who was now, as Brant said, "worm take-away."

Brant asked, "So do we have any suspects?"

Roberts sighed. You were around Brant, you got to sigh.

A lot.

He said, "We checked out the all usual perverts, but a biter, no, we haven't had one of those . . . before."

Brant gave the wolfish smile, said, "Okay, a challenge as it were. I like a case I can . . . how would you put it, Guv, sink me teeth in?"

Jesus.

Brant stood, an imposing figure when he stood to full effect, the bulky frame, all muscle, the black Irish face and those hard eyes, pure granite and he had the aura of,

"You wanna fuck with me?

. . . . Bring it the fook on."

Roberts, twenty years on the force—all of them rough— knew one thing: when you had nothing, you did the one reli- able, you went to a snitch.

Trouble was, Brant's snitches had a history of coming to vi- olent ends, the most notable being one poor bastard who was literally kebabbed.

Testicles first.

Say what you will, London villains had a sense of humour, balls in the wringer you might say.

Caz, a guy who claimed to be from South America, a profes- sional dancer, had lasted longer than most. He was actually from Croydon but what was a little geography?

They got outside. Brant suggested they use his own car, say- ing, "We don't want to frighten the natives."

His car—well, his latest one—was a BMW . . . on a sergeant's salary?

They got in and as they pulled out, Brant said, "This motor purrs, Guv, you oughta get yer own self one of these babies."

Yeah, right.

Brant lit up one of his beloved Weights, a cigarette almost

impossible to get anymore and dragged deep, his Zippo flicking like a bad prayer, said, "Wanna hear some music, Guv?"

Without waiting for a reply, he hit the speakers and here came Tom Waits, a-wailing and a-moaning, Brant saying, "I tell you, guv, this bollix, he's had some wild nights. I'd love to have a pint with him."

Roberts, who liked his Sinatra, wondered if there was any reply to this and decided no, not if it involved sanity.

They parked outside a pub in Balham, not exactly a dive but not flash either, Brant looked at his watch, a Rolex, naturally, said, "Caz should be having his eye opener about now."

They walked into the pub and it had that awful morning-after aroma, cheap booze, nicotine linger, and dashed hopes.

Brant said, "I fucking love this hole."

The clientele consisted of a few elderly women, sipping on sweet sherry, an elderly guy, already slumped over a pint of mild, and Caz.

You couldn't miss him. His shirt—he favoured the most garish type that even Elvis wouldn't be, pardon the pun, found dead in. He had the shirt open to his navel; a large gold medallion filled the blank space.

He was wearing shades, though it was dark in the place. Deliberately.

The customers were not fond of light.

Much in common with vampires.

He had a tall glass of what looked like Coke but was sure to be loaded. His body language on their entry had been relaxed.

Not no more.

He'd tensed up, ready for flight, but he knew from sad experience there wasn't anywhere to hide from Brant. He took a deep gulp of his drink, shuddered, and waited.

Brant was in jovial tone, boomed: "Caz, me oul mate, how are you doing?" And sat right next to Caz. He took the drink, sniffed it, said, "Jesus, paint off a gate."

Roberts sat, watched as Caz lit a cig with a slight tremble in his hand—Brant or the booze or probably both.

Brant said, "This is my Guv so you be on yer best behaviour, I'm trying to impress him."

Brant had never tried to impress a living soul.

He looked at Roberts, said, "Guv, hop on up there, get us a large G and T, no ice. We need to like . . . blend."

Roberts moved, and the bar guy, looking like an over-the-hill bouncer, all tattoos, wasted muscle, sneered, "What can I get you, officer?"

Roberts gave him the look, said, "One tonic water."

The guy debated this then slurped a tonic into a far-from-clean glass, asked, "Anything else?"

Roberts, leaned over the counter, said in a very quiet voice: "Bit of fucking civility wouldn't go astray."

The guy, realizing he'd read Roberts all wrong, tried, "On the house, sir."

Roberts put the glass in front of Brant who raised his eyebrows then fired up a cig, said, "Caz believes he might have our case solved . . . already! Isn't that right, matey?" Brant took a swig of the tonic, grimaced, asked, "The fook is this?"

Roberts was delighted, said, "The proprietor had what you might term . . . an attitude."

Brant's face darkened then he suddenly walloped Caz on the back, nearly sending him across the table, said, "Don't be shy, spill all."

Caz took a large swallow of whatever concoction he had, and shuddered, looking like he might throw up. Roberts moved well back. Then the internal battle waging in his stomach eased and Caz, wiping sweat from his brow, said, "Phew, close call there."

Brant gave him an elbow in the gut, which wouldn't have helped the very recent healing, said, "Fascinating as your belly is to us, tell my Guv what you know."

He did.

A guy in his late twenties, recently back from Iraq, always dressed in black, was muttering in the clubs about vampires, creatures of the night, and a righteous cleansing.

His name was James Martin.

Roberts was highly skeptical—the southeast of London was jammed with nutters like this. He asked, "That's it, for heaven's sake?"

Brant was irritated, snapped, "Jesus, Guv, hold on, there's more."

There was.

The said Mr. Martin had lately been trying to sell jewelry, saying his new *followers* had bestowed it upon him.

Suddenly Roberts was keener; the victims had all had their rings, earrings ripped from them. He asked, "And where does said Mr. Martin hang his . . . cape?"

Caz sat back, a positive glow in his cheeks, the cure kicking in, big time.

Roberts asked, "What?"

Brant gave a tolerant shrug, said, "He needs paying, Guv, the poor man has to live, them shirts don't come cheap."

Roberts got his wallet out, saw he had two twenties and pulled out one.

Brant said, "Aw, Guv, don't be like a cheap date," and grabbed the other twenty, but didn't give it to Caz.

Roberts, all out of patience, asked: "You might want to contribute yourself . . . Sergeant?"

Brant said, "My gratitude is never soiled by mere cash."

Caz, surprised to have received anything at all, put the twenty away, said, "He lives with his mother—19, Clapham Terrace."

Brant said, "Hope he hasn't taken a bite out of her, least not yet." Brant was on his feet, said, "Guv, we can't sit here all day, let's hit the road."

Caz, well on his way to a whole new inebriation, offered Roberts: "I can get you one of these shirts, special rate, you'd be XL . . . right?"

The XL hurt, Roberts had been on a diet, thought it showed.

Brant said, "Get him a half dozen, he might not seem it but he's a pretty colorful guy."

Outside, getting in the car, Roberts was surprised that Brant had let the bar guy fuck with him when Brant said, "Just a sec, Guv, left me fags on the table."

He was back in a few minutes, carrying three bottles of gin, said, "Nice guy that barman, wanted us to have these on account."

Roberts, getting into the motor, asked, "On account of what?"

Brant was putting the bottles in the backseat, said, "On account of I only broke one of his fingers."

As they pulled away, Roberts said, "Give me my twenty, you only gave that poor slob one of them."

Brant, cutting off a black cab, said, "You know, Guv, I don't mean this as a criticism but you're a bit mercenary, a little too obsessed with material things. You ever read 'Desiderata'?"

Roberts, horrified lest Brant recite the bloody thing, said, "Turn left, it will bring us on to the terrace."

Brant lighting a cig and doing a rapid, illegal U-turn at the same time, said, "You'd look good in one of those shirts, you have the weight to carry it off."

They were coming up on the terrace when Brant asked, "Think we should swing by a grocery?"

Roberts, seriously pissed now, unable to get past the twenty—forty—quid near-screamed, sarcasm leaking over his tone. "What, you need a fucking apple, that it?"

Brant, adopting mock hurt, went, "Whoa, big fellah, what's with the sour grape?"

Let that awful pun hover then:

"Garlic . . . you know, can't be too careful."

Roberts might have punched him then but they'd arrived at the house. Brant said, "Ah, de Count."

The house was unremarkable, well-kept but all the curtains were drawn.

Roberts said, "Now for once, you shut the fuck up, hear— I'll lead this investigation."

Brant was reaching in his jacket, took out a Ruger, checked the clip, slammed it home then eased it into the right pocket of his jacket.

Roberts could have reamed him a new one right there for carrying but shook his head, said, "Try not to shoot me."

Brant said, "Friendly fire you mean?"

Roberts had a moment; he knew Brant was more than capable of it. Roberts rang the doorbell, Brant behind him, whistling . . . *there were seven Spanish angels.* . . .

A woman in her late sixties opened the door; she had snow white hair, a pleasant expression, but her eyes were terrified.

Roberts produced his warrant card, said who they were and might they come enter.

She moved aside and seemed to curl in on herself.

Roberts asked, "You were expecting us, weren't you Mrs. Martin? You are Mrs. Martin, mother of James?"

She began to cry, Roberts tried to soothe her, said, "It's okay, everything's going to be fine, we'll take it nice and slow. You want Sergeant Brant to make you a nice cup of tea?"

She was shaking her head, and between sobs, managed, "Ever since he came home from Iraq, he's been different; he used to be such a good boy."

Roberts was glancing round the front room, as cops do, taking in everything and noticed no mirrors, and a blank space on the wall still held the trace where a crucifix had once hung.

Roberts asked, "Where is James now?"

A voice answered, "Who trespasses in the house of the undead?"

A tall, good-looking man was coming slowly down the stairs, dressed in a long black cape and nothing else. He had flowing blond hair and looked completely deranged. He was carrying a lethal-looking sword.

Brant muttered, "Fucking loony tunes."

And Mrs. Martin fainted.

Neither cop tried to catch her, their full attention on the advancing figure, Roberts ordered: "James, come on, mate, you don't want to do anything silly, put the sword down and we'll have a cuppa, bit of a chat, and . . ."

Martin lunged with the sword, catching Roberts in the shoulder, cutting a wide gash across it, blood spurting in an arc.

Brant said:

"Fuck this."

Shot the guy twice in the head.

Martin fell backwards on the stairs and Brant moved to him, pulled down his bottom lip, said, "No fangs, huh?"

When the various emergency crews had arrived and Roberts had been loaded into an ambulance, Superintendent Brown said to Brant, "Did you have to shoot him?"

Brant looked him straight in the eyes, said, "I was all out of stakes, sir."

Roberts was released from hospital the following evening, bandaged to the hilt, given painkillers and warned not to drink. Brant was waiting outside, asked, "Want to get drunk?"

Oh yeah.

They did, massively.

It was a week later when Roberts woke from a fevered sleep, felt a sharp pain and at first, thinking it was his shoulder acting up, he staggered to the bathroom, got the light on and then as he looked in the mirror, to his horror, he saw two puncture wounds in his throat.

They heard his howl as far away as Clapham.

The Long Count

Sam Edwards

*P*onk.

That was the sound in Rusty's head. Just like one of the cartoon sound effects on the *Batman* show. Unfortunately, it was also the sound of the big guy's pinky ring as it bounced off his upper left canine.

When the chirping birdies cleared, Rusty managed a response to the somewhat unexpected blow. "Ow."

The shot to the mouth was only somewhat unexpected since Hermes, the flyweight who had been working the heavy bag under Rusty's tutelage, took the first swing. Hermes was on his back, down for the long count.

"Aw, hell," Rusty said, less in pain from his mouth than at seeing yet another prospect unconscious on the mat. Granted, Hermes was a flyweight and the puncher was clearly a heavyweight, but still. He should have been able to take one goddamn punch. Or had the reflexes to get the hell out of the way. "Look what you did to my boxer. That ain't right."

"Do I have your attention, Mr. Cobb?" The voice was a syrupy Texas drawl. Rusty leaned around the heavyweight to see its owner. Jesus, Rusty thought, I'm being rousted by Hopalong Cassidy. The guy was standing in a Brooklyn gym wearing an embroidered western shirt and a brown ten-gallon hat.

"Chaps."

"Excuse me?"

"You need chaps to finish that outfit, *pardner*."

The cowboy nodded at the heavyweight, who grabbed Rusty by the front of his sweatshirt and backhanded him across the mouth. Small blessing, but the second shot cleanly knocked out the canine that was cracked in the first punch. At least he'd save on the dentist bill.

"Nobody likes a smart mouth, Mr. Cobb."

"Please, we've shared so much already, call me Rusty." He spat and his tooth bounced once and landed on Hermes's limp glove.

"This isn't a Sunday social, Mr. Cobb." The cowboy took his hat off and wiped his sweaty brow.

It was hot in the gym. Rusty kept it that way on purpose. A page he stole from the old Kronk Gym in Detroit for conditioning fighters. Maybe if he waited long enough, his two visitors would pass out from heat exhaustion. "So I shouldn't bother with the fine china, then. You mind telling me what this is about?"

"Don't insult me by pretending you don't know why I'm here." Cowboy bit the end off of a cigar the size of a biscuit can. He spit the wet tobacco right on Hermes's forehead. Hermes didn't even stir. One time contender, now human spittoon. The goon whipped out a lighter that looked like it cost more than a Buick. Cowboy puffed a few times, rolling the cigar for an even burn. "Don't insult me by telling me you don't know who I am."

Rusty tried. He didn't have to try hard. He was sure that he'd remember such a ridiculous character. Something about the goon itched at the back of his head, but that was it. As far as Cowboy was concerned, nothing. "Sorry, Hoss. Never really listened to The Village People."

Cowboy waved his hand wearily at Rusty. "Hurt him," he sighed.

The goon palmed the lighter like a roll of quarters and came forward for round three. Rusty was ready this time. It had been almost two decades since he'd been in a ring, but the moves were still there. Like riding a bicycle. A middle-aged bicycle in desperate need of oiling, but still able to out-speed a heavy-weight. Rusty ducked the haymaker, crouching low and bringing his fist up and under the big guy's ribcage. The goon *woofed* as Rusty drove his fist deep into his sternum. Then Rusty brought his left straight into the guy's balls. What the hell. They weren't in a ring, so Rusty wasn't worried about losing a point. The goon dropped to his knees.

God bless steel-toed boots, Rusty thought as he punted the goon's chin. The kick lifted him off the floor and on his back, splayed out next to Hermes. Knockout, Rusty thought proudly before he put weight on his kicking foot. Not being in fighting condition, the kick had wrenched his ankle. "Ah, shit," Rusty yelled as he dropped, clutching his foot.

Either way, he was just about to get up and hobble himself over for some cowboy ass-kicking when he heard the unmistakable click of a gun.

Jeez. The guy was actually carrying a six-shooter. Cowboy had it pointed directly between Rusty's eyes. "Nice moves, Mr. Cobb. I'd applaud, but I might accidentally pull the trigger and blow your face off."

"Please then, hold your applause until intermission."

"There is no intermission, Mr. Cobb. This is a one-act. At the end, you either return what you stole, or you disappear."

"Oh, it's like *Tony and Tina's Wedding*, then."

Cowboy didn't get that one. "You have three days." The big

guy groaned and got up groggily. Cowboy shook his head disgustedly at his thug.

"That's a long play."

"You seem to be the only one playing here, Mr. Cobb. I'm not." Cowboy pushed the still staggering goon out the door.

Rusty was a thief. A petty thief, at best. Stole petty items. Petty cash, for instance. Nothing worth the trouble that Cowboy seemed intent on causing him. No fine art. No heirlooms. Shit, more often than not, the jewelry that he pocketed fell into the categories of costume or out-and-out worthless.

Like a lot of serviceable but non-contender boxers, Rusty needed work not long into his thirties when it became obvious that his minor talents were heading south. He delivered packages for a messenger service. Sometimes, those packages were C.O.D. When the receptionist went into the little metal cash boxes, Rusty made mental notes. The next day, dressed in his only decent suit, Rusty would walk into the offices early while the cleaning crews were still working, stuff the box in his valise and walk right out. If he had to sign in at the security desk, he just wrote in S.R. Leonard. Rusty wondered if Sugar Ray had ever been questioned about the thefts.

His record low was $14.75 at a small dot com. His record high was almost a grand out of some big shot literary agent. Fuck 'em, Rusty would think. He'd worked with a manager/agent for a few years. The sonofabitch dropped him faster than a handful of shit the second the ref counted to ten in Rusty's last fight. Rusty got a quiet enjoyment out of burglarizing agents. They were all a bunch of bloodsucking thieves themselves.

If he came into an office that had expensive little laptop computers, Rusty would help himself to a few and pawn them for a couple extra hundred. It was that money that eventually enabled him to buy the old gym in Brooklyn. Nowadays, if he pulled a grab, it was more for shits and giggles than actual need.

Some people liked blackjack for their gambling; Rusty enjoyed a little trespassing and B&E.

And it was all little. Little was the operative word. Worst came to worst, Rusty would only have to suffer minor legal consequences. Even when he hooked up with Dante, they made sure they took only cash and easily pawned items. For reasons he couldn't figure, Cowboy seemed to believe that he had something that belonged to him. And he wanted it back.

Unfortunately, Rusty didn't have clue one what that item could be.

"A cowboy?"

"A cowboy," Rusty sighed. Dante wasn't an idiot. He sometimes could be slow, or dull or . . . ah hell, who was he fooling? Dante was an idiot. But he was an idiot that could open safes faster than the people who knew the combinations. He was like Rain Man, if Rain Man was a thief.

"Like cowboys and indians?" Dante asked.

"No, like cowboys and spaghetti-o's," Rusty yelled into the phone.

"Cowboys and spaghetti-o's? I don't get you, Rusty."

Jesus.

"Just listen to me, will you, dipshit? Has anyone been into the shop lately? Maybe wearing a cowboy hat? Walking his pet gorilla? Carrying a six-shooter and a lot of questions?"

"A gorilla?"

Rusty slammed the phone down. Dante was obviously off of Cowboy's radar. By Rusty's estimation, Dante had accompanied him on his last five jobs, going back three years. One morning, Rusty walked into an office and found Dante under the desk, looting a floor safe. He was dressed in a jumpsuit and looked as scared as Rusty felt. They stared at each other for a few seconds before Dante offered Rusty the glittering contents in his left hand.

"Halfsies?" he offered, hopefully.

From that point on, they worked as a team. Rusty would scout the offices, determine which ones were worth hitting and bring in Dante for the safes. Dante brought his skills and Rusty brought his brains and helpful advice. Such as the suggestion that the retard didn't wear his A-1 Computer Service jumpsuit when he was going to rob a fricking office.

So Dante was out. Stupid, maybe, but Rusty doubted that he would just forget encountering the cowboy.

Next step. Information. Information meant Jameel and the candy boys. The candy boys were a scam that ran its fingers through most of the city. A small army of kids roamed the streets, selling candy bars for their sports team at a buck a pop.

There was no sports team.

Jameel was the local sergeant for the Brooklyn troops. The kids got five dollars for each box they sold. Each box had forty candy bars in it. Buying gross, the boxes cost five dollars each. Thirty dollars in profit on every box sold. There were more than a hundred kids selling box after box 365 days a year. Nobody knew who was at the top of the heap, but whoever he was, he was one rich bastard.

Now the underbosses, like Jameel, had a side business. That business was information. Hundreds of little eyes and ears across the city was an amazing resource. For the price.

"Two hundred."

"One hundred, just for the name." Rusty was uncomfortable standing on the open corner. Even though Jameel probably had a couple of thousand on his person at the time, Rusty wasn't worried about getting caught in the middle of a robbery. A while back, one of the sergeants got rolled. Less than twenty-four hours later, three teenagers were found under the bridge, throats cut, cheeks stuffed with M&M's. No, Rusty just worried what his neighbors might think.

"Don't have a name. Got something else. A hundred-fifty for it." Jameel scratched at his belly. The front of his basketball jersey lifted, showing the hilt of a butterfly knife in his waistband.

Rusty took the money and palmed it into Jameel's hand. Christ, he hoped nobody was watching.

Without even looking, Jameel rolled his fingers around the paper. "The top bill's fake."

"What?"

Lifting up the hundred to the sunlight, Jameel said, "See? No watermark. It's counterfeit, yo. You trying to play me, Rusty?"

Rusty looked at it. Shit. He reached into his pocket and pulled out a crumpled wad of bills and handed them to Jameel.

"Only eighty-three here, Rusty. Falls a little short."

Rusty gritted his teeth. "That's all I have."

Jameel thought about it, then stuffed the money away. "Okay. The man's a Bleecker Street player. Don't know what his business is, but my boys see him at that blues club all the time."

"The Queen of Diamonds?"

"It's on the second floor, right? Above that Thai place with the big ugly ass orange awning?"

"Yeah."

"That's the one."

Rusty knew the club, but for the life of him still couldn't figure any connection. "How did he get pointed in my direction?"

Jameel chuckled. "Shit, man. How does anybody get information in this town?"

Rusty swallowed the hard lump that formed in his throat. "You told him."

Jameel grinned wide. "Damn right." Jameel could see the tension in Rusty as he clenched his fists. "What?" Jameel opened his arms wide, challenging. "You got a problem with that? The man had the cash and he paid. Not the bullshit scratch that you got, either."

Following his best survival instincts, Rusty turned and walked away fast, before he did something stupid.

"Nice doing business with you, Rusty," Jameel catcalled down the street.

Rusty wanted nothing more than to turn back and beat the snot out of the punk. He knew however, besides being suicidal, it just wouldn't look right, roughing up a twelve-year old like that.

"Ah! My friend!" came the deeply accented bellow from the back of Abboud's Pawn. Rusty never liked the way Ali called him "friend." First off, he called everybody friend. Secondly, there was a slight undertone, as though he could replace it with "sucker" without missing a beat. "What do you bring for Ali today?"

"Just got a couple of questions, pal-o-mine." Rusty walked over to the plexiglass and chicken wire cage that Ali cocooned himself in. For such good friends, Ali never even unlocked it to so much as shake Rusty's hand in twenty years.

"This no good information booth, Rusty. Maybe you try Times Square." Ali cackled at his own joke. Rusty felt blood rush to his ears. "Maybe you go see *Rent.*" Ali cackled harder. The only thing that ever emerged from Ali's box was his breath. The laughter pushed a wave over Rusty that smelled of yogurt and chickpeas.

"I'm serious Ali."

"So am I. *Rent* very good show. My children love it."

"I'm more interested in cowboys."

"Then see *Annie Get Your Gun.* Why do you bother Ali with no business? I'm busy man."

In those same twenty years, Rusty had rarely seen another human in the shop. More often than not, it was Ali's wife, who was usually screeching Arabic at him in a voice that reminded Rusty of a cat with strep.

"I don't want to see a fucking musical, Ali. I got guys asking questions."

Ali's eyes made a quick flash from their usual greedy glow into fear. "What? What questions? What did you tell them? I run honest business."

"No you don't."

"Doesn't matter."

"Yes it does. They think I took something from them."

"What did you take?" Ali scratched his stubble, intrigued.

"I don't know."

"They no tell you?"

"They seem to think I should know."

"Ah! Is like movie *Marathon Man*. Great movie. 'Is it safe?' Did they ask you that? Did they ask you if it was safe?"

"Goddamn it!"

"Never mind. Okay, okay. What do you want to know from Ali?"

"Have I ever brought you anything . . . ? Was there anything that you ever got from me that might have wound up worth more or wasn't what I thought it was?"

"No, Rusty. Ali would never cheat you like that."

Truth was, Ali would cheat anybody like that. But the reason that Rusty did business with Ali, apart from his moral ambiguity regarding purchase and resale of stolen goods, was that despite it all, he was a terrible liar. He was too greedy. Whenever he tried to pull a fast one or short-change, he would break out in a sweat faster than a pig in a sauna.

Ali wasn't sweating.

Rusty fingered the hundred-dollar bill in his pocket. "I need a gun then."

Ali brightened back up. "Ah! Ali have many guns. Give old friend deep discount. How much?"

Rusty held up the hundred.

"Hundred is fake."

God*damn* it! Rusty muttered a stream of curses as he stormed out the door.

Ali was still yelling as the door shut behind him. "Ali give you nice set of steak knives for bad bill! No gun, but you stab somebody good!"

As he walked down Houston, Rusty turned into a quiet bar. He ordered a scotch, downed it, ordered another before the cute bartender put the bottle back. First luck he had all day. The bartender didn't catch the fake bill. God bless New York's bar scene, where perky tits outweighed brains and skill any day.

He sat in a cloud trying to think. Who was he kidding? He had nothing. He was five miles north of nothing and three west of clue one.

It couldn't have been anything that the cowboy wanted public, or else why not just send cops?

Weapons? By his best estimation, he'd acquired about a half dozen guns or so over the years. All of them went to Ali. Maybe one of them would have been evidence in a murder case? Nope. Figuring in the cowboy's style and readiness to draw, none of the guns he'd stolen were six-shooters.

Drugs? Nope. Couldn't have been. In many a safe, Rusty found the gamut from Valiums to what looked like a half pound of uncut Colombian. They always left it behind. He and Dante agreed that drugs weren't any direction they wanted to head in, business-wise. Dante may have been an idiot, but he wasn't stupid.

Computers? Dante took care of the computers. He wiped out the hard drives, then sold them in his computer shop. Maybe there was some kind of damaging file on one of the computers. It still amazed Rusty that someone as mentally and physically clumsy as Dante could have such careful fingers on a keyboard.

Deft fingers that were capable of pocketing something before Rusty knew what was in the safe. Jumpsuits had lots of pockets.

Before Rusty could leap up and run over to strangle himself a retard, the bartender squealed and ran to the door. "Yancy! Get in here! You better not be walking by without saying hi." In the doorway, she leapt into a pair of arms, peppering the face with affectionate kisses. Very big arms. The cowboy's goon carried the girl back into the bar, placed her down, and sat in the stool next to Rusty.

"Hiya, Rusty," he said.

"Hiya, Yancy. Funny coincidence, isn't it?"

"What? Oh. Well, to be honest, yeah." Yancy actually blushed.

The bartender started pouring a pint before the keg sputtered and died. She clucked her tongue. "I got to go down and change the keg. Don't you leave." She pointed an admonishing finger at Yancy before she walked out back.

"Cute kid," said Rusty.

"Yeah. I used to work the door here. I was following you. The coincidence was that you came in here."

"This before or after Tua?"

Yancy looked surprised. "I guess it wouldn't have taken you long to figure it out at this point. Did you see it?"

"In person." Yancy Benevides was a young heavyweight who made the mistake of running into six too many of David Tua's hooks one night in Vegas. Rusty watched the whipping from the front. The fight was on the same card as one of Rusty's not-so-hopefuls. That was why he looked familiar. "Was that your last?"

Yancy tapped at his right eyebrow. "They removed part of my ocular bone. Nicely dislocated my cornea, too. Fucking Hawaiian hits harder than a mule kick."

"He's Samoan."

"Either way. Was Hearns your last?"

Now it was Rusty's turn to be surprised. "Yeah. The famous right. Did you see it?"

"Over and over. Broke my Dad's heart. You were his Great White Hope. In a way, I was kinda honored when you punched me in the gym. Until you hit me in the balls."

"Sorry." Rusty wasn't sure if he was apologizing for the low blow or for Mr. Benevides's heart.

Yancy shrugged. "S'okay, I guess. I'm gonna stop following you now, since you know I'm here and all."

"All right."

"Mr. Queen wanted me to tell you that you got one more day." Yancy caught himself. "Forget I said that." He tapped his eyebrow again as he stood in explanation of his gaffe.

"Already knew," Rusty lied. "Queen of Hearts. That where you met him?"

"Yup. Working the door."

"So, boxer to bouncer to goon? Dad must be proud."

Yancy shrugged. "Pays better than either of the first two. How much does thief pay?"

"Touché."

"Oh, and I owe you this." Yancy brought his huge fist into Rusty's crotch, mashing his testicles into the bar stool. Rusty moaned and slumped to the floor. When he found the strength to open his eyes, he was looking up at the bartender.

"You're gonna have to leave, Mister."

They were remarkably perky tits, Rusty thought as he wondered whether his balls would ever work again.

The hole was small and right between Dante's eyebrows. Dante's vacant eyes were crossed, as if trying to look up and into the hole that had opened there. Rusty fought the crazy urge to look in the hole for any evidence of a brain. Instead, he rooted through the pockets of Dante's jumpsuit. Seventeen-hundred dollars. Not bad. Rusty knew the old adage to be true. Nobody was more paranoid about theft than a thief. Lucky for him, Dante wasn't bright enough to find a hiding place anywhere but on his body.

It all came together in Rusty's mind. He'd been fighting the wrong fight all along. Never go toe-to-toe with a puncher when you're a boxer.

Last round.

Ding.

Rusty left the message at The Queen of Hearts that he'd meet them there at five a.m. After closing, but before Bleecker Street would have any morning traffic. Rusty got off the train at Second Avenue and jogged the remaining mile, feeling his blood pump, the muscles loosen up. He felt good. He jogged up the stairs to the club, marveling at the god-awful orange awning as he passed it. He knocked on the wooden door. Yancy opened it and stepped aside.

Mr. Queen smiled a big Texas grin as he came in. "Mr. Cobb. I'm so glad that you decided to do business here, clean up the mess you made, and such."

Rusty pulled the metal box out of his backpack. "First of all, let me apologize for any inconvenience this has caused you. I didn't know what it was when I took it and I sure as hell didn't know how important it was when I did."

Queen smiled wider. "Bygones and such. Yancy?"

Yancy took the box from Rusty and with his other hand grabbed the hood of Rusty's sweatshirt, choking him.

Queen took the box and stepped back. "Just so's we're sure you're not trying to pull a switcheroo here."

"Suit yourself," Rusty croaked.

Queen thumbed the lock on the box.

Three.

Queen opened the box. Rusty spun, catching Yancy with a

hook right on the eyebrow he'd pointed to. Yancy let go of the hood and wobbled noticeably.

Two.

Queen looked up, his face a mask of rage. "You sonoafa . . ." He dropped the box and reached for his gun. Rusty threw the dazed Yancy into the space between Queen and himself. Yancy stumbled and fell into the gun. His body muffled the shot, but a red blossom opened on his back.

One.

Rusty dove out the second story window into the ass-ugly orange awning.

BOOM

The explosion blew out all the windows facing Bleecker.

Rusty never figured out just what he was supposed to have stolen.

Dante's money had been enough to buy a timing cap and a small quantity of plastique from Ali. Small, but enough for one good bang. With ultimate caution, Rusty attached the cap to the lock on the box and stuffed the lower part of the tiered box with the explosive, turning the metal casing into a great big shrapnel grenade.

The concussion nearly threw Rusty over the awning, but he caught the edge, rolled, and came down hard on the street. He was covered with shards of glass, but the thick sweatsuit had protected him from any major cuts.

He lay on the concrete for as long as he could afford, did a quick mental inventory of his parts, decided they were intact and carefully got up. Time to go. His ears rang loudly and he feared he wouldn't hear approaching sirens.

On the corner of Lafayette, Rusty found a slightly burned cowboy hat. He stuffed it into his backpack and started the jog back to Brooklyn.

Johnny Cash Is Dead

Jordan Harper

I drove all the way across town to cut up this son of a bitch, but it's these three flights of stairs that got me worried. Usually when a man goes to see another man on business, it's the other fellow that he needs to keep his eye on. But my leg was my problem. My left knee started stinging something fierce while I was coming from old North Springfield to the southeast where they built all the malls and new apartments. Some old folks just like to complain for being left alive so long. I'm not like that, but my knee is. I smashed it thirty years ago at Marion, wrestling with a convict and taking a tumble down some stairs. Never liked long stairs since.

In the Ozarks we get about two weeks of spring before it gets hotter than a whore in church, and this was one of those fine April days after the cold and before the thunder and the heat. The whippoorwills were still singing when I got to that big apartment building on the corner of Glenstone and Cherry, and there wasn't any stirring in any of the apartments I could see. The building was cheap yellow siding with concrete decks for each apartment. Most of the decks had little black grills and a few beer bottles on them. Mostly young folks from the school lived there, and not many that age see the sun rise unless they didn't sleep at all.

There was a tiny red sports car, just like Mandy told the police, parked across two spots. And above it sat three stories worth of concrete steps to the door of his apartment, number 309, just like it said in the arrest report I had there in the truck. There was a good chance I'd be using both hands on the railing before I made it to the top and out in the open where I could look like an old man in front of God and the world. I parked the truck next to his car, cutting off "Don't Take Your Guns to Town" in the middle. My grandson tells me that folks his age are listening to Johnny Cash, but he's just a man in a costume to them. They can't feel the music in the aches in their bones. He's dead now besides.

I pushed the .38 in my pocket so I wouldn't have to hunt for it, made sure that the rope was in the bag, along with the knife and stone, the gauze and the papers I'd taken from the courthouse. I reckon that was stealing, taking those files, but the court already decided that they'd done all they'd cared to with them. One of the papers was paperclipped to the photo of Mandy, her eye blood-clotted, that they'd taken at the hospital. I shut the bag.

The climb burned hellfire on my knee, and my lungs started to feel like they were coated in molasses. Lucky not to have keeled over on the landing between floors, I leaned over against the wall a spell, thinking Louise would curse me for a fool for climbing them at all. I knew damn well she'd call me a lot worse than "fool" if she learned what I had planned for the rest of the morning. So I pushed her from my mind, got up that last flight of steps and knocked on number 309.

It took a few times before I heard some rustling from the other side of the door. Heath Jackson opened it, looking all gummed up in the face and confused, wearing nothing but a pair of drawers. In court, he'd been spit-shined and in a suit, but standing there in that doorway he looked gruff and dumb just like the sorry bastard he was.

I guess he didn't get too many old men with guts hanging over their belts and faces full of sweat coming to see him. He just stared at me without a "hello" or nothing. And he didn't see the gun until it was right there in his face.

"Son, you and I have a little business to take care of."

When I walked the turn at Marion, I fought a lot of convicts bigger and meaner than Jackson, and I'd always gone man to man. I figured that although it might feel easier to clout the man with my club, he might just figure the next day he could whup me in a fair fight. I finished that idea before he even got it. You get the best of a man because you had a piece of iron and he didn't, well, you didn't best him at all. The fellow who shot Jesse James proved that. So it pained me to have to use this gun to get Jackson's attention. It was all bluff anyway. I had the drop on him, but the .38 wasn't cocked and there weren't but two feet between us. That young fellow could have snatched that gun from me right quick before I could have pulled the trigger and spoiled my day.

He was a big son of a bitch, too—played ball in school, and had those fancy-cut muscles the young men have these days. They look real nice, but to me they're like flowers grown in a hothouse. In my time I knew some big farm boys who baled hay all day long, and maybe you couldn't pick out every muscle they had, but you'd sure as hell know they were there if that fellow pasted you.

But, just like I figured, he couldn't make a move. It don't look like much from the side, but a barrel can look awful deep when you look straight down it. It grabs your attention. So I pushed my way inside, brushed right past him and shut the door.

His place was painted real nice and filled with fancy furniture, so that you knew he hadn't picked none of it himself. And it smelled like an old barroom. Empty beer cans with bits of ash around the hole were piled next to the phone on the counter that separated the kitchen from the rest of the room. That's where the sink was, and a garbage disposal, and I was going to be needing that later. The bigger part of the room had a couch facing a TV four times the size of the one I have, and a small little dining room table with two chairs, which was just what I needed.

"Now you just have a seat and mind your manners and I won't paint the walls with you," I said. "Don't get smart."

He might have been half-asleep when I got there, but he sure was awake now. "What is—? Who are you?"

"Don't remember me? Well, a man sitting in the dock has other things to do besides look for old men sitting in the stands, so I don't take offense. I'm John Mashburn. Mandy Pearson is my granddaughter."

Every day he was in court, I was there. Just watching him, whispering with his lawyers. Looking all smug and serious and innocent as the judges and lawyers read motions and whispered at the bench. I sat there every day because Mandy needed representing and she wouldn't stand to be in the same room as him, and her mother was barely able to make it through the day and her father is worthless and lives in another state now besides. I was there until the very last day. Charges just thrown out the window because Mandy had to go and take a shower to wash the stink of his touch off her before she got the nerve to call the police. "He said, she said," they said, and that's all they were going to do about it. I saw Jackson's cute little mask come off when the judge rapped the gavel. I saw that smile bloom on his face like a flower growing on cow shit. And I saw that prosecutor not look me in the eyes as he walked out of the room and that's when I knew that if someone was going to stand up for Mandy then it was going to be me.

"Now, sir, I think we'd better talk about this."

"Oh, we're going to talk about it alright," I said, "but you're going to sit down now or you'll be laying down in a second. Now take that seat."

The chair looked maple but wasn't as strong, but it didn't feel like he could bust it, either. So I got him sat down and had him put his hands behind his back and got the rope out. The whole time he was still talking a blue streak, but I didn't pay no mind. I worked the rope through the slats of the chair and around his wrists. I had him lace his fingers together behind his back so his thumbs were pointing up in the air and got to work tying the knot. My fingers aren't so nimble as they were, but I got it as tight as I could. I gave my hands a shake to get the sting out, picked up the pistol and pulled another chair so I was facing Jackson from about six feet away, close enough to hear him good but far enough away to get a shot off if I had to. He was still talking.

". . . and I want you to know the truth. I mean, don't you think you should hear the truth first?"

"Alright, son. Let's hear your piece."

I can't remember all of what he said, but you should have heard it. A preacher caught in his neighbor's bed couldn't have talked any faster. He said, "I don't blame you for coming up here, either. In fact, I think Amanda has every right to be proud of you for sticking up for her, but I just don't think that this is what you want to be doing with yourself right now. I don't know what you're planning to do to me, sir, but you know you won't get away with it. I don't think Amanda wants her grandfather to go to jail," and just kept going.

He was wearing that mask again, but I saw where it didn't fit him around the eyes. Those were just cold. They didn't move or change with the rest of his face. You spend enough time around convicts and criminals, you learn these things. It's the eyes every time. He thought he was going to sweet talk this hillbilly old man and he slipped on that mask like it was nothing. You might think it's brave to be able to smile at a man who's got you tied up and covered cold, but it wasn't, not this time. Even though I had the drop on him, he'd taken a look at my old jeans pulled up past my belly and my work shirt older than he was and didn't see a man like him staring back. He was just saying "good dog" to a bad one.

"Look, I know you treasure your granddaughter. She's a beautiful, smart girl. But times are different now. You might think she's innocent, but she's a normal girl. And maybe we got a little rough, but she told me she liked it rough, you know. And yeah, we got a little out of control, but there was a lot of alcohol involved and it was just a misunderstanding between two consenting adults. That's all it was."

"Maybe you think that you can try and tell me things are different now than they used to be, but I lived back then and I live right now and I'm the one who knows both. So let me tell you, there's always been fellows like you who think they're slicker than owl shit. Folks always wanted to get a piece of action before they were married, and quite a few always have. There's always been whiskey and beer and girls who like to try it as much as a man does. And there's always been bastards like you who thinks that's the easy way to get in a woman's drawers." I opened up the bag at my feet and took the whetstone out, just to watch him eye it. "I saw Mandy that morning. I saw her face, goddamn you."

"Now, wait a minute!"

"Be quiet now. I know that Mandy's telling the truth and you ain't. But even if I wasn't sure, it wouldn't matter to me. She's my blood and under my care, and you're not. So you're the one who's answering to me." With that I pulled out the knife, long with an elk horn handle and hard iron blade. That got him sitting up.

"What are you doing?"

I liked to hear the fear that he couldn't keep under control anymore. I scraped the knife against the grain of the whetstone, real slow, just for show. The blade was already sharp enough to split a hair, but I liked watching the scraping sound run up and down his spine with each pass.

"Well, now, I thought a long time about what to do with you. First thought, of course, was just to blow your goddamn head off, and it's not much more than you deserve. Not much more, but more just the same. So, like I told you, you just sit still and take what's coming to you and you'll wake up tomorrow. So I thought about cutting your pecker off to make sure you can't ever do again what you did to my Mandy. And I like the sound of that." I let him stew on that for a second. "But it wasn't your meat alone that did what you did. It was your hands that held her down and let you get your way. So that's how I decided I'd make sure you'd never hold another woman by the throat again. I'm going to take off your thumbs."

The chair proved itself right then; it didn't break. Jackson was breathing hard and high now, and his mask was gone and he looked cold and crazy at the same time.

"You must know you can't get away with this."

"Did I say how I used to be a prison guard?"

A second full of nothing passed, so I went on.

"Well, back in 1959, I was still pretty green, I drew the short straw for some serious overtime, driving a convict to Kansas so that he could be hanged. That's a long road, taking a man to die. Jimmy Carson and I drove Convict Rodriguez for six hours and he never said a word to either of us but 'please' and 'thank you.' He'd killed his wife and the man she was in bed with, so many shotgun shells that neither of them had a head left on their necks when he was done. And they were going to hang him for it. He knew he had to answer for what he did, so he didn't hold it against us for doing what we had to do. And my whole life I've thought more of that hanged son of a bitch than a lot of people who never did wrong, but never did right either."

While he chewed on that I turned my back to him and cocked the pistol. I didn't want him to see I needed two hands to do it. Then I went to the phone on the counter and dialed three numbers.

"911 emergency services. What's the nature of your emergency?"

"Miss, my name is John Mashburn. You need to send an ambulance and a squad car over to 1526 Glenstone, apartment number 302."

"Sir, what is the emergency?"

"Well, there's going to be one bleeding man here in a few minutes. I'll try to sop it up, but you better send that ambulance quick. The squad car will be for me. Tell 'em I won't kick when they come."

"Sir . . ."

"I'm John Mashburn."

I heard the noise behind me and just got the gun in my hand before Jackson hit me from behind. My knee gave out with a pop I could feel inside my head and we were down on the ground, me on my stomach and Jackson on my back. My arm was trapped under my chest, the pistol in my face and gun oil in my nose.

Damn old fingers too rotten and sore to tie a goddamn knot the right way, that's what did me in. Jackson had gotten himself untied while I was talking, and now he was breathing in my ear as loud as a lover. His left arm wrapped around my windpipe and squeezed. The world turned white at the edges. And I didn't see my whole life like they say you do. No, all I saw was what Louise was doing right at that moment, sitting on the porch with a cup of coffee wondering where I'd gotten myself off to. Right then I wished hard that I could be pulling onto the driveway with a bit of breakfast for her. But there wasn't any time left to feel sorry for myself.

I got my head lifted up the floor until the back of my head touched Jackson's cheek. That just made it easier for him to choke me and he squeezed and whooped. But it gave me enough room to lift the pistol off the ground. I had to twist my wrist as hard as I could and my fingers were shaking with the strain but I got the end of the .38 in my mouth. One hard push and the barrel scraped the roof of my mouth until the angle felt right. I pulled the trigger.

The bullet blew out the back of my head and smacked right into Jackson's face. He stopped the choking and fell on top of me and we both bled out and died there on his living room floor. Which is good enough, I guess.

Juanita

Tim Wohlforth

Juanita Hopkins lay naked on her bed in a pool of sweat. She twisted and turned, flailing at the dirty, rumpled sheets. It was 2:30 AM. She had never experienced such heat so late in a Nevada night. The only sound she heard was the clicking of a Big Ben clock by the side of the bed.

Where was the bastard? Albert should've been in bed by now. The last skin flick went on at midnight in that porno house he manages. I shouldn't give a shit where he is, she thought. But I do. Damn it, I do.

Juanita couldn't lie in that soggy stinking bed one more moment. She got up and threw a threadbare pink robe over her plump body. Distractedly, she ran a hand through her coarse bleached-blond hair. She stuck her stubby toes into her bunny rabbit slippers, and shuffled, only half awake, across the room and down the stairs to the living room of her unpainted ranchette. "Probably shacking up with some bimbo on the couch in that office of his," she muttered under her fetid breath.

Then she saw him, lying on the floor, gaping hole in his chest. He lay face up, a surprised look frozen on his face. A lake of blood had formed around the body. He wore his baggy black trousers with shiny knees, braces hanging loose. Stained undershirt. No shirt. He had pissed in his pants.

"Shit," she shouted to no one in particular. "Somebody finally got the bastard. Calls for a drink." She staggered over to the bar, its black laminate peeling off, and grabbed a grimy glass. She scanned the bottles lined up in front of the discolored mirror, framed in gilded white. Most of them were empty. She spotted a half-full bottle of Old Crow and filled her glass to the brim. She plopped down on the couch, facing Albert's body.

No hurry. He ain't going no place. Gotta be dead. If not, will be soon. Even in this heat, it'll take a few hours for the bastard to start stinking. God he had a lot of blood. Would have guessed he was made up entirely of fat. For now she'd just sit there, stare at the asshole, and think about all the rotten times they'd had together. Juanita had seen just enough of the inside of a church as a child to know she wasn't supposed to speak ill of the dead. She was damned if she could think of anything good to say about Albert. Okay, he stuck around. The others just stayed for a night or two and then left her. She'd gotten used to him.

Too used to him. She took a deep gulp of her bourbon. Too damned used to him. Scratchy beard. Huge beer belly, covered with hair and tattoos. Kind of like fucking a decorated gorilla. Only way she could ball him anymore was when she was drunk. He'd bring home a porno flick, bang her around a bit with his fists, huff, puff, and grunt. Then go soft. The asshole.

Boy did he stink. Did he ever shower? The only time he smelled decent was when he was covered with cheap perfume from some whore he had bedded on that goddamn couch of his. Well, no more fucking him. No more being slapped around. No more hollering at him for money. No more picking up after the slob. Not that she bothered much anymore. He didn't notice how she kept the place.

She grinned. The whiskey was having its effect. She lifted her glass and toasted Albert.

"Here's to you, you old bastard. You stinking desert rat. May you burn in the hottest damned flames in the deepest fucking sweaty hole in all of Hell. Let the devils stick their pitchforks into your balls and twist."

Juanita dropped her glass to the floor and passed out.

Bright light burned into Juanita's face. Salty sweat dripped into her eyes, stinging them. Her mouth was parched. Her head ached. She needed a drink. She forced open her eyes. What the hell was Albert doing lying on the living room floor in a pool of congealed blood?

Hundreds of flies covered the body, pigging out on the motherfucker's blood. Buzzing, licking, fighting each other for the choicest mouthfuls of Albert. The shitface was finally doing some of God's creatures some good. Maybe they'd finish him off and that would be that.

Juanita found herself watching a single fly. It had gotten stuck in the ooze, its wings covered with red goo. The more it flailed away, the deeper it sunk into the mess. All the time it ate away, gorging itself to death. It moved less. A single wing vibrated. Then it was still.

She returned her attention to Albert. Just couldn't leave the peckerhead there. She looked longingly over the body in the direction of the bar. No, she told herself. Later. First she would have to give Albert a proper burial. She forced her large body up and out of the cavernous hole she had created in the weak-springed couch. She waddled upstairs, took off her bathrobe, and threw on a faded, sleeveless, rose-patterned housedress. She replaced her slippers with work shoes and came back downstairs to tackle Albert.

She grabbed him by his two legs and slowly dragged him out of the living room, through the small kitchen, and into the backyard. No neighbors to worry about. Nothing but sand, rock, rich green creosote bushes, a sickly bent Joshua tree, a massive tangle of a prickly pear cactus, and mesquite as far as she could see. Bare rock-covered hills surrounded the gulch on three sides. She found a shovel and started to dig. Most work she'd done in years. She was determined that the burial be proper. And proper for her meant deep enough so that the vultures, the coyotes, and the sheriff couldn't find him.

She dragged Albert alongside the trench she had dug. Then she rolled him in. He landed face up, eyes open, staring at her. God, what an ugly puss. Puffy red face. Mouth stained by chewing tobacco. Dribbles embedded in his scraggly beard. Mean black eyes staring right at her. She hoped he could see her. She wanted him to watch her bury him—one spadeful of gravel and sand at a time. She spit in his face. Then she started shoveling in the dirt. As each mound of dirt hit the body she shouted a different refrain.

"For your two-timing with all those sluts. For that time you punched me black and blue. For that goddamn wad of money my sister sent me that you stole. For the time you fucked my sister."

An hour later she patted down the last shovelful of dirt on the unmarked grave. The sun was high in the sky. No wind. Must be over a hundred degrees. She looked around her. She could actually see the heat, layers of haze pressing down upon her. She felt faint. Knew if she didn't get back into the house she'd collapse. What a place to live! But not a bad place to die. Juanita stood there drenched in sweat. In minutes, the top layer of dirt would dry in the sun and blend in with the thousands of acres of sand around her.

"Even a rotten bastard like Albert deserves some kind of service," she muttered to herself. Then she smiled.

"Asses to ashes. Lust to dust. Try fuckin' around in hell, if you must."

Rivulets of dirty liquid that looked like the Tijuana River passing through the city's slums flowed down her tanned face. She wiped her brow with the back of her rough-red hand, entered the house and started to clean up the bloody mess in the living room. Luckily Albert never got around to buying carpet. Never got around to anything. She got down on her hands and knees and scrubbed the floor with a stiff brush. She enjoyed the work, rubbing memories of Albert out of her mind with each stroke. Heavy doses of Clorox bleach and Lysol completed the job. For the first time all week, she washed the dishes in the sink. Then she went upstairs, took the stinking sheets off the bed and threw them in the washing machine. She stripped off her clothes, added them, and turned on the old chipped-enamel Maytag wringer washer. Then she took a shower.

She walked out of the shower stall, dripping wet, and looked at herself in the mirror. God, she'd gained weight. Her massive breasts were sagging. So what, she said to herself. Men go for quantity not quality. She'd never been quality and she'd never wanted for men. She forced her boobs into a halter, put on her best lace pink panties, and shorts. She went downstairs to think.

She sunk into the couch, bottoming out on the floor. She wanted a drink so damned badly. No more silent, lonely drinking. She'd save booze for partying with friends. Did she have any friends?

She'd drive into Lovelock and find friends. Men friends. She could be in luck and they'll have a wet tee-shirt contest at the Half Dollar. She always won that one. She could hear the whistles from the horny crowd, Johnny Cash on the jukebox, the smell of pickles and popcorn. Life. Fun. Excitement. Escape from this damn empty desert and that rat Albert.

Her thoughts finally returned to Albert's murder. Who, she wondered, had killed him? Whoever it was deserved a goddamned medal. Silver Cross or Purple Heart or something.

Don't they have some medal to honor the hero who kills the worst wife-beating, two-timing, double-crossing, porno-pimping, white-trash, desert rat there ever was? She could remember so little from the previous night. Images returned. The heat, smelly sheets, Albert's body. She couldn't remember anything that happened earlier that evening.

She glanced around the room, searching for something that might spark a memory. She spotted a gun, her gun, sitting on the corner of the bar. Whoever killed the bastard must have used her gun. A thought hit her hard, like a tire iron across her skull.

Could she have been the killer?

"Now, that's an interesting possibility," she said out loud. She laughed. "Never thought I'd have the guts to do something like that. Not saying I did."

Just in case, she'd better bury the gun. She picked up the pistol and carried it outside. She dug a little hole next to Albert's grave, placed the weapon in it, and filled the hole in. That's when she noticed Albert's rusting pickup truck sitting next to her old fin-tail Chevy.

"Got to get rid of that goddamn truck," she said to herself. "Sooner or later, old Sheriff Walton will come poking around out here. Don't want anyone to know Albert came home last night."

She started to think. Everybody thought she was stupid, but she knew she wasn't. Just saved thinking for what was important. This was important. She scratched her rump and thought some more. Of course, she could ball old Walton. She knew he wanted her. Then she shook her head. That was okay for beginners, but the old bastard was gonna look around after he screwed her. A fast fuck meant nothing to men.

A plan formed in her mind. She'd take his old truck, tie the Chevy onto the hitch in back, and tow it to the junction. Leave the truck there with the keys in the ignition. One of the Indians from the reservation would find the truck and steal it. He'd be the one with some explaining to do to the sheriff. She'd drive on into Lovelock to report that Albert had never returned from work the night before. Then off to the tavern and a man.

"No, got to wait a suitable mourning period," she said, in a solemn voice, like the preachers of her childhood. "Be suspicious if I'm seen off drinking with someone so soon after he disappeared. Anyways, need to give the thieving Injuns time to thieve."

She decided to modify her plan. She'd drive home after she dropped off the truck and wait for the Sheriff to turn up. He'd show, sooner or later. Either looking for Albert, or maybe, noticing Albert wasn't around, looking to take advantage of his absence.

Juanita took the shovel and put it in the workshed in the back. She found an old chain Albert used to pull out mesquite stumps. She started up the Chevy, lined it up behind the truck, jumped out and attached the chain. She climbed into the cab of the truck and reached for the key.

"Fuck!" she screamed. "The key must be in the bastard's pocket, six feet under."

The situation required a lot more thought. No way was she going to start digging him up. She had had enough trouble the first time around. One burial a day was her quota. There had to be another way. But she was coming up empty. Too damned hot. God, she was thirsty.

"I think I better have a drink," she muttered as she staggered toward the house. She found an unopened fifth of Old Crow. She took off her halter, shorts and panties. Too hot for clothes. She collapsed naked on the couch. She filled to the brim the dirty glass she found lying on the floor. She took a deep gulp. No thoughts came to her. Sweat dripped from every pore in her body, staining the couch. She downed the rest of the glass.

She had some fuzzy thought about jumping the ignition

wires. Albert talked about things like that. That's how the ass-hole used to earn his living before he got into the porno flick racket. He showed her once. If only she could remember how he did it.

She filled her glass again. Another drink, she told herself, and it will all become clear. Just needed to lubricate the brain cells. The liquor made her sweat all the more. She felt sticky, nauseous. The room started spinning around her. She saw a huge fly with Albert's head, licking blood off its legs. Dizzy. Darkness.

She awoke to find a smelly, grizzly, panting mound of flesh on top of her. Her clammy body stuck to his fat belly. Like they were welded together by sweat. Albert, for Christ's sake. No, it couldn't be. That bastard was six feet under. Sure as hell was some fat man. And he was poking the hell out of her. It was Walton. The bastard hadn't even showed the courtesy of taking his clothes off. Just pushed down his pants and pulled up his shirt. His goddamn badge was digging into her left breast.

"What the shit do you think you're doing, Walton?"

"What does it look like?" he panted. "I'm fucking you."

"So who gave you permission?"

Maybe the bastard would have a heart attack, the way he was going. But then she'd have another body to bury. Didn't think she could drag this one. Too much for one day. What a motherfuckin' day it had been.

"I don't need permission." He slapped her in the face.

"Where's Albert?"

"Dunno." She gasped for air. Her face stung, pain breaking through the haze in her mind. "Don't look like you want him back. Anyways, not now."

The sheriff continued to huff, puff, wheeze, and screw, as he questioned her. Juanita wondered if this was how all his inter-rogations went.

"Won't do. Supposed to be in Lovelock at noon to open up his porno house. Got some horny geezers lined up outside waiting for him."

"Dunno."

He slapped her face again without pausing in his humping. Shit. She was sober enough now to really hurt. He was enjoying beating her. Getting off on the violence just like Albert. But Albert was her husband. He had some rights. This asshole had none.

"Why is your Chevy tied to the back of Albert's pick-up?" His breath stank of whiskey. The bastard had found her Old Crow.

"Had trouble starting it. Was gonna tow it into town. But Albert had the keys."

"I'm going to ask you one more time only. Nicely. Where's Albert?"

"Maybe he wandered off in the desert."

He yanked her hair violently back. She screamed. Suddenly the pervert grew really stiff. He cummed. He lifted himself from her body. The horny dickhead had finally finished. He slapped her backside and smiled. Like he had been doing her a favor. Then he pulled up his pants and made an attempt to tuck in his shirt.

She breathed easier. The old buzzard weighed a goddamn ton. She reached for her clothes. He pushed her hand away and shoved her back down on the couch.

"Maybe I get some deputies out here and dig up the place."

He stared at her naked body, raping her with his eyes. She didn't give a shit. He could stare all he wanted to. Gave her an edge.

"So go ahead," she taunted him. She sensed he had something besides justice in mind.

"Maybe Albert's not worth the trouble. It all depends on you."

"What do you mean?"

"Suppose I get rid of that truck for you. I know somebody who will tow it away. No questions asked. Used to work with Albert in his old racket. He'll sell it in another county. Suppose, in return, you let me put in my own guy to manage that theater you and Albert own. Then, I visit you from time to time."

"What would Myrtle think?"

He hit her again, this time in the stomach. She groaned. Almost puked. But she didn't really care. She was used to rough treatment. She just wanted Walton to know he didn't hold all the cards. She could always go to his wife.

"Myrtle is a saint. Don't you ever mention her name again."

"But you like sinners," Juanita was about to say. She swallowed her words. No sense provoking him now that they were getting down to business. Shit, no sooner did she get rid of one asshole when another moves in on her.

"You've got a deal," she said.

Walton smiled and began to unbutton his pants. The horny old bastard. At least Albert left her alone most of the time. Preferring the whores he ran. Her fate. Like the damned fly caught in the blood. God, she needed a drink. A thought came to her. Who benefited from Albert's death? Not her. She had traded one fat bastard who beat her for another. Walton, that's who. He's taking over Albert's business and fuckin' her to boot. Maybe he killed Albert. Her new thought helped clear the fog from her mind. It all began to come back to her. She replayed the events of the night before in her mind as if they were a movie. She had been drinking upstairs in her room. Too hot. Maybe, she had thought, the Old Crow would put her to sleep. And it had. But she had awakened by shouts coming from downstairs. Two men were arguing in the living room. She had thrown on her bathrobe and stumbled down the stairs. She saw Walton and Albert, but they didn't see her. Shouts. Something about money. Walton was shaking down Albert. She stood at the top of the stairs and watched. Walton grabbed her gun from the table. Shots. A door slammed. Then quiet. Good, she had said to herself. Finally she could sleep. She staggered back to bed.

Why, that *asshole*. That's how come he was so damned quick to show up out here. Why he assumed from the first that Albert was dead. That she had buried his body. Shit. And she had wasted all that time and effort digging that hole. That was Walton's job. No doubt why he came back here. Must have been surprised to find the body gone. And relieved. But what could she do about it now? Who would believe her?

Juanita looked at Walton with a knowing smile on her face.

"I remember last night," she said defiantly.

"Nothin' to remember, you drunken whore."

She was sure he knew she knew.

"Take your damned pants off," she commanded. No way was she going to be fucked with clothes on anymore. He did as he was told. Walton lowered himself back down upon her. She opened her legs for him. Part of the deal. She gave him a little pat on his fat rump.

"Now, no rough stuff."

At least she would get some respect. If not, she knew where the gun was buried.

Jack Jaw and the Arab's Ape

Ryan Oakley

"So you want thirteen then?" Jack said and kicked the side of the cage. The chimp cowered in the corner. Its face looked pale and snot mixed with drool on its chin. Jack looked back at the Arab who smoked a green hookah and blew smoke out of his nose. It smelled like apples and Jack hated apples. "The thing looks sick to me. I'll give you eight."

"Eight?" The Arab sat up, his eyes wide. "Eight? You offer me eight hundred for Mr. Skippy? Eight?"

"That's right." Jack adjusted his top hat and leaned forward on his cobra-headed cane. He kept a careful eye on the big man behind the Arab. "And I'm being generous." He tapped the cage with his cane. The chimp hardly moved. "He doesn't look like any sort of fighter to me."

The Arab slowly shook his head and relaxed back into his seat. "I assure you that Mr. Skippy is in the best of health. He's just tired after his long voyage and disturbed by the activity of this most busy port."

"Seems quiet enough in here," Jack said and looked around

the dim bar. It was empty except for the man who was passed out at a distant table; snoring like a locomotive with his head resting on his arms. Even the bartender was gone. Jack had paid him ten bucks to take a walk.

He looked at the drunk for a long moment and said: "I tell you what. You let him at that piss-head and if I like what I see I'll give you a thousand."

"What if Mr. Skippy gets hurt?"

"If Mr. Fucking Skippy gets hurt fighting that drunk son of a bitch, then I don't want him anyway." Jack felt his blood getting up and took a deep breath. If this bastard thought he could rip him off he'd learn a sharp lesson at the tip of Jack's cane sword. "Are you game or not?" He tapped the cage again and looked at the chimp. "How about you, champ? You figure you got what it takes?"

The Arab tilted his head back and, keeping his eyes on Jack, said something in a coarse, coughing language. The big guy behind him stepped forward and bent down in front of the chimp's cage. He grunted at the ape and pointed at the drunk. The ape put his hand on the top of his head. The big guy looked at the Arab and nodded.

"Okay, Mr. Jaw. We will try things your way. Step back and we will release Mr. Skippy. I think you'll like what you see."

Jack did as he was told. The big guy pulled open the cage door and Jack realized that it hadn't even been locked. He expected the chimp to go crazy, to run up and down the bar smashing, crashing, and hooting, but it just stepped forward and slowly stood up.

"It's a bonobo," the Arab said. "They're bipedal."

Whatever that means, Jack thought.

The ape crossed the bar, its long arms swinging at its sides like meaty pistons. It was a short beast, about three feet tall, but it looked strong. As it approached the drunk, Jack felt his jaw tighten. He heard his molars grinding against each other and cursed the third-rate cocaine he had snorted before this meeting.

Mr. Skippy didn't do anything fancy. He just raised his right fist high above his shoulders and then brought it down in fast arc upon the back of the drunk's head. It made a noise like a watermelon being hit with a hammer.

The size of the man's skull seemed to halve and the chimp grabbed him by the hair, lifted his head up, (Jack couldn't help but notice that the man's face was a flat red mush) and slammed it back down. One, twice, three times.

The chimp turned around and shuffled back towards his cage. He sat down in the corner, squealed like a baby and was given an orange by the Arab. The blood on his hairy hand streaked its rind and he shoved it into his mouth, eating skin, blood and all.

"You like?" the Arab asked, his voice as sweet as the juice that dribbled down the chimp's chin.

"Yes."

"Then you give me eleven."

Jack didn't hesitate. "Deal."

"You know what happens if you fuck with Jack Jaw?" Jack said to the filthy little, barefoot kid, who was nodding his head like his neck was a spring.

"Yes, sir."

"Good." Jack reached into his pocket and gave the kid a roll of money. "You know what to do with that?"

"Yes, sir." The kid smiled. He was missing a few teeth, but at his age it was hard to tell whether they'd been knocked out. Either way, Jack didn't like his smile. It looked like he might be up to something. He slapped the kid across the face. The kid's lip trembled.

"You gonna cry, you little shit?"

"No, sir."

"Then get out of here and watch your step. You fuck with me kid and it's the last thing you've done."

"Yes, sir." The kid hung his head and scampered out of the room, slamming the door shut behind him.

"Little fucker," Jack said and tapped a bump of cocaine onto his fist. He snorted, smacked his lips and turned towards the ape that sat on the bench, wearing leather shoes and a pair of ragged pants held up by suspenders.

"Lookin' good, Mr. Skippy," Jack said and ground his jaws.

The Arab had trained the chimp well. He was a placid creature who hardly resisted when Jack shaved him. But once—just once—he gave Jack a look that turned his spine into a brittle icy rod. Other than that he was always very still. He didn't move except to eat, shit, or fight. To make him fight you had to grunt twice (the big guy had shown Jack how) and point at the victim. So far they had all been victims. The odds were stacked in Mr. Skippy's favor. As long as they got those rats out of the pit, the fight should go off without a hitch.

Jack heard the call for final bets outside and the crowd getting loud. He took a few steps towards the chimp and pulled a syringe out of his jacket pocket. "Now keep calm, Mr. Skippy," he said. Jack knew it was goofy but he figured the ape understood him. He looked so damned human. "It's gonna be a tough fight tonight and Daddy's got your medicine."

He took the chimp's hand in his and stretched its arm out. Without going through the usual work of putting a strap around its arm he found a fat vein and carefully slid the needle in. "Now that don't hurt too much, does it, champ?" The ape grunted. Jack pressed the plunger down, pumped the monkey full of dope and stepped back.

He'd only used half on the chimp (it should be enough) and wiped the syringe off on his pant leg before rolling up his own sleeve and injecting himself. The morphine hit nice and warm through his chest but it made him a bit too dopey. He fumbled through his pockets for some more coke. Snorted a few good bumps just to get his shit back together.

"C'mon now, Jack," he said, then paused. "No, I'm Jack. You c'mon now, Mr. Skippy. We gotta make Jack some money."

He took the chimp's hand and walked out the door. A collage of growling, scarred faces appeared before him. Sweaty bodies parted to let him through. He half-felt people patting him on the back; half-heard them shouting encouragement. Then they were in the pit, sloping dirt walls around them. Across the filthy, blood-soaked expanse, where a man had just fought fifty rats, stood a big drunken bruiser named Blade.

Nice name, Jack thought. Real original.

He heard the shouter announcing the fighters. They all thought Mr. Skippy was a midget, probably a retard, too. But they had seen him fight and knew what he could do with his fists. Beside Jack, the ape swayed in his shoes.

"Annnnnnnnd *FIGHT!*" The shouter shouted.

Jack grunted twice and pointed at Blade. Then he scrambled up the ladder and out of the pit. Someone beside him pulled it up.

He sat on the edge, not concerned about getting his suit dirty, his legs dangling into the pit. He was a bit too fucked up to stand. Across the fight zone he saw the kid staring at him. The urchin gave him the thumbs up, which Jack ignored and looked down. Blade was approaching Mr. Skippy, who was swaying back and forth. Good. The animal could feel the morphine. Jack hadn't been sure that it would affect him.

He just hoped it was enough to make the ape lose for a change. He wanted this bet to pay big and the way the odds were stacked, it should. If Mr. Skippy went down fast then Jack would walk out of here a rich man.

Blade grabbed the chimp by the shoulders, picked him up over his head and threw him against the dirt wall. Mr. Skippy bounced right back up and faced the charging brawler. It looked like he was about to get run right over but he lifted his long arms, grabbed Blade by the waist and threw him over his head. The man hit the ground, skidded, and quickly stood.

Shit, Jack thought. Mr. Skippy shouldn't be moving that damn fast.

The brawler hit the ape in the head but Mr. Skippy didn't seem to feel it. He just grabbed both of the man's arms and yanked down. Hard. Jack remembered when he was a kid and got his boot stuck in mud. He had slowly yanked it out and it made a great slurping noise. The brawler's arms made that noise—except louder and shorter. He suddenly looked like he had two long red wings and Jack realized that it was spurting blood. The fucking chimp had ripped his limbs off at the shoulder.

Mr. Skippy waved one arm over his head and used the other to bash Blade in the face while he fell to his knees, his countenance pale and screaming in the suddenly silent room. He flopped forward and the ape jumped on his back. He tossed an arm into the crowd. It cartwheeled over Jack's head and he heard people gasp and try to scatter out of the way. Mr. Skippy started to shriek as blood puddled below him, sinking into the already saturated dirt. It stank like iron.

I've gotta calm him down, Jack thought. There's no telling what he'll do. He slid down the side of the pit and stumbled into the blood, getting his hands all wet and sticky. Shit. As if losing the money wasn't bad enough.

The ape was yanking its pants off and they bundled up around his feet. It squatted on Blade's back and took a shit. Jack willed his legs to take a step towards the beast but they would not cooperate. He was fucking scared. This goddamn monkey was coming down. He should have used more dope. Mr. Skippy picked up his steaming pile of crap and flung it into the crowd, baring his big angry teeth and beating his chest.

"Okay Mr. Skippy," Jack said, trying to sound calm although his heart was having a seizure. "Okay. Just be nice and easy. I've got a nice orange for you."

The ape looked at him with that foul-eyed glare. Jack patted his pockets and tried a smile. The chimp growled. The noise took form and Jack could swear he understood it. The fucking thing was talking. *"More! More!"* It stepped forward.

Jack reached into his pocket for the needle and pulled it out. It was empty. The chimp hooted and took another step. "Easy," Jack said. "Easy. Dad's just gotta buy some—"

"MORE!" The ape sprang forward and into Jack's chest, hitting him like a bag of wet sand, knocking the wind out of him. Jack hit the ground and the chimp raised its arms. *"MORE!"*

Jack's hands were in a panic and they searched through his pockets until he found a little paper package marked "five." There was no time to cook it, so he just held it up, closed his eyes and waited to be beaten to death. Nothing happened. Then he heard a slurping noise and dared to look. The chimp had opened the package was licking the powder out of one of its big hands.

"Umph," it said and relaxed.

Jack stood up and looked around the pit at the people staring down. They were a stupid lot but he thought he could see understanding slowly dawning on them. He had to get out of this part of town by tonight—before they figured it out. He took Mr. Skippy by the hand, demanded that someone lower the ladder and when they did, climbed it.

It had taken a month to find the Arab and two weeks more to arrange a meeting. At least Mr. Skippy's hair had grown back. "He seems different," the Arab said.

Jack nodded. "He is. I was right. The damn ape was sick. You sold me damaged goods."

The Arab looked up from the cage and into Jack's eyes.

"I will give you two hundred for him back," he said.

"I paid eleven hundred," Jack protested.

"Yes. But I had him off the dope then. You've put him back on it." The Arab shook his head. "You didn't think I could tell? You think you're the first to try this? I bet you had him mugging pushers until you realized that he would not share."

Jack hung his head and looked at his shoes. They were scuffed and he needed a hit. He was broke and cold. Two hundred wasn't much but it was enough to stay high for a week. "All right," he said. "You have a deal."

A Sleep Not Unlike Death

Sean Chercover

Gravedigger Peace was already sitting up when his eyes opened. It had been years since the nightmares, but his face and forearms were clammy with perspiration and his heart was racing, so he assumed there'd been one. Truth was, Gravedigger Peace didn't remember his dreams these days. Not ever. Not one.

A sleep not unlike death.

Gravedigger drank from the water glass on the bedside table. The digital clock said 3:23. He stood, peeled off his moist T-shirt, wiped his face and arms. Tossed the shirt into the laundry hamper, then shuffled to the kitchen. Instant coffee with a couple ounces of Jim Beam. Final drink of the night.

He sat on the couch in the living area and drank his bourbon-laced coffee and listened to the rain drumming on the metal roof. He stared at the dead gray television screen. No point turning it on; he knew what he'd seen and nothing would have changed in the last three hours. He turned it on anyway. The set came to life right where he left it, tuned to CNN. The news hadn't changed. The bodies, what was left of them, were back in the

United States. Next of kin had been notified, and the names of the five civilian contractors slaughtered in Ramadi had been released to the public.

Civilian contractors. A family-friendly euphemism for mercenaries. The euphemism had never bothered him when he was in the business, but it bugged the shit out of him now.

The television screen showed heavily compressed digital video that had originally aired on Al Jazeera. Five bodies, dumped together in a heap in the middle of the street. Burning. A couple dozen young Iraqi men dancing around the fire, chanting *God is Great* and *Death to America* and other things Gravedigger could not understand. Then the television showed photos of the five Americans. Four white kids in their late 20s, and one black man in his late 40s.

Gravedigger took a deep breath, blew it out, and consciously relaxed the white-knuckle grip that threatened to shatter the coffee mug in his right hand. He didn't recognize the younger men on the television screen, but he knew Walter Jackson and had served under him in Nigeria a decade earlier. Back in another life, when Gravedigger Peace was still Mark Tindall.

The barracks smelled like cigarettes, stewed goat, and the collective body odor of seven testosterone-rich men. No breeze came through the screened windows and the cigarette smoke hung like a fog in the dim light.

Mark Tindall tossed three .45-caliber bullets into the center of the table. "Raise it up, ladies."

"Fuckin' Africa," said Walter Jackson, and tossed his cards in. "I fold." He wiped his ebony torso with an olive green T-shirt. "Never cools down, not even at night."

"I thought you were from the Southland, Sarge," said Raoul Graham. "Heat shouldn't bother you." Then, to Mark, "I'll call your bullshit." Raoul tossed three bullets into the pot.

Walter Jackson leaned back in his chair and grabbed a Coke

from the cooler, "Milledgeville's hot but you get a break every now and then." He popped the bottle cap with the edge of his Zippo, gulped down half the bottle. Then held the cool bottle to his chest, rolling it across a faded blue tattoo. The insignia of the 1st Special Forces was still legible—two crossed arrows with a fighting knife in the middle pointing skyward, above the motto: *De Oppresso Liber. Free from Oppression.*

Underneath the motto, Walter Jackson had added: . . . *Or Not.*

Mark Tindall never asked what had turned Jackson's army life to dog shit, but he knew that Jackson was bitter about it and saw the military as no more noble than the world they now inhabited. Fighting for whichever side offers the most money.

Mark had never served in the military, and he hadn't become a mercenary for the money. He just wanted to kill things. To inflict pain on others. Like his dad inflicted pain.

Around the table, the other three men folded their hands in turn, and Mark shot a hard look to his only remaining opponent.

"How many?"

"Three," said Raoul, and Mark flicked three cards face-down across the table.

"And dealer takes one," said Mark.

"You're gonna miss that straight draw," said Raoul, grinning.

God, Raoul had a knack for pissing him off without even trying. "Flush draw, asshole," Mark sneered. He separated six bullets from his pile, added them to the pot. "And it'll cost you six to find out I made the nut."

Walter Jackson stood and got a fresh shirt from his footlocker, put it on. "Tindall, when you're done taking Graham's money, I need you. Perimeter survey. Bastards are gettin' closer every day."

Brian Billings sat up on his cot and closed the book he was reading. "I'll go, Sarge."

"No you will not."

"Aw, how come Golden Boy always gets the glamour jobs?"

"Fuck you, Billings," said Mark, without looking up from his cards.

Jackson spoke before Billings could answer. "Tindall goes because Tindall is better than you. Quietest white boy I've ever seen outside Special Forces."

"Thanks a heap, Sarge," said Mark Tindall. "Raoul, you gonna play, or what? I gotta go."

"Just trying to decide between a call and a raise."

Mark Tindall dropped his cards facedown. "Take it." He stood from the table and strapped on his sidearm.

Raoul giggled and raked in the pot. "I *knew* you missed your flush."

"Wrong again, genius. I was bluffing all along. Didn't have shit."

Walter Jackson slung an M-16 over his shoulder, "Let's go, Golden Boy."

In the morning, Gravedigger avoided the television altogether. Queasy from the hangover, he made a solid breakfast. Three eggs, four rashers of bacon, three slices of whole wheat. And coffee. Always coffee. He considered a slug of bourbon, just to smooth out the rough edges, but the urge itself was a red flag. Sure, he'd been drinking the night before, but now it was morning. It had been years since he drank before the day's work was done. He deferred to his better judgment, taking his coffee black. He could feel Mark Tindall creeping around in the back of his skull, and it worried him. He'd killed that guy years ago, and he was fucked if he'd ever go back.

I am Gravedigger Peace, he reminded himself as he washed the dishes. *That's who I am.*

It had been raining for two days straight and it was still falling at a steady pace. He put on a plastic poncho and walked to the groundskeeper's shed where he assigned the day's muddy tasks to his crew. There was his assistant, Sam, who'd worked at Mount Pleasant Cemetery for longer than anyone could remember, and Sam's son Bobby, who was approaching 30 but had the mental capacity of a 12-year-old. Larry and Jamie were a couple of black kids who'd just graduated from high school and were working to save money for college.

And then there were the losers—Tweedledum and Tweedledee, Gravedigger called them. They didn't get the reference and seemed to enjoy the nicknames. A couple of teenage metalhead stoners, they'd barely made it out of high school. But most people don't want to work in a cemetery, and Gravedigger had given them a chance. The latest in a long series of small acts since he'd killed off Mark Tindall. Small acts to confirm his status as a member of the human race.

So far, the stoner kids had worked out okay. Just barely. They weren't going to set any records for speedy work, they sometimes called in hungover on Mondays, and he suspected that they often smoked up on their lunch breaks. But graves were getting dug, bodies buried, and the grass was getting mowed. So he'd decided to keep them on for the rest of the summer, but wasn't planning to invite them back next season.

Gravedigger made it through the morning meeting on autopilot and dismissed his crew. The walkie-talkie on his belt crackled to life, summoning him to the office. He hopped on an ATV and drove through the hot summer rain to the main building near the cemetery's entrance. Without a word, the receptionist ushered him in to see the boss.

"Thanks for coming, Gravedigger. Can I get you anything? Coffee?"

"No thanks." Why thank him for coming? And why the solicitous tone? The boss sounded like he was talking to a customer.

"Reason I called you in, we have . . . well, we have a body, just arrived for burial. No funeral, just burial. Employer's picking up the tab."

"Okay."

"The deceased put it in his will, to be laid to rest here, because you're the head groundskeeper." He looked at a sheet of paper, put it aside. "His name was Walter Jackson. I guess he was a friend?"

The room spun and Gravedigger closed his eyes.

"I'm sorry, Gravedigger. Take a few minutes to collect yourself, I'll wait outside."

A silver sliver of a moon provided just enough light to move. More light would make them more vulnerable, while a moonless night would force them to use flashlights, which was even worse. This was perfect.

Mark Tindall and Walter Jackson made it out to the perimeter—five hundred yards from the barracks—at an easy pace. But the perimeter survey would be tediously slow. As Jackson so often said, "You can go fast or you can go quiet, but you can't go both."

Silence demands a kind of slow that very few men have the discipline to achieve. The vast majority of military men could never sustain it, but it is mastered by Navy SEALS and Special Forces. And few mercenaries. Mark took a justifiable pride in his ability. Still, he berated himself for every cracked twig underfoot, for the rustle of his pant legs, for the very sound of his own breathing. But there was none quieter, and even Walter Jackson could not hear him.

It took over an hour to make one hundred yards along the perimeter. Mark walked point, with his commander ten yards back, following—quite literally—in his footsteps. The night vision goggles were a necessity, but in this heat Mark had to take them off every few yards and wipe the sweat out of his eyes. Each time they made twenty yards, Mark stopped and Jackson slowly closed the distance between them. They used hand signals to communicate the All Clear. Then Mark started again, ever so slowly.

At two hundred yards, Mark saw the camp. Both the sight and sound of it had been blocked by a small hill, and by the time it appeared, they were close. Too close.

Mark held up a hand to stop Jackson from approaching, hunkered down in the tall grass, and took stock. Five small tents stood in a circle, a campfire in the center. Nine men sat around the campfire. Six wore sidearms and three cradled machetes on their laps, but Mark saw no long guns.

And then came the soft breeze. It blew gently across the campsite, and the fire crackled and threw off more light. But it blew the smoke straight toward Mark, and his eyes began to sting and water, and his nose tickled.

Mark Tindall sneezed. The night shattered.

Gravedigger stood in the rain and, using a spade, separated the grass from the earth below. The area around the head groundskeeper's residence was taken up mostly by old mausoleums, but he wanted to bury Walter Jackson nearby, so he commandeered this spot, about ten yards from his front door. Once he'd placed the sod to one side, he used a small backhoe to dig the hole, dumping the wet soil on a tarp to the other side.

The casket arrived, and the crew lowered it into the hole. Because of the persistent rain, the ground was waterlogged and there were a couple of feet of standing water below. The sealed casket floated aimlessly in the grave.

Gravedigger sent Sam off to get the sump pump, and then retreated to his residence, where he rummaged through an old shoebox and found a photograph of Mark Tindall and Walter Jackson. It was the only thing he had kept from his former life. He'd thrown everything else away when he killed Mark Tindall and became Gravedigger Peace, but Jackson had saved his life and he could never bring himself to get rid of it. Now he would lay it to rest with his old friend.

He left the photo on the kitchen table and, in the bedroom, stripped off his sodden clothes. Walter Jackson would have no funeral, only a burial. But at least he would have one mourner. Maybe it was a useless gesture, but Gravedigger didn't care. He opened the closet, and put on his only suit.

He tied his tie in front of the bathroom mirror, and tried not to look beyond the knot. But he couldn't help himself. Avoiding his own eyes, he examined the thin white scar that ran from his left cheek down to his jaw. The scar made by a machete in Nigeria. And when he made eye contact, Mark Tindall stared back at him. *Shit! Fuck!* He swung open the door of the medicine cabinet, displacing the mirror, and fled the bathroom, thinking *I know who I am. I know who I am. I know who I am . . .*

Photograph in hand, Gravedigger headed back out into the hot summer rain. Fuck the poncho, he would stand in his suit in the rain and give Walter Jackson a proper sendoff. It was coming down harder now, blowing in his face, forcing him to look at the ground as he walked to the graveside. He looked up and dropped the photograph.

They were coffin-surfing. Tweedledum stood on top of the casket, rocking it with his legs, creating a wave beneath. He struck a surfer's pose, and sang the theme from *Hawaii Five-O.* Tweedledee stood off to one side, laughing.

Gravedigger screamed and lunged forward, then caught himself. He trembled as adrenaline coursed through his veins.

Tweedledee stopped laughing and said, "Oh, shit."

Tweedledum jumped off the casket and out of the grave. "We were just having some fun, man."

"You're fired. Both of you."

"What difference does it make?" said Tweedledee. "Dude's already dead."

It took all of Gravedigger's willpower to keep his voice from breaking. "Get the fuck out of my graveyard. Now. Before I hurt you."

Nigeria is a very bad place to do prison time, especially for a white man. Walter Jackson endured his share of torture, but his cell had a cot, and a hole in the floor served as a toilet. Mark Tindall did harder time. The guards beat him daily, sometimes breaking ribs and once breaking his left arm. He was given just enough food and water to keep him alive and days would sometimes pass between meals. His cell had nothing in it at all, not even a drain in the concrete floor, so he lived in his own filth.

Sometime around the fourth month, the guards took Mark Tindall's boots away and whipped him on the soles of his feet. His feet soon became infected, purple and swollen and oozing pus. He was given no medical attention and his fever soared. Hallucinations came regularly, and he started to lose himself. Some days he would be lucid, but other days he was stark raving mad, smearing himself with his own shit, howling at the walls and twitching like an epileptic having a seizure. Then he would pass out, and wake up relatively sane again. Until the next time.

On the six-month anniversary of their capture, the guards hauled Mark Tindall from his cell and hosed him down and put him in the cell with Walter Jackson. A man in a crisp military uniform came into the cell.

"Tomorrow morning," the man said, "one of you will be sent back to America. It is for you to decide which one." The man handed a pack of Marlboros and a book of matches to Walter Jackson, and left.

Jackson lit a cigarette and put it between Mark Tindall's lips, then lit one for himself. They smoked in silence for a few minutes.

"You don't look so good, Golden Boy," said Jackson.

Mark Tindall let out a crooked smile. "You're lookin' a little skinny yourself, Sarge."

"Hey, I'm livin' high on the hog. This is the fuckin' Ritz Carleton compared to your crib."

"Yeah. It's pretty nice. I could stay here awhile."

Walter Jackson stubbed his cigarette out on the floor and lit another. "Shit. You gonna lose those feet if we don't get you out of here."

"Might lose 'em anyway." The two men nodded at each other, and silent tears began to stream down Mark Tindall's face.

Jackson slid over and put his arms around the younger man's shoulders, holding him like a protective father. "When you get out of here tomorrow, put it behind you, Mark. Don't look back."

Mark didn't even try to argue.

Gravedigger Peace woke to the sound of his own voice. "Sorry I sneezed, Sarge." *Sorry I sneezed. Shit. Sorry I left you behind. Sorry I lived.*

The bedside clock said it was just past midnight. He had slept only three hours. After the stoners had left, he'd sumped the water out of Walter Jackson's grave and covered it with earth by hand, using the spade. He needed to work off the adrenaline. Once the grave was filled, he went home, tossed his ruined suit into the trash, and lay in the bathtub with a long drink. He tried to make himself cry a little, but he hadn't cried in years and he couldn't summon the tears. Finally he gave up, finished his drink and went to bed.

Now he was up again, and his nerves felt raw, exposed. He tried to read, couldn't. He got a beer from the fridge, but didn't open it. Sat in front of the television, but didn't turn it on. The rain had stopped at last, and the silence rang in his ears.

Then he heard it. A sound from outside. Voices.

He opened the coat closet and reached for the Mossberg shotgun that he kept there, then reached deeper into the closet and pulled out a machete instead.

The moon was almost full, and Gravedigger's eyes adjusted to the light as he walked toward Walter Jackson's grave, holding the machete in his right hand and a flashlight in his left. Tweedledee stood pissing on the grave, then put his dick back in his pants. Beside a nearby mausoleum, Tweedledum stood with a can of spray-paint in his hand. Painted on the wall was, *I rode Gravedigger's bitch!*

Gravedigger flicked the flashlight on, and both boys froze. They should have run away. But instead, they charged.

And Mark Tindall cut them to pieces.

Burning Ring of Fire

Hana K. Lee

Before I met J, I had never really listened to Johnny Cash. I knew who he was, but I wasn't into that kind of stuff. I was more into the electronica/dj scene. Or "faggot music" as J called it. He was such a sweet talker.

He bought me my first Johnny Cash CD, and I fell in love with both of them that night. While we were fucking, J would sing "Ring of Fire" in my ear. I never knew that Johnny Cash could be so hot.

For the longest time, that was our song. Our love was just like burning in a ring of fire. If we weren't fucking, we were fighting over something stupid. Fight, drink, break stuff, drink, fuck, start all over again, fuck some more. Still it was love all the same. We were the same kind of animal. A few parts quiet, more parts wild, uncontrollable at all times.

Love is a burning thing.

I listened to that song over and over until it seared into my memory. It hid behind the memory of J's mouth, his harsh jawline, his crooked grin. It hid behind the pale blue eyes that I used to call corpse eyes. Because I had never seen a white person with eyes so pale. I always liked the white boys with the light blue eyes. That was what made me notice him. The way he held me down on the bed made me come back for more.

Some people think that if someone you love dies, a part of you dies with them. Or it makes you want to die with that person. At least that's how they portray it in the silly picture shows. That's sentimental bullshit. When a person dies, your love dies, too. That's it. Ashes to ashes, love turns to dust.

The sadness only lasted for a brief flicker. He had never spoken of any family or friends, so I was the only one there in the end. After I collected his ashes, I drove down PCH towards the Huntington Beach pier. We had talked about cremation a couple of times. Neither of us wanted to be buried underground if no one would even visit our graves.

I took a fistful of ashes and let them drift towards the water. Fistful after fistful into the cold Pacific water. It's something that he had mentioned once, but I remembered. He loved the surf lifestyle, and he wanted to be one of those surf junkies. He loved all that RonJon, Billabong, and other surfwear. He never said anything, but I knew that water freaked him out. I didn't like to pry, but he freaked out when I suggested we take swimming lessons. Like it was his worst nightmare.

They must have known that. That's the only reason why they didn't use something easy like a gun or a knife. I know he must have put up quite a fight. He was skinny like a junkie, but he was deceptively strong. He had a lot of force behind that wiry frame and those lean forearms.

When I found him, I almost didn't call the cops. He was soaking in the bathtub. Marinated in a tub full of water, blood, and shit. At first I thought maybe the assholes had shit in the tub as some form of humiliation. I'm pretty sure that J shit himself as he was dying. I didn't want anyone to see him like this, but I couldn't lift him out of the tub.

They carved up his arms real good to make it look like he went crazy and offed himself. The cops wrote it off as a suicide, and I didn't fight them. The lazy fucks didn't even ask why the bedroom was torn up. Didn't matter. I didn't trust them, and they were happy to get out of there. Another junkie gone under. Case closed.

And it burns burns burns.

He never told me about what he did, but still I knew everything. I was never one to pry into a man's business. He had his life, and I had mine. I could read all the details in his eyes. I knew when work was kicking his ass. I knew when he had an easy day that made it all worthwhile. I knew when the others were ragging on him.

I knew he liked to share the perks with me, and I let him. Fine dining, trinkets, Fendi bags, $500 bottles of wine. I was never into the junk, and he used to tease me about that. I never tried anything stronger than Ketel One shots. That's all I needed then. I didn't like to be too out of control.

There were a couple of times when I wanted to warn him. When I noticed that he was skimming more merchandise than usual. When I noticed that his sampling habits were becoming more noticeable. I never said anything. My mama always taught me that a good woman doesn't stick her nose into a man's working life. That's the number one reason a man will turn against womankind. She also wants to butt in where she doesn't belong.

That little piece of advice had always worked until now. It always made the guy want to open up more and spill his guts. J wasn't like that. He liked to simmer and figure things out on his own. I let him simmer. Maybe I should have said something.

At first I thought about fire. I didn't know which ones were involved, so I would get them all. The more I thought about it, the less I liked the plan. Arson is complicated, and I don't understand chemicals. Even if I did know that stuff, I wasn't exactly sure where to go.

J was always getting mad at me, because I didn't like to plan. He liked to write things down in little notebooks, charting, diagramming, thinking on paper. Just because I didn't do that, he thought I wasn't a planner like him. He thought I didn't think over the details. I do, but I keep it all in my head. I never left a paper trail like he did.

J never mentioned any names, but I knew where to find one particular guy. I pulled out my fetish gear, and I headed to Club Octane. I walked in at midnight, and the dance floor thumped old goth-industrial crap. Everyone was dressed in black, so I was able to blend in with the other poseurs and wannabes.

I didn't have to look for him. He found me at the bar. I had seen that face in one picture that J ripped from my guilty fingers. It was the only time I had snooped in his stuff, and I got caught. I didn't know if he was a friend or associate.

My leather corset pushed my tits up and out, and I leaned towards him. He glanced towards my stiletto boots.

"Those look dangerous," he joked.

I didn't respond. I pulled out a Marlboro Light, and he held his lighter up. I took a drag, and I let my fingernails graze his wrist. I caught him licking his lips once. I was dressed with purpose, so I know he couldn't help it.

I let him do all the talking, all the schmoozing. After a few minutes I was getting bored, so I just sighed and gave him that look. If he was too stupid to recognize that look, I was going to give up. I wasn't going to be the aggressor. Too many witnesses around, and a woman coming on too strong is memorable.

He understood the look. Twenty minutes later, I made him pay cash for the motel room. I was down to a push-up bra and black lace garters. No panties. He was on the edge of the bed, and he was practically drooling. His hard-on pointed at me.

I pointed at his feet. "I am not fucking you with your socks on."

He bent over to remove one, and I slid the needle into his neck.

When he woke up, I was hovering over him, still in my fuck-me outfit. He couldn't move because I tied his wrists and ankles to the bed. I had a Domme friend who taught me how to tie unbreakable knots with simple hemp ropes.

He didn't really understand his situation. That's why he never screamed for help. He probably didn't want word to get out. How he got tied down by some psychosexual bitch with bondage fantasies. His struggles only made the knots tighter, and his hands started to lose color.

I said a name, and his eyes got really big. Now he was thinking that maybe this wasn't a game. He tried to get all tough and spit into my face. I wiped it off on my glove, and I took the towel off his crotch. He was still semi-hard.

I grabbed his cock and jerked him until he was hard again. He started cussing at me, and I put my panties deep into his mouth.

I asked him two questions, and I told him that he would answer right after I took the panties out of his mouth. He cussed at me through the panties. He was trying to shake his hands loose, but the ropes cut into his wrists.

I pointed his cock straight into the air, and I cupped his balls in one hand. They fit nicely into my palm. I let go off his cock, and I got out my kit. I soaked some cotton balls with kerosene, and I rubbed them across his balls. I made sure the hairs on his balls were drenched.

When I lit up a cigarette, he finally understood.

Even after he told me everything I needed to know, I didn't stop. I sang in my best Johnny Cash voice:

". . . and it burns burns burns . . ."

I think the smell of his burning cock must have taken him over the edge. When he started to choke on his vomit, I took my time in cleaning up.

By the time the cops arrived on the scene, my night would already be complete.

* * *

I glanced at the dash. 1:20 AM. I was flying down the 15 freeway. I would be able to reach Vegas in two hours or so.

After I burned both of his nuts off, the guy had started telling me all kinds of stuff. At first I wasn't sure if any of it was reliable. I've read somewhere that torture victims start to get confused, and they make up stories just to stop the torture.

I double-checked with J's notebooks, and I knew that most of the information had weight. Even if the names were different, the descriptions seemed right.

I had been kidding myself. I had been so blinded by love and maybe grief that I couldn't see the truth. All this time I had imagined that someone high up in the operations had put a hit on my man. The truth was so much simpler.

Even if J had been skimming a little here and there, the top dogs wouldn't have been able to catch that. They had much bigger things to worry about. In that world, J was a peon, and he only knew other peons. Any fool could have figured that out in two seconds.

The truth is always much more simple, more black and white.

The first guy became even more cooperative after I said I would let him go. I know he didn't believe me, but he wanted to. Even though he should have passed out from the pain, he hung on. He still wanted to live. That's human nature. Despite the worst pain, the natural instinct is for survival. He would have drawn me some maps if I had wanted them. It turns out that the others were local.

I found the second guy sleeping in his bed. It was over in two seconds. A gun makes everything so much easier.

The last guy, supposedly the one who cut J's arms to pieces, recognized me right away. I don't remember J ever taking a picture of me, but I remember him messing around with his new camera-phone. He must have sneaked a picture while I was reading.

He recognized me, but he was still slow to react. He saw a petite woman standing in his bedroom, and he was confused more than scared. He wanted to know how I got into his house. It's not my fault that he used a cheapie security system.

He didn't understand the situation until he saw the gun. He turned away, perhaps to get his own weapon. The first bullet hit the back of his head.

This one, I wanted this one badly. He was bigger and stronger than the other two, so I know he was the muscle. I know that it was those hands that held J down in the bathtub. Held him underwater until he was begging and pleading. Held him underwater until he couldn't hold his bowels anymore.

Right before it happened, J and I had gotten into a huge fight. He said things he shouldn't have said, and I cracked a table over his head. I meant to come back. He knew I always did. Instead of the usual day, I spent four days away from him. I was out drinking with my girlfriends and hitting the clubs. It felt good to be single again.

When I came back, the apartment stank of shit and rot. J was stewing in that filthy water for four days. He was purple and bloated to twice his normal size. His eyes and mouth were open, and he continued to drown in that water.

That's when my love died. I'll still remember his touch, his smile, his stupid jokes, and all the little things. But those memories hover in the background. What I remember most of all is how he looked like as he died. I'll forever remember the eyes bulging out of his head. His tongue hanging out of his mouth, forever bloated and lapping that filthy water. The same mouth that used to send kisses all over my body. Forever polluted in that death water.

The last one went down with one bullet, but I emptied the rest into his face. It wasn't enough so I went back to my car and carried a gallon milk-jug into his house. I poured the contents all over him, and I lit a match. I didn't watch the news, so I don't know if the entire house went down. When I left, he was turning black so that was enough for me.

I rolled down the window, and the night air felt good against my face. We had always joked about eloping to Vegas. He wanted to do it in one of the Elvis wedding chapels. As long as it wasn't in a real church, it was fine with me. We always joked about it, but he never got me a ring. He got me plenty of other jewelry but never an engagement ring.

I felt moisture on my face, and I rolled up the window. I glanced at his suitcase sitting next to me. It was the just-in-case suitcase. *In case anything bad ever happens to me, I want you to take this suitcase and run to Vegas.* I had never opened it until tonight. It was full of cash, some fake IDs, and a few weapons.

I used to always make fun of him for being such a worrier. Always thinking about the worst case scenario. He always said: *I worry about you. I'll always worry about you.*

I always responded: *But I'm a big girl, and you've taught me well.*

He'd have that same pinched look on his face and say: *But I haven't taught you everything.*

When I first glanced into the suitcase, I was confused at first. He had packed all the wimpy guns that he never used. They were all close-contact pistols, only slightly more dangerous than my knife collection. Then I realized that he had packed the lighter guns. Like he thought I wouldn't be able to handle something heavier.

I switched on the Man in Black, and I started to sing with him, "I went down, down, down, and the flames went higher."

I lit another Marlboro Light. I quit smoking two years ago, but I still had a bunch of cartons left from J's stash. I had been chain-smoking since Barstow. So I smoked and I sang and I wept all the way to Vegas.

McHenry's Gift

Mike MacLean

There was a knock at the door. Dillon Leary grabbed the .45 from underneath his mattress and pressed himself flat against the wall. He thumbed the safety off then racked the pistol's slide, jacking a round into the chamber. It was a big sound in the little apartment.

"Who is it?" Dillon called out.

"UPS. Got a package out here."

"Leave it."

"I need a signature, sir."

Dillon glanced through the peephole. The man outside was dressed from head-to-toe in brown. Brown shorts. Brown shirt. Brown cap. Standard issue UPS uniform. He even had one of those electronic clipboards to sign. The kind that looked like an Etch-A-Sketch toy but that recorded names into a vast computer database. From all appearances, the guy seemed like the real thing. But appearances could be deceiving.

Taking a deep breath, Dillon caught a whiff of the mildew and grime that permeated his little apartment. On Saturday nights the elevators smelled like vomit, the halls like piss. Dillon snuck another look out the peephole. The UPS guy stood motionless, head down, cap low over his eyes.

Screw it, thought Dillon. He held the .45 low behind his back and opened the door an inch. "Pass me the board."

The guy did as he was told, slipping the Etch-A-Sketch toy through the crack of the door. Dillon scrawled his name on the monitor screen and handed it back. "Take off," he said.

Shaking his head, the UPS guy disappeared down the hall. Dillon waited two and a half minutes. Then he quickly swung the door open and swept the package up from the floor. It was lighter than he thought it would be. He shook it gently. It made no noise.

Who could've sent such a thing?

Great efforts had been made to conceal Dillon's whereabouts. His dingy little hideaway sat surrounded by government housing projects, pawnshops, and liquor stores. It was a place where people minded their business and kept their mouths shut. Dillon had grown up in a neighborhood like this. He knew how to blend in, how to disappear, become another face in the crowd. No one had a clue Dillon was here.

So how did the UPS find him?

As he turned the deadbolts behind him, Dillon scanned the box's surface, reading the return address. Printed clearly in the upper left-hand corner was the name Wilson McHenry.

Dillon's blood went cold, chilling his veins. The box nearly slipped from his grasp.

He had just received a package from a dead man.

Wilson McHenry didn't look like a drug runner. He was tall and thin with stooped shoulders and a salt-and-pepper beard, a little more salt these days than pepper. Sometime in his late thirties he'd gone bald. Now, at 60, he was rarely seen without his trademark black fedora. It wasn't a look many men could pull off, but it seemed to suit McHenry fine.

It was the hat that Dillon first recognized as he trudged over a hill at Cedarbrook Park. He spotted McHenry on a bench facing the lake, feeding ducks from a brown paper bag. Along with the fedora, the old guy wore a pair of khakis and a tattered tweed jacket. More like a college professor than a career criminal. Dillon took a seat next to him and stretched out his legs. The lake smelled like wet grass.

"You ever eat one of those things?" asked Dillon, nodding towards the ducks.

"Every Christmas when I was a boy," said McHenry. He pulled a handful of breadcrumbs from his bag and threw them into the pond. A pair of silky green mallards plucked them from the water and quacked for more.

"What'd they taste like?"

"Like a greasy turkey. But greasy in a good way. Maybe I'll make one next holiday. You can come over and try it for yourself."

"I'd like that."

McHenry finished with the breadcrumbs, crumpled the bag, and sky-hooked it into a trash can a few feet away. There was a simple grace to his movements. McHenry was no athlete, not anymore. But he was comfortable in his skin, comfortable in his aging bones. He propped the fedora high on his head and squinted in the sun. "So why am I here?"

"Estaban sent me. He wanted us to talk."

"Estaban, huh? You on his clock now?"

Dillon went silent.

"I have to admit," said McHenry, "never saw that one coming."

"Writing's on the wall," said Dillon. "You've had a good run, Mac. Longer than anyone I know. But Estaban is a Colombian. And this is a Colombian's game."

McHenry smiled sadly. "And it's a young man's game too, is that it?"

Dillon peered out at the water. Gray clouds reflected off its glimmering surface, a bit of sunlight fighting through. "He wants thirty percent. And you have to chip in to pay off the *federales*. Maybe an extra five a month."

"That sound like a fair deal to you?"

Dillon shrugged. "It's what he's offering."

"And if I say no?"

"This is Estaban Gomez we're talking about. A Mexican judge said *no* to him once. They still haven't found the body."

The old man leaned back against the bench, letting out a long sigh. "You know, I was only nineteen when I started in this business. I'd fly a little Piper Cub back and forth to Mexico a few times a month. It was pot back then, a little cocaine here and there. God, I was a cocky little shit. Did it more for the thrills than anything else. Now it's all about the money. Been that way for some time."

"It was always about the money, Mac. You just never noticed."

"Maybe so."

"So why not get out?" said Dillon. "You've got enough put away. And Estaban won't bother you as long as you're not competition."

"Sorry, kid," said McHenry. "Not ready to give up the reins yet."

Dillon closed his eyes, listened to the ducks as they drifted away on the water. "Is that your answer then?"

"I'll talk to the boys. Let them decide for themselves. But I'm still in it."

Dillon stood, brushed off the seat of his jeans, and rolled the kinks out of his shoulders. He looked down at the old man, seeing his steel blue eyes, dark in the shade of the fedora's brim. "I wish you'd change your mind."

McHenry shook his head. "You know me better than that."

Dillon nodded and headed back up the hill. Just as he was about to disappear over its edge, McHenry called out to him.

"Hey," said the old man, "you still flying?"

"No. Too busy on the ground."

"That's a shame. You always were pretty good at the controls. Had some real talent up there."

"It wasn't talent," said Dillon. "I had a good teacher."

Night fell and the apartment filled with gray shadows. Dillon barely noticed. He sat in a dark corner, silent and unmoving, staring at the package on his kitchen counter. He'd been sitting that way for over an hour.

When the package first arrived, Dillon almost opened it. Then he noticed the overnight sticker. The parcel had been sent within the last 24 hours, sometime after McHenry's death. Which meant someone had sent it on the old man's behalf, possibly someone looking for revenge. If that was the case, maybe opening the package wasn't such a good idea. It wasn't ticking, but that didn't mean anything. Digital timers didn't make noise, Dillon told himself. And neither did trip wires.

Now, sitting in the dark corner, Dillon finally willed himself to move. He went to the kitchen and pulled a Budweiser from the fridge. Taking a drink, he circled the package a few times, trying to guess what could be inside.

A small block of C-4 would do the trick, he thought. *Or maybe a stick of good old-fashioned dynamite.*

No, the old man wasn't like that. McHenry saw killing as a necessary evil, but one to be avoided at all costs. Pure and simple, he didn't like to hurt people. And he certainly didn't have the heart to order Dillon's death.

Did he?

Dillon thought back to their last moment together. He had seen a father's love in the old man's eyes. Even in the end.

Setting his bottle down, Dillon found a box cutter in a cabinet over the range top. He just had to know. Carefully, he steadied the package and gripped the box cutter tightly. He was sweating and the plastic handle felt slick in his hand. Once he made his first cut, there was no going back.

He placed the blade lightly against the box top, about to slice into the tape. Then the phone rang. Dillon let out a heavy breath and went to answer it.

"Yeah?"

The voice on the other end was frantic, speaking rapid-fire English with a thick Colombian accent. "Leary, is that you? I have bad news. Very bad. *Dios mio*, you not going to believe it."

Dillon recognized the voice instantly. It belonged to Miguel Ortiz, one of Estaban's L.A. lieutenants.

"Miguel, slow down," said Dillon. "What're you talking about?"

"It's Señor Gomez. He's dead."

"What?"

"Estaban is dead," said Miguel, this time louder. "Someone blew up his Mercedes. Right in front of that house he bought in Brentwood. You hear me, Leary? You there?"

Dillon didn't answer. In a daze, he set the phone back on the receiver and looked once again at the package.

Maybe he was wrong about Wilson McHenry. Maybe the old man was as cutthroat as Dillon himself had been.

Dillon had put McHenry's prize Dobermans to sleep with a pair of drugged T-bones, then scaled the south wall of the old man's estate. The wall's razor wire cut into Dillon's work gloves, but left his skin unmarked. He would leave no blood at the scene, no DNA, no fingerprints.

Once inside the walls, Dillon carefully made his way across the grounds, sticking to the shadows and avoiding security cameras. He moved very slowly, very patiently. When he finally reached the main house, he saw McHenry sitting alone outside on the deck, drinking a margarita. The old man looked strange there for some reason. Dillon couldn't put a finger on what it was. Then it occurred to him that McHenry wasn't wearing his fedora. He looked unnatural without it, like he was missing a limb.

"You didn't kill my dogs, did you?" asked the old man.

Dillon stepped into the glare of a flood lamp, his shadow stretching across the lawn. "They're just napping."

"I appreciate that." McHenry took a sip of his margarita and eyed Dillon from head to toe, pausing briefly at the .45 automatic in Dillon's hand. "I've let the boys go for the evening," he said, "so you won't have any trouble."

"I'm sorry about this."

"Don't be. In a way, I'm glad it's you and not some punk kid. So how much is Estaban paying anyway?"

"Not enough. But I've got family. A sister out in Pasadena. Estaban knows where she lives."

"I understand. And, believe it or not, I don't hold a grudge. This is all just part of the deal."

A cool breeze swept across the old man's back yard, rustling leaves in the tree branches. McHenry shifted in his chair, set his drink down on the deck floor. "Hey," he said with a smile, "you remember your first run? Down in Colombia?"

"It was Peru. Eight years ago."

"That's right, Peru. We landed that old twin-engine prop on some god-forsaken airfield up in the mountains. In high wind, too. You were what, twenty-three, twenty-four maybe? Christ, I don't know what scared you more, the landing or them guys waiting for us."

"Bunch of mountain men with automatic weapons," said Dillon, chuckling. "Almost wet my pants when I saw them. Kept seeing scenes from *Deliverance* run through my head."

"But how did you feel after it was through?"

"Like I'd won the lottery," said Dillon.

McHenry's smile faded. "I miss that feeling. Miss the rush. I guess it was over for me a while ago."

The old man stared blankly into the night sky, not looking at anything in particular. All the life seemed to drain from his eyes. "I've made some arrangements," he said.

"We're not taking about a will, are we?"

"Estaban's a snake, always has been. Play with a snake, sooner or later you'll get bit. But I'm not going down alone. I've seen to that."

"What're you saying, Mac?"

McHenry faced him. For the first time, Dillon noticed the deep lines of age etched into the old man's brow, like time had run a razor across his skin. "In this game, every move is a risk," he said. "Everything you do has repercussions. I want you to remember that."

Dillon nodded. "I'll remember."

"Good," said McHenry. "Now let's get this over with."

The old man rested back in his chair and closed his eyes, as if he was about to take an afternoon nap. His face held an eerie calm.

Slowly, Dillon raised the .45 and took careful aim. Never in his life had a gun felt so heavy.

McHenry's boys had been busy. Within an hour, Miguel had phoned Dillon's apartment three more times, the panic in the Colombian's voice growing with each call. Three of Estaban's former lieutenants were dead. One went by bomb. Two others were shot. Then the phone calls stopped altogether, and Dillon began to wonder if Miguel himself had gotten hit.

Silence hung in the apartment like a poisonous gas. Walking to the fridge, Dillon dug out another beer and tilted the bottle back. Four empties sat on the kitchen counter.

What the hell was he still doing here? He should've taken off by now. Yet something kept him. Dillon tried to tell himself he was just biding his time, waiting for things to cool down before he made his run. But that was a lie, and he knew it. It was the package. He had to know what was inside.

Dillon took one last swig of beer then set the bottle next to its empty brothers. He grabbed hold of the package with both hands, carefully lifting it off the counter, testing its weight. It felt light. He shook it a little, hearing no hint at what was inside.

If it was a bomb, it would've gone off by now, thought Dillon. He picked the box cutter up and repeated the words in his head, over and over. *It would've gone off. It would've gone off. It would've gone off.*

Hand shaking, Dillon ran the cutter's blade along the box top, slitting the tape wide. Nothing happened. He closed his eyes and quickly ripped open the package's flaps.

There were no explosives, no wires, no timers. Instead, the package was filled with paper shreds cut from the *L.A. Times*. Nestled among the shreds was Wilson McHenry's old, black fedora.

Dillon let himself breathe again. He lifted the fedora out by its brim and looked at it hard. He recalled his last conversation with McHenry—the old man sitting on the deck, talking about "arrangements" and "consequences." Dillon had thought it was some sort of threat, a last ditch effort by the old man to stay alive. He should've known better. McHenry didn't play that way.

So what was McHenry's game? The answer came to Dillon as he pulled the hat on over his brow.

McHenry was tired of the business, he had said so himself. But he'd held on so long, he didn't know how to let go anymore. He needed Dillon's help. That was why he said he didn't hold a grudge. McHenry wanted out, and he understood that Dillon was just protecting himself and his family.

The fedora then was a symbol. McHenry was passing the baton. By having Estaban and his men killed, he was clearing a path so Dillon could take over. Run things the way the old man would have.

Dillon couldn't help but smile. Christ, McHenry was crazy. He wished he could see him now, have a drink together, tell a few jokes maybe. But all Dillon had left of the old man was the hat.

Tossing the empty package in the trash, Dillon smoothed out the brim of his new fedora. He wouldn't be anyone's muscle anymore, or a pilot running product. He was going to make something of himself, he decided. He'd make a deal with McHenry's boys and reorganize what was left of Estaban's crew. March right out and take control. After all, that's what the old man would've wanted.

Two of McHenry's boys sat in a Plymouth parked under a dead street lamp, waiting. They were both big men with square jaws and shoulders cut from stone. A sawed-off shotgun rested in the passenger's lap, out of sight below the window.

"Someone's coming," said the driver, nodding in the direction of the apartments across the street.

The passenger peered through the front windshield, catching sight of a figure stepping out the front entrance. "That's him."

"You a hundred percent?"

"Trust me, it's him."

"We don't got a picture or nothing. How can you be so sure?"

The passenger pumped the shotgun. A 12-gauge slug cranked into the chamber, ready for business. "The old man left clear instructions," said the passenger. "Told us to look for a guy wearing a funny old hat."

Capacity to Kill

Donovan Arch Montierth

I am not who I appear to be.

I've been playing this game for so long, I've almost forgotten who I was when I started. But then again, I doubt if I ever really knew who I was, even then. Do you ever truly possess an identity . . . or does it possess you, I wonder.

At the end of a hallway, lights are broken, casting deep dark shadows in a corner next to a stairwell. A single red dot flares in the center of the darkness as a cigarette shrinks in length. The figure with the nicotine fix leans against the wall and waits. He is a huge man. A hulking figure in leather, he is consumed by tattoos and his seething demeanor. His eyes are as intense as the ember of his cigarette. He has the eyes of a predator.

You would have to be a predator in my line of work. A successful predator in the wild has to pick up certain abilities. Intelligence, adaptability, camouflage, keen senses, steely nerves, misdirection, and patience are all important tools for a gifted predator. A lethal combination when used together. Strength and pure raw force help, I can see. But without the others, they become useless. A single rhinoceros will often fall prey to the strategy of a lone tiger. It may put up a valiant effort for awhile, but they all fall sooner or later. Strength and power make the animal over-confident, often separating itself from the herd in an invisible sense of self-security. The tiger's best tool is patience. He just sits and waits for the moment when the rhinoceros makes himself vulnerable and open to a single solitary attack.

It's all part of the game.

The figure waits. An elevator bell dings.

When the elevator doors open, a little man steps out. The figure smiles and examines his prey closely. John Gant can't be taller than five foot four, he figures, a hundred and forty pounds, maybe a little more for his soft looking tire around his mid-section. He's in his mid-fifties, balding with wire-rim glasses, a briefcase, and a small brown lunch bag. He looks like he jumped through a time machine from the nineteen-forties, as he has tan gloves and his suit is a brown three-piece.

It's very important that I study my prey. I need to know that one thing that drives each person. I find that one thing and I have control. I do my homework. There is so much to learn about people. How they carry themselves, how they act, their desires, their needs, and most of all their capacities.

Much of what drives us as humans is our capacity. Our capacity to love, our capacity to hate, our capacity to feel empathy towards another human being. This capacity drives us and motivates us. Most of all, I want to know of a person's capacity to kill. Not everyone has it. But in my line of work it's important to know how far a person can be pushed before they will reach inside their souls and find that capacity within themselves.

John walks down the hall and stands in front of door 453, which has a glue strip where the name plaque should be. He absently fumbles for his keys. He has a slow lazy way about him. He finds the keys and unlocks the door. He shuffles in and closes the door.

The predator smirks and drops his cigarette into a pile of half-smoked butts on the floor and steps on it. He walks up to the door and opens it without knocking.

John Gant stands at a single metal desk facing the door in the middle of a completely sparse office. He is startled when the figure opens the door suddenly. The figure looks around.

The office has very little furniture. The desk has a phone, computer, and one file folder on it. A single folding chair sits in front between the desk and the door. John has his hands on a plush roll-back chair as if he was about to sit at his desk. The figure notices there is nothing in the room that signifies personal belongings of any kind; no pictures, no name plaque, nothing on the walls.

The figure comes in dramatically and slams the door, then sits in the folding chair.

"So you wanted to see me?" he rasps dryly.

John Gant tries to regain his composure, "Excuse me, can I help you?"

"Now I am truly hurt that you don't recognize my voice, I should be unforgettable. After all, we just talked yesterday." His eyes curl up in question. "Are you senile?"

John squints in recognition. "Mr. Preston?"

"That's right, here I am after all . . . Brophy Preston!" He yells triumphantly.

"I'm terribly sorry, Mr. Preston, I was unaware that we had set an appointment. I was under the impression that you did not want to meet with me." John sits down.

Brophy smiles, slaps the table and points at John. "That's not it, I just had to see you for myself, you know, make sure you're not the cops or nothin'. In my line of work, you have to be careful, you know."

John's brow furrows as he reaches for the file folder on the table. He flips it open to reveal a mug shot of Brophy and pages underneath. He thumbs a few pages until he comes to what he is looking for. "Line of work, Mr. Preston? I didn't realize you were currently employed . . ."

Brophy furrows his brow in response. "Hell, just 'cause I don't have a time clock to punch in and out of doesn't mean I'm not dedicated to my work. Don't think of it as blue-collar work, think of it as black-collar work. A little breaking and entering here, a little kidnapping there, it's all the same. I still get paid."

John flips the pages back and taps the mug shot. "Black-collar . . . well, it's reassuring to know you still have your criminal ties." He smiles, trying to loosen the tension.

Brophy doesn't smile. "Ties. A pun. I get it. I like that. You sure are an interesting man, John, don't get me wrong, you are funny, but you and I both know why I am here . . . ," he winks at John, ". . . so how about we *both* get down to business."

John reaches down for his briefcase and places it on the desk. "I assume you are talking about the one hundred thousand dollars I mentioned on the phone?"

Brophy laughs loudly. "Ha! That's it, now you are definitely more interesting. John, you got me here, I am all ears and terribly eager to know more. So let's have it."

"Right. Thank you, Mr. Preston. I guess I should start at the top." John takes a big breath.

"I sure would appreciate it." Brophy breathes sarcastically.

"I work for an inter-continental agency called the N.A.P.C. or the North American Peace Coalition."

Looking around impressively, "Well, they do have beau-t-i-ful offices. Or is it orifices."

Embarrassed, John says, "Oh, I'm only here temporarily, under assignment. This is just for a few days. The regional office is out of Vancouver, British Columbia. It is a little agency partially funded by the U.S. and Canadian governments to find and apprehend certain individuals that make up a very low percentage of criminals that are considered by both governments to be the most dangerous."

"Unsavory types."

"That's right. Serial killers, terrorists, and bombers seem to make up the majority of these."

Brophy suddenly yells, "My brothers . . . and how do I fit in?"

John pauses a second and looks at Brophy. "We would like you to help us catch them. Well, one to be specific."

Brophy says quietly, "I don't think I heard you right. You said what?"

John nods. "We have a known suspect here in town that we would like to apprehend, his name is James Renault, a Quebec national wanted for the bombing of the court building in a small town in Canada."

Brophy's eyes turn into slits and he looks around the room again closely. He suspiciously says, "You're a bounty hunter?"

In surprise John says, "Oh, no, Mr. Preston, I'm not. I'm a clerk. I go out and recruit locally for jobs, then disappear. Most people don't even seem to notice me. I go into one area and move on when the job is done."

Brophy nods in satisfaction. "You didn't look like one. Do you realize who I am?" Brophy rambles on without waiting for an answer, "I'm one of the bad guys. I take pride in that. I love what I do. You might as well be speaking French. You want me to be a bounty hunter?"

John opens his briefcase and pulls out a thick envelope. He lays it in the center of the table seductively. He smirks as if ready to lay down his cards. "I have one hundred thousand dollars that says I do."

A smile flickers across Brophy's face and his eyes play tag with the envelope. "Now you're speaking my language." The smile disappears with a snap. "Why me?"

"Who better to catch a criminal, than another criminal?"

Brophy thinks about it. A battle rages inside—as if he is torn between which capacity to give in to. His capacity for hate seems to win over greed. "I think bounty hunters are worse than cops. They aren't even doing it for the right reasons. It's all about the money with them," he eventually says.

"That makes you ideal for the job. You get paid when you do a robbery or a kidnapping. Only when you do a job for us, no one will hunt you down for it."

A dark look sets the embers off in Brophy's eyes. Brophy stands up, trying to get a reaction from John. "I've killed a few bounty hunters in my time. I know how they operate and there is a distinct difference between me and them . . . I LOVE what I do," he says with conviction.

He reaches into his coat pocket and John flinches as he pulls out his cigarettes. Brophy smiles as he seems to feed off the energy of John's fear, as if sunbathing in the glow of a forbidden sun. He takes out his Zippo lighter, lights the cigarette, and takes a deep breath of death as his hand slowly drops the lighter back into his pocket. He pauses to enjoy the tightness in his chest and he focuses on John again. "I LOVE the look of fear in people's eyes." He leans forward and places his palms on the desk and blows the smoke into John's face. John coughs uncomfortably. "I LOVE getting in their faces and seeing their pain up close. It's like a game for me. Like Kick The Can. You remember that one, a group of kids gather around a can and you have to kick the can before someone tags you. Only this game . . ." He points to the table, "I play by myself and I'm kicking someone else's can all over the street." He twirls his fingers around the table.

John nods. "Think of this as a game then. Only the can you have to kick is James Renault. The list I have here is for DOA." He reaches into the briefcase and pulls out a clipboard. He taps it. "DOA. As in Dead or Alive." Brophy shows some genuine interest. "That's right. I am giving you the right to kill someone, and it's legal." John raises his eyebrows, looks at the clipboard and waves it above the table. "Have all the fun you want, all we want is the thumb."

Brophy's eyebrows collide. "The thumb? Why the thumb?" He walks over to lean on the wall.

"It's been our experience that most people are a little partial to a thumb being taken, whereas some people will accept twenty thousand for any other digit. We also need the newspaper from the day after."

"Newspaper?"

"A thumbless corpse usually raises enough eyebrows to be listed in the paper the next day and it shows the date of the kill." John throws the clipboard back into the briefcase. "Excellent for our records and we match the thumbprint to the fingerprints on file. If they mention the name of the victim in the paper or show a picture, you get a twenty-thousand-dollar bonus."

"How do I get my money?"

"You give me the thumb and newspaper and I give you the money." He taps the envelope.

"Let me see it."

John opens the envelope and spreads a few tightly bound thousands on the table.

"How much is that?" Brophy asks.

"Hundred thousand." John nods.

"Where's the rest. The twenty thousand for the bonus?"

John pats his coat pocket. "I have that if you get it. This should give you enough money to leave the country if you so wish. Find a nice place in the Bahamas or something."

Brophy thinks about it. He looks at John with a tight stare. Slowly, he walks around the table like a tiger stalking a rhinoceros. He leans over the back of John's chair behind him and puts the cigarette out on the desk in front of John. John's body tightens like a spring coil.

Brophy breathes in John's ear. "I think you may have misjudged me." Brophy brings an unsheathed switchblade around in front of John and taps it on the table in front of John. John looks at the blade as if wondering where it came from. "What if I just kill you right now and take the money for myself?"

John takes a deep breath and blows it out slowly as if to steady his nerves. "That is one option, but where's the fun in that? You've left your handprints on the table . . ." John taps the table ". . . and who knows how many other places. People saw you come in here and people will see you leave. Unlike me, Mr. Preston, people notice you. You stick out like a sore thumb, no pun intended."

"That may be true, John," Brophy places the blade on John's throat and John starts to shake, "but it sure would be fun. And in the end, it's all about the game."

John takes one last stab at a bargain, "How about this Mr. Preston . . . unlimited free rein to play your little games—all you want. All financed by us. I need a good regular. I can send you all over the country playing tag with all of the people on my list. The money is good and you will never be hunted again. How is that for benefits?"

The room is still. John and Brophy both seem to hold their breath. Brophy says quietly, "Now that may be something to think about." He abruptly stands back up and the blade disappears inside a pocket. He steps around to the front of the desk and smiles.

"Do you like to play games, John?"

John breathes slowly and cracks a smile of relief. "Only when I was a little boy. But it has been a long time."

"I bet it has. Only you might be really good at them, you have a poker face . . ." And with that, Brophy leaves the office with a flourish.

Quietly, John starts to flip through Brophy's file once more, wondering what he got himself into.

＊　＊　＊

They made me what I am today.

I often wonder how I got here. Then I meet another one, just like the first and I remember why I'm here. They fill the need within me. The need I have to play the game.

Some people say the first time a person sees blood spilled, they're never the same. I can remember my first time. It was a moment of sheer terror, and somehow ... thrilling. That moment changed my life forever. They call this feeling bloodlust. Adrenaline replaces the blood in your veins before a kill. I was on the edge, waiting for the time to strike. Waiting patiently for the prey to spring the trap.

A small parking garage, dimly lit and vacant, sits quietly, no trace of the savage tableau that's yet to come. Two cars sit in the small underground brick structure. A beige rent-a-car sits in a far corner, while a dark ominous van sits in the middle.

In the opposite corner, an elevator bell dings.

The doors open and out steps John Gant. He is still in his three-piece suit, wearing his gloves and carrying his briefcase, paper lunch bag, and his clipboard. He walks across the parking garage toward the rent-a-car, unaware of the eyes peering at him from inside the van.

He walks past the van. Half-way to his car he hears the van door open, then close. "John, I think it's time we play a little game of our own," a ragged voice says behind him.

John stops and peers back at the van. Brophy Preston emerges from the shadows. He is in all black and wearing gloves. Light glints off the steel blade in his hand. John is startled. "Excuse me ... Mr. Preston?" he says curiously.

Brophy walks toward John slowly. "I said, I think it's time we play a game of our own. It's called, Hide and Seek. I know you've played it before, only about a hundred years ago."

John is confused. "I don't understand."

Brophy continues, "This particular Hide and Seek is a little bit different though."

"Mr. Preston, is this about what we discussed earlier? Have you made your decision?"

Brophy stops a few feet away from John. "Oh, yes, I have." He points the knife at him. "My decision is for you and I to play a game. Drop your stuff. Now."

John looks at him for a second and slowly puts his briefcase, clipboard, and baggie on the ground.

"Stand up. Don't move. I wouldn't want to cut you. Not yet. Put your hands up." John does as he's told. Brophy comes around and pats John down quickly, looking for something. "Do you have any weapons?"

"Mr. Preston?"

"Do you?"

"No."

"The envelope's not in your pocket. Where is it?" John doesn't speak. "Is it in the briefcase?" Still nothing. "OK, then we'll do this your way." Brophy Preston backs up a few steps, puts the knife away and smiles at John. As if scolding a child he says, "The rules are very simple—somewhere you have hidden a hundred thousand dollars. I'm here to find it. Is that becoming clear? Will you give it to me?"

John tries to reason with him. "Mr. Preston, we've discussed the terms of our agreement; I can't give you the money until the job is completed."

Undeterred, Brophy continues. "That's what I thought. And I do appreciate your honesty, John, I really do, but I think it would be a lot easier if I just take the money myself and move on. That vacation does sound good, believe me . . ."

"I can't give you the money."

"Yes, I know that John, and you are a strong one." Brophy laughs. "So let's just play the game, shall we? Now, I'll introduce a few more players to the game." Brophy suddenly raises his right hand. John flinches and Brophy laughs again. "Not so fast, we haven't even started the game. This is player number one. His name is Mr. Right." Brophy says as condescension drips from his every word. He balls his fist. "He is an aggressive player and very competitive. He hates to lose." He suddenly raises his left hand. "This is player number two. His name, unusually enough, is Mr. Left." He balls his left fist. "He is also very competitive and hates it when he loses to player number one." Brophy holds his fists up in front of John for him to get a good look. "Their job, rightly so, is to Seek for that check. Seek and ye shall find!" Brophy puts his hands down. "Will you give me that money?"

Softly, John says, "No."

"OK then, let the games begin. Mr. Right?"

Brophy quickly punches John viciously in the stomach. John doubles up and gasps for air. Brophy holds his right fist in front of himself and asks, "Did you find it, Mr. Right? No? Well, then it's Mr. Left's turn. Mr. Left?" Brophy punches John in the face. His glasses fall to the ground. John grabs his face in pain. "Did you find it, Mr. Left? No? Damn. That's a shame. No winners yet . . ."

In obvious pain John says, "This really isn't necessary."

Brophy's playful facade drops and he yells, "Well, you're right there, I gave you a chance to think rationally, but you didn't take it! So here we are playing a game that you are unequipped to handle. Let me just fill you in on a few things. I am perfectly happy the way things are." He pokes John in the chest, "I make the rules. I play the games. And I don't have to answer to no whiny-ass scrawny clerk for any of it. I will take your money though. That is appreciated."

John chokes in obvious disgust, "You won't get away with this. We'll catch you."

Brophy puffs up his chest and says in a kid's voice, "You and what army?" He pokes himself in the chest. "I've been doing this for too long, I know all the tricks. Hey, you know what this game needs? More players. Right now, there are only three. Me, Mr. Right, and Mr. Left. So let's introduce two more players to the game and make it five, shall we?" He holds up his right foot. "This is Mr. Toe. Your turn, Mr. Toe."

He kicks John in the side and John falls to his knees clutching his side. "Oh, that was a good one Mr. Toe, but did you find it? No? OK, then—on to player number five." He holds up his left foot. "This is Mr. Heel. Heel? Your turn." He kicks John in the stomach. John yelps and goes down on the pavement hard. "Did you find it? I didn't think so."

Brophy bends down to speak into John's ear as if scolding him. "Now, John, you are the only player not showing any enthusiasm for the game. The other players and I are holding up our side. We expect some participation from your team. It's time to pull your resources together and produce the item we are playing for." Brophy pulls out his blade and opens it slowly. He's tiring of the game. "Now, I will only ask you one more time . . . where is the money?"

John coughs for a few moments and wheezes, "It's in the bag."

"What? I can't hear you." Brophy strains to hear.

"It's in the lunch bag."

Brophy smiles. "Sneaky. Lunch bag. I figured it was in the briefcase." Brophy taps the blade on John's forehead a couple of times. "Now, go get it."

John finds the strength to crawl over to the bag. He reaches into the bag, pulls out a small pistol and instantly shoots Brophy in the left foot. Brophy shouts in surprise and falls to the ground, clutching his bloody foot.

John takes a deep breath and stands up. He dusts off his suit and rolls his neck as if letting out the kinks. John breathes normally and smiles at the man lying on the ground at his feet. Brophy is stunned, glaring up at John in amazement. John calmly walks over to his glasses, blows on them, folds them up and puts them in his pocket. His demeanor has changed and he takes on the appearance of a different man. Confidence shines in his eyes and face.

John says in a voice deeper and without the whine, "Now, let me introduce you to someone." He holds up the little gun so that Brophy can take a good look at it. "This may sound very hokey, but let's play in your world for a little while, shall we?" As if teaching a class, John says, "This—is the great equalizer. I know, trite, but true. He's not the best, but overall not a bad player to have on your team. The wonderful thing about him is that he doesn't care what race you are, what gender you are, what size or age you are. He is the great equalizer." John puffs up his chest, "Makes even the littlest man as strong as ten." He pokes himself in the chest. "Makes the older feeble man, that's me, as young and as agile as any younger man," he says as he pokes Brophy in the chest, "that would be you."

John taps the gun on Brophy's forehead. "This makes me fast. This makes me strong and this makes me powerful. This makes everything fair. This, Mr. Preston is my Army as you so playfully put it. Are you listening Mr. Toe?"

He swings the gun around and shoots Brophy in the right foot. Brophy screams as the blood rushes from his face.

"What's wrong Mr. Preston? You no longer have any more passion for the game that you so thoughtfully started. If you start the game you have to be fully prepared for the unexpected. The problem, Mr. Preston, as I see it is that you simply did not bring enough players to the game. Right, Mr. Left?"

John shoots Brophy in the left hand.

"Me? I have myself and five other players—tiny players, but players nonetheless. Three have had their turns."

He shoots Brophy in the right hand. Brophy screams in agony and struggles to hold on to his bloody body.

John nods. "Four. Now, Mr. Preston for someone who professes to be so well equipped for this game you forgot one vital rule. Do you know what that is?"

Brophy gurgles, "What?"

"Anyone not bringing a gun to the game, will lose." John drops the playful façade and says, "Now, Mr. Preston, let us go back to the main issue, shall we? You still have a few minutes yet until you bleed to death and it is important to me that you understand this. Are you comfortable?"

Incredulous, Brophy says, "I'm bleeding . . ."

John continues, "Then you should be numb in no time. Anyway, let me teach you something about being a bounty hunter, because this is something I know a great deal about."

Brophy's stunned again. He looks at the little man kneeling before him as if seeing him for the first time. "You're a bounty hunter?" He manages.

John nods in affirmation. "That's right. You misjudged me. The best hunters always make the bounty come to them. The biggest tool for a bounty hunter? Eh?" he asks.

"I have no friggen idea . . ."

"Estimation. How do you estimate the strength of a man? By his looks? By his mind? By his resolve? No. By his experience." He taps the gun on Brophy's head again. "It's called research, Mr. Preston. You research your opponent. So you know him well enough to bring him to you. What is his capacity? How far can you push him? What motivates his desire, feeds his monster?" John looks Brophy deep in the eyes. "A man's character cannot be defined by what he chooses to show you. It's what he doesn't show you that counts."

He reaches down and picks up Brophy's knife. "My research, for example, has shown me that you like to beat up on your victims before you kill them. Also, that you have an affinity for knives not guns. You could care less about money judging by the amount left behind at several of the jobs and how at every opportunity you played and taunted your victims and the police. I was able to catch you where others had failed because I fed your need to dominate your victims."

Brophy squeezes out, "Why did you wait so long?"

John shrugs. "Hey, don't blame me if I played the game better than you. You seemed to like it so much, why not give you a taste of your own medicine? You had a chance to ask questions. Your first question should have been, am I on that list?"

Brophy laughs and finds some strength to say, "Go ahead and take me in. I'll just get loose again, and we'll throw that can right back into the air and start all over."

John looks at Brophy just as a tiger would a defeated rhinoceros. "It's easier to take a thumb than it is a prisoner."

John shoots Brophy in the forehead. He falls back on the concrete, dead.

John throws the gun on the ground next to the body. He reaches down and meticulously cuts off Brophy's thumb with his blade and throws the blade on the body. He takes his leather gloves off to reveal his hands in plastic gloves underneath. He throws the leather gloves next to the body.

He walks over to the briefcase and takes out plastic bag and puts the thumb in the baggie and places it into a pocket of the briefcase. Grabbing the clipboard, John reads, DOA TARGET and underneath that, "Brophy Preston." He takes out a pen and crosses out the name. "There's your money," he says as he puts the clipboard in the briefcase. John stands and walks toward his rent-a-car, gets in and drives away.

In this business, you have to have a little bloodlust. Otherwise, how could you do what I do. You have to have a killer instinct, and a little bit of the tiger in you. Does this make me any better than the men I kill? Probably not, but there definitely is a difference between me and them. I do this for the right reasons and I HATE what I do.

False Alarm

J.D. Smith

Fucking car alarms.

A stiff breeze and they go off. A shotgun blast around the corner and they go off. One time, when I was in Mexico on some import-export business, shockwaves from the fireworks for the festival of Saint Whoever-the-Fuck-It-Is-This-Week Week set off every car alarm for a three-block radius around the main plaza. If you didn't know any better you would have thought bombs were about to drop. Shit.

I can't blame that guy in California who emptied his Magnum into a Camaro that seemed to go off whenever somebody sneezed. It was keeping him up at night. A few more guys like that and the world might actually become a better place.

In the meantime it is about 10 p.m. on a weeknight and I am stuck on a side street in a leafy-ass neighborhood where doctors and lawyers live. I have about a thousand decibels pouring out of the hood while I'm fumbling for the right button or switch to kill the *whooing* and *cranking* that sounds like the bastard love-child of a squadrol and an ambulance.

Maybe I bumped the door with my bag of tools. Maybe I gave the sedan a dirty look.

I hate working with borrowed cars. But that's what I've got, and I am in the seat punching all the remote buttons on the keychain and digging around in the dead zone between the steering wheel and the driver's side door to see what will keep me from becoming an even bigger Neighborhood Watch magnet than I already am.

Too late.

A front door on the other side of the street opens and out of the piss-yellow light of his living room walks a respectable citizen who makes up in gut for what he lacks in hair. He is carrying a two foot-long police brutality flashlight almost as if he knew how to use it, and he is prepared to defend his property values.

I'm not too keen on being looked at like some kind of criminal just because I'm having some technical difficulties, but I have to put myself in his place for a minute. Telling him that I'm having a bad enough night as it is only going to make him suspicious. And that if he gives me any guff about it I'll turn that flashlight into the second coming of Abner Louima's broomstick.

I already have the windows down—the only thing on this car that's manual—by the time he waddles over.

He raises his voice over the whanging of the alarm and says, "Can I help you, sir?" in the way that means, "You have thirty seconds to get out of here before I take down your license plate number and call the cops."

I'm sorry to cause all this trouble (he'll never know how much), so apologizing comes easy enough.

I throw in an explanation, too.

"This has never happened with this car before." True that. "It must be a short circuit."

This guy might look soft, like he spends most of his time behind a desk, but it's clear that he's read at least one volume of the *Time-Life* series on auto repair and now he wants to prove it.

"It can't be that," he says, "or none of your electrical system would be working." All of the sudden he is going from Clint Eastwood in his *Dirty Harry* days to Bill Cosby in the Huxtable years. This might be the kind of guy you'd want as a neighbor.

"Why don't you let me take a look at the manual? I might be able to figure this out."

I lean over and pop open the glove compartment and there the manual is, right where it's supposed to be.

I pass it over to him and he turns on the D-cell nightstick. I'm blinded for a second and he has the drop on me, but he's too busy leafing through the booklet.

A flick to the back of the book, and then the middle, and with his middle finger he points out a set of instructions on a right-hand column. He walks me through the steps. With one button punch on the keychain and the turn of a switch at the base of the steering column, we put the alarm back to sleep.

You could grab a handful of the quiet that comes after that.

By now my shirt is soaked, and I'm surprised I can't hear the sweat drip off of me. But our upright citizen can't see that. One more reason to wear a jacket and tie, like any other businessman.

I thank the man, and apologize again. I even mean it. There's no reason to bother innocent people and I don't like attention when I'm not looking for it.

The Good Samaritan/Neighbor takes me at my word. "I'm glad I could help. Nobody wants to end their day like that. Just remember what I showed you. I dog-eared the page in your manual for you."

He thought it was my manual. They were definitely his prints.

"You have a good night now."

It was getting better by the second. My small-s savior waved and made a beeline back to his home and castle, probably to watch *Law & Order* or some other show about bad things that happen in other places. He goes back into the piss-yellow light and shuts the door. The curtains stay closed as I roll out. He's not interested in checking the plates; I'm just a guy in a jam.

Well, not anymore. I've got all the time in the world to boost whatever I can scoop up and pry out before I leave the rest of this tank at the chop shop. The boys will know what to do with the bodies in the trunk.

Rescuing Isaac

Frank Zafiro

"So your guy got pinched. So what?" Angelo's voice coming out of the telephone receiver was thick with New Jersey accent. "Everybody gets pinched."

Dominic Bracco lowered the pay phone receiver away from his mouth and rubbed his eyes. "I'm worried."

"What's to worry about? Get a lawyer. He gets off or he does a little stretch. No big deal."

"It won't be a little stretch. It'll be a dime."

"Ten years for theft? You're kiddin' me, right? And speak up, I can barely hear ya."

Dom moved the receiver closer to his mouth. "The charge isn't theft. It's robbery."

"Don't tell me your guy flashed a gun."

"No, he had it covered with a paper bag. But it doesn't matter. In the State of Washington, all you have to do is act like you got a piece and if the other guy believes it, it's robbery."

"Yeah, sure, it's like that most places," Angelo said. His tone took on that of a teacher whose patience was wearing thin with a slow student. "But that's the letter of the law, not how they charge it. As long as he didn't actually show them the gun—"

"That's how they charge it here." Dom didn't like his uncle's tone. *He* lived here in River City. *He* knew the score. Angelo didn't. All his uncle did was get a little taste of everything he did. And for that little taste, he was supposed to help out in situations like this one.

"Okay," Angelo said, "if that's the way they do it, that's the way they do it. Get the kid a good lawyer."

"He's got a good lawyer." Dom scratched his hairy forearm.

"And?"

"The lawyer says he's fucked."

Angelo chuckled. "The lawyer actually said that?"

"Not in so many words."

"Why's he so sure?"

Dom suppressed a sigh. He shouldn't have to explain. Angelo was supposed to help, no questions asked. "They caught him in the hijacked truck, with the gun in the cab. The driver picked him out of the lineup. Then instead of clamming up and waiting for the attorney, which is what I told him to always do no matter what, he goes and lies to the cops instead."

"Stupid," Angelo observed. "How about the judge?"

"No chance."

Angelo whistled. "He *is* fucked."

"Like I said."

"So he does some time."

Dom could almost hear the shrug that accompanied Angelo's words. He gritted his teeth. "He might not do the time. That's why I'm worried."

"You think he'll turn state's witness?"

"I don't know. He might."

"I told you to only hire Italians," Angelo admonished him. Dom rolled his eyes. As if Italians never turned on each other. "Uncle Angelo, there are no *paisans* out here, you know? It's not like Jersey. Any Italians in this town, they shop at The Gap."

"Whatever. Look, if he rolls, this guy, what can he give the government?"

"A lot," Dom conceded. "Too much."

"Too many eggs in one basket, Dommie," Angelo said. "What did I tell you about that, huh? You don't trust no one guy with too much."

"I know."

"You say you know, but now this guy is in jail and you're calling me, shitting water about it." Angelo sighed. "Can you get to him while he's in jail?"

Dom hesitated. Traffic whizzed by behind him. He'd never used this pay phone to call Uncle Angelo before, so he knew it was safe. But Angelo—

"Is this line okay?" he asked.

"New cell phone," Angelo told him. "Out of the box this morning. Now answer the question."

"The answer is no. I've got no people inside and the jail security is tight, too."

Angelo was silent for a while. Finally, he said, "I guess your only option is to break him out."

"Break him . . . what?" Dom sputtered.

Angelo didn't seem to notice. "I'll send two guys. They're gonna need a wheel man. You got a wheel man?"

Dom shook off his surprise. "Yeah. But who are you going to send?"

"Doesn't matter. It'll be a coupla guys from Kansas City. You can call them Mr. Johnson and Mr. Peterson. They'll take care of the details."

Dom gritted his teeth. Kansas City? Compared to Jersey, that was the minor leagues. And River City was even lower than KC on the pecking order. By sending troops from there,

Angelo made a clear statement—Dom's problem wasn't that important.

"Thanks," he managed to say. "I'd use my own people, but—"

"But they gotta disappear after. I know. Don't worry. Time will come I need your guys for something out this way. Just tell them not to wear no flannel shirts." Angelo laughed at his own joke. The laughter dissolved into a hacking cough.

Dom pulled the phone from his ear and waited.

Angelo finished clearing his lungs and grunted. "How's my restaurant doin'?" he asked.

"Fine. It's a hot spot in town. How's things in Jersey?"

"Getting dark, Dommie. But there's money to be made. Always money to be made."

For the thousandth time, Dom thought about asking to come back, but he held his tongue. Now wasn't the time. Not when he was asking for help instead of solving his own problem in the piss-ant city he'd been sent to work.

Instead, he listened carefully while Angelo told him what to do.

Isaac looked thinner to him. Dom wondered if he'd eaten since the arrest. The young man's usually perfectly gelled hair was a tangled mess. His eyes darted warily left and right as he sat down on the other side of the thick Plexiglas window and picked up the phone receiver.

Dom did the same. "You know they tape these?" he asked, pointing to the phone.

Isaac nodded.

"Don't ever say nothing to anybody except your lawyer," Dom told him. "And him only what he needs to know."

Isaac hung his head. The act made him look much younger than his twenty-three years. "I'm sorry, boss."

"Don't be sorry," Dom said. "Be smart."

Isaac bobbed his head, not meeting Dom's eyes.

"Look at me," the older man said.

Isaac looked up. His eyes brimmed with tears.

Christ, you'd think he'd never gone to jail before. No way will he do the dime without rolling over. "Listen, kid, I'm going to take care of you."

Isaac's eyes brightened. "How?"

"Never mind how. You just worry about what I need you to do."

"Sure, boss, whatever you need."

"Tomorrow, you call your lawyer and tell him you want to petition the court for new counsel. You want a hearing, understand?"

"Yeah. I want a new lawyer."

"No. You want a *hearing.*"

Isaac squinted. "Why?"

"Just do it."

Isaac Rainey sat on his jail bunk, his knees drawn to his chest. He thought about everything Dom had told him, running it through his mind over and over so he got it right. Relief had washed over him as soon as he realized that Dom was going to bust him out.

Dom had been his second visitor that day.

The first was the bitch detective again, the one working his case. McLeod was her name. She laid it all out for him on the table. All the evidence. Him in the cab, the gun, the witness, his own stupid fucking lies. All of it was worth ten years in Walla Walla State Penitentiary, she said.

When she was done, she put all her papers back into a file and said she could help him out. Dom's contacts went all the way back to the East Coast. She could call in someone from the FBI who worked organized crime and they could work some sort of deal. He refused her, but after the long walk back to his cell and the hard stares from the other inmates, he'd wondered if maybe that was his best option.

When Dom came to see him and told him he'd get him out, it made him feel guiltier than hell for even thinking about turning on the man. Dom had given a job, trusted him, been like a father to him. You don't repay that kind of loyalty by rolling over.

Isaac allowed himself a smile. Everything was going to be all right.

In the small office at the rear of Angelo's Restaurant, Dom counted out the contents of the envelope and cursed. He began counting again. Joe Bassen stood in front of his desk, rocking from foot to foot.

When he'd finished counting the second time, Dom cursed again. Ever since Isaac got popped, earnings were down. Some of it was because Bassen didn't have a partner to work with him. Isaac was a sharp worker, and productive. He did Dom no good sitting in jail. He needed him back on the streets.

He glanced up at Bassen. The former boxer swayed and waited, probably replaying a fight from the past in his head. Was he skimming? Naw, Bassen was loyal. Not as smart as Isaac, but loyal.

"You hit the auto body shop out east yet?"

Bassen broke his reverie and nodded. "Yeah. They didn't have it."

"None of it?"

"Not even the vig."

Dom swore. Missing a payment was one thing, but not even paying interest? "What'd you do?"

Bassen blinked. "Gave the foreman a little reminder. And said I'd be back tomorrow."

Dom nodded. Collecting was Bassen's forte and he did it well. The bigger operations—that's where Isaac came in.

Trish knocked at the door and poked her head in. The nu-

merous bracelets on her wrists clinked with each motion.
"Coupla guys to see you. Said they're from out of town."

Dom slipped the envelope into his desk. "Sure, Trish. Send
'em in."

When the pair ambled into the office, Dom raised his eyebrows. Both of them were smaller than he was and neither one
looked Italian.

"Peterson," said the first, a wiry man with muddy brown
hair. He held out his hand and Dom took it. The grip was firm.

"I'm Johnson," the second man said. His frame was well
muscled and his grip even firmer. He wore his hair gelled like
Isaac.

"Dominic Bracco," he told them both, then motioned to
Bassen. "That's Joe. He'll be your wheel man."

Johnson nodded to him, then turned back to Dom.

"When's the hearing?"

"Ten tomorrow."

"Courthouse security?"

"It's tight. Ever since nine-eleven, they've got just one entrance."

"Metal detectors?"

Dom nodded.

"How about in the courthouse halls?"

Dom shook his head. "They've got security guards at the entrance and a couple that I think are on call, but no roving patrols."

"And in the courtroom? Bailiffs?"

Dom grinned. "Not like back East. Bailiffs are nothing more
than secretaries. Most of them are women in their forties or
fifties."

Peterson and Johnson exchanged a glance. Johnson raised
his eyebrows slightly. Peterson shook his head. "Too many
witnesses in the courtroom."

Johnson shrugged and turned back to Dom. "How about
transport from the jail?" he asked.

"Two corrections officers."

"Not cops?"

"No. Jailers."

"Armed?"

"Yeah, they carry guns."

"The route?"

Dom pulled out a piece of paper and drew. "They have a special entrance and exit from the building right here. Once they're inside, there's a short hallway, a pair of double doors and they're in the courtroom hallway."

Johnson pointed to the outside door. "Where's this lead?"

"Just outside, onto the Public Safety campus. They have to walk him about a block to get back to the jail."

"They transport him *outside?*" Peterson interjected.

Dom nodded.

Peterson shook his head in wonder. "Who plans their security? A retarded monkey?"

"Is the campus closed?" Johnson asked.

"Only from cars. It's open to foot traffic."

"No checkpoints?"

"Uh-uh."

"How close can you get a car?"

"From this exit? About a block."

The two men from Kansas City exchanged another glance, both with slight smiles.

"Your boy going to be wearing a suit for his hearing?" Johnson asked.

"Brand new one, yes."

Peterson and Johnson nodded at the same time.

"This will work," Johnson said.

Back at the hotel, Peterson asked, "Whattaya think?"

Johnson shrugged. "I think that if this mope wasn't the boss's nephew, I'd be banging a showgirl at Taps right now."

"No, I mean the plan."

Johnson shrugged. "Like I said, it'll work. We snatch the guy, turn him over to his crew and we're out of here."

"I wish we could fly back. It's a long fucking drive."

Johnson put his bag on the bed. "We got satellite radio. It'll be fine."

"I wonder what they're gonna do with the guy once we snatch him."

"Who cares?"

"I didn't say I cared. I said I *wonder*."

Johnson considered a moment. "This ain't Jersey, or even KC. They'll probably make little frosted cupcakes together and have a good cry."

Peterson laughed. "Probably."

Johnson removed a roll of cash from his bag. "Come on, we gotta go to the hardware store."

The next morning, Isaac dressed slowly in his cell, relishing the feel of real clothing against his skin. Especially the shirt. It wasn't silk, but the material was cool and smooth. Nothing like the rough, ill-fitting orange jumpsuit he'd been issued after being booked.

He ignored the prying eyes of the guard at his door and took his time knotting the tie, adjusting his belt, and slipping into his shoes. Finished, he put on the jacket and smoothed the lapel. Even in the misshapen reflective film that served as a mirror, he figured his reflection looked good.

He fussed with his hair for a few moments, wishing he had some gel.

Dom waited in the car sipping his mocha while Bassen checked out the house. It was one of the rentals he owned and was supposed to be empty, but sometimes kids or druggies broke in and camped. When Bassen found them, they didn't come back, and word spread.

Bassen appeared in the doorway and waved him in.

Clutching his coffee cup, Dom climbed out of the car and went into the empty house.

Peterson slid his pant leg down and tossed the masking tape into the courthouse bathroom trash can.

Johnson hefted a wooden hatchet handle, smacking it into his palm.

Peterson slid his own handle up the sleeve of his jacket and held it in place by bending his wrist. He met Johnson's eyes and flicked his wrist. The wooden handle snapped into his hand.

Johnson grinned.

Judge Petalski looked up from the short legal brief and stared at Isaac Rainey. Isaac smiled back at her. She considered him for a moment then dropped her eyes back to the brief.

Isaac leaned toward his lawyer. "That judge is hot," he whispered. "No wonder they called her Judge Petals."

His lawyer shushed him.

Isaac watched the judge read, admiring her long black hair and pretty face. Even the librarian glasses she wore were sexy.

When she pushed the brief aside and looked back at him, he shot her another smile.

"Mr. Rainey," she said, "this brief contains no legal reasoning for your lawyer to be removed from the case."

Isaac nodded, enjoying the sound of her smoky voice.

"It is your prerogative to dismiss him if you wish, since he was not assigned by the court. But I will not rule that he has provided inadequate counsel."

"Thank you, your honor," his lawyer said.

Isaac tried to appear hurt.

Judge Petalski acknowledged the lawyer's thank you and turned her attention to Isaac. "Frankly, Mr. Rainey, this hearing has been a waste of the court's time and, I suspect, nothing more than a ploy on your part to spend some time outside of your jail cell. While I intend to ensure that you get a fair trial in the matter before this court, do not think that I will tolerate any chicanery or manipulation of the system. Is that understood, Mr. Rainey?"

Isaac cleared his throat and stood. "Uh, yes, your honor. I'm sorry."

She regarded him for a moment, then gave them both a curt nod. "Very well. Dismissed."

When she banged her gavel, Isaac couldn't help smiling.

Johnson expected the transport deputies to flank the target. He was pleasantly surprised when he saw the large wooden courtroom door swing open to reveal them walking single-file. The thin kid in between the two had his hands in front of him, the cuffs hidden by the length of his jacket sleeves. He kept the pace slow, but Johnson wasn't sure if it was just simple defiance or him playing to the plan.

Peterson stood near the exit door, looking at some legal paperwork they'd downloaded off the Internet. He did his best to plaster a confused look on his face.

Johnson fell in behind the second deputy, glancing at his watch and playing the part of a harried lawyer. He double-checked and saw that both deputies were armed.

The first deputy, a lumbering fat slob with a scraggly black mustache, stopped at the exit door. He removed a ring of keys from his belt and unlocked the door. Peterson lowered his paperwork and gave a frustrated sigh.

The deputy swung the door open wide and walked into the hallway without a backward glance. The second deputy, red-haired and red-faced, stepped forward and grabbed the door, holding it open for the target.

Peterson made eye contact with Red. His face brightened and he stepped toward him. "Hey, officer, can you help me out? I can't figure out where I'm supposed to go for this hearing."

Red shook his head. "Sorry, I can't. I'm transporting a prisoner."

"I'm a lawyer," Johnson said, stepping close. "I can help."

Red looked over his shoulder at Johnson. "Thanks, sir—"

Peterson flicked his wrist and the short axe handle appeared in his hand. He drove it into the deputy's sternum and followed it up with a wheelhouse uppercut beneath the deputy's chin.

Johnson grabbed hold of Red and forced him into the hallway. Peterson bounded past him after the lead deputy.

The door slammed shut behind them.

Johnson let the wooden handle drop into his hand. He struck Red behind the ear, delivering three hard shots. The deputy collapsed and lay still.

Johnson looked up in time to see Peterson reach the fat deputy. The deputy half-turned, his expression bored. When he saw Peterson bearing down on him, his eyes flared open wide in surprise. His hand flew to the gun at his side, but Peterson cracked him on the jaw before he was able to grab the handgrip of the pistol.

Peterson swung several times in rapid succession, choosing a different target for each blow. The deputy crumpled to the ground, rolling in agony. Merciless, Peterson dropped his knee onto the deputy's back and struck him in the head until the deputy went limp.

Meanwhile, Johnson plucked Red's handcuffs from the case and cuffed the deputy's hands behind his back. He pulled the deputy's Smith & Wesson from the holster and tucked it into his own belt. Then he glanced up and down the hallway, searching the ceiling and above both doors for a security camera. He saw none.

"Unbelievable," he muttered. This place was definitely Hicksville.

Peterson cuffed the fat deputy and took his keys and gun.

The target stared at them both with wide eyes. "Wh-who are you guys?" he asked in a tremulous voice.

"Never mind," grunted Johnson. "Walk between us. Don't look at nobody."

The men from Kansas City took up a position in front and behind the target and walked confidently out the door and into the courtyard.

Isaac struggled to keep his face neutral. Adrenaline coursed through him as he walked between the two suited men.

I can't believe Dom just broke me out of jail!

He realized he was smiling and forced his grin into a frown. The two men walked quickly but casually and he kept pace with them. No one approached them or even seemed to give the group a second look.

Despite the cool air, sweat trickled down his back. The weight of events settled on him and his stomach churned. He kept expecting to hear yelling and gunshots from behind them. He glanced over his shoulder and saw nothing but people going about their business.

"You look back again," one of his escorts growled, "and I'll break your fucking arm."

Isaac snapped his eyes forward, focusing on a point on the ground about fifteen yards ahead. He kept his eyes lowered. The trickle of sweat turned into a flood.

A block from the courthouse, Joe Bassen waited in the driver's seat of a white Ford Crown Victoria. Isaac heard the engine rumble to life as they approached. One of the suited men broke off and went to the passenger side. The other opened the back door and pushed him in.

"Move across," he grunted at Isaac.

Isaac slid across the seat to the passenger side. The man climbed into the backseat and closed the door.

"Go," he directed Bassen.

* * *

Dom sat in the canvas folding chair and watched the small TV on the kitchen counter. When he heard footsteps on the back porch, he snapped the TV off.

Johnson walked through the door first. He ignored Dom and his eyes swept the room.

Isaac came next, rubbing his wrists and smiling.

"Hey, hey!" Dom said, holding his arms open wide. "He's free!"

Isaac leaned into the bigger man, who slapped him heartily on the back.

"Thanks, boss," Isaac whispered into Dom's chest.

Dom pulled Isaac away and held him by his shoulders. "You're my best earner. I couldn't let you take a fall."

Isaac beamed.

Johnson cleared his throat. "Everything went off clean," he told Dom. "We're done."

Dom let go of Isaac and offered his hand. "Thanks."

Johnson looked at his hand for a moment, then shook it. "It was the job," he said simply.

Peterson opened the door and the two men strode out to the car.

Assholes, Dom thought, watching them go. *Arrogant assholes.*

"Who are those guys?" Isaac asked him.

Dom shrugged. "Professionals."

"I believe it. You shoulda seen it, boss. They kicked the shit out of those two guards."

"They kill anybody?"

Isaac's face fell. "I . . . I don't think so."

"Good."

Isaac swallowed. "What do we do now, Boss?"

Dom grinned and clapped him on the shoulder. "We get you a fake ID and send you on a vacation. You like San Diego?"

* * *

The Yukon rolled slowly through River City. Bassen navigated the SUV along the streets, careful to obey all traffic laws. Isaac hunkered down the backseat, wearing sunglasses and a River City Flyers ball cap and smiling. He felt like whistling, but he knew he'd never be able to pucker his lips with the perma-grin plastered on his face.

He glanced at the hulking figure of Dominic Bracco in the front seat. Another rush of gratitude washed through him. Dom could've left him hanging, abandoned him to do ten years, but the big Italian didn't. He rescued him instead. He called in *professionals* to break him out. Isaac's throat constricted a little and his eyes misted. The man in the front seat had showed him more love than his own father ever did.

He leaned forward. "Boss? What do you want me to do in San Diego?"

"Huh?"

"San Diego. What am I supposed to do there?"

Dom cleared his throat. "Keep your nose clean, that's what. Hang out on the beach. Chase trim. Get a tan. Just don't get busted."

"What about money?"

"Deliver pizza or something," Dom said. "I don't care. But stay clean. And grow your hair out, or cut it off."

"Cut it off!" Isaac's hands flew to his tangled locks.

Dom laughed, a booming sound that filled the car. "Fine, fine. Grow it out. In a year or so, we'll bring you back home. I want you clean and looking different. Everything will blow over by then."

"A year? That long?"

"Better than never," Dom said.

Isaac squinted. "You really think this'll blow over, boss? I mean, it's a robbery beef, right? And then those guys clubbed the shit out of the guards. Plus—"

"Fuggedaboutit," Dom said, slipping back into his old Jersey accent. "In two or three months, the Russians will pull something twice as big and everyone will forget. Trust me." He reached back, rested his hand on Isaac's knee, gave it a hard squeeze.

Isaac nodded, satisfied. He sat back and thought about bikinis and beaches.

Dom sat quietly in his seat, watching traffic pass. When the Yukon dropped down toward the T.J. Meenach Bridge, he pressed his elbow against the hard metal of the .45 tucked in his belt under his jacket.

"Turn here," he directed Bassen, who took the narrow exit before the bridge. It led to a small two-lane road.

"Where we going?" Isaac asked.

"I told you. To see the guy about your fake I.D."

"Nobody lives out here," Isaac said.

"It's a shortcut," Dom told him. "I wanna avoid traffic. You're still pretty hot."

"Oh."

Bassen guided the Yukon along the wooded, two-lane road. The land on either side of the road belonged to the small state park along the Looking Glass River, which flowed on their left.

They passed the sewage treatment plant and kept on.

A half-mile before the Bowl-and-Pitcher picnic site, Bassen turned onto an access road that led north, away from the river.

"This guy live in a cabin or something?" Isaac joked.

Dom grunted.

Bassen drove the Yukon along the road for another two minutes. A heavy silence settled in the cab. When Bassen slowed the vehicle without any houses in sight, Dom heard Isaac's frantic voice from the backseat.

"Oh, no," he whimpered. "No, no, no, please, no."

Dom turned, but Isaac kicked the door open and scampered

from the backseat. He landed on the ground awkwardly and fell in a heap, but bounced back up immediately and broke into a run.

Bassen stopped the Yukon and got out.

Dom swung his door open and stepped out, drawing his .45. He took careful aim at the center of Isaac's back and fired.

The sharp crack filled the air, but the echo died on the trees and brush along the road.

The force of the bullet threw Isaac forward. He collapsed face-first in the dirt.

Dom strode purposefully toward the fallen man. His designer shoes snapped small pine needles with each step. He reached Isaac, who was struggling to drag himself forward, moving like a man in slow-motion. A gurgle rose from his throat.

Without hesitation, Dom leaned forward and snapped off a second shot right behind the ear. Isaac jerked and lay still.

Dom turned to Bassen, who lowered the hammer of his own gun and went to the rear of the Yukon. He swung open the rear door, tossed his gun into the truck and pulled out a shovel.

"I only brought one," he said.

"Good," Dom said, "because I ain't digging."

Kill Posse

Victor Gischler

Monica

The groupie couldn't have been more than sixteen, bottle blonde, good legs blooming into a chubby ass. Breasts trying to overflow a purple tank top. Too much makeup. She clung to the emaciated rock star. Billy Cage was big stuff in Sweden and had started getting fans in the States. Now he was touring the South, filling fifteen-hundred-seat halls. He'd pulled the teenager up from the crowd and onto the stage. She'd been adoring and giddy.

Monica Chase had seen it before, although none of the other girls had been quite so young. Chase had no tolerance for little girls who threw themselves at men. Especially at a punk like Billy Cage. Chase put the kid out of her mind and concentrated on the job.

She scanned the crowd, the roadies and stagehands and publicity hacks and hangers-on all jamming the long hall from the stage to the limousine parked in the back alley. Loud. Shouting and hoots. Flash bulbs. In the old days, Chase would have been nervous with so many strangers this close to the client. But nobody was after the skinny Swede. The protection was all show.

Still, it was supposed to be her job. She touched the throat mike. "I need the door guys to make a hole. Limo driver, be ready to pop the door locks. I want a clean shot out of the alley, so make sure nobody's parked illegally."

Up ahead, Chase saw the door goons open the back door and push the crowd back, clearing a short path to the limousine. The goons (and she thought of them as goons) were not her people. They'd come with the job. The goons were trying way too hard to look tough, shaved heads, black turtlenecks, mirrored sunglasses.

Chase darted ahead of the band to be first out the door. The crowd was small but loud, mostly young girls screaming for Billy. Billy ran past the crowd into the limo followed by the drummer, two guitarists, and a bass player. All had groupies in tow. The teen in the purple tank top looked like she'd won the lottery. A limousine ride with a rock star. Chase was thirty-four and tried to remember what it was like to be sixteen. Vaguely embarrassing and anxious. Flashes of tomboy, the track team, awkward sexual encounter on prom night.

Chase climbed into the passenger side of the limo and thumbed her throat mike. "We're secure. Get the advance car ahead of us to make sure it's clear up to the hotel rooms." She glanced in the rearview mirror, saw the partition already going up, so the band could start groping the girls.

She reached into the jacket pocket of her pantsuit for the pill bottle. The pantsuit was gray. A burgundy blouse. Competent and professional. The .380 automatic made a slight bulge under the jacket. She found the bottle, spilled a pill into her palm, looked at it a second before popping it into her mouth and swallowing it dry.

They arrived at the hotel, and Chase escorted the band to their rooms without incident. From behind closed doors, she heard the party begin, raucous laughter and techno-pop music turned up too loud.

Chase touched the throat-mike and checked in with the goons. They were all in position. None of them would do anything more strenuous than turn away over-eager groupies and autograph hounds. The whole setup was a big waste of her skills.

The publicity people had concocted a story that some archconservative moral types were gunning for Cage and his band because his saucy songs were driving the youngsters to sin. It had made a medium splash in the tabloids. At least it was a paycheck.

Chase went to her room, splashed water in her face. She hadn't been sleeping well. She popped another pill, washed it down with half an Amstel Light from the honor bar. She looked out the window, the cityscape blazing with promise. Was that Dallas? Yes. It took her a moment to remember. Six cities in the past seven days.

She poured out the rest of the beer and tossed the can into the trash.

Chase decided to walk the band's hall one more time. By now, if the band followed the routine, they'd each retreated to their separate rooms to give the groupies something to remember. In the early morning, the groupies would slip out, holding their shoes, mascara smudged, haggard and bleary-eyed, hungover and half-ashamed. Live it up, girls. Rock and roll.

Chase passed Billy's room and heard the scream.

She was at his door in a split-second, pounding. "Mr. Cage, is everything all right?"

A pause.

She pounded harder. "Mr. Cage, are you—"

"Go away." Cage's voice, muffled by the door, slurring, part Swedish accent, part booze. "All is okay."

Chase heard the sobbing. The teenage groupie.

"Mr. Cage, I'd feel better if you could open the door please." Nothing.

"Mr. Cage!" She took a step back, readied herself.

"Go away, bitch. I tell you all is fine. Fuck off."

Oh, really?

She kicked hard, the doorframe cracking. A Swedish expletive. The groupie screaming. Chase kicked again, and the door flew open. In her peripheral vision, she saw one of the goons at the end of the hall sprinting toward her. She thought about drawing her pistol, decided it wasn't needed and would only alarm everyone further. She went into the room.

Billy Cage leapt away from the groupie like he'd been zapped with a cattle prod. He was skinny and pale, genitals bunched in leopard-skin bikini underwear. The groupie huddled on the sofa, plain white panties. Old bruises on her white shins. Half her tank top pulled down, a breast exposed, raspberry nipple. Eyes red from crying.

"Get your clothes on," Chase said.

She didn't move.

"Do it!" Chase barked.

She jumped, half-fell off the couch, crawling for shoes and jeans.

Billy Cage was red all up through the face, shaking with feeble rock star rage. "You bitch. Get out of here. She's fine."

Chase sensed the goon arriving behind her, standing in the doorway.

"Mr. Cage, it's time for the young lady to go home." Chase bent, picked the groupie up by an elbow. She held her clothes and shoes tight against her chest like they might shield her.

"No!" Cage shook a bony fist. "Get out now. You'll be fired. I say to get out. You hear me, stupid bitch?"

He took a step toward Chase, his fist out in front of him, and Chase's reflexes kicked in. She dropped the groupie, knocked Cage's fist away with one hand and struck with the other. Chase's fist popped Cage on the bridge of the nose. Cage squawked, eyes wide. He stumbled back, blood rushing from his nostrils.

The goon behind her moved, and Chase realized the situation. The goons worked for Cage, not for her. She spun to see a heavy fist coming at her face. She ducked, dropped to the floor and swept the goon's legs. He upended, landed hard on his back, air whooshing out of him. He got up on his elbow, made like he wanted to have another go at her, but Chase was on her feet first. She kicked, the heel of her boot smacking his chin. The goon's eyes rolled up and he fell back, didn't move.

She stamped hard on the downed goon's hand, heard at least two finger bones snap. *That's what you get.*

Chase wheeled about to face Cage, but the rock star was curled into a corner, holding his bloody nose with one hand, jabbing an accusing finger at her with the other. "Bitch. You will pay for this." The words came out: 'Bidch. Youb bill bay ford dis'. "You are fired. You will never work again."

"Uh-huh." Cage fired her about twice a week. It meant nothing. Chase worked for the record company, not the snotty little Swede.

Chase went to the groupie hiding behind the bed. "Are you okay?"

She nodded slowly. "I'd like to leave now."

"Right."

Chase watched while she got dressed. The groupie walked out fast, didn't look back. Chase hoped she'd go straight home to her mother. Maybe she'd learned a lesson. Maybe not. It wasn't Chase's problem.

"I will sue you. I will sue you for every money you have," Cage shouted.

"Get some sleep, Billy," Chase said.

Chase went back to her room, washed down two Vicodin with another beer. Almost immediately, she felt her anger and tension drain away. Cage and his ridiculous band. Hell.

The call came thirty minutes later, the record company exec, sounding tired and impatient.

"If you're not satisfied, you can send me packing any time," Chase said.

"We're appreciate your continuing to protect Billy from his own . . . uh . . . impulses," the executive said. "But try not to mark his face please. He needs to perform."

"I want a raise."

The executive sighed. "Okay."

The Old Man

Imagine someone who'd been shot twice, stabbed four times. Form a picture in your mind. His left eye had been gouged out during an earnest "discussion" with the *Federales*. Two fingers missing from his left hand. Interrogation some called it. He'd even been set on fire once. Lived through it all. You'd probably think of a hulking great monster to survive all that. Not only survive, but return to wreak terrible revenge, those who'd wronged him buried to their necks in sand. The desert took them, the ants and vultures and always, always the unforgiving sun.

But Carlos Alvarez wasn't a hulking man of steel. He was a stooped, brown little man with thin, white hair who held his Camel cigarettes in a trembling, ruined hand. It was hard for him to play Mario Karts on the GameCube with that hand, but he managed it, just liked he'd managed so much in his eighty-one years.

He thumbed the pause button, froze his speeding Mario Kart in mid-race, so he could discuss killing a man with his grandson.

"You wanted to see me, grandfather?" Miguel was tall and lean, dark hair and moustache, broad shoulders, angular features, good-looking in a hungry, gaunt sort of way. He worshipped the old man, ran many of the organization's day-to-day operations for him.

The old man paused, looked out over the fenced-in pool, various members of his extended family soaking in sun, the gardens, fence, and desert beyond. His mind was relatively good, only a little slow sometimes. *Ah, yes,* he remembered.

"I want you to pick a few of the boys to kill somebody in the States."

"The rock and roll singer, yes?"

The old man's eyes veered to the eighteen-year-old girl in the thin dress by the pool. His great-granddaughter Maria, so beautiful, hair midnight dark. Her belly rose tight and round from the lounge chair. Her thin fingers laced together, resting on the pregnant belly. Her laughter drifted up to them and she watched the younger children splash in the pool.

"He has insulted us. Insulted our Maria."

"Of course," said the grandson. "It shall be done."

The old man restarted the Kart game, leaned in his chair as he took a tight curve. "I want the golf game, the one with Tiger Woods."

"You can't get it for GameCube. You need an X-box."

"Damn." The old man *tsk*ed. "You'll have to pick one up next time you're in town."

Miguel cleared his throat. "Grandfather, about—"

"I'm thinking." He drove another lap, the digital ape in the kart ahead of him lobbing bananas into his path.

Miguel waited patiently, hands clasped behind his back.

"Perhaps, we need professionals," suggested Alvarez. "I don't want anything linked back to us."

"I know our men can handle it, Grandfather."

Alvarez said nothing. Think first, then talk. The benefits of age. He must let his grandson handle this. It was part of grooming the boy to take over one day. Sooner than later, Alvarez reminded himself. There had been bad news his last visit to the doctor. Time was so short. Alvarez had his doubts, but he would let Miguel handle it.

"Very well."

"I will see to it," said Miguel and left.

Carlos Alvarez looked at the desert again, so flat and vast. He owned the land in all directions for fifty miles, every stone and cactus. A mile and a half to the south, there was a small village of maybe a hundred inhabitants. Alvarez owned the village also. The men and women who lived there cleaned Alvarez's estate, tended his gardens, husbanded his cattle and goats and chickens and pigs, cleaned the pool. There were women who entertained the men. There was a small cantina and two or three modest shops that catered to the villagers. Alvarez was like a king to these people, his holdings a little fiefdom. And he loved his people. He didn't know them, but he loved them the way a king loves his subjects.

The old man imagined if he squinted hard, let his eyes go fuzzy that he could see all the way to the village, see the young boys in white, herding goats with a stick and a yapping dog. Yes, he could see an old woman in a rocking chair on the porch of her little house, little girls playing, old men on opposite sides of a checkerboard discussing the coming harvest. He saw it all, this bright utopia for his people.

He was eighty-one, so few years left. If he could live forever he could spread his benevolent reign over the region, all of Mexico. The whole world. Was he insane to think thus? No. He'd heard somewhere that if you wondered if you were insane, then you weren't.

A figure coalesced in midair. He hovered over the desert, an old man in brown robes, a blue glow around him. A vision. It was not any saint Alvarez recognized. His sister had claimed to see the Madonna once at the end of a hot day in the desert tending goats, but everyone just said she'd been dehydrated. Now, Alvarez wondered. He looked hard at the vision which seemed so familiar, the white beard, the kind face. The old man beckoned to him, then dissolved into the wind.

Alvarez blinked. Shut his eyes hard and opened them again. The vision did not return.

Satisfied, he pressed the start button and began another race. Apes and mustached wops and prehistoric turtles bombarded him with fruits and nuts.

The Juans

Miguel entered the small house on the other side of the Alvarez compound. The clubhouse everyone called it because all of Alvarez's gunmen congregated there, passed the time, and waited for orders. Miguel walked into the living room, coughed.

A thick cloud of tobacco smoke. The place stunk of stale liquor and armpit.

"For the love of God, open a window," Miguel said.

Two grubby men in recliners looked up as Miguel entered. They faced a fifty-inch plasma television, video game controllers in their hands. A World War II game in which they shot Germans with various weapons was turned up to a deafening volume.

Miguel grabbed the TV remote, hit MUTE. "Where is everybody?"

"There's just us," said the fat one. His name was Juan and he had sleepy eyes, ruddy skin. He wore jeans and flip-flops. His toenails were long and yellow. His T-shirt didn't quite cover all of his belly.

"They're all working. Smuggling something over the river," said the other one. His name was also Juan. Alvarez employed many men, and at least a dozen were called Juan. This one wore track shorts and an L.A. Lakers tank top. Gold teeth. Rings. Many gold necklaces. If he fell into the Rio Grande, he'd sink straight to the bottom.

"I'm sending you somewhere. A job for Grandfather. Pack your bags. You're going to the States."

"The States?" asked Fat Juan. "Just us?"

"I haven't decided yet. What is that?" He pointed at the TV. "Do you have X-Box?"

"Yes," said Golden Juan. "We just got this yesterday. Medal of Honor."

Miguel asked, "Do you have Tiger Woods Golf?"

"In the case," said Golden Juan.

Miguel picked up the leather case, went though the selection of games, he found Tiger Woods, took it out.

"What are we supposed to do?" asked Fat Juan. "Will it take long?"

"Just be ready to go. I'll give you the details later."

Miguel grabbed the controllers from their hands, unhooked the X-Box from the TV. "I need this."

"Hey!"

"And clean this place up." Miguel left, the X-Box under his arm.

Monica

Billy Cage's tour bus left Dallas late, arrived in Baton Rouge late. Everyone was road weary and pissed off. Monica's back ached from sitting so long in a crappy bus seat. She popped a Vicodin and set about securing the hotel, the Sheraton at the Convention Center on the Mississippi River.

Cage was scheduled to play for the World Horror Convention, a crowd of people dressed like vampires and punks, goth kids and oddballs with tattoos and piercings.

Sure.

Chase expected little or no trouble, but she went through the procedures by the numbers, located the exits, made sure all the goons had their assignments, coordinated with hotel security. Shipshape. All her ducks in a row.

She sighed. Probably all wasted effort.

The Juans

Fat Juan and Golden Juan sat in the front seat of a Grand Marquis, waiting in the long line of cars at the border between Juarez and El Paso, the border crossing closest to Alvarez's vast property. The bored officer on the Mexican side saw who it was and waved them through automatically.

They made a point to get in the lane all the way to the left for the Americans. It was hot, but they'd rolled down the car's windows because the man in the backseat smoked a cigar the size of a railroad tie.

His name was Juan also.

Smart Juan had been put in charge of the other two Juans. Fat and Golden Juan were ruthless, efficient killers. Clever and imaginative they were not. They possessed no aptitude for leadership. They could be trusted to follow clear, direct orders and to show up for meals on time. Thus, Smart Juan had been sent to keep things on track.

All three wore Mexican gangster chic. Dark suits without ties, white shirts with the top three buttons undone. Fat and Smart Juan each wore a gold crucifix on a single gold chain. Golden Juan, of course wore several chains as well as a ring on each finger. The rims of his sunglasses were covered by cheap gold plate. Smart and Golden Juan wore cowboy boots. Fat Juan wore sandals, his yellow toenails sticking ahead like the horns of some alien animal.

They pulled up to the checkpoint and Smart Juan leaned out the window, waved to the customs officer on duty.

The officer came over, leaned down to the window. "You guys again, huh?"

"Hello, *Señor* Williams," Smart Juan said. "Please feel free to search the car. We know you're just doing your job, and we wish to cooperate fully."

Officer Williams winked. "Right. Pop the trunk, okay?"

Fat Juan popped the trunk.

Officer Williams circled to the rear of the vehicle, looked both ways, then lifted the trunk. Inside: Nine semi-automatic pistols, four revolvers, two shotguns (one pump-action, the other a side-by-side double barrel), two Uzi submachine guns, a hand grenade, three giant knives, two keys of hash, a canister of pepper spray, and the May issue of *Hustler*. Atop the pile of contraband sat a fat, white #10 envelope. Williams picked up the envelope and opened it, thumbed through the cash within. He looked around one more time then pocketed the envelope.

Back at the car window, Williams said, "Everything seems to be in order. You guys have a nice stay in the United States."

"*Muchas gracias*," Smart Juan said. "I'm sure we will."

The Old Man

After the vision, Alvarez revisited the subject of his sanity.

Alvarez woke up before the sun as is the wont of many old men. He sat on the veranda looking out over the desert at night, glittering and seeming so close, marveled how the dark expanse met the night at the horizon, stars blazing. The vision hovered there. The man with the white beard had looked so familiar, the long brown robes.

Your men will fail, Alvarez. They aren't up to this task.

"Who are you?" Alvarez *knew* he'd seen the man's face before.

They are on a mission of death, said the vision.

"What the hell are you talking about?" Alvarez asked the apparition.

But then a fiery orange smear broke over the horizon, turning the desert into a landscape of hellish desolation. The sunrays struck the vision, and the old man in brown robes dissolved, spread himself across the universe.

Alvarez sat on the terrace thinking about his sanity and the vision. Was it possible that the vision was merely a manifestation of something Alvarez knew subconsciously?

Alvarez would think on it.

In the meantime, a very old woman waddled onto the terrace with a plate of dry white toast and a small cup of very strong coffee. The woman was older even than Alvarez, who thought of her as coming with the Creation. She seemed to belong in the same category as the rocks and the sky.

The contrast of his great-grandaughter's expanding belly

and the life within sent shivers of joy and rage through his body that Alvarez could not quite explain.

The old man scanned the sky for the vision. Nothing. He felt disappointed, wanted to see the wise old man in brown robes. He willed the ghost to appear without result.

Alvarez shifted in his seat, turned his good eye northward, let it go out of focus. Yes, it was happening, his gaze lifted up over the desert, beyond the river. Beyond Texas.

He could see them. Juan, Juan, and Juan. They were in trouble. Peril. *Madre de Dios!*

Great peril!

The Juans

"Oh, no," Golden Juan said. "Oh, no, no, no, no, NO!"

"What the hell is it now?" Smart Juan asked.

"They put cheese on my hamburger. I specifically said no cheese. I told them, didn't I? You heard me." He nudged Fat Juan. "You heard me tell them."

"I heard you," Fat Juan said. "No cheese."

"Goddamn them to hell. I should go back and burn the place to the ground. Fuck Wendy's."

"Just scrape it off," Smart Juan said.

"It's melted all over everything."

"I like cheese," said Fat Juan.

"I hate this," Golden Juan whined. "I want to go home."

"Shut up," snapped Smart Juan. "You're both driving me crazy. Eat your damn burger."

They'd put Texas behind them and were over the line into Louisiana. To celebrate, they'd gone through the Wendy's drive-thru. Travel had been excruciatingly slow. Fat Juan and Golden Juan wanted to stop nearly every hour. Golden Juan wanted to stop and buy sports jerseys of the local teams all the way up from Texas. Fat Juan had a bladder the size of a pinto bean.

"What are we supposed to do when we get to Baton Rouge?" Golden Juan asked.

"Find the place. Kill the singer."

"You really don't like cheese?" Fat Juan asked. "You had pizza yesterday for lunch."

Golden Juan shook his head. "No, pizza doesn't count."

Fat Juan frowned. "Why not?"

"Shut up," Smart Juan said. "Just drive quietly for a while, okay?"

They went along the highway. The quiet lasted a total of seven minutes.

"I have to go to the bathroom," Fat Juan said.

Monica

An hour before the show and the place was chaos.

The horror fans had already pushed up against the stage and were screaming for the show to start. The opening act was a vile display of body piercing. A fat guy with a devil beard shoved needles through a woman's body parts until she left the stage, bloody and grinning.

The riotous circus kept Chase busy with minor concerns, rowdy groupies trying to get backstage at Billy Cage, kids whacked on the latest narcotic. The whole convention center writhed like a fistful of worms.

She issued orders to various goons, keeping the Mexican in her peripheral vision the entire time.

She'd spotted him twenty minutes ago, lingering near one of the exits. The Mexican was out of place among the horror conventioneers, just standing with hands in pockets. His eyes darted side to side, taking in the crowd, and Chase didn't like not knowing what the guy was about. He was dressed too good to be kitchen help.

Chase delegated one of her goons to approach the guy and tell him to move on if he didn't have a convention badge. She watched the encounter unfold, the goon confronting the Mexican, the Mexican shrugging and slouching toward the exit. The Mexican spared Chase a glance before leaving.

Probably just curious about the horror freaks, Chase thought.

She went backstage, found the band guzzling Budweiser. Billy Cage slung the guitar over his shoulder and belched. "Almost showtime, yes?"

"Yes."

The conventioneers were screaming their asses off for Billy to take the stage. A chant of "rock the bayou" along with stomping boots shook the convention center.

Billy's nose was still red, but the makeup artist has covered most of it.

"I found out about you!" Billy grinned idiotically, pointed at Chase, a cigarette smoldering between two fingers. "You were an Army spook in the Gulf War. Land mine metal shredded your leg, eh? Tough lady."

"Ancient history."

"Don't try that tough stuff again with me." Billy puffed out his bony chest. "I make you sorry, eh."

"Go sing your songs, dumbass."

Billy sucked on the cigarette, blew smoke at her and winked, then led his band onto the stage. Chase heard the crowd roar. *I don't need this shit.* She rubbed her temples, blew out a ragged sigh and fished the pill bottle out of her jacket pocket. She swallowed one, considered a second. She shook her head and put it back in the bottle. Put the bottle back in her pocket. She'd gotten on the pills after the doctors put her leg back together. The Vicodin was a key ingredient in her ability to cope. Her teeth hummed with Billy Cage's voice, the jerky song like the screech of the world dying.

The Juans

Smart Juan returned to the car, ducked his head into the open window. Golden Juan and Fat Juan sat in the front seat, drinking cans of Diet Dr. Pepper.

"They have some bouncer types around the exits," Smart Juan told them. "Not very professional except the one in charge, some *puta*."

Golden Juan snorted. "You want to do it now?"

"We need to get backstage," Smart Juan said. "Between sets when they come back for a break, eh? It's noisy. Don't do anything until I signal. I'll take care of the woman."

"We'll need some things," Fat Juan said.

Smart Juan nodded. "Pop the trunk."

The Old Man

The house was full of children. Alvarez liked it that way, the noise of life overflowing every room. So many grandchildren and nephews and nieces. Family was everything.

In the sprawling den, they all watched *Star Wars* again on the enormous plasma screen television. Alvarez had seen the film a hundred times. He paused now to watch a scene, Obi-wan Kenobi showing Luke Skywalker proper light saber technique. Alvarez started to walk away then froze. He turned back to the film. Looked at Obi-wan. Alec Guinness.

Oh no.

Alvarez walked onto the veranda. The night was cool, and the stars were bright. He attempted to summon the vision, making his demands to thin air. The old man in the brown robe shimmered and appeared before him.

"You're from my imagination, aren't you?" Alvarez said to the face of Alec Guinness. "You only live in my head."

"Yes," said the ghost. "I'm sorry."

"What's wrong with me?"

"You're going to die, and I'm the part of you that knows it. Remember what the cancer doctor said?"

Ah, yes. His visit to the hospital last month. They warned him his brain would deteriorate.

"What do I do?" he asked the ghost.

The ghost motioned to the pool. Alvarez's great-granddaughter sat in a lounge chair, looking up at the moon. Maria always sat in a lounge chair. It was so hard for her to get comfortable. She would pop any day now.

"Go to her," said the ghost.

He did.

Monica

Everything seemed under control, so Chase ducked into the restroom for a quick piss. The restroom door shut, muffled the concert to a distant racket. Some slight relief. She eased herself into a stall, sat, and peed. She did not leave right away. It was good to sit quietly. She cringed at the thought of going back out, the whole post-concert cycle starting again, groupies and parties. She felt like a zookeeper.

She sighed, stood, and flushed.

She pushed open the stall door and caught a momentary blur of red before her world exploded white hot with pain. Her head spun, the world twirling and flopping upside down, darkness swallowing her.

She floated in the darkness, other colors swirling. It seemed like a long time, but she couldn't be sure. Her face against something cold and hard.

She opened her eyes, saw she was on the rest room floor. Her face throbbed. She got up on her elbows, looked down. A puddle of blood and saliva on the tile. Three teeth. She tried to stand. Dizzy. Tried to talk, but half her mouth felt frozen, the skin and muscles on one side seeming to sag.

Chase grabbed the sink, pulled herself up and looked at the horror show in the mirror. The left side of her face dented in and red, a dark gap in her smile from the missing teeth. She glanced around, saw the red fire extinguisher on the floor. Somebody had used it to knock her cold. How long? She heard the music, so the concert was still in full swing.

Chase splashed water on her face. Rinsed out her mouth. The sting of cold water on her empty tooth sockets made her knees wobbly. She took out the Vicodin bottle, her hands shaking, got the lid off and spilled them, the pills clattering across tile.

She went to her hands and knees, scooped up three and popped them into her mouth, washed them down with more stinging water.

Come on, baby. Do your magic.

Within seconds she felt the calm ease through her body. There was still terrible pain, but it seemed muted now, wrapped in cotton.

She drew her automatic and ran for the backstage area.

Chase almost tripped over the body of one of her goons. He lay in a widening puddle of blood leaking out of his throat.

Three men stood backstage, facing away from her, watching Billy Cage screech a song about heartbreak. She paused, deciding if she should approach them or call for backup. Then the middle turned, and Chase saw it was the Mexican. He nudged his pals, and all three turned, lifted automatic pistols toward her.

She fired.

They fired.

The fleshy part of her right thigh exploded in a spray of blood. She kept squeezing the trigger as she went down, caught the fat one in the chest, the other two across the legs. The wounded men screamed curses at her in Spanish.

They lay on the ground, firing at one another. Finally, she caught one of them on the top of the head. He twitched and went still.

The final attacker emptied his magazine at Chase as she pulled herself behind some lighting equipment.

A commotion from the stage. They'd heard the shots and the band had stopped. The Mexican grunted to his feet, limped toward her. She slapped a new magazine into the .380, rolled from behind the lighting equipment, already squeezing the trigger. Something slammed into her belly. And again into her chest. It was hard to breathe. A hot buzzing in her ears.

She turned to see the Mexican lying dead. She'd hit him with her last burst of fire. Chase's hand went down to her belly, came back glistening red.

Things went fuzzy. She blinked. Suddenly the band was standing over her, and security guards. Somebody yelled for an ambulance.

Chase could feel it, the life draining out of her, like she was a balloon deflating. She looked up into Billy Cage's confused, stupid face. Her mouth worked open and closed, but she couldn't make words come out.

I died for you? Protecting you, you little punk shit? For what? They say your life flashes before your eyes. For Chase it was a little montage of bad choices and missed opportunities. It wasn't fair. She wanted it all back. She wanted a do-over.

Too late.

The Old Man

"What are you doing out here all alone, child?"

Maria smiled, and Alvarez felt his heart go gooey.

"It's so quiet, Grandfather," said Maria. "And the night is cool."

Alvarez scooted a lawn chair next to hers, reclined, his legs stretched out. "Have you decided what to name the baby?"

"After you, naturally." She laughed.

He laughed, too.

They were quiet a moment, and then Alvarez said, "You seem sad sometimes when I look at you."

She nodded. "I'm sorry."

"Don't be sorry. Tell me."

"A child needs a father."

Alvarez said nothing to this.

"I was thinking," Maria began, "well, maybe if we went to Billy Cage, told him about the baby. I know he would do the right thing."

She was so young. How does one answer such a thing?

"Maybe," Alvarez said. "Perhaps when the child is born. Who could resist a beautiful baby?"

He knew the lie had been the right thing when she reached over and squeezed his hand.

The moon hung gigantic in the sky.

"You know, I was watching a science documentary last night," Maria said. "Did you know that the moon is moving away from the earth an inch every year? Centuries from now it will have gone."

"Amazing," Alvarez said. "It's escaping then. Somebody should do something."

They laughed again. They sat quietly together a long time. After some time, Maria fell asleep. Alvarez put a gnarled hand on her tight belly, felt it rise and fall.

At once things began to shut down inside of him. There was no pain, just a strange awareness. The doctors had warned it could happen suddenly. He felt light, like he was floating. Soaring faster up and up and into the stars.

Chasing after the moon.

Sweet Benny and the Sanchez Penitentiary Band

B.H. Shepherd

It's a Thursday night and Sue's is packed. Old buddies are trading dirty stories over pitchers at the top of their lungs and the bartenders are earning their tips—been shaking out fruity martinis since eight-thirty. The dance floor, the dark corner where the tables are pushed back, is crowded with necking kids and single girls in miniskirts sending out the signal. Jukebox hasn't worked since I got here in '72, so half the floor is taken up by some college band murdering the memory of a blues musician nobody ever gave a fuck about.

It didn't used to be like this; one time Sue's was a whiskey and beer hole. If you were on the other side of my bar, it was a while since you had friends to drink with. I was just another one of those bums when Big Earl died and left me the place in '86. He was a professional alcoholic, so I guess you could say he died on duty, which is as honorable a thing as a man could hope for. He always used to say that sometimes in life it's hard for a man to hold his head up and keep on walking, and if he's walking through El Paso, he stops at Sue's for a drink. Everyone in Sue's had a story about those times; it was that time for me when I started working here, and it was that way until just a few months ago. A few months ago I never knew margaritas came in strawberry, and Thursday night was slower than the last highway out of Hanoi. But all that changed when I met this young con name of Sweet Benny.

Sue's had many regulars, some more like furniture than customers, but Benny was the closest thing I ever had to a favorite. The yat-spittin' son of a bitch first swaggered in here not even a year ago, dressed in a boot-marked and blood-stained blue tuxedo. He ordered a beer and asked me for work before I was even done pouring. I told him the first round was on me, but he best look elsewhere for that job. Whistler's Place over on San Jacinto used to hire boys fresh out of Sanchez because they would drink their wages, but then every night the bar was full of hammered ex-cons. One rowdy weekend the place burned to the ground, Whistler turned up missing, and nobody asked any questions because we didn't have any. Sanchez was like an asshole factory built on Hell's own oasis in the desert, distilling men into the most vile and ruthless bastards ever to roam Texas. Benny seemed harmless enough, a skinny little mulatto with a voice as light as his skin, but I'd seen Sanchez do worse with less.

It took him the better part of a week to drink through his gate money, and after that he just hung on to the end of the bar like it was the last thing floating on a sinking ship. See, Benny was one of those drunks who's your best friend, full of dirty stories about seducing rich white ladies and then ripping them off, leaving them naked and broke. His stories always ended with "But I ain' shawmin' none no mo'," and his jagged grin would sag until someone bought him a drink. But it wasn't long before Benny ran out of stories and the bar ran out of generosity.

When he asked me if he could trade me anything for drinks

and I said, "Money," I knew that wasn't what Sweet Benny had in mind. He couldn't have been older than twenty, but he talked like he'd been selling cars for thirty years. Everything he said made you want to keep talking to him; he'd draw you into his story by asking what you thought about it, and before you knew it you actually cared about what happened. All his questions had the force of statements. He was completely full of shit, but Benny's main selling point was that there was no car. I had no idea what he was pushing, and the only way to find out was to buy it.

A week later this jig was back with a whole band of one-note losers, saying they'd play for free drinks. I said they could have the first round free and have to earn the rest. He promised me they'd play more than drink, and I said this way I'd know for sure. I was assured that would be no problem, no problem at all, and Benny scurried back to warming up his "band." Benny was singing, backed up by a big old nigger name of Bo Ghost on bass; reckon he got the name because he was blind as a bat and twice as black—when he sat in that dark corner all you saw were two hollow gray eyes floating above a shock of white beard. He wasn't much on talking, that was pretty much Benny's department, but after every set he drank like his next stop was the morgue, and left before it showed any effect on him. Somehow I learned that Ghost was actually Benny's cousin, and so I asked one night if everything his relation sang about was true, and he replied in a voice so soft I could have slept on it: "Benny is a fine storyteller. He never lets the truth get in the way of a good story." And when I asked what Benny really went away for, he just chuckled and asked what he told me. I had to take it all with a bag of salt, because Ghost didn't look like he'd been out long either—but I didn't want Benny's hard-luck tale to be a half-truth.

Playing guitar was some kid they called Zig Zag, his handle

inspired by the jagged black tats that sleeved his wiry arms and curled around his throat. He always placed his guitar in a chair next to him like a lady, and his eyes were always shut when he strummed her. During the week I always saw that drag rat playing his guitar out by the highway, or on the corner by Salado's place tweaked on some lab junk, wearing a cardboard sign that read FAMILY SLAIN BY NINJAS. NEED $$ FOR KARATE LESSONS—GOD BLESS. He'd stumble into Sue's about an hour after the rest of the band finished warming up, twitchin' and itchy, talking so fast he forgot his words and barely able to hold his head straight. Double Beam could usually put his feet back on Earth, but he stopped taking them because he always played his best when he was coming down the hardest. That's what he told me, whatever the fuck it meant. For a few hours every Thursday and Friday night, Zig was a genius, but you could always read the junk in his eyes, cracked and stained like church glass.

There was also a shadow-faced cowboy in a straw hat called Dodge, though he never introduced himself—real strong and silent type, but he could make a harmonica cry. They even got Pedro, the kid I'd been paying a dollar an hour for the last six months, to play drums and haul all their gear around in his van for nothing. Turns out his name was Vijo. I didn't ask where they got the gear. The band always warmed up with blues tunes, and then the show was mostly BB King and Johnny Cash covers, but Benny always traded Folsom for Sanchez. It wasn't bad. No overnight success, but there were no fights and nothing burned down. It was a good night. And just like that, one good night lead to another. My patrons had friends, and before long some even had women, and they all came to Sue's to shake it to the sounds of Sweet Benny Pace and his Sanchez Penitentiary Band.

They didn't come up with the name, but it's catchy, ain't it? Wish I could take the credit, but it was actually some kid named Tucker or Chad who first gave them ink in a community college newspaper. Within a week, Sue's was crawling with students and wannabe musicians who just couldn't wait to hear a bunch of ex-cons hammer out a fourteen-minute Freebird at last call on a Friday night. For the city bitches that come out here to slum it, it was just a way to blow off some steam, an end to their week. But Benny and his boys from inside played from pain; you could tell they didn't have much else going on but singing for their booze. If it weren't for Sue's, I doubt Zig Zag would bother crawling out of his gutter.

On the night they were "discovered," Zig unplugged as soon as he finished his last note, shaking like a drug store pony, but Benny grabbed him by the arm because the crowd was still clapping, and if the crowd ain't gonna stop, why should the band?

"Gimme some sad da singduh, Zig," he slurred. "Make the ladies cry." An original encore by Sweet Benny was a rare thing, but only because none of them were ever worth repeating. Nothing but clever country rhymes about selling dope on Bourbon Street and dirty little tunes about stealing from women he seduced. But that night he did a little ditty with a chorus of "Goodnight Sally," about the one girl that was so pretty he just couldn't rip her off, and so he slips out the window empty-handed and heartbroken.

Now, no one who knew Benny longer than ten minutes believed this story, but that didn't stop him from getting laid every time he sang it. It was the song that was going to make them famous, because the bright-eyed journalism student on the beat couldn't get two words from anyone but Benny.

Like I said, Ghost weren't much on talking, Dodge never said anything but, "Whiskey, straight," and Vijo didn't even speak English. That left Benny and Zig Zag, who was already itching to get somewhere. The dumb kid went for the guitarist interview, trying for that A+ no doubt, and walked right up into his face and just started spitting questions at him. Zig Zag didn't even break his stride as he grabbed the nearest mug and smashed it over the kid's head. The dumb kid crumpled to the floor, bleeding and cursing and that just made Zig even madder. He kicked him over onto his back and started to go to work on his face with a piece of broken glass, but big Bo Ghost pulled them apart like a teacher in a schoolyard.

"Easy friend," said Ghost.

Benny carried the poor kid off to the commode to lick his wounds while Zig Zag stood there staring daggers, his hand still gripping glass. "Go take a nap, Grandpa," he snapped. "This ain't between me and you."

"No, it ain't," Ghost replied calmly. "I am between you and him." That pretty much settled it. Zig may have only had a pile of ash for a brain, but he could still see that Bo Ghost was easily five times his size; the guy had to duck his head just to stand up inside.

I put his cut on the counter and watched him stuff it in his tattered camo pocket without even a count. He slung that axe over his shoulder like a shotgun and hustled out the door hissing, "Fuck all this noise, I got shit to do." Once Zig went slinking off to his alley to burn, Sweet Benny spent the rest of the night giving the young journalist an earful. He was all smooth-talk and smiles, telling tall tales about living by the sweat of his hustle and his big music ambitions. Benny made himself out to be a real penitentiary poet and the kid ate it all up, taking notes like he thought there was going to be a quiz. That article goes to press and suddenly a week later I'm not doing them a favor anymore—Sweet Benny is actually putting money *in* the register.

One night near closing, after Zig and Vijo had disappeared to their respective nowheres and Benny had left to touch a few co-ed souls with his poetry, I shared a few shots with Bo Ghost, just to finish the bottle. I forget how it came about, but he told me Benny was his cousin from Zana, that they had strayed a bit, but were trying to play their way back, do their part.

"Benny's no problem," I told him, "but that Zig Zag should be on a leash. Can't keep him around the children."

Old Ghost was the picture of seriousness when he replied, "Just because I did not wish to see that boy die does not make me his keeper. I'm just here to play."

"Way he handles that ax I might think about keepin' him. Am I right, cowboy?" I passed the question down to Dodge, who sat at the end of the bar with the other regulars—silent, smoking, islands of men.

"A man don't know better than to shit where he eats is just a dog," he replied.

Bo Ghost stood up kind of quick to that. "What did you call me?" he asked.

Dodge didn't look up from his glass as he replied, "I said it loud."

There was a tense moment, like that whistle just before a mortar hits and you're waiting for a whole piñata of blood, guts, and fire—but this shell was a dud. Ghost grabbed his money and stormed out the door, and the only conversation I got out of Dodge the rest of the night was: "Whiskey, straight."

They weren't exactly friends, all the players of the Sanchez Penitentiary Band. If you didn't see them on stage, you would've never guessed they even knew each other, but when they played it was like they'd been on the road for years, cracking jokes and beers between songs. The band's drink jar sat on top of the old jukebox, and would fill up with singles as folks made requests. After that article, they started having a little more left over at the end of the night. But I never saw Benny handing it out. They all tended to go their separate ways after the show, except for Dodge—he never missed a last call.

"You ever go home, cowboy?" I asked him.

He passed a dry glass back to me and muttered, "Whiskey, straight," but the bottle was as empty as the bar, one last sliver of amber.

"Time to call it a night," I said. "Go get some sleep."

"Ain't tired." He grabbed the bottle off the counter and downed what was left. That's when the phone started to clang like a fire alarm. I knew it meant trouble, this midnight call. I'd owned Sue's for thirty years and this was the first time I ever heard the phone ring. On the other end was a Miss Veronica Featherstone with the ACL Office and she wanted to confirm the venue, but I didn't know what the fuck that was. She huffed impatiently and asked if the Sanchez Penitentiary Band was playing here tomorrow night and I said sure, why not? After she hung up I asked Dodge if he knew Miss Featherstone.

"Nope." The door slammed shut behind him.

That Friday night Benny showed up looking shiny, smiling and shaking hands with his band like they just won a ballgame. He bought a round for the house, made an enthusiastic toast no one could understand, and only got more excited as the college kids started to filter in early. Vijo had to help me serve beer 'til showtime, I was getting so backed up. When I finally got two words with Benny, they didn't make any sense; he just shoved a folded up flyer in my shirt pocket and said, "Alla bess, m'mayun. Is owl happnin."

In between pours I was keeping an eye out for this Miss Featherstone, but that night it was like trying to find a drunk in an El Paso alley—the place was packed with dolled-up chicks, and she coulda been all or none of them, far as I knew. But it didn't matter, because she never got a chance to hear the band play. Soon as Bo Ghost struck that deep blue bass groove, the guitar should've come trailing along behind—but Zig's attention was elsewhere, buried in the tits of some bus stop bitty whose fella wasn't paying her enough mind. But you better believe he noticed some tatted junkie trying to play his woman like a guitar in front of everyone.

Benny tried to intervene. "C'mon, bruv. Do ya thayn layduh. Less blazum music."

". . . back the fuck up you fucking butterhead Benny bastard I'll fucking kill this fucking bitchcunt is *mine*," Zig hissed, burnt on some new lab junk. He grabbed at this girl by the fistful and suddenly she wasn't digging it anymore; that's when Joe Boyfriend decided to play Joe Hero. He had balls, I'll give him that, but then he got kicked in them and wasn't much good to anybody. The girl pushed at Zig, darkened tears streaking down her cheeks as she begged to be let go. The crowd was quiet as a cemetery—it never occurred to most of them that hardened criminals might actually be dangerous, and in any case they had no idea what to do about it.

But me, I've got a few. My hand was sliding over the familiar wooden grip of Earl's old crowd-pleaser, duct-taped under the bar just for special occasions, but then Dodge got up, no harmonica and no drink in his hand, and stood toe to toe with their misbehaving guitarist, so close the crooked straw brim of his hat almost scratched the tip Zig's nose.

"Lady asked to be left alone," he said evenly, stating a fact. "Think you should listen to her."

". . . the fuck ever man just wanted to get my what was fuck man . . ." Zig's head dropped as he shoved the girl back at the crowd and shuffled off to the corner like a kid caught breaking his own toys. My hand relaxed, but the crowd grew restless and began to make for the door. Benny tried to coax Zig Zag back onstage, but he just flipped everyone the bird as he hollered over his shoulder, ". . . best watch yourself bitch."

"Howya gone sed no to money?" Benny screamed.

The answer was lost as someone kicked down the mic stand with a deafening crash and the cackle of feedback. I covered my ears and I could see all the players jump. I also saw some ass-hole in a tan trooper's hat come up behind the stage, pointing a gun and hollering at the band. Whatever he yelled was lost under the feedback, Dodge didn't even hear him put two bullets in his back. The hat tumbled from his head and he hit the floor like he'd been tackled, good arm grabbing for something to pull himself up. Vijo bolted out the back door before anyone could look at him twice and Zig Zag wasn't far behind him, while Benny and Ghost put their hands up. Terrified college students were stepping on each other to get out the door and even fleeing through open windows. The crowd-pleaser tore free with a good yank, but then I saw the shooter was waving around a badge as well, still yelling as he walked over and kicked the power cord out of the amp. Suddenly he was coming through in stereo.

He was Sheriff R.P. Coolidge and he had a score to settle with the murdering son of a bitch whose music we all seemed to love so much. He shamed me for employing ex-cons, he shamed them for not doing more with their second chance, and he shamed the system for letting such a vile and ruthless bastard as Dodge Hardin roam free when he'd put so many officers, in-nocents, women, and children in the ground. I just kept my mouth shut through the whole mess, hoping I'd make it through the day without getting shot or arrested. When he fin-ished his little speech, Sheriff Coolidge dug his bootheel into the wounds he'd inflicted, kicked Dodge over on his side, cocked the hammer of his gun, and demanded to know if his victim had any last words.

"Yup," he said from behind a big shit-eating grin. His good arm shakily placed his hat back on his head. "You're a lousy shot, Coolidge."

There was a shot, blood hit the drum, and a badge clattered to the floor beside a tan trooper's hat with a burnt and bloody hole through its center. I didn't even see Dodge reach, but there was a gun smoking in his hand, a Colt six-shooter so old it had probably shed Union blood. He used the gun to push himself to one knee, and then Benny and Ghost helped him to his feet. I could hear the sirens on their way as they staggered out my back door into the alley. That was the last I saw of Sweet Benny and his Sanchez Penitentiary Band.

I told the cops the whole story, but they insisted on grilling me two more times at the station and showing me lots of mugshots that all looked the same. I positively identified Sweet Benny Pace, a Louisiana con man, and Roger Hardin, a notorious gunfighter, but could provide no info as to their current whereabouts. Though I can't really say I was surprised, what could I have expected? I was just glad the bar was still there when I got back. Had to shut down for a week or two to clean up the mess, and when I re-opened Sue's was even more popular than before. Bands came by and begged me to let them play, kids started to frequent the place like it was just another college watering hole, and after a month or so, it was. They chased out all the regulars—Sue's used to be a whiskey and beer hole, now it's a place to come sip fruity margaritas and hear "indie" music, whatever the fuck that is. Just sounds like a whiny kid with a guitar to me. Sometimes one of them will ask me when Sweet Benny's coming back, and I always tell them he's booked a lifetime gig in the steel motel, but I don't really believe it. See, when the cops were asking me all those questions, there was something I didn't quite recall till I got home that evening.

The flyer Benny had shoved in my shirt pocket; it was for Austin City Limits, a live music festival so big even a loser like me had heard of it. In almost microscopic type under "Local Bands" there they were—Sweet Benny and the Sanchez Penitentiary Band. I was sure then that they weren't on lockdown. They were on a mission, and if we heard from them again it was gonna be just what Benny wanted, on a stage in front of half of Texas, or on a special six o'clock news bulletin. Only time would tell . . .

Trim

Vinnie Penn

It's funny, I thought she'd be shaved completely. She was certainly trendy enough, or at least tried to be—a dangling Playboy bunny swinging from her belly button, her half shirt just about touching it. One hundred percent blonde, with blue eyes and big breasts, Inez was total centerfold material. But, not with that thing between her legs.

Early on in our fooling around she began biting my nipples. At first I thought it was a good thing, the appetizer to a meal whose main course might be some spanking with a side order of hair pulling. But, as time went on it became clear that she was a one-trick pony. She chewed and chewed and chewed, and the sensation flew right past erotic to psychotic.

As she lay before me, legs spread and veritable horse's mane glistening in the candlelight that came off her nightstand, I wrestled between faking an emergency and opening a condom.

Inez was intriguing enough, the kind of exotic bounty I figured I wouldn't get to experience once the age where young people typically backpacked through Europe passed me by. Yet, here it was, the dalliance with a foreigner I presumed was now never to be.

Afterwards, in the bathroom, I tried to avoid the mirror as I splashed cold water on my face. What's left of my hair was matted, the bald spots coming across as this total contradiction to the life I was living. Infomercials say I couldn't possibly score the way I do. So how, then, was I? And how long could it possibly last? My face was nothing but jowls. There was stubble everywhere and I had shaved just the night before. "Why am I the worst shaver?" I actually said out loud. My love handles spilled out over my Calvin Klein boxer briefs.

"What?" She shouted from the bedroom. That could be it. Maybe she didn't understand the word "shave."

It is a difficult subject to broach, as delicate as the flower that blooms beneath it. If you've undone her button-flies and discovered a hornet's nest, encouraging the landscape may just leave you stung. Straight outta *Cosmo*, huh?

Fact is, in an age where shaving it off is completely all the rage, anything more than a tuft seems like too much. Generally, these days, if there is anything at all, it is a perfectly coiffed landing strip, at best.

Such is the state of the nether region. Unfortunately, getting some trim sometimes involves someone who needs to *get* a trim. And striking up that little exchange can lessen your opportunity for any other type of exchange unless you do it just right.

Adding insult to potential injury, we men have discovered that taking a shear to our own shrubbery only results in us looking larger somehow, rendering negligence in this department incomprehensible.

But, a woman doesn't want to look larger, obviously. Nor may she want to be so vulnerable, so revealed. And ultimately, gentlemen, this is their decision.

It does not mean the discussion cannot take place, however; that a subtle suggestion cannot be made. Along the lines of the commercials where a woman and her mother stroll down the beach talking hygiene, a meeting can come to order.

You are not her mother, though. Contradictorily, you may just be the man her mother warned her about.

Tact is your ally. A mutual shave is an ingenious route to go. Suggest a bath, light some candles, and then turn up in the tub with a razor in one hand and a dollop of cream in the other. Keep a pair of scissors at arms length if unruly happens to be an understatement. Then once it begins to grow back you can say you prefer it shaved completely, or at whatever point along the way you prefer.

This was how I broached the subject with Inez, her protests notwithstanding. "There's supposed to be hair there," she kept saying.

Despite Off-Broadway's urging that all women embrace their vaginas, many remain apprehensive to do so, some even viewing their pubic hair as a beard covering an ugly face.

Such was the case with Inez, who, unfortunately, was correct. Her . . . "area" went from looking like Abe Lincoln to a tomato that'd been left on a windowsill too long. It looked downright *angry*. Plus, Abe's mole was still there.

It was not happy to see me, was not ticklish, had no sense of humor whatsoever. It was a disgruntled vagina.

How could I say any of this to Inez, though? "Thank you for letting me shave you, but we've gotta wait 'til it grows back to fool around. It's mean-looking."

Of course, Inez had decided she liked it. So, the next time we took a bath together I put some Rogaine into the tub—after all, I had cases of the stuff (to no avail)—and Inez got some sort of infection. Worse, she leapt from the tub in pain, slipping on the tile and fracturing her ankle.

I kept my fingers crossed the entire time in the waiting room at the hospital that I wouldn't have to come clean, but the doctor was closing in on the culprit—damn CSI shows. So, I told

Inez everything in the emergency room. She looked at me as if I were insane.

Later that night, back at her apartment and not speaking to one another, I passed a special on the *Discovery Channel* about angry beavers, and I snickered.

"Wot is so funny?" Inez asked angrily—as angry as the creatures that were filmed for the special—and I didn't know if she just didn't want me laughing, period, didn't want me happy at all, or if she knew "beaver" was slang here in America for ... well, you know.

"Nothing," I said timidly.

Timid was a new thing for me, too. A bail bondsman by trade, I spent my days, or moreover, my nights, bailing scumbags out of jail—imploring them not to skip out on their bail and pending court dates. And when necessary, tracked them down with my bounty hunter, Conk, a six-foot-five monster—much of it due to a pituitary problem—who liked when my threats didn't intimidate enough and he got to crack some skulls.

One particular bounty used to truly test Conk's already limited patience. A pimp who abhorred the term, but nonetheless set prostitutes up with the dregs of society and took seventy-five percent of the earnings (so what else could he be called?). He used to face Conk's bashings with a smirk, all the while telling him he needed to get laid, maybe even fall in love, and that he was just the guy to facilitate that. Conk punched him in the face so hard one time a piece of the pimp's eye was in Conk's enormous ring afterwards.

I'd stand there, after my threats and pointed fingers did little to procure cooperation, and watch these beatings, nary an eyelash batted, sometimes making phone calls, ordering pizza.

The last time I bailed this pimp out he told me there'd be no problems this time around. That Conk, he suspected, was only partially human, and lectured me on women on the way to his plush digs in the ghetto.

"Somewhere along the way we lost sight of the fact that women are beautiful, graceful creatures who deserve to be put on a pedestal and respected," he said, dabbing his eye repeatedly due to what I thought were tears, but was really just that one eye watering endlessly because a piece of it was still lodged in Conk's lion-head ring with rubies for eyes. "What's worse," he said next, "is that they did, too."

I thought of that the night of the Rogaine incident, after changing from the Discovery Channel to *The Bachelor.*

Two months or so later, after Inez's bandages were removed and crutches returned, I was watching television once again while she was in the bathroom. The water had been running in the bathtub for a bit, the resulting steam creeping out under the bathroom door, filtering into the living room like a fog.

"Can you help me?" She beckoned from beyond the door. Assuming her foot was still hurting, and that she required some help getting into the tub, I hopped to my feet and went in. I hadn't seen her naked since the last bathtub folly, so there was at least that in it for me.

I was surprised to see her already in the tub, lather between her legs like whipped cream atop an ice cream sundae. She had let the hair grow back in, this patch of blondish curls, like a beard of cotton a child uses for Santa's face in art class in Kindergarten.

She held a razor in her hand, waved it around, grinning, inviting me in. Disgruntled vagina or not, tender nipples the next three days or not, I wanted some—and Inez did have some other tricks in her repertoire, that was for sure.

I peeled my clothes off frantically, reminiscent of when I lost my virginity to a hooker me and all my friends took turns on. I was in such a rush I pulled my pants off over my shoes, taking them off after the pants. All the while Inez laughed and laughed.

Once I got in and we got situated—one leg up alongside the

rim of the tub here, one of hers tucked under one of mine there—she proffered me the razor. "Shave the way you like," she purred. And I did, slowly, gingerly, if you don't mind me using such a word. Sculpting. Careful not to cut her. One of my fingers close to going inside of her at one point, which she promptly declined. "After," said she.

When I was done, a palm tree sort of thing happening, (which rendered that mole a coconut as far as I was concerned) I leaned in to kiss her. Pulling back, away from me, she reclaimed the razor, saying: "Now it is your turn."

As I mentioned, I already had a fairly regular grooming regimen in place that kept my region from being unkempt. Inez sprayed some shaving cream into her hand and then massaged it onto my pubic hair. And I do mean massage, her fingers alternately grazing my balls, causing the skin to tighten considerably.

She began shaving me, dunking the razor into the water and then bringing it back up, all the while still cupping me with her other hand. The head of my cock rose up from the water, like a mini-Loch Ness Monster, and I lay back against the tub, at once enduring a spa treatment and some primo foreplay. Closing my eyes, I could hear Inez purring, "Mmmm." Then, she said, "I loved you, you know."

A smile emerged from my ecstasy, eyes still closed. But then I reconsidered.

Loved.

"D."

Past tense.

That fifth letter, like the ominous final chord to a composition. Then the razor, in a swift motion, cutting open that major vein, artery, whatever it is, that runs through a man's scrotum. I shrieked, and heard it, like a teenage girl shrieking during a horror film.

Inez scrambled out of the tub immediately after wielding

the razor and my hands went down into the bloody water, grabbing myself, causing overflow onto the bathroom tiles.

"What . . . the . . . *fuck?*" I heard myself gasp. I, too, scrambled to get out but couldn't. Slipping, banging one knee, maybe shattering it, my legs numb and lifeless anyway.

She just stood there, right outside my reach, toweling herself off leisurely. The blood kept coming, draining, and my vision was becoming blurry. She lit up a cigarette, propped herself onto the sink, all the while still, "Mmmmm."

I clutched the washcloth draped over the side of the tub and pressed it against my sack but it only succeeded in making me shriek again. Then, for whatever reason, I began trying to tie it around my leg, as if there was enough material, in an effort to stop the bleeding. It was futile, pathetic, and Inez even giggled.

"Fucking . . . bitch," I sputtered.

Then the blackness began. I could only keep one eye open at a time and not for very long at that. Out of the corner of my right eye, peripherally, the last time I was able to open it, I saw Inez dialing a number on her cordless. *Beep*, I heard. Then *beep*. And then *beep* again. That was it, no more buttons.

I was fading fast, and that's when I heard Inez, like I had never heard her before: "Oh my God! Help! My boyfriend! He is hurt! I am afraid he may be dying!" I was dead before she even finished the 9-1-1 call.

A year later, to the day, my family put a prayer of remembrance in the paper for me. "Before his time" was one of the lines. In that very same paper, only a few pages away, in the Wedding Announcements section, there was a photo of Inez and a man who looked very familiar.

"The groom-to-be is a physician who, ironically, treated his intended last year for a burn" was one of the lines.

The Neighbors

Bill Fitzhugh

Monday
September 10, 2001

"Barry . . ." Vic's voice came over the line in a strangled, halting, whisper. "I'm . . . cas . . . trated."

"What?" Barry nearly dropped the phone so he could wipe his hands.

"They're . . . cut . . . off." Vic sounded as if he were struggling for breath and life itself.

"What? Why?"

"Bleeding's . . . bad."

"Why are you calling me? Dial 9-1-1!"

Vic wanted to go on, but he couldn't. That was all he could take. It hurt too much to continue. He had to laugh. "Jesus," he said. "I'm kidding. You think I'd call you if I was sitting here bleeding profusely from my crotch? What the fuck good would that do?"

Barry, sitting in his Santa Monica office, smiled as he raked a hand through his thready hair and said, "Vic, you had me goin' there. You oughta be an actor."

"Who's acting?"

A slight pause before, "Whaddya mean?"

"You don't listen to a word I say, do you? And just so you know, that's a bad thing for an agent. I told you I was getting this done months ago."

"Getting castrated."

"My vasectomy."

"Oh, that's right," Barry said. "The trial of the century."

After nearly being trapped in a paternity suit by a woman who had studied at the Bonnie Lee Bakley School of Shakedowns, Vic had undergone the operation. Given his tenuous grip on the bottom rung of the middle class ladder, Vic could scarcely afford another lawsuit, let alone a wife or a kid. When served with the papers, however, Vic and his agent had briefly entertained the notion that they might be able to turn the proceedings into a boost for Vic's sagging career, but the press didn't bite. Vic's star as a screenwriter had never risen to the heights necessary to have this qualify for the *schadenfreude* derby that was Hollywood.

"The only way to make something out of this would be to kill her," Barry had said.

"And get caught."

"Sure, focus on the down side."

Barry had a soft spot for Vic, even if he wasn't much of an earner. Vic's odd sense of humor was as refreshing as his genuine gratitude for the work Barry did on his behalf. And the fact that Vic didn't seem to have anyone else—no family or friends—always triggered something in Barry. It wasn't compassion exactly, more like pity. So he said, "How'd it go? You feeling all right?"

"Fine," Vic said. "Yeah, I got back about an hour ago. Sitting here with a big martini and a bag of cracked ice on my sack. Or a sack of ice on my cracked bag, take your pick."

"That's lovely, thanks."

Vic giggled as the vodka and narcotics seeped into his blood. "Consider it your ten percent," he said. "And they gave me some award-winning narcotics, too. Best of show. These little yellow fuckers, whatever they are, are fantastic!"

"I'm happy for you," Barry said. "Is this going to delay your second draft?"

"What do you think? You think you'd get anything done in this condition?"

"Fine, I'll tell them you had, uh, emergency surgery. You need some more time."

"You out of your mind?" Vic spilled some vodka as he eased himself into his lounge chair. "Those fuckers get so much as a whiff of sickness they'll drop me from the project faster than you can say 'numb nuts'."

"You know they're not like that," Barry assured him. "They're people. People with testicles, I might add. They'll understand." He had a thought. "Or I could say it was like a chin tuck, something like that."

"Do me a favor," Vic said, the insinuation clear.

"Fine, I'll lie."

"Atta boy."

Vic had given himself the week off to recuperate. He planned to spend some quality time watching daytime TV and getting drunk. And not just tipsy either. He was aiming for peanut-brained and legless, squiffy-eyed, starched, monkey-sucking drunk. What you might call a serious bender. Something to mark the end of a rough patch and the start of something new. The paternity suit had tapped another nail into Vic's financial coffin. He was hoping the new script would be his revival. And he wanted to come at it fresh, like starting a new year. But as it was September, he had to create an artificial starting point. He figured the back end of a drinking binge would do fine.

So he kicked back and took another sip, a good one, and allowed himself the luxury of thinking back on his moment of glory. After a decade of struggle, Vic had broken through when one of his scripts sold for good money, got made, and did well at the box office. After that, the offers poured in. He cherry-picked the good ones. He bought a little house out in Canoga Park and figured the money would keep coming as long as he wrote. It was a common mistake.

His tax returns said Vic was a writer but he preferred the older term: scenarist. He came up with scenes. Circumstances with dramatic possibilities. Scenarios. He'd tried actual writing once but boy, what a pain in the ass that was. And no money in it either. Hell, Vic didn't want to be Faulkner, Fitzgerald, or Mailer—which was fortunate since such desires would lead only to crushing disappointment for someone with his skills. And he had skills. They simply wouldn't be described as of the literary variety.

Vic wrote for the citizens of the cineplex. The popcorn crowd sucked his stuff up like so many crack whores. Nasty, violent stuff. Stories with secretly planted bombs. Paranoid fantasies come to life. Children trapped in dark, moist places, being chopped, drilled, and sawed into gruesome bits. A regrettable pastiche of pornographic savagery. Blood, flesh, nerves, and teeth. Awful compositions of explosions, exploitation, and horror punctuated by counterfeit moments of shock created by sudden, loud noises rather than anything remotely resembling genuine tension.

At least that's how Vic described his work. Hell, he knew what it was. It was software for a machine that needed more every week. It was escapism, cheap thrills, and a way to make a living without a commute. It was commerce, by God, nothing more, nothing less. As the old saying goes, they don't call it show *art*, they call it show *business*.

And business was good. Life was good. At least for a while.

But then he turned down some offers and demanded too much money and started talking about gross points, and before he knew what had happened, the offers started going elsewhere. Somebody else got hot. People forgot Vic's name.

Well, fuck 'em, Vic thought. The business was all about cycles. He'd been up, he'd been down. Only one place to go from there. He figured the new script would put him back in the game. He was looking forward to getting back to it, almost as much as he was looking forward to his bender.

After the surgery, Vic bought four bottles of vodka. And not just any vodka. Something new for the new economy. Forty bucks a pop. Made from rare seedless albino grapes or the dew of Danish virgins or something equally esoteric. Vic put the bottles in his freezer along with half a dozen martini glasses. After his first one, Vic had to admit, it was the best drink he'd ever had.

And the pills. Hoo-boy, the pills were great.

So he sat in the leather recliner all afternoon slurping vodka like a Massachusetts senator with his dick in a sling. He stayed there into the night, getting pickled in the comforting blue light of his big-screen television.

The last thing he saw was a late night sports recap with the biggest news story of the day: Michael Jordan hinting at another comeback. After that Vic drifted off, or passed out.

Tuesday
September 11, 2001

Vic woke up in the chair, dehydrated as a piece of dried fruit, a thrumming hangover like rodent teeth gnawing on his optic nerves. He rubbed the crusty sleep from the corners and brought his eyes into focus so he could check his scrotal support. He was shocked at first, primarily because he'd forgotten that he'd shaved himself for yesterday's operation. It looked like a featherless, newly hatched bird of prey or maybe a small boneless chicken. He couldn't decide. His fevered imagination had allowed that he might wake up with a pair of grotesquely bruised eggs, yellow-brown as they approached gangrene. Strangulated, with a sweet smelling discharge, ready to pop like overripe figs.

But no. Everything seemed all right down there. No discoloration, no swelling, no nothing.

But the pain. The pain was in need of management.

But first things first. He shuffled wobbly down the hall, cupping himself as he moved toward the can. A deep breath. He stood in front of the toilet, over-abundant in his caution, treating his cock as if it were a contact-explosive. Carefully now. No wiggling. Gently. Ahhh.

Then to the kitchen, bowlegged as a cowboy. He gave the coffee machine a passing glance but decided the answer lay in the hair of the dog. Specifically a greyhound. He juiced a grapefruit, fresh from his own backyard, then pulled a chilled glass from the freezer, glugged it full with the special edition vodka and splashed it with the grapefruit juice, pink as a lip. Ahhh. The California lifestyle.

He wobbled back to his lounge chair, leaving small puddles in his wake. He took one of the yellow pills for breakfast and chased it with the greyhound, oblivious that the world had changed while he slept.

And slept.

Even considering the previous night's consumption, Vic was surprised how late it was. His eyes rotated slowly to the ceiling, then out the window. Something was odd. Then it occurred to him. It was so quiet. Unusually, weirdly, quiet. That's why he'd been able to sleep. But why the hush? The skies above Los Angeles were usually brawling with police, news, and traffic helicopters, private planes coming and going from Van Nuys, big jets leaving LAX or approaching Burbank.

But right now, nothing. It was eerie.

Still, it was nice. Vic took another sip on his breakfast bracer and felt the yellow pill dissolving in his system. Calming the synapses. Relaxing the muscles. Slowing his breath.

Then he turned on the television.

At first he thought nothing of it, assumed he'd tuned into a movie-of-the-week disaster story. All shaky hand-held video footage of panic and destruction. Billowing clouds of mucking gray dust stampeding office workers through a canyon of a street like shotgun pellets down a barrel. The script sounded improvised but had a genuine urgency. Vic changed the channel a few times only to find the same story everywhere he went. Even the words *Breaking News* splashed across the screen, Vic assumed, was part of it. But part of what? Intellectually he knew they wouldn't be showing the same movie at the same time on every channel. But the alternative refused to register. The alternative didn't make any sense. Slowly though, the truth began to find its way past the impossibility of itself.

And then he accepted it, or tried to. This was real. This was happening. Or, as the facts began to organize in his mind, he understood that it had already happened. Back East, New York, D.C., somewhere in Pennsylvania. Hours ago. All flights grounded. That explained the quiet.

He drank heavily as he made a few calls of the can-you-fucking-believe-it variety. But mostly he just sat there, growing sick from the news, yet unable to turn away. He'd never felt anything like it. It was shock, disbelief, not knowing who, what, why. Why? He spent the day going from channel to channel as if hoping that someone eventually would say something to explain it all.

But he never found that channel.

No one knew anything for sure, so they just kept talking. A blur of chattering heads. Wolf Blitzer with Madeline Albright. A cowardly attack, yes. And it was tempting to speculate on state sponsorship, but let's not. Aaron Brown with one senator calling it an international crime. Judy Woodruff with another senator saying it was an act of war. Jeff Greenfield guessing 22,000 dead, on the order of the Battle at Antietam. Worst in American history. All that death once again in the name of God. Allah. Call it what you will. Three or four hundred fire-fighters running toward the thing everyone else was running away from. Pearl Harbor for a new generation. Our hearts go out. Rumors of heavy volume on put options for airline and in-surance stocks. Did someone profit on this? Premature to point fingers. It's still unfolding. We don't know. But early finger-pointing is this guy bin Laden.

And the awful footage over and over and over, dripping on his mind like Chinese water torture. Relentless and more sick-ening with each replay. The planes striking the buildings. The unfathomable, consuming fireballs. Small white flags waving from smoking windows.

It was odd. Vic felt sickeningly, viscerally connected to the events while at the same time feeling completely disconnected from them. As if it had happened to him but without his being involved. Maybe it was too much to absorb from 3,000 miles away. Maybe if he were there, Vic thought, if he could look out his window and see it, smell it, taste it in the air, maybe then it would make more sense or seem more real. If he could be there to do something, maybe it would be different. But he couldn't be there. All he could do was watch the images hour after hour after hour. What else was he going to do? He had to watch. All the death, the loss, the grief. The magnitude.

He drank two more greyhounds. After that he stopped bothering with the grapefruit juice altogether. He just stared at the screen, sucking the vodka down wholesale, pummeled by each new fragment the networks hurled his way. FAA radar data for United Flight 93. A call from a cell. Passengers voting to take the plane back. "Let's roll." The heroes augering into a field minutes later.

Wednesday
September 12, 2001

The television was still on when Vic woke up. Material witnesses had been arrested. Raids on apartments in New Jersey and Del Ray Beach, Florida. FBI agents seen wearing protective suits as they carried boxes from the apartments.

The word hangover was no longer adequate to its task. Vic's brain had shrunk from the walls of his skull, the nerve endings swollen and throbbing, his mouth dry and gummy as a two-year-old glue stick.

He started drinking immediately. He checked the prescription and saw he had refills. He found a pharmacy that delivered. Then he returned to the television news and the relentless assault on his emotions. He knew there was nothing he could do. Knowing more couldn't help, wouldn't do anyone any good, but Vic wanted every scrap they came up with. The attacks and the coverage had churned up a ravenous hatred that needed to be fed.

The hijackers had seventy-eight virgins waiting for them. Nobody else did. Flight training in Florida. No red flags. No instruction on landing or take off. No red flags. Names on terrorist watch lists. No red flags. Security camera capturing Mohamad Atta breezing through security at Portland Airport. No red flags. Al Qaeda sleeper cells in forty U.S. states according to the FBI. No red flags.

Fifty billion didn't buy as much security as one might hope.

The stunned sensation that had held Vic in its grip began turning to rage. It was a delayed reaction, like being somewhere, minding your own business, when out of the blue someone sucker punches you. It takes a minute to put things together, to figure out the who, why, and the what-the-fuck. You're stunned for that moment. But then you're furious and can't be stopped. Someone has to pay for it. That's how Vic felt now. Something had to be done. Somebody had to die. Lots of people had to die. What were we waiting on? "Let's roll!"

The feeling of helplessness—was that the right word?—his inability to be in New York to do something, to move rubble, to give blood, to do anything simply increased his rage. Was it helplessness or impotence? He thought of his operation. He looked at his boneless chicken, drank some more, and took one of the yellow pills.

Flight attendants, passengers, pilots. Throats and box cutters. Jihad! Desperate, wrenching phone calls from 30,000 feet. People jumping from 90 floors up. Someone in a wheelchair trapped in a stairwell. Jihad! The footage again and again of the terrorist training camp that looked so ridiculous. Men with their faces covered by the head scarf carrying Kalashnikovs as they jumped over a comically low barrier and crawled through a corrugated culvert pipe like some grammar school obstacle course. Jihad! *This* was the enemy? We can't stop *these* guys? The government couldn't find, or at least fake, better footage of a terrorist training camp?

A feeling of doom settled into his gut.

A car's horn startled Vic from his drunken stupor. It started the neighbor's dogs barking. It was late now, eleven-fifteen. The news was still infecting the nation.

The horn sounded a second time.

It's that guy across the street again, Vic thought. What sort of asshole has . . . ?

And all of a sudden, it hit him like a truck full of explosives. Fuck! Vic sat bolt upright. His eyes and his mind narrowing all at once.

That guy across the street. That dark-skinned, secretive son of a bitch with the odd habits.

Vic had never thought about it before. He'd never had *reason* to. But now. Now he had a goddamn reason.

The FBI estimates there are sleeper cells operating in forty states. Son of a bitch.

The horn sounded again and Vic went to the window to look. Same as before. A car had stopped at the end of the man's driveway and honked. The man came from his house out to the street. Vic snuck outside for a closer look, creeping along his hedges, out of sight. There were no streetlights. It was too dark to see details. The driver got out and met the man from the house. The trunk popped open. A transaction of some sort. They spoke but Vic couldn't catch the words, wasn't sure of the language. The man returned to the house. The car drove off in the night.

And that got Vic to thinking.

He hurried inside, fueled by adrenaline, vodka, and a new sense of fear-driven duty. He grabbed a legal pad and sat in front of the tube marshaling his evidence from memory, all the things he'd seen from his window that didn't add up now that he thought about it, now that he had some context, now that someone had told him what was going on and what to be on the look out for. The suspicious deliveries, unusual driving habits, scraps from personal letters cross-cut by a paper shredder on the street after spilling from the recycling, the list grew long. As he wrote, Vic continued subjecting himself to the televised barrage of the hideous, the appalling, and the grim.

Jihad! The messages left on the answering machines of loved ones, play on the air. Doomed voices Vic would never get out of his head. Stories about the rain of body parts from the towers. Jihad! Grim administration insiders with we-told-you-so's and talk of preemptive strikes. Get them before they get us. Let's roll!

Hell yes, Vic thought. That's exactly what we have to do from now on.

Jihad!

Friday
September 14, 2001

"Can you fucking believe it? They've got these sleeper cells in forty states," Vic said. "They're here. They live all over the damn country."

"Yeah, I read a story about it in *The Times*," Barry said. "Pretty scary stuff."

"Scary as all hell," Vic said.

"And this has happened before? The car late at night, the weird business in the dark?"

"Hell yes," Vic said. "A bunch of times. At *least* a dozen, probably more. I wasn't counting. And they've only lived there about nine months."

"Maybe the driver just doesn't like to back up," Barry said.

"What?"

"Maybe it's just easier to stop at the end of the driveway, rather than pulling in and backing out."

"It's a circular fucking driveway!" Vic said. "That's my point! Actually it's shaped more like a lower-case *h*, you know, with a spur leading to the garage in the back. The house is set back thirty or forty feet and there's a big circular drive, so why not just pull up to the front door, do whatever the deal is, and drive straight out? Saves the guy in the house from walking all the way to the street and the driver never has to back up or anything. None of it makes any sense."

"What I don't understand is, if it was some sort of terrorist thing, why would they do it right there on the street? Why not be more secretive?"

"But it *is* secretive," Vic said. "It's pitch black out there at night. They never do it during the day when anyone could see them. You know me. I'm here all the time working. I can't help but see everything that goes on around here. I know every dog that's walked, every FedEx, UPS, DHL, and Sparkletts delivery that happens on this street. But this car only comes late at night. They probably figure no one's watching, figure they're being as secretive as they need to be."

"And you're sure it's not pizza or Chinese?"

"Yes, I'm sure," Vic said. "Jesus."

"Are the streetlights burned out there or what?"

"No, this stretch never had any, which is great. Kids don't even come down here on Halloween. Keeps things quiet."

"Well," Barry said. "I admit, it's a little weird."

"A little? Listen, I can see half a dozen of my neighbors' houses from here. You know how many of them I've seen do anything remotely like this? None. Zero."

"Maybe it's a drug deal," Barry said.

"Maybe," Vic said. "According to a thing I saw last night, that's one of the ways they fund their activities. But I was thinking it might be money laundering. Have you heard about the *hawala* thing?"

"The what?"

"It's a way they transfer money without involving banking systems. No records, nothing. They've been using it for centuries in the Middle East. Maybe this guy's one of the paymasters for the sleeper cells."

"You've been doing your homework," Barry said, sensing a project. "You think there's a story here? Something for a spec script?"

"Listen," Vic said. "I've got a whole list of their weird behavior that I never really thought about, until now. Now some of it makes sense. Like when the guy walks out to his driveway for these long, agitated phone calls? I have no idea what language. I tried to listen but that's twenty yards even if I'm right behind the bushes. I was thinking about going to this spy shop and getting one of those parabolic mikes, but, not that I understand Urdu, but . . ."

"He speaks Urdu?"

"Urdu, Farsi, I don't know what he speaks," Vic said. "But I've never *heard* him speak English."

"Have you ever talked to him?"

Vic peeked out the window and said, "No, he doesn't make himself available like that. I've never seen him talk to any neighbors either, now that I think about it. But my point was about the way he wanders around while he's out in his driveway. I swear this guy's on a satellite phone and he's trying to get a better signal."

"Like he's calling his boss back in Afghanistan," Barry said, wheels turning. "At a terrorist training camp. The reveal is that the call is coming from a sleeper cell in suburban America. Something like that, that's good. Of course it'll be a while before we can pitch anything. Everybody's a little sensitive right now, but that'll pass. This guy lives alone?"

"No," Vic said. "There's a woman, his wife. I mean I've always assumed she's his wife. They both look Middle Eastern of some sort. Shit, I couldn't tell a Sunni from a Kurd. I mean, face it, we wouldn't be having this conversation if they looked like Swedes. But check this out, the woman does this all the time. She'll get in her car, drive to the end of the driveway, and stay there while she puts on her makeup."

"Maybe she's just trying to save time."

"No!" Vic said, as if admonishing a dog. "That doesn't make any sense. Think about it. If you want to save time by putting makeup on in the car, you do it while you're driving or while you're stopped at lights on your way to wherever you're going. Not while sitting still in your driveway. You might as well stay inside and do it."

"I see your point," Barry said.

"The more I hear about the Taliban, the more I think it's got something to do with the fact that their women are supposed to keep themselves covered and are absolutely forbidden to wear makeup. *But* if they're a sleeper cell, this woman can't very well be running around in one of those *burkas,* can she? So maybe the man is trying to keep things as close to Islamic law as he can. Have you seen the stories on Sharia? Jesus, these people are nuts, makes fundamentalist Christians look like *Girls Gone Wild.* Anyway, maybe he refuses to let her put makeup on in the house. Makes her wait until she's out of his sight or something, I don't know. Regardless, the behavior is weird."

Barry said, "So you called the FBI?"

"Hell yes. Talked to Agent Ron Phillips."

"What'd he say?"

"He was busy."

"That's it?"

"Well, he asked me to fax over my list of stuff, any information I had. So I did."

"Okay," Barry said. "I guess you did your part."

"I don't know," Vic said. "He didn't take me as seriously as I would have liked."

"Well, what else can you do?" It was a rhetorical question. "Just think about the spec script idea, okay?"

"I'll just wait and see if he gets back to me," Vic said. "And meanwhile, I'm keeping an eye on the son of a bitch."

Sunday
September 16, 2001

By Sunday, Vic had seen the planes hit the towers over two hundred times. Replays in slow motion, at full speed, and freeze framed etched into his mind's eye forever. He found

himself crying once at the terrifying, intimate emotion of trau-
matized husbands and wives, mothers and fathers, brothers and
sisters, wandering the streets of lower Manhattan holding photos of their loved ones. *Please. Have you seen her? Have you
seen him? Can you help?*

Image rules the landscape, and the cumulative effect of the
images repeated over twenty-four hour cycles was having its
way with Vic. It fed the hatred and stoked the fires. And even if
he turned it off, no matter how much he wanted them to stop,
he couldn't get the doomed voices out of his head.

Mostly, Vic wanted somebody to do something. He wanted
missiles launched, bombs dropped, Special Forces infiltrating.
He wanted populations decimated. He wanted the full wrath of
the U.S. military visited upon the heads of everyone responsi-
ble and anyone who had celebrated the moment. What were
they waiting on? Why hadn't there been any preemptive strikes?

Let's fuckin' roll!

Vic pushed his recliner across the room to the window
where it was easier to keep an eye on the guy across the street.
He dusted off his old binoculars and kept them on the side
table next to his drink. When the vodka ran out he started on
the scraps of his liquor cabinet beginning with half a bottle of
Crown Royal and another yellow pill.

It was early afternoon when an unmarked panel van rolled
slowly up the street. It was big enough to deliver any number
of things. It pulled into the man's driveway. Vic had seen this
before, too. The driver, furtive and dark, glanced around before
unloading something. The man from the house didn't sign for
anything. The van left.

Vic got the plate number, picked up the phone, and called
the FBI.

"I don't know if you call it a step van or a panel van or
what," Vic said. "But it was sort of like a UPS truck, maybe a
little smaller. It looked like it used to have a logo on the side but

it's gone now. Oh, and it had Nevada plates," as if that cinched the deal.

"Anything else?" Agent Phillips asked sluggishly.

"No, that's it," Vic said. "Pretty suspicious, though."

"How so?"

Vic couldn't believe this guy. What did he want, the man on his prayer mat in the front yard five times a day? "Well," Vic said, "everybody else on the street gets deliveries from UPS, FedEx, and DHL. This guy has a second-hand, unmarked truck with out-of-state plates bringing stuff. And it's not the first time either. That's what's suspicious."

"All right," Agent Phillips said. "Thanks for the call. I'll put this with the rest of your stuff."

Barry didn't sound too surprised when he said, "That's it, huh?"

"Yeah, can you believe it? The fucker blew me off," Vic said. "I'm out here doing his goddamn job, handing 'em one on a platter and this is how they respond. That's why the terrorists could hijack those planes in the first place, you know? FBI, CIA, NSA, they all had the information they needed to stop it, they just didn't do anything with what they had."

"I don't know, Vic, maybe there's an innocent explanation for everything," Barry said.

"Yeah? I'd like to hear it," Vic said. "I'd sure as fuck like to. Hit me."

"I didn't say I *had* the explanation," Barry said, trying to sound calm, hoping it would be catching. He could tell Vic had been drinking. "I'm just saying, that's all." He paused before continuing, "Listen, have you thought about the spec script idea?"

Vic sensed that Barry wanted more evidence. He said, "Let me ask you. When you get home every day, I mean in your car. What do you do?"

"What do you mean?"

"I mean what do you do, park on the street? Pull in to your garage? Do you go in head first or do you back in? Do you alternate every other day? It's a simple question."

"I pull into the garage headfirst. Why?"

"Every day?"

"Yeah, every day."

"What about Cindy?"

"Same."

"Every time?"

"Yeah, every time. I mean, unless we've been to Costco or something, you know once every few months we might back in to unload stuff."

"Exactly," Vic said. "Same as me. Same as everybody else I can see from my house. Same as everybody I've ever fucking known. Except for these people. Some days they park in front of the house, sometimes they pull head first into the garage, but a *lot* of the time they back into their garage like they're loading or unloading something from the trunk. Explain that."

"Maybe they go to Costco a lot. They have kids?"

"Yeah, that's another thing," Vic said. "About once every six weeks since they've been here, they'll trot these two young boys out on the front lawn to pitch the baseball with "Dad." I've never see them coming home from school or riding their bikes on the street, nothing. The other kids in the neighborhood? See 'em all the time. But these people? It's like they're renting these kids to make it look like they're an all-American family. To blend in. That's what they said these sleeper cells do. They try to blend in."

"That seems a little far-fetched." There was something in Barry's tone that said he wondered if the pins had come out of Vic's hinges.

But Vic was past listening. "And the *parents*," he said. "They come and go all day, like neither one of them has a job. But they've got to have a job or they couldn't buy a house, right?"

"Maybe they're independently wealthy."

"And they live here? It doesn't wash."

"Maybe they're writers."

"Writers? They don't sit still long enough to write anything."

"I was joking," Barry said. "I admit, it's all pretty strange but don't get too caught up in watching them. You've sent the information to the authorities, just let it go at that. But think about the spec script idea. You know, fade up: a Middle Eastern man on his satellite phone in an American suburb, talking to a terrorist in Syria, something like that."

"I'll tell you something else weird." There was something spooky in his voice now. "I've never seen the two of them in a car together," he said. "Ever. Period. Doesn't that seem weird?"

"Vic, I've got to go. Warner Brothers is on the line."

Writing had taught Vic a few things about people. It was axiomatic in his line of work that the way one acted under pressure revealed a lot about one's character. If a person talked a big game when things were copacetic but folded under stress, it was the folding part that told you who they really were. And, after that last shot of sweet whiskey, it was beginning to look to Vic as if Barry and Agent Phillips were both lacking in certain aspects of character now that the pressure was on.

It was good to know who you were dealing with, Vic thought. Then he heard someone on the news say you're either with us or you're against us. And everybody seemed to agree with that and so did Vic right at the moment.

But it left him feeling like he was on his own.

He'd been blown off by everyone from his literary agent to an FBI agent. Everyone treating him like he was overreacting. (And it wasn't just Barry and Agent Phillips either. LAPD and the LA County Sheriff's Department had both put him on hold and left him there.) *Over-reacting?* Vic poured what was left from a bottle of Tia Maria, about two fingers worth. He looked at the dark liquid and said, "I bet everybody on those planes and in those buildings wished a few more people had over-reacted." He drank it like a shot and looked back in the cabinet, rooting through the remaining bottles like it was a crowded chess board.

Vic didn't think he was asking for a lot. He just wanted to see the FBI knock on his neighbor's door and ask a few questions. Stick their nose in. It wouldn't take ten minutes. A quick look around the guy's house. Maybe test the trunk of his car for explosives. Just do something.

He was down to the liqueurs. He grabbed the brown square bottle. Drambuie. Scotch sweetened with heather honey, flavored with herbs. He made a Rusty Nail and stood at the window, watching. His own little department of homeland security.

Vic had given Agent Phillips what—in light of recent events—he considered to be credible information. But had the man acted on it? No. Had he so much as bothered to come and interview this guy and the woman? No, he hadn't. So the question in Vic's mind was: *How can I get the FBI over here? What can I do to get Agent Phillips's attention?*

Vic found his idea at the bottom of the Rusty Nail, under the ice. Preemptive strike. He looked out his window again, like Gladys Kravitz on steroids, bug-eyed and twitching. *Subtle's not working*, he thought. *These bureau guys need something they can get their bureaucratic minds around. Something more than a list of unexplained behavior that requires them to make connections that aren't obvious enough. The list I sent merely suggested terrorism. What I need is something that shouts it.* As Vic chewed on a piece of ice he thought, *You want terrorism? I'll give you terrorism.*

He grabbed the goose-necked bottle of Galliano, opened it, and gave it a sniff. Licorice. But not enough for a whole drink. So he mixed it with some ouzo and a little sambuca as he thought back on something he'd written into one of his scripts after the Oklahoma City thing. He remembered the research. It was pretty simple. Yeah, he could do it. That would work.

It was dark when he staggered out to the garage. Under the work table, a dozen open sacks of fertilizer, some for St. Augustine, some for fescue, some for the vegetable garden. Perfect. He looked around for a container. Something to hold the thing, to *be* the thing. He picked up coffee cans filled with nails and screws and dumped them on the floor. They were too small. Paint cans were better, but still not enough volume. He settled on a big ice chest. It had a nice seal, almost airtight. Probably hold forty or fifty pounds of the mixture. With some duct tape, he thought it would work. In case of earthquake he had a can of diesel for a generator. He mixed it with the bitter fertilizer.

Coming on the heels of the anise-infused Galliano-ouzo-sambuca mixture, the banana liquor was a refreshing change. Vic served it to himself in a frosted collins glass. It was sweeter than he expected, more like candy or medicine you didn't mind taking. He drank from a straw as he sealed the fertilizer-and-fuel mixture in the cooler using every inch of one hundred yards of duct tape. Being an intricate pattern, it took a little while.

The final problem would be rigging a booster to detonate the thing. A simple fuse wouldn't work. Vic remembered that much from his script. He'd need something concussive, a small explosion to trip the large one. Maybe gas fumes in a glass jar, set by a spark. Sure, why not? He stumbled back into the house to a jumbled closet filled with dusty sports equipment, outmoded stereo gear, and other boy toys. He ripped the guts from a remote control monster truck that only turned right anymore. He crossed some wires hoping to cause a short.

It worked.

The bomb did everything Vic had hoped for, and more. Three LAPD units were there within five minutes. The bomb squad arrived two minutes later, followed by a S.W.A.T. team, the fire department, and paramedics. Most of the neighbors stood on their lawns with their robes and their mouths open, wondering what had happened. The most popular guess was a natural gas explosion. But no one came out of the house across the street.

Several news helicopters circled overhead, their powerful cameras zooming in on the smoldering remains. There were newspaper and television reporters on the ground as well. One of the bathrobed neighbors was already negotiating to sell the home video footage he'd been shooting since the explosion.

Vic's name would definitely be in the news tomorrow. He would make the front page of both the *Hollywood Reporter* and *Daily Variety* as well as the *L.A. Times* and *The Daily News*. The DVDs of the movies he had written would soon be flying off the shelves. Two of his scripts, which had stalled in development, suddenly got green lights. He was finally one of Barry's biggest earners.

Agent Phillips, a stoic fifty-year-old, arrived and took charge of the scene. He was standing near the crater where the explosion happened. A guy from the bomb squad who was nearby gathering evidence looked over at him and said, "Do you smell . . . like . . . banana?"

Agent Phillips looked at him. "Funny you say that. I keep getting licorice." He tilted his head back and sniffed with his eyes closed.

"Huh." The bomb guy sniffed again. "Yeah, yeah, a little bit."

Agent Phillips told the paramedics they wouldn't be needed. "Coroner's on the way," he said.

"Hope he brings a spatula," was the paramedic's only comment.

Agent Phillips looked up and down the street, his suspicion aroused. Everyone on the block was standing outside their homes, except the people in the alleged sleeper cell. He began to wonder if Vic had been right.

As he crossed the street and approached the house, he saw a curtain fall back into place and the light in the front room went off. His pulse quickened. He walked up the circular driveway, to the door, rang the bell. After a moment when no one answered, he knocked with his fist.

A second later, a voice from the other side of the door said, "Yes?"

"Open up," Agent Phillips said. "FBI."

The door opened just a crack. A dark-skinned man peered out, nervous and shifty. "Yes?"

Agent Phillips flashed his ID saying, "FBI. I'd like to talk to you."

The man's eyes darted back and forth, looking past Agent Phillips, as if for possible witnesses to what might happen next. He closed the door slightly and whispered to someone.

Agent Phillips slid his hand toward his gun. "Now," he said.

"Okay, okay." The man opened the door. "Come on in."

Agent Phillips stepped inside and stared in cold disbelief at the phalanx of computers and electronic eavesdropping equipment filling the room. A listening station. He said, "What the hell?"

The dark-skinned man reached inside his jacket and produced an ID of his own. "Agent Alvaro," he said. "National Security Agency." He gestured at a woman—presumably *the* woman—sitting at a computer, with headphones on. She wore a lot of makeup and gave a cursory wave. "That's Agent Raphael."

Agent Phillips gave her a professional nod then looked to Agent Alvaro for an explanation.

"We've been watching this guy ever since he wrote that script about domestic terrorism." Agent Alvaro crossed to a table stacked with files. "We have people inside all the networks, studios, and agencies keeping an eye open for anybody with, uh, subversive intentions." He pulled a thick folder from the bottom of the pile and handed it to Agent Phillips. "See for yourself. That's from the case officer who opened the file."

Agent Phillips opened it and read. It described Vic's script as, "*A nasty bit of treasonous propaganda, a blame-America-first narrative that painted the various federal security and policing agencies as inept bad guys, more concerned with budgets, political considerations, and protecting their turf than with protecting Americans. Possible security threat.*"

Phillips closed the file, shaking his head. "I had no idea. The guy said he was a writer, but . . ."

"Writers spread ideas," Alvaro said. "And ideas can be dangerous. So we moved in. Tapped his phone, found out every library book he'd checked out, and started monitoring all his Internet activity. You should see all the stuff this guy researches. Weird, off-the-wall stuff."

Agent Phillips gestured at the eavesdropping gear and said, "So you guys knew that he'd called us, saying he thought you were a sleeper cell?"

"What?" Agent Alvaro tried to hide his embarrassment with some incredulity. "Well, no, we didn't. Really?"

"Really."

Alvaro sounded somewhat defensive when he said, "Well, obviously, we couldn't listen to every single call the guy made." He gestured toward the outside world. "We have to come and go like an average family, keep the guy from getting suspicious, you know? Of course, even if we're not here the computer records and transcribes all the calls. Sooner or later, we'll get around to reading all of them, you can count on that."

Agent Phillips waved off his concern. "Listen, I understand how hard it is to do this without the necessary resources. We've been so swamped with tips, I haven't had time to do any background checks on you guys. I mean for all I knew, you could've been a sleeper cell." He peeked out the curtains at the emergency vehicles lining the street.

"Well, it's a moot point now," Alvaro said.

"Boy howdy. But listen, I'm curious about a couple of things," Agent Phillips said. He asked Alvaro about some of the items on Vic's list.

Agent Alvaro wagged a finger at the eavesdropping equipment and said, "Oh, well, I have to go out to the driveway to make cell calls because this gear screws up my signal."

"He said you seemed pretty agitated during some of the calls."

Agent Alvaro laughed. "Probably when I call my mom. She's in Lisbon, going deaf, only speaks Portuguese. You have to gesture a lot."

"He thought it was Farsi or Urdu."

Agent Alvaro chuckled at that. "Hell, I don't think we have two people in the agency who can speak Farsi." Asked about the kids Vic had seen pitching the baseball, Alvaro said, "That was my idea, something to make us blend in. Keep him from getting suspicious."

"Nice touch," Agent Phillips said. "So now what? You guys pack up and move to another job?"

"No," Alvaro said. "We've picked up a few things on some of the neighbors. E-mails, phone calls, whatnot, a surprising amount of anti-American, anti-government stuff. We're going to stick around, keep an eye on 'em for a while."

Agent Phillips shook Alvaro's hand. "These are scary times," he said.

"Nine-eleven changed everything."

"Be vigilant," Agent Phillips said with a nod. "The enemy's all around us."

The All-Night Dentist

Vincent Kovar

Working nights is one of the many things I did to make my marriage work. The money is exceptional, it's why Antonia was with me in the first place, and once I started there was no stopping. I see a few patients in the late afternoons, mostly to keep my tax returns from sending up red flags. But my business, like my clientele, is largely nocturnal.

You've probably heard that dentists have the highest suicide rate of any profession. No one is quite sure why but we do seem to be a depressive lot, even those who get out into the sunshine with greater regularity than me. Still, as long as I had my clinic, I didn't have much to whine about, except my ex-wife.

I had her dead to rights for marital infidelity. I came home one morning and found Antonia honking like a goose under the undulating ass of our accountant. He blurted out the usual line, "This isn't what it looks like," while she, crisp as a credit card, just said:

"Don't stop."

She said it to him. Antonia had already stopped speaking to me directly and all subsequent communication during the divorce was transmitted through her wooden-faced lawyer. After those two words, "don't stop," she became the greatest ventriloquist alive. Her lips never moved.

Still, I let her take almost everything. I handed over the house, my BMW and virtually all of our liquid assets, just so that she would leave my practice alone.

I don't whine about driving a Chevrolet Citation two decades old or living in a cramped apartment where the hallways smell of cabbage. Especially not to my patients. However, sometimes when they're on the chair, I do describe how nice it would be if they took care of Antonia for me.

"*Ihh hoo essy,*" my patient says, his mouth full of my fingers. Too messy. Too many deaths. Too close to me.

He should know. Underneath the pretentious black leather and crushed velvet, this guy wearing the blue paper bib is a predatory killer, darker and more voracious than any twelve Dahmers or Bundys put together. He killed my former accountant while I was at a conference in Wichita. At least I'm pretty sure it was him. They are all pretty tight-lipped about this sort of thing. The body turned up burned to ash in a car fire. The murder wasn't any great favor to me. My night clients count on me and since the accountant was the one cooking my books, they figured he had to go after the divorce. Good dentists are hard to find, especially ones who are open all night.

Both of his canines have cratered brown patches along the first inch, but the left also has a crusty mush of black, gingival decay nearer to the gums. It's a form of meth-mouth particular to my clientele. Even undead enamel can't take the toxic traces of sulfuric acid, phosphorus and lye that lace the veins of nearly every junkie in America.

"You have to lay off the meth-heads," I say, though I know it will do little good. Telling a vampire to stop feeding on drug addicts is like telling my day patients that they need to stop eating fast food. Everyone knows it's bad for them, but like fast food, junkies are on every corner, easy to pick up and ultimately, disposable.

From the chair, the blood drinker hoots his contrite agreement, "Ay-oe, Ay-oe . . ." I wonder if they get something out of it, some secondhand high tinged with lost mortality but such questions cross the boundaries of our professional relationship. Besides, what am I supposed to say? "It might kill you?"

I'll bond some Optec HSP onto his right cuspid (I refuse to call them fangs) but there isn't much to save on the left. It looks like it's been soaking in battery acid so I'll have to pull it. I finish the right onlay, clean him up and make an extraction appointment for Tuesday night. We'll start the implant procedure immediately after.

Getting into undead dentistry was easy. They'd been watching me for a long time. I think they were watching Antonia, too. I was a plain but upwardly mobile, yuppie mercenary with a wife way out of his league. She was an insatiable swamp leech—bloating herself on the hemorrhage of my affection and fortune. I lost so much of both, I was dizzy, intoxicated. It felt like love.

Getting that first "special" patient made me feel the same way. Each time I work on one of them I still get it. Learning how the supernumerary cuspids fold down from the palate. Watching them stack up piles of cash, sometimes even gold, on the tray when I'm done. It all pushed me up higher toward the rarified air where I was good enough for a woman like Antonia.

Once I had enough, I figured I'd be out and breathing that same air before my hands got too dirty.

My apartment is close enough to walk, but I usually drive to avoid the near-constant drizzle of Seattle's weather. The place is on the third floor, with no elevator, above a Starbucks and across the street from a Thai restaurant that doesn't serve breakfast. I'm too tired to climb the stairs and too jazzed up for coffee so I follow the tail end of rush hour traffic out to the suburbs.

Antonia's new place in the suburbs is in one of those end-less, curving rows of white tract mansions chewing up the land-scape, crammed in with the smallest possible interproximal space. Its only advantages, from my perspective, are that, one: most of her neighbors are double-income households with both spouses off to work, and, two: Antonia's house is mostly glass, devoid of secrets and affording ample vantage points for me to look in on her.

Some days I stay in the car, jerking off and waiting for her to walk past the windows. Other times, I sneak into her bushes for a closer view. I'm looking for a flaw, some crack in the surface of her that reveals some humanity, some regret or some weakness.

She has an affinity for white. Even after the charred body of her lover was pulled from the wreck of his Lexus, Antonia never wore the widow's weeds. Someone told her once that black was slimming, so she forever after referred to it as "the color fat peo-ple wear to fool themselves." She even wore white to the funeral.

The place is white on the inside as well, so minimalist and clean it is almost featureless. I gave her an expensive set of porcelain tooth veneers about halfway into our marriage. Her décor reminds me of those veneers—unstainable, artificial, and nearly unbreakable.

She's bright and shining and perfect. And I want her dead.

The obvious question is, when did I become such a loser? Was it before our divorce or am I suffering through some kind of emotional and financial aftermath? Was I always such a putz, such a balding, paunchy freak vainly attempting self-pleasure in my ex-wife's manicured bushes? Maybe.

I live in the times when normal folks are asleep, tucked safely in with lovers or spouses. By contrast, my world is pop-ulated by drunken college kids, by hospital shift workers and, of course, by vampires. We see things differently at night, float-ing through a sea of alcohol, fatigue, or undeath.

Basically, I'm only a little pilot fish, swimming alongside sharks and cleaning the leftover bits of life from between their teeth. Someday I'll have enough stored away to retire. Someday Anto-nia will be gone and my world will be white and shining and per-fect. I'll spend half the year in Alaska and half in Tierra Del Fuego, following the midnight sun and living where it's never night.

At two the next afternoon, I get a call from Antonia's lawyer, or more precisely, his paralegal Chet. I don't rate a call from the big dog. I get the guy who cleans up after him. I wonder if Chet has his own Antonia somewhere. Somebody he is trying to win over by going for the big bucks. I feel a strange bond to Chet. This is a guy like me—a remora swimming alongside sharks, trying to get by.

He is as cheerful as an exposed nerve. "I need to have a cleaning. When is your next opening?"

I start thinking about crystal meth again. Wondering if this kid is smoking it or snorting it or shooting it directly into his veins. What kind of masochist wants a dentist from the wrong side of a messy divorce? Chet usually calls to have something signed, sent, or paid for but is never actually rude. So I tell him the number of my service and hang up. I give money to Anto-nia, she gives some to the lawyer, the lawyer pays Chet and he dribbles the last of it to me. It's life's trickle-down theory and somehow I always end up at the end.

After I fall back asleep I have that dream where all my teeth are falling out. Freud wrote that this was one of four basic dreams that all humans have. I wonder if vampires have it, too.

My neo-gothic tooth extraction shows up early, so I don't have time to check to see if Chet is scheduled. The vampire looks nervous and vaguely hostile so I talk him through the implant procedure one more time. After removing the rotten tooth, I'll drill a titanium screw up into his jaw and attach the new porcelain cuspid. Dentistry has totally changed for this type of patient due to the advent of ceramic and titanium. During the decades we used silver, vampires avoided the chair.

His tooth is so corroded I'm afraid it might break, but it pops out on the first yank. That's when he rears up, eyes blazing, and I am pretty damn sure he's gonna bite me. I wait a few long minutes before picking up the drill.

This is not the night to lobby for an undead cadre to exterminate my ex-wife or quibble over my fees. The patient depends on those teeth. Even a partially edentulous vampire will have trouble getting the right incisal occlusion, and therefore enough blood flowing to feed. He'd end up gumming at food that someone else has cut open for him.

That's when I hear the outside door. I turn up the gas and quickly excuse myself to the front.

It's Chet.

He spells out the deal a little too quickly and it spoils his tough guy routine. He's found my offshore account in the Canary Islands and now wants half or he turns me over to Antonia.

"Are you sure you want to do this?" I ask and he looks confused, not realizing I am trying to give him a way out.

He pulls on the best mobster face a skinny, twenty-five-year old paralegal can muster and says, "Are you sure you don't?"

Then he sweeps out with a flourish of his coat. He probably thinks it's impressive, but I get that sort of thing all the time. I've seen it done by the best.

It's reasonable to assume Chet is having me watched, so I decide to stay away from Antonia's house. Getting caught in her bushes with my pants down would be the final indignity.

The office is closed on Friday nights, so I wolf down some triple garlic chicken at the Thai place across the street.

While I eat, I ask the waitress to bring me a phone book. Chet is listed. So is his address. Amateur.

I take half my order in a to-go bag and drive over to my blackmailer's apartment. He lives in an expensive building in the gay part of town. The art in the hallways is screwed to the walls but the orchids are fresh and the carpets are clean. Chet answers the door in a track suit.

"Hi Chet, can I come in?" I walk in without waiting for his answer. He went to a lot of trouble to bring our lives together. If he is real, real nice, I might try to save his.

I let him talk his shock out of the way. During the speech, I look around his apartment. The place is huge and crammed with expensive, no-credit-check-to-buy kind of stuff: plasma television, leather furniture, and a dozen small speakers dangling like dead bugs off the glittering spider web of a stereo system. Chet is in debt. Chet is in a lot of debt.

I say, "Look kid, whoever you're spending this on, whoever you're trying to impress, it's not worth what you're getting yourself into." Then, as he eats my triple garlic leftovers, I give him version number two, the one about how my night patients are actually members of an Italian fraternal organization. It's a good routine; clean, seamless, polished.

Monday afternoon, the woman calls from my appointment service to tell me I have a string of cancellations. It's a bad sign. A really bad sign.

There's a knock at my door a few minutes later and two men are standing in the cabbage stench outside my apartment. Neither of them are neo-gothic types like my implant patient. They are not a type at all really. No capes or accents; no renaissance collars or monochromatic black. They are dressed in grays and browns; average men of an average height and average build. They're the type who can kill a hundred people in a park, rob a bank, and then fade into a crowd.

I pat the folder of papers that Chet gave me; even show them the hard drive I took from his laptop computer. They're not reassured.

"It's a good story you told him," says one.

"But it's also too interesting," adds the other.

"That type is attracted to danger."

"He likes to see how close he can get to the edge of the cliff."

"It makes him feel alive."

"He's like you."

For a minute I think they are considering adding a paralegal to their stable of help. If vampires need a dentist, surely they also find occasion for legal advice. Is there a secret phone book of night plumbers, furnace repairmen, and barbers? Are the undead ever hunting around for a late night back waxing?

They're afraid Chet knows too much. Getting the file and the hard drive was a good start, they say, but my would-be blackmailer is too unstable. Chet is about to go the way of my former accountant, minus the goodbye screw from Antonia.

Let's face it. I'm a bottom feeder and Chet is higher up the food chain. We both may be remoras or pilot fish or whatever but in the descending order of Antonia-Lawyer-Chet-Me, the paralegal is an obstacle to my getting a bigger chunk of life. I should feel crappy for what I do next. But I don't. Whatever nerves inside me which might register such subtle regrets are long gone. The betrayal is like meth, a corrosive acid eating away whatever enamel is left around my soul but the euphoric rush of it keeps me from noticing. Almost. With four little words I go from being a sucker fish to something with teeth.

"Antonia's in on it."

They stare at me a long time. My macabre obsession with gruesomely killing off my ex-wife is famous among my special patients. They've always denied me the pleasure. Too many bodies equal too much attention equals substandard dental care for the living dead.

So I do the routine again, version three. I do the routine with my testicles clamped up tight next to my body. I do the routine thinking that at any second they're going to smell bullshit.

My story goes that both Antonia and Chet are going after my Canary retirement account. They might even go after my practice next and my patient records. They might even find the vault where I keep x-rays of my patients who happen to have two-inch canine teeth. Chet backed out, I tell them, but Antonia . . . Well, she is turning out to be a bit of a problem.

Antonia and Chet are already dead when I pull the teeth from their corpses. I didn't see the killing. The two nondescript vampires showed up at my office each carrying a body.

"No one will find them," one of the vampires says, "But let's be sure."

Their story, version four, goes like this. Antonia and Chet were embezzling money from me for years. The police would figure my ex-wife and her new, incongruously gay lover murdered me in my office and disposed of the body before fleeing. Chet's homosexuality doesn't seem to concern anybody. For enough money, they figure, anybody will fuck over anybody.

There is no midnight sun for me, no Alaska or Tierra Del Feugo. Handing over my retirement fund is the price for holding Antonia's twenty eight, flawlessly white, veneered teeth in my hand.

The vampires decide to bring me on full time, citing both the increased occurrence of meth-mouth and their need for long-term stability. They really don't give me a choice. They do me right there in the office.

I'm still only a sucker fish. My new two-inch canines get pulled a few minutes after they make me. They don't want another shark swimming in the ocean. They want an undead, after-hours dentist in a very small bowl.

So I try not to whine. Instead, I work through every night dreaming about the suicide I can't commit and a midnight sun that never sets.

The Replacement

Duane Swierczynski

"SURRENDER."

This is what I heard through a haze of alcohol.

"SURRENDER AND I WON'T KILL YOU."

I looked out of my windshield and saw a surly, body-armored police officer pointing the business end of a .357 at my unprotected face. Desperate, I tried to piece together the evening. I remembered bikinis and Alabama Slammers in test tubes and Foster's. For a second, I imagined the police officer wearing a bikini over his body armor but the image quickly dissolved as he plunged his fist through the windshield and yanked me out of my car.

The cop dragged me across the street, broken glass spinning into my face like tiny wheels. I felt cold steel trolley track on my cheek.

"I WANT YOU TO SEE WHAT YOU'VE DONE."

I knew that my ex-wife's car was a wreck—a shattered windshield being the least of my worries. I shouldn't have tried to drive home from Escape in my state of mind. I probably really screwed up the fender and the bodywork on the passenger side. God, but for the grace of bikinis go I.

"GO AHEAD, LOOK."

The police officer hoisted me to my shaky feet; flashers filled the air around me. I couldn't focus. But finally I did. And when I did, my heart stopped. My eyes wanted to suck themselves back into my skull.

No.

"LOOK."

A young woman's body, slightly bent, lay in the middle of the road. Blood pooled around her head.

"Oh God," I muttered, and started crying. I turned away. All I remembered was my car spinning, bright lights, and a horrible thud I thought was a speed bump.

"LOOK!" The police officer forced my head back around and jammed my eyes open with his gloved fingers. "LOOK, YOU BASTARD! LET THAT BURN INTO YOUR WASTED LITTLE BRAIN! LOOK!"

I looked.

And looked.

Until I looked long enough to try to take the cop's gun from his hand and shoot myself.

My lawyer tried to reason with me. "You don't want this. Trust me, man, you don't fuckin' want this."

"I do."

"This is barbaric, this new death penalty. Christ, it ain't even a death penalty. It's a torture-slowly-for-hours-then-kill-you penalty."

But I'd made up my mind. For taking a life, even as unintentional as that taking was, I must give my own life, no matter how painful. My life for hers. Amanda Sue Patterson.

Age 20. College student. Majored in English Lit. Pretty green eyes, strawberry blonde hair. Liked Beatles records. Loved Ayn Rand books. If I hadn't killed her, I would have fallen in love with her.

"Bro, take the deal. It's the best thing. Think of your ex-wife."

I said, in the strongest and surest voice I could muster, "I'm thinking of Amanda Sue Patterson."

The Judge frowned at me, then looked down at his desk. "This is unusual."

"I want to pay for my crime," I said. My lawyer kicked me under the table.

The Judge looked my way. "Shut up. I'm trying to read here." He looked down again and kept reading. "Something new from the Supreme Court." He looked at me. "You've got a choice, you little bastard."

I held my ground. "I don't want a choice. I want to pay for my crime."

Amanda Sue Patterson haunted my every waking moment. She said to me: *I know you didn't mean to kill me. You were just drinking to forget the alimony payments you have to make at such a young age. You're young, you got stupid, I died. I forgive you.* She was so sweet, so forgiving. God, I wanted to pay.

"You're going to pay, all right," the Judge said finally. "In fact, to set an example for this court, I'm going to sentence you to the new penalty for vehicular manslaughter in the Eastern District of Pennsylvania. You're going to the Replacement Program."

"I want death!" I said. "My life for hers!"

"Exactly," the Judge said.

The Replacement Program is justice in its simplest and purest form, nearly Biblical in execution. An eye for an eye, the Bible said. Good-government lobbyists recently agreed, and it passed Congress—not without help from anti-death-penalty activists and other assorted religious do-gooders. A life for a life.

I was sent to live with the Patterson family.

The program was created by a lawyer/philosopher/talk show host Harold Amis-Bowe. His theory? The only way to compensate for the taking of a life was with another life. The death penalty wasn't the answer, Amis-Bowe argued. That merely gave society an easy out. No, Amis-Bowe maintained, true compensation could be brought about by the surrender of the murderer's life in place of his/her victim.

I arrived on a Thursday.

Amanda's mom—sorry, *my* mom—was understandably cold. She said, simply, "Hi." Her blonde hair was drawn back in a cruel babushka. She'd been drinking. The smell of vodka was on her breath as she leaned to kiss me on the cheek.

Amanda's brother—*my* brother, fuck, I've to get this right— wasn't exactly chummy, either.

"You're going to regret every moment you have left alive," he said.

"Nice to meet you," I said. I had to be kind. It said so in the manual.

"I'm going to skull-fuck you with a chainsaw."

I was shown to my room. The closet was full of old-fashioned gowns, floral skirts, and funky blouses with spinning discs. Amanda had spent untold fortunes on antiquated post-modern clothing, it seemed. But her bureau drawers were filled with the usual suspects—panties and bras and love letters. I collected the letters in a pile and put them under the mattress. I planned to save them to read when I was feeling particularly masochistic.

I'd barely finished adjusting to my new surroundings when I was called for dinner.

Amanda's seat was in the corner of a long dining room table. Even though two older brothers had gone their own way, two places were left empty, as if waiting for a pair of Elijahs to show up. Mr. Patterson sat at the head of the table, Mrs.—damn it,

Mom—at his left side, and my brother Patterson, Jimmy, at his right. The places across from me and to the right of me, remained empty for the duration of the meal.

I felt funny asking for another refill of iced tea, so I didn't.

"Phone call," Jimmy said. He threw the phone at my head.

"Hello?"

"Yeah, uh, Amanda? I thought you were, like, hit by a car or something."

"This isn't Amanda. I'm Amanda's replacement."

"Yeah, so you're okay. That's cool."

"No, actually, Amanda's dead. I'm her federally-sanctioned—"

"Funny, babe. I was wondering if you wanna party with us tonight. The hot tub's free, and I've got, like, a fuckload of Oxys."

"Perhaps you didn't hear me, I'm—"

"Get here about eight."

I decided to give up, just like Mr. Amis-Bowe's manual suggested, and *surrender*.

"Sure, whatever."

"Cool. See ya."

I hung up. Jimmy poked his head into my room.

"You gotta go, Amanda," he said.

"Were you listening?" Did this little bastard listen to all of his sister's conversations?

"No choice, *Amanda*," he insisted.

"I don't have the address."

Jimmy threw me a piece of tattered paper. "Phil Randy. There's his address." He smirked. "Amanda would've been there."

Jimmy had obviously read the Amis-Bowe manual cover to cover.

Amanda's boyfriend was named Bob. He stopped by not long after reading about the Replacement Program and subsequent articles about me.

"Mister . . . ?"

"Come in. And you can call me Amanda. It's my name. Federally-sanctioned Amanda, if you like."

Bob smiled and walked through the front door. He was a sweet guy, really. I felt horrible for him the moment he'd called three days previous. He wore a plaid polo shirt and comfortable-looking khakis. Bob probably would've been the kind of guy I hated in high school years previous—confident, smart, gorgeous girlfriend, college-of-his-choice—but now I could feel nothing but pity.

"Amanda," he said, in a sweet, passive-aggressive kind of way.

"Yes," I said.

He laughed nervously, then recomposed himself. "This is crazy, but I've got to do this. For my own peace of mind."

"Go ahead," I said.

"Uh—"

"Don't be afraid, Bob. Tell me."

"Okay." Bob swallowed. "Amanda, since you've died and the government has replaced you with a heterosexual man in his late 20s, I'm breaking up with you."

I understood, but something bothered me. I shouldn't have done this—God, the kid was through enough—but I owed it to Amanda.

"How can you do this?" I asked. "After everything we've been through?"

Bob looked angry and hurt. "What?

"You heard me. How can you?"

"How do you know?"

"I've read Amanda's journals. God, Bob, she—uh, *I*—loved you! What about marriage? California?"

"What?"

"You're sitting there ready to end something just because of death? Death? God, Bobby, on the first night we made love you promised me you'd love me 'til death and beyond! Do you remember that! Do you? HUH?"

"You're a man!"

"I'm still your girlfriend!"

I went too far, I know.

Bob started crying. He cried and cried until I put my arms around him.

"I just," he sobbed, "wanted to do the right thing."

"It's okay" I said. I hugged Bob until he felt embarrassed enough to leave. I think Amanda would have been happy.

Mr. Amis-Bowe isn't a cruel man. His manual allows for phone calls, and once a year, visits. Who visits me? My ex-wife.

She's pretty. Blue eyes, dark hair. Perky figure. She's no Amanda Sue Patterson, though. Her name is Alicia.

"You're pathetic," she said.

"Nice to see you, Allie."

"Do you realize how utterly ridiculous you are? How ridiculous all of this is?"

Alicia was always to the point. Maybe I was being ridiculous, but this was not ridiculousness of my own making. Besides, I thought that I had been finding ways to transcend the ridiculousness with a kind of sublime acceptance. I was learning everything I could about Amanda. Mimicking the emotions gleaned from her journals. Capturing her facial expressions. This was a full time job. This was Vocation with a capital "V."

I looked at her the way Amanda would have, the way I saw in the family DVD library—with head cocked slightly to the side and lips pursed and eyes partially winced, and I said, "Is it *really* now?"

Alicia didn't visit the Patterson household again.

Some things in the manual bother me. Like the penalty for multiple-murderers. It's essentially a time-share plan, where families have their loved one replaced only certain days a week. Like, huh? Please. And take the penalty for murdering bachelors and spinsters: the so-called "No-Escape Clause Plan." In this one, you've got to stay at the victim's job and live at their apartment forever, never advancing, never gaining. What if the murdered would have gone on to greater things, like finding the cure for cancer?

I hear Amis-Bowe is reconsidering these sections, and thank goodness. It'd be none too quick.

Passing final exams was difficult, and the English Department social wasn't all that fun (no one asked me to go, *sob sob*) but summer came quickly and the mood in the Patterson family seemed to be changing. Mom stopped scowling and her breath didn't always reek of vodka. Dad and I shared a few close moments watching ball games—"Get me a beer, and I guess one for yerself"—something I was sure he'd never done with Amanda. But brother Jimmy was still the stickler. Just when I thought I'd pulled the psychic blanket over my head and they'd accepted the Replacement, he'd be there to yank it from my fingers. One day, however, I made a breakthrough.

"Amanda would have never done that," Jimmy had said, when I'd finished mending the broken slats of a picnic table.

"The manual says not all Replacements are perfect fits," I reminded him politely. "The idea is to give the energy, the spirit, the love . . ."

"Fuck your love. You're a murderer."

I looked at him, trying to pierce through. "Did you love Amanda?"

Jimmy was silent.

"Did you ever tell her that you loved her?"

This was perfect Amis-Bowe, and it was working. Jimmy was silenced. He shuffled his feet and quietly moved to the corner of the garage.

"Did you ever think you'd get a chance?"

Jimmy ripped a spider's web from a lawn chair and left the garage, silent.

I was making progress, sure enough.

Mr. Amis-Bowe himself came for a visit yesterday, except it wasn't Mr. Amis-Bowe. The original was gunned down by a fanatical death-penalty activist six months previous, and the thug was condemned to fill his spot.

"How are you doing, uh . . . Amanda Sue?" He started giggling, looking down at his clipboard chart.

"Fine, just fine. I got into Penn."

Amis-Bowe's replacement looked at me long and lean, then erupted into paroxysms of laughter. "Do you realize how utterly ridiculous you are?"

"You sound like my ex-wife."

Amis-Bowe removed a pistol from his briefcase and put it to my head. "You know I could snuff your life away faster than it would take your body to realize it should piss itself?"

"Then you'd be me," I answered sheepishly.

He paused. "Then I'd be you." He wiped his nose on his sleeve. "You're damned right I'd be you. 'Cause that's the American Way, right? Isn't it?"

"Yes, it is."

"I could pump you so full of lead that you could sharpen your head and do the *New York Times* crossword puzzle."

"You could." I did a quick mental search, then called the right Amanda-ism to mind. "But *really* now."

Amis-Bowe left soon, but not after stripping me of all my visitation rights for the rest of my life and conducting interviews with the other members of the Patterson family. He must have gotten them all riled up, because things reverted back to square one, emotionally speaking, for weeks after that.

* * *

Not long after my spot-assessment Jimmy started trying to kill me. At first, it was just verbal threats:

"I'm going to cut your head off and put it in the washing machine."

"You're going to wake up and find your legs broken."

Going to Mom and Dad didn't do any good. "So fucking what," Dad would say. Mom wasn't a ball of sympathy, either, unless she were drunk. Then she would say: "Now Jimmy, don't threaten to kill your sister. It's just not nice." Then she would laugh and laugh until she started slobbering on herself and fell off the kitchen chair.

I wanted to protect myself, but I knew the moment I struck back I was dealing with the Replacement Program's Time-Share program, and being Amanda was difficult enough. Besides, I felt for Amanda. I wanted to be her, to live her life for her. It was the most important thing I'd ever done. But being Jimmy? That loser?

For the first time, I think I truly understood what I meant—what Amanda meant—when she wrote in her journal:

No one understands me in this house. I really want to love them all, be like families on TV. But I can't. I wasn't trained that way. None of us were. We were trained to hug in the most superficial, kiss-goodnight-because-I-have-to way. You don't know how much I just want to hug my father. But I can never. Nope. I'm trained to rebel against my parents at every turn, to hate my siblings. That's what families are all about.

Amanda Sue Patterson, I love you, and the darkest day that humanity ever saw was the day I killed you.

I was sleeping—no, actually I was reading but pretending to sleep when the light in my bedroom flicked on and a figure lunged at me. It was Jimmy, with a pistol—a pistol that I would later discover was registered to Mr. Amis-Bowe's replacement. He pressed the business end beneath my right eye.

"*I'm going to blow your brains out.*"

I should have replied with a sample from the Amis-Bowe text on Aggressive Situations, but the heat of the moment caught me. I flipped him off the bed. He shrieked and landed on his stomach—and on his gun, which went off.

Goodness—what had happened? I sat up in bed and looked at Jimmy. His head, cocked to one side, was shaking. His lips were spritzing blood. I leapt to his side and tried to find the wound, but his stomach was a mess.

"Jimmy, hang on. I'm going for help."

I was barely up when Mom burst into the room and began screaming.

"MURDERER! MURDERER!"

I looked at her with Amanda's martyr eyes. "No, Mom. Jimmy didn't mean it. I'm sure he was just playing around."

"MURDERER!" Once her hands were around my neck, I realized she was talking about *me.*

Mom was strong. She dug her nails in deep, and actually had me on my knees and seeing polka dots when Dad burst in. He looked around the room, trying to comprehend everything. "FUCK ME!" he finally hollered.

I would have hollered, had I enough air in my lungs. But I was blacking out. And Dad was prying Jimmy's pistol from his trembling fingers.

"KILL THE MURDERER!" Mom shouted. "KILL! HIM!"

Dad took a few steps back and lined up a shot at me. "This is for our children, you hateful son of a bitch."

Unfortunately for Mom, Dad was a bad shot. Mom released my neck as she lost the front of her chest. I went crawling across the room. Dad lost his mind. Jimmy started throwing up blood. Air was cascading back into my body in large, hurtful gasps.

I saw Dad kneeling with the pistol to his head, right in front of his family's bodies—mine included. But I was alive! Alive! I sat up when my head finally cleared and tried to tell him so.

"No, Dad!" I said weakly. "You can't. You've got to be Mom. I'll be your children." I swallowed hard, and mustered as Amanda-like as possible, pretty and swollen-lipped: "Really."

His eyes turned to mine, went wide, and then he blew the top of his head off.

Dad was a bad shot the second time, too. He's still alive. Missing a good part of his face, but alive.

Jimmy lost his liver and large intestine. He's hooked up to a machine. But it's nowhere as big as the machine Mom's hooked up to—permanently.

I guess I can stop calling them "Mom," "Dad," and "Jimmy." The courts—which don't take attempted murder of a Federally Sanctioned Replacement lightly—have commuted my sentence. I'm back to my old self, my old life. The Pattersons are doing hard time in a Federal Prison/Experimental Cybernetics Laboratory. Their sentence is six consecutive life sentences—each. With the machine, Mom . . . er, Diane Patterson's hooked up to, she might actually complete each one.

I moved home to Alicia, who, believe it or not, took me back. We fixed the car, had a couple of children. We named the littlest one—a girl—Amanda. I've started teaching her Ayn Rand. We listen to the Beatles. But she'll have none of that—at least for now.

As a father, you see, I've learned a few things. I used to think you could shape your kids any way you wanted. I thought they'd always look to you for guidance and understanding. Goodness, I thought that having kids meant replacing your own childhood.

Boy, was I wrong.

Eight Guns Over a Dead Girl

Patty Templeton

Chapter 1

Savi was a purse snatcher, a wallet grabber, a *fuckyoufirst* then steal your green, heartbreaking bitch. Her stems climbed high to a mix of dynamite and heaven. She had been known to allow victims to smell her black curls or, if you were lucky, tongue the outline of the inked cobwebbed wings taking location across all of her back before she sent you to the six foot drop. She was a barroom tall tale, the poetics off the bathroom wall:

> *You grabbed some tail, you brought it home.*
> *Yer hard, she's wet, yer all alone.*
> *Ask her her name, that's what I said,*
> *but if it's Savi, yer already dead.*

And Savi hunted at the Blind Staggers Inn.

The Dame was blonde and looked like a burlesque librarian: hair in a high bun, gin in small hands, and a tight brown sweater wrapped around an eyeful. Savi could've fallen in love with her,

but she fucked her instead. The Dame was more than half behind the cork and all it took was Savi nuzzling into her ear,
"Oh, you just need to get home. I'll take you before one of
these surly sonsabitches tries to take advantage of the situation."

With a hand precariously close to a posterior, Savi led her to
a cab.

It was all giggles to The Dame's northside bungalow.

Savi followed to the door, went for the hug goodnight, grazed
lips across an ear and gave a kiss on the cheek. Said Dame invited Savi in.

Coffee was had, footsy played, and many a mark knows
how creeping delicious Savi's delicate toes can be. At bedtime,
The Dame said, "Why don't you come tuck me in?"

So up the stairs and Savi knew this broad had dough.

In the bedroom—and there were the jewelry chests.

Onto the bed and The Dame smiled and said, "Why don't
you grab me a little something from that drawer," while she's
unbuttoning and swinging down her tresses and this is where
Savi almost backed down, almost tossed the knife from her
sneaking thigh and pledged eternal I'd-take-a-bullet-for-you-
firecracker-love for this gorgeous piece.

Sitting in the top drawer, elegantly straddled by silk under-
things was the thickest, meanest strap-on Savi had seen, but
Savi saw the pearls sitting underneath the monster.

Savi unzipped as she slinked to The Dame who said, "My
Atty won't be home till tomorrow."

Savi strapped on as she climbed onto the bed and The Dame
had one hand in the wet and the other at Savi's breast.

And Savi gave The Dame a squeal as her tip played around
the lips and finally pushed in and it was thick and it was in, but
The Dame, she said *deeper* and Savi gave her the crimson jim-
son and the blonde was at her neck, doing this thing to her ear

and Savi had her knife under the pillow, but this blonde goddamn she made her horny and Savi was rethinking the whole
kill-the-bitch attitude, but she caught out of the corner of her
eye the glittering rocks on the nightstand, but fuck she was in
this bitch so fucking deep and The Dame whispered *fuck me
harder* and bit Savi's bottom lip, and Jesus K. *Rist*, Savi was
coming all over the place and The Dame was laid back, arching
her back, Savi's left on a breast and right behind her neck, and
goddamned if Savi didn't want to fuck her seven times till
morning, but fuck, fuck, there, there, right fucking, *there*? Was
that a Van Gogh above the bed? And Savi's knife came out with
the dick still deep and The Dame's eyes opened up as the blade
plunged in.

Savi rolled over, unstrapped and wiped off, reaching for The
Dame's purse on the oriental carpet.

Atticus the Itch's goddamned wife.

Savi had screwed the best wet of her life and it was the best
gal of a man who had just got out of prison for punching a hole
through a cop's fucking head. Atticus the Itch who owned the
city, who owned the damn hotel she lived in. Atticus the Itch
who, if he saw her, would kill her, *then* fuck her, then toss her
out the goddamned window to let the cops clean up after because the cops knew better than to ask questions anymore. Ask
questions and you either get sodomized and strangled or a hole
punched through your head—a serious hole the size of a peach
from the Itch's bare knuckles, just like Jimmy What's-His-
Name now sitting in a wooden kimono waiting for God to take
him home.

Only The Itch owns God, too.

Good side: She could get lost off this score.

Bad side: Getting found out by The Itch and having ap-
pendages slowly hacked off between dickings, whereupon fi-

nally she would pass out and The Itch would skin her back to keep as a wall hanging.

Coin toss: The Dame said he wouldn't be home till tomorrow. This score would last her years.

Savi nuzzled naked up to Mrs. Itch who coughed up her last, the knife still in her heart, and kissed her on the mouth for the good fortune. Savi felt those stirrings and The Dame dropped dead, so Savi reached for the soggy strap-on, laid back, and tucked herself in thinking about the pearls in the drawer. There was the first moan. The rocks on the table and Savi pushed deeper. The painting above her and goddamn this was a good, f . . . f . . . fucking score, naked in The Itch's house.

Naked and the door creaked downstairs.

Savi pulled out, looked up, only 4 AM. That little cunt, *my husband won't be home till tomorrow, my ass.*

This is all explainable. Dead wife. Wet strap-on. All parties naked.

Twenty steps left, The Itch was coming up the stairs.

Tell him his wife was a bitch and he deserved better.

Eighteen steps and The Itch was past the Tiffany window.

Tell him The Dame killed herself.

Fifteen steps and Savi could hear Mr. The Itch humming.

Tell him; screw telling him anything, Savi grabbed the purse, grabbed the rocks, and went for the pearls.

Twelve steps and good, his feet were heavy, he sounded drunk, sounded slow.

Ten steps and the hall Edisons flicked on and Savi had Mrs. The Itch's tight little sweater barely covering her ass, shoving her dress, shoes, everything into another bag from the closet.

Five steps and Savi was out the window, bags tossed and trying to climb down the vines like a two-bit porch climber, with a flash of a January breeze climbing between her legs.

The door creaked open as the window creaked shut and Savi

almost broke her ankle from the half-asinine jump as Atticus
the Itch started yelling from above.

It was four in the morning and decent girls weren't out this
late.

Savi walked down the block, lugging bags towards the El.

Too bad somebody saw her.

Chapter 2

Max had a penchant for gory three-penny comics and big tits, neither of which his mother allowed him to be around.

This was not an issue.

Joey Fitz smuggled him comics and Max saved a month's worth of allowance and ordered binoculars from *Boy's Life*. *Yeah mom, I got 'em for birdwatchin'. Sure.*

In fits of thirteen-year-old rebellion and boredom, Max leaned his gangly frame on the window sill and spied on the neighbors, keeping a journal of findings:

1. *Mrs. Fitz wears black garters.*
2. *Miranda Marley and Paul Hock were tonguing behind her daddy's shed.*
3. *Shelby: tomboy, age 14—NOW HAS KNOCKERS.*

And so it went with savory tidbits that any respectable citizen should know about his neighbors, numbered and often scribbled out and renumbered in order of importance.

It was on an iniquitous night of peeping across that street that one Max Z. Glaester with brown eyes did see a raven-haired woman with the curves of country roads climbing into bed with Atticus the Itch's big-tittied wife, sexing and sweating at four in the morning. And though Max didn't quite understand how or why Raven was packing a dick bigger than his, he was excited nonetheless and quite possibly, in love. *Why couldn't girls around the block look like that broad?*

About when Max's binoculars were fogged and he was swollen and ready, Raven stabbed the Wife and down the street The Itch walked home, surrounded by his gang of large shoulders.

This was not OK. Max loved this woman. This was not in-

fatuation. She was evil. She was beautiful. She'd probably read comics with him. She—she was perfect. The Itch finds her and he'll kill her. Kill his Raven, with the boobs and the tongue and, and, no one was killing his girl.

But while Max was getting brave, the broad was getting away and Atticus the Itch's squall could be heard till Jersey.

As his Raven shimmied and jumped down from the Itch's house, Max struck a match, dangled a cigarette, and climbed out his own window, thinking about the tux he would wear at their wedding, about the whiskey, the dancing, the caving honeymoon at Yosemite, and he shadowed her long legs to the El.

The El car shook back and forth, weaseling to the southside and all the five AM businessmen were in other cars. It was Raven and him. Alone. Together. *Should I propose now? Wait till she gets off?* Max pulled his cap down, and watched Raven's way. She put on these wraparound stiletto numbers *and the* legs *on his girl, hot biscuits.*

"Kid? Kid you got an issue I need to smack outta you?"
She talked to him. His Raven, his betty, his angel.

"Kid if you don't quit gawking I'm gonna cut you up like a chink's dog."

And she could curse. Atta girl. He knew she was perfect. The train swayed back and forth or maybe that was his heart punching his body around. Max pulled his cap off and squinted.

"Last chance kid to button your lids before I toss you from this train," she pulled her black curls into a ponytail.

"Yeah, well, yeah . . ." *Dammit, he was squeaking.*

"What of it?"

"I—well . . . I saw, you have a . . . Do you really . . . ? I mean, The Itch."

"Did you say The Itch?" Seventeen demons shot out of her eyes and crawled at him.

"Um, you—"

"Did you see me at The Itch's house?" She reached for something.

"I . . ."

" 'Cause if you did, slick, I might have to throw you out the window after slitting yer throat." Max saw a blade sing from one of the bags she sat by.

She was so tough. She could piss all over Kate the Cow who stole three of his comics. Perfect, perfect, perfect.

"I, well, I wanted to give you a place to hide out. You, yer . . . perfect."

The train was irate; it lurched past the Loop and his Raven was headed to a dirty part of Chicago. Max pulled out another cigarette and offered her the Luckys.

"Hideout? Kid, what reason do you think I have to hide out?" She put the blade back and grabbed the pack.

"You, well . . . I think you—" He stopped and lit up.

"Alright then, so, we've established that you ain't seen nothing, right?"

"I saw you naked." Max's eyes tacked on her chest.

"Well, you ain't the first, kid." *She was smiling at him, smiling those red lips at him, Max Z. Glaester.*

"I, well—" Max went down on one knee after he stumbled the two feet to Savi and accidentally ashed on her knee, "Will you marry me?"

Yes, that heavenly noise was her laughing at him.

"Kid, get lost while I still let you."

He would tell his mom it was a spur of the moment thing, getting hitched.

Max was up off the grit and leaned back on the El door, "Well, I'm pretty handy. I mean, I could do stuff for you."

His Raven stood up, grabbed her bags, her sweet little sweater sheltered that rear, and she pointed at him, pointed at HIM.

"What's your name, kid?" Her nails were red as her lips.

"Max Glaester, at yer service. I mean, I would love to . . ."

He didn't get any further, the door opened up and his tail-bone made friends with the El platform. His Raven stepped over him to get out *and did he just, he did just, thank God she wasn't wearing any underpants.*

"Well, Mr. Glaester, seeing as you know things, and seeing as you want to be useful, grab the bags and quick step. We got someone to meet."

"Umm, hey, hey lady," he picked up the bags and watched her sweater ride up in the early morning light as she tried to pull it down.

She turned back with a little bit of a glare, more of a smirk, her top lip slightly, adorably crooked.

"Should I call you Mrs. Max Glaester?"

"Savi, kid, the name's Savi." And yeah, that time she smiled at him.

Chapter 3

Bars ain't the place to be at six AM—especially when you're hungover, recently sprung from the joint, and want to boink the wife till you fall asleep on her. But bars are the place to be, if you get home to damn well see that you've been half-ass robbed and your wife is sprawled out naked in the bed, not all *come-fucking-hither*, but rather swabbed in the cum of some other creep while a godless piece of strap-on shit winks at you from beside her dead hand. And more to the point, the Blind Staggers Inn with its ragtag piano, cheap beer, and velvet booths is where to be if you're known as The Itch and you told the bartender to keep a good goddamn eye on your wife till you got back round to her.

"Smitts, didn't I tell you? Didn't I tell you to watch the bitch?" The Itch was thick in a suit, head shaved, no eyebrows, always in a black hat.

SMACK.

Smitts head rolled to the side; there was blood in his eye. Two goons held his arms back. His feet weren't really touching the ground so much as playing ballerina.

"*Smitts, I said, didn't I fucking tell you to watch the god-damn wife till I was around?*"

SMACK. Backhand this round.

The Itch wasn't even punching him yet. Smitts knew he was dead; dead dead dead. He never got around to fixing the cracked mirror behind the bar either.

"Smitts, you piece of shit, *who did she leave with, Smitts?*"

Smitts opened his mouth, blood drooled onto his buttondown.

SMACK.

Two more weeks and he woulda been in Minnesota fishing the bend in the river this time of morning.

"*Smitts, are you fuckin' crying? Are you goddamn well*

cryin? Cuz I'm a fuckin' widower right now and I should be cryin'. But can I cry, Smitts? Or do I have to be a man, come to your southside piece a shit bar and be a man?"

SMACK.

Mothballs and curtains kept the dark in the bar and the goons held tight, fingers laced between Smitts' scrawny arm muscles. There was a gun behind the counter, but no way for Smitts to reach it.

SMACK, and The Itch had a hand wrapped around a suspender.

"Can I cry, Smitts? Over my dead wife still in my fuckin' bed? Probably raped in the ass by some *sick fuck. Took against her will. Can I fuckin' cry too, Smitts?"*

Smitts opened his mouth again, "She left with—"

SMACK. Smitts wouldn't ever see outta that eye again.

"What? You dirty piece of fly shit, you think you can talk about my dead wife? My true fuckin' love? The bitch who waited it out for me while I was upriver? You think I'm gonna let you even say shit about her, Smitts?"

"She, left with . . ."

Then came the first wind-knocker to the gut.

"Smitts, this bar is done. You are fuckin' done."

The second wind knocker, this time to the jaw. Smitts could hear the angels close in as the bones splintered.

"Smitts, I might let you live. I'm gonna fuck ya. I'm gonna cut off your dick and I'm gonna take your bar, but I might let you live." The Itch lit a cigarette and smoke gathered as he pulled a rope out of his briefcase. The goons wore daisy smiles.

Smitts tried one more time to talk. "She left with some broad." He spit out a tooth. "They were dyking."

SMACK.

"Excuse the fuck outta me, did you just call my dead sainted wife *a fuckin' dyke? Drop him boys. Drop him in that puddle of piss he's making."*

Sure enough, Smitts had pissed himself, and a goon wing-tipped Smitts' head into the yellow iron liquid. A siren passed outside the bar, but kept going south.

"Smitts, you saying my wife left with a dyke?"

Smitts tried to nod, piss and bar grit went up his nose.

"Smitts, *you saying my wife was a dyke?*"

Smitts waited for the blow, a kick this time, to the ribs, at least two were broken. He shoulda went into insurance like his mother wanted.

"*Put this on the sonofabitch.*" The Itch tossed the rope at his boys who wrapped it round Smitts' neck and hands; splintering threads roughed into his jugular and Smitts lay half hogtied.

The Itch had a calmer look as he polished the blood off his knuckles, "Hey Smitts? Smitts, you ever been fucked in the ass before?"

Smitts looked up with the one eye that worked as Atticus the Itch pulled down his zipper.

Chapter 4

"Where we going?" The kid lugged the bags, hissing glares at men who rubbernecked as Savi walked past. Market carts were out and a few old men sat on porches. It was still early.

"Jack Seven Maps." She didn't even turn around, but Max liked the view regardless.

"The legend?"

"Sure kid, the legend."

"Where we meeting him?"

"Carry the bags, cut the tongue, and keep up."

Max didn't know how she could walk so quick on pencil thin heels. It made her ass bounce and he wondered when he could get his tongue in her ear.

They stopped at a travel agent place across the street from the Blind Staggers Inn.

"We going on a trip?" Max imagined going down on Savi in a pyramid, *makinglongsweetlove* in the jungle after killing natives, grabbing a fistful of her hair as she put her mouth around . . .

"*Max*, get your goddamned ass inside."

They were in the basement and Max was standing in front of Jack Seven Maps. Jack Seven Maps, who could break outta any prison, who could bust anyone else outta prison. He had comics written about him. He had a Clark-Gable-looking mug shot in the *Trib*. The papers said he shoulda been in movies instead of jails and ladies fainted for him. They called him Jack the Map, when he cracked out of his first joint and kept adding numbers to the title as he kept busting out. He was dumb and unlucky at robbing banks, but genius at weaseling outta architecture. Max stood in front of Jack Seven Maps and Jack Seven Maps was hugging his girl.

"Hey," ... yeah, that was Max. "Hey, get your goddamn hands off my girl!" Max dropped Savi's bags and balled up his fists as he stumbled down the stairs.

Savi and Seven Maps turned with dropped jaws.

"Savi, who the hell is this kid?" Seven Maps' paw was still on her shoulder.

"Kid saw me and followed, I didn't have the heart to break his cute little face yet. He carried my bags."

"*I said get yer hands off my girl!*" Max took a step forward. Shit, he was crazy. He was challenging Jack Seven Maps who supposedly bit a man's eye out once, somehow or something.

"Savi, is this twelve-year-old piece a shit your new dick?" Jack Seven Maps was grinning teeth. Max wasn't. What could he use to kill this bastard? Three chairs, one crate table, tea, bare bones—nothing—but he might be able to reach the hanging light bulb and cut Seven Maps' throat.

"No, it's better than that Jackie. Max here proposed on the El. I might settle down with him."

Savi said yes? Did she just say yes? Shit, he was getting married, wait till Joey Fitz heard.

Jack Seven Maps' hand went to squeeze Savi's, "In that case, dear, good luck."

Before Seven Maps finished, Max rushed him trying to get out a good punch before Seven Maps could kill him.

Seven Maps grabbed the punch and swung Max in so they were back to chest, both looked at Savi. Max wiggle-stomped, red-faced in a chokehold.

"Hey Savi, how's about you explain to your *fiancé* that we're cousins and there ain't no reason to be going to an early grave." Max slouched, somewhat thankful.

"Kid, this here's Jack and he's a cousin. Don't worry little man, my heart is all yours." She smirked and Jack let go.

"I'm thirteen." Max grunted.

"What?" Jack Seven Maps' voice sounded like stray dogs getting into whiskey.

"Not twelve," Max picked up the bags as Savi sat down.

"My largest apologies. Have a seat by your lady."

They gathered round the crate table with a tea set. Max dared to put a hand on Savi's bare white thigh, Seven Maps laughed at the audacity, and Savi could give a good goddamn as long as they got down to business.

"So, what's the mire that brought you home? Tea?" Seven Maps was an unusually graceful tea pourer and Max tried to indifferently slide his hand upward, millimeter by millimeter, every two minutes.

"I scratched someone bad, Jacky. Someone real bad."

"Who?"

"The Itch's wife."

Seven Maps spit tea out of his face, it reached Max's knee. Max weighed his options—let go of Savi to clean it, or not?

"Well hell, we do have some business, eh?" Seven Maps regained his calm. "How long?"

"About two hours ago."

The bulb got scared and flickered.

"Anyone know?"

"The kid."

"You gonna kill him?"

"Nah, seems useful." Max's heart fisted around, his hand squeezed her thigh.

"I can get you out on a 7:30 train. Gives you forty-five minutes to pack. You are going to pack, right? Or at least change? You look like a Seventh Street whore taking two-penny dick for breakfast."

"Yeah, you look well yourself. How's about I don't pack, you sell whatever's at the hotel and send me the funds later? I don't leave this hole till I have to and you get me some clothes.

I know you keep an ugly little harem with those jabbering travel secretaries upstairs. Grab me some respectable garb off one of their tails."

"Well dear, whatever will one of those ladies wear home then?"

"Your dick for all I care, get me some clothes. Let the kid get the clothes. I don't care."

"Was it a good score?"

"Woulda been if the sonofabitch hadn't been walking up the stairs while I climbed out the window."

"Kid, you saw all this?" Seven Maps' hair was slicked back, his mustache somewhat twitchy.

"Most."

"Well, ain't you a man today?" Jack Seven Maps got up. "Please, do help yourself to more tea. I'll find clothes that'll fit your rack."

"It is a nice rack, ain't it?" Max smiled at Seven Maps and put his hands behind his neck, kicking back to a two-peg chair lean. Seven Maps shook his head. Savi stood up, pushed Max over, and kicked him in the ass.

"Kid, it's comments like that that make me not wanna marry you so much."

Shit thought Max, but all the same, he was on the floor looking up at Savi, thanking God again that she didn't have time for panties.

Chapter 5

"Smitts, you took it like a man. A crying, vomiting, bleeding man, but a man." The Itch held up the wallpaper, flicked his square and watched the boys put Smitts' pants on.

"See Smitts, I'm not gonna kill you and I'm not gonna hurt you—until I find the bitch that fucked my wife and to do that, you gotta nod me to her." Smitts had smears of The Itch all over his legs, pants, and back and tried to crawl to the gun behind the bar.

"Grab him, boys." The Itch walked out, humming towards the car.

The goons grabbed Smitts, who didn't have a voice to whimper, and dragged him head down out the door. Not even locking the joint up, sonsabitches. A new round of prickling tears started glazing the dirt around Smitts' eyes. It was full-on day and the sun brought his torn short sleeves and pus-leaking lips to light.

Savi changed into this two-piece skirt suit and Max grabbed an eyeful, tilting his head back so he could see underneath the blindfold.

"Quit being a pervert." Savi threw the sex-scented sweater at him.

"Not like I ain't seen it before." Max went to pull the blindfold down.

"You touch that for another ten seconds and I'm gonna break your sex off before you can see." Savi was being tough, but she didn't sound all that mad.

"Long as yer touching it, sister, I'll die a happy man."

Jack Seven Maps came down the stairs. "Lover's quarrel?"

"Don't be a jackass, kid's a peeping disgrace. If you're gonna do it kid, do it well. Christ, kids don't know nothing these days." Savi was done, her tits barely held in by the V-neck suit jacket. She shimmied the skirt up a little bit.

"Well, car's out front and I got a naked secretary to deal with, how's about you and the sidekick scram?"

"You'll take care of the hotel?"

"Already half done."

"Keep half the money for yourself, Jacky."

"I wouldn't dream of it. You'll need it for your wedding."

"Aww shut it."

Savi went up the stairs and out the door as a pissy naked woman yelled at Savi from the closet. Max brought the bags and Jack Seven Maps saw them to the car.

Smitts didn't want to die today. He didn't necessarily want to get pulped and taken in the ass and thrown in a car, but he didn't want to die. Ain't the fates great when they agree with you?

Smitts could barely see, but he saw Savi. Saw the bitch saunter out the door, busting her chest out a cute little suit like she was respectable or something, pretending to be a mom with a kid in tow.

With a bloody hand, Smitts tugged on the sleeve of the goon who shoved him into the car as The Itch and his other smoked outside.

"Dammit Smitts, this's a new suit—*new*, get your goddamn hand—"

But Smitts pointed. Pointed, and with any guttural ability he had left nodded towards and eked out the word *DYKE* as his head banged against the car window towards Savi.

Savi saw The Itch and shoved the kid into the car.

Max's head hit the far door hard and as his forehead leaked, he fell to the floor.

The Itch heard from the goon who heard from Smitts and grabbed for his gun.

Jack Seven Maps had two barrels on him.

Savi pulled out one.

The goons had four guns.

The sun got scared and hid behind clouds. The kid was out cold and the grown-ups all had pistols pointed from twenty feet across the street. Five guns to three on a sweet summer day.

None moved and suddenly there were no neighbors.

"You the dyke that fucked my wife?" The Itch asked, his voice coating the street with gravel.

"You the son of a bitch who came home early?" Savi could take the bastard with Jacky around.

Smitts leaned low in the seat and cars know when to not drive down certain southside streets.

"Ya know, all you need is a little bit of my dick and it'll clear up all that dyke." The Itch began to itch, his finger getting warm.

"Can't be that good if your wife wanted me to fuck her with a strap-on."

Atticus the Itch shot Savi in the heart, but it never worked right anyway.

Savi shot The Itch in the crotch, just to be a bitch.

Seven Maps shot both the goons as both muzzled him.

All parties were bleeding and the pavement felt cold for summertime.

Smitts climbed outta the car and laughed to joy in the sunshine. He kicked the gun away from The Itch.

Savi couldn't breathe and Seven Maps had already stopped.

Max flung outta the car at Savi; God must have woke him up.

Smitts kicked the shit outta the Itch, *"You fucking piece of shit, come into my bar, try to fuck me up. FUCK YOU!"*

KICK.

"FUCK YOU ITCH!"

KICK, KICK—and Smitts picked up the Itch's gun and shot him in the face.

Savi had a trail of red leaking between her breasts. The kid teared up over her.

"Kid..."

"Yeah?"

"Quick." Her voice was a dying kitten.

"A doctor... I'll get a doctor." His forehead still bled as well.

She grabbed his sleeve, "No, kid." This time a cough came up bloody. "Kid, go hold up The Itch's place." Her eyes searched high, somewhere over Max's head and stopped moving. He wiped at the snot and blood mixed on his face and got up.

The sun went back to simmering as Max Z. Glaester ran to the train and Smitts hung The Itch's gun above his bar.

If There's a Hell Below, We're All Gonna Go

Stephen Allan

Hillary woke in the motel room to the sound of sirens. He sat up and grabbed the Remington shotgun lying in the bed beside him. He pumped it. Red lights flashed from behind the heavy curtains like bright artificial flames. In his drowsy state, his first thought was of the looters; but he realized he was too far north for anyone to be crashing through storefronts. He left the city when the levees broke. Used his light and siren and got out fast.

He checked the clock. 3:00 AM. He brought the shotgun to the window and peeked out. A Honda Civic was crushed against a concrete barrier. Smoky waves of orange flames flowed from it. A fire department hose team was taming the fire. Hillary moved away from the window and checked the bump in the rug. Satisfied that the cash was still there, he tried to go back to sleep; but only lay there until the gray of dawn.

When he realized he wouldn't be able to fall asleep again, he sat up and turned on the television. Everything was about the hurricane. News reporters talked about the devastation and loss of life. Hillary lit a cigarette and watched.

Video showed Hell on Earth: thousands surrounding the Superdome, looters carrying away televisions and groceries, roving armed gangs and dead bodies floating facedown. There were reports about the lack of government response and the failure of the local police, many of whom had abandoned the city. Hillary glanced over to his detective's badge sitting on the nightstand. *Fuck 'em.*

Then Hillary saw him, wading chest-high in the water holding a half-full garbage bag and a suitcase of beer. Jasper.

"Son of a bitch." Hillary thought the little prick had died in the fire. What good was the arson job if Jasper didn't burn? He was the only one who could rat Hillary out about the stolen cash. Hillary knelt down to the slit he made in the carpeting the night before and pulled out the money belt. Seventy-five thousand.

There was no luck in hoping the fucker would drown. Hillary would have to finish the job. He would have to go back into the city.

Hillary's aluminum boat glided through the floodwater up Asylum Drive toward the brick bank that held his mortgage. As he approached the building, he noticed the broken windows and a tall man with a rifle standing watch. Hillary twisted the Evinrude's stick back to the right and slowed the boat. Inside were three other figures standing around the giant vault door. One of the men held a sledgehammer and pounded on the vault. Hillary idled the motor and reached to his hip where his police-issued semiautomatic lay. He pulled his weapon out an inch as the rifleman called to the others. All four men came out of the bank. Hillary took his 9mm out, but aimed it down at the water.

"Don't be stupid," Hillary said. "Just keep as you were. I ain't here to stop you."

"You a cop?" the one with the rifle asked.

"That's neither here nor there right now," Hillary said.

"Fucking police ain't nothing no more," the rifleman said. "We the ones in charge. We the ones deserve respect. Carrying your gun around like you still something, white man. Guess what? You ain't. You can't come in here and fuck with us no more. There's no law. We the forgotten down here, law don't care 'bout us."

"You may be right about that," Hillary said and spit into the dirty floodwater. "I don't give a fuck what you do, as long as you don't shoot me in the back. Take the place for all it's worth, what do I care?"

The rifleman looked at Hillary, as if judging the cop's fate. He finally nodded.

"Get, old man," the leader said and motioned for his men to follow him back into the bank.

Hillary revved the boat's engine and continued down the street as a dead man floated past. The cop looked away from the floater. The body was destined to rot in the humid sun and there was no sense in pulling it into the boat. Let the demons and angels fight over the poor fucker's soul.

Jasper's place was around the next corner, so Hillary cut the engine and paddled the rest of the way to the house. All the shades were drawn. Hillary watched for any movement in the windows as he glided to the front steps. He tied the boat with a loose knot, and then grabbed the shotgun. He walked onto the front porch and knocked on the door. He moved to the side and waited for an answer. Nothing came, even after knocking twice more. He tried the knob, but found it locked. He was walking to the side of the porch to find another way in when the front door erupted into splinters. Hillary jumped over the porch and into the water. He went under and came back up covered in the shit floating in the vile water. He found his footing and aimed the shotgun at the front, waiting for Jasper to pop his head out.

Gunshots sounded from the back of the house. The bullets missed Hillary, but hit only a few inches away. He didn't anticipate Jasper having any friends. Hillary swung around and volleyed with his own shots, but only hit the side of the house. Whoever had shot at him had moved.

He heard the blast from the porch before he felt the hot sting in his side. Hillary let out a cry as he turned around to face the porch and fired blindly. He heard a body drop.

Hillary climbed out of the water and onto the porch, ignoring the pulsing hurt in his side. The dead gunman was face up. It wasn't Jasper. Hillary recognized the guy—a minor dealer from down on Bourbon Street, one of Jasper's pot buddies. Hillary took the revolver beside the body, but it was empty. He threw the gun into the water and looked into the house. The front door was left open. Hillary checked the foyer and entered with his shotgun ready.

"Police," Hillary shouted. "Come out with your hands up."

He walked through the house, checking each corner he came to.

"Stop right there and drop your gun," Jasper's voice came from above. Hillary looked up. The scumbag was holding a sawed-off on him. Hillary did as he was told and let his weapon fall out of his hands.

"Ain't no fucking cop coming around here for routine patrols," Jasper said as he walked down the stairs. He looked into Hillary's face and smiled with recognition. "Well, you may be police, but this ain't official business is it?"

Hillary remained silent.

"Yeah, I know you. The fucking thick neck from Vice who stole all that money; the one with the girl's name. Shirley? Marley?"

"It's 'fuck you'."

"Doesn't look like I'm the one's fucked," Jasper said, walking toward Hillary. "You thought you could shoot a couple of big time dealers in front of me and get away with that shit?

Man, you're lucky the world came to an end around here, 'cause I'd have been on somebody's front door ratting you out; somebody big, willing to part with a little reward money."

Jasper kept inching toward Hillary, until he was within reach. Hillary grabbed the barrel of the shotgun and twisted it out of Jasper's hands. Jasper brought his foot up hard into Hillary's crotch. The cop dropped to his knees, but was able to keep a hold on the weapon.

Jasper ran into the kitchen as Hillary struggled back up. His balls were on fire and he couldn't stand up straight. Gritting his teeth, he aimed the shotgun toward the kitchen and fired until all the shells were gone. There was as sharp cry, followed by an agonizing moan. Hillary hobbled into the kitchen and found Jasper slumped against the bottom drawers of the kitchen counter.

Hillary stood over Jasper. As he threw the empty shotgun down, he pulled out his Beretta. But before he could get a shot off, Jasper jumped up with a long kitchen knife and sunk it into the cop's belly. Hillary dropped the gun on the counter as he grabbed the knife and pulled it out of his stomach.

Jasper stood up and reached for the Beretta. Hillary looked into the knife drawer and saw a meat cleaver. As Jasper slipped his hand around the pistol, Hillary brought the cleaver down on Jasper's wrist, separating it from its arm. The gun fired once from the reflexive twitch of the trigger finger, shooting the 9mm off the counter and onto the floor. Jasper held his stump up and blood spewed an arc into the air. Hillary knocked Jasper onto the floor and went for the gun—and the hand still attached to it. He pried the severed hand from the weapon and threw it on the linoleum.

Hillary aimed the blood-soaked gun at Jasper.

"Turn around," Hillary said. His voice was strained, as if the words were forced out of the mud.

Jasper was on his knees, wrapping his stump in a greasy dishtowel.

"My fucking hand." It came out in sobs of anger and pain.

"My fucking balls," Hillary said as he adjusted himself. He kicked Jasper in the ass. Jasper fell onto his side and rolled over on his back.

"Shoot me like a dog?" Jasper said. "Ain't man enough to kill someone on his feet, gotta wait until he's on the floor?" Jasper's eyes rolled and his head swayed a bit as the dishtowel turned red.

Hillary looked down. Without medical attention, Jasper would simply bleed to death. He didn't want to wait that long. In a city of total silence, the gun's eruption cracked into everywhere.

Hillary tried to keep his balance as he climbed back in the aluminum boat, but he fell. The combination of the kick to the nuts and the knife wound played havoc on his ability to walk straight. He sat up, keeping a hand on his gut to stop the bleeding. The knife had missed the cash in the money belt. Bad luck. The bills might have stopped the knife. Now he had to get out of the city and find a doctor.

He placed one shoe against the back of the boat and pulled the cord. He did it to near exhaustion before the motor came to life.

He directed the boat back down Asylum Avenue toward downtown. The heat and humidity of the afternoon made it difficult to breathe. Sweat ran off his face. He tried to wipe it away, but each time he removed his hand from the wound, more blood flowed out.

The adrenaline of fighting was seeping out of his veins. It was replaced by pain and weakness. His eyelids drooped and the hand steering the Evinrude slipped off the stick. The boat made a sharp turn to the right, causing Hillary to fall out of his seat. He tried to regain his footing, but the out-of-control boat made it difficult. He was forced to use both hands to pull himself up.

Then he looked where the boat was heading: the red brick bank. He reached for the engine's stick, but it was too late. The boat struck the concrete steps at full speed. Hillary was thrust forward against the bank's moss-covered wall. He dropped to the cement with the sound of cracked bones.

The pain was so horrible, Hillary wished he would just pass out.

The rifleman and his cronies ran out of the bank. Hillary looked up at the looters and saw the fear in their eyes. All the tough guy facades had drained away and Hillary realized that they were just kids.

"Christ," the rifleman said.

"Jimmy, what's that hanging out of him?" the one with the sledgehammer asked.

The rifleman crouched next to Hillary. "Intestines," he said.

One of the other kids pointed to a hundred-dollar bill hanging out of Hillary's ripped shirt. "The dude may be fucked, but he's rich."

Hearing those words, Hillary tried to bring the revolver up and point it at the kid. He thought he had, but his arm lay still on the steps.

"Try it," Hillary said, blood seeping from the side of his mouth. The words slurred out like whispers, but he could tell the kid understood.

Jimmy stepped on Hillary's gun arm and pulled the weapon out his hand.

"Grab the money belt," Jimmy ordered. "Billy, man, take the cash from this corrupt motherfucker and dump him in the shit."

"Jimmy, the guy's a cop."

"I don't care who he used to be. He ain't nothing now," Jimmy said. "You forget, ain't nobody no one now in the floodwater."

Hillary tried to roll away from Billy as the punk lackey

crouched down and opened his shirt. Billy took the money belt and stood up, handing the cash to Jimmy.

"Nah," Jimmy said. "You hold onto it for now." Jimmy took his sneaker off Hillary's arm and kicked the cop off the concrete and into the water.

As Hillary floated away from the bank, he felt the dirty water enter his body. He drifted toward the floater he had seen earlier. Its lifeless eyes stared into the roasting sun and Hillary noticed the unnatural orange burn of its skin. He knew he would soon be that same color. Maybe when the water was gone and people actually searched the area, they would find his body resting among some tree branches or the top of an abandoned car.

Hillary's nerves turned numb and the pain disappeared. He tried to spit the contaminated water out of his mouth, but the polluted taste stayed on his tongue. As he passed his fellow floater, Hillary noticed the television helicopter flying above. A cameraman strapped in the open doorway pointed his camera at Hillary. He tried to wave for help, but slipped beneath the surface. Unable to hold his breath, he inhaled the dirty water. There was no fight left. All he could do was sink beneath the grime, mud, and shit and just let go.

Counterfeit Love

Jeffrey Bangkok

I went to the hospital but not for me. The nurse at the front desk had blond hair, gray eyes and a firm ass, the kind that dared the insertion of foreign objects.

Unfortunately, I wasn't there for ass so I asked where he was and how he got there. She told me my old man fell off scaffolding at a construction site. She fluttered her eyelashes as she gave me the room number. I fluttered too, and didn't bother to readjust. She saw the bulge, blushed and said he was in intensive care and that the doctor would tell me more and paged him. Not a good sign. I looked at the bright side; if I told her a sob story maybe I'd get a sympathy fuck. But first I saw the old man. I entered his room. The rotten feeling chewing on my guts was confirmed once I saw and heard the whirl and whoosh of the machines hooked into him. He looked like an abused android ready for the scrap collector. I cursed life support and its series of mechanical monstrosities. My blood pressure rose as I watched the ventilator go up and down. I pulled back the sheet and examined the bruises on his ribs. Accident my left nut, I thought as the surgeon strutted in like a peacock. He was short, in a hurry, and smug. He told me the old man wasn't as hard-headed as I thought.

He put it this way, "The trauma induced by the fall caused irreparable damage to the frontal, parietal and temporal lobes of the brain, rendering your father incapable of higher function and greatly impairing his lower functions."

I translated. A tomato has more horsepower; he's fucked as an alkie hunting for a fix on a Sunday morning in a dry county. I laughed, reached down, gave the old man's hand a squeeze. He was a bastard, but he was my bastard.

"Did I say something humorous? Are you all right?" asked the surgeon.

"All the king's horses and all the king's men couldn't put Humpty Dumpty back together again," I said as I walked out.

"Mr. Harlan," he called after me, "if you're interested, we offer counseling on the third floor."

"Piss off, Napoleon, I've all the psychology I need right here," I said taking a long pull off my flask. The burn felt good. I savored it like revenge as I made my way out of the building.

I pondered what I knew. Pop was part mountain goat so I knew the falling part was bullshit. I'd told him not to marry Jean but he had a prescription for a new erection pill so he was as happy as a twelve-year-old boy watching his first porno. I told myself he'd be on to someone else but a couple of weeks later they were married. Not long after, I got word I was out of the will and she was in. Now she'd grabbed for the cash and left him to wither like a misplaced turnip. She didn't even have the decency to pull the plug and finish it.

Wanna go skydiving, bitch? I'm fresh out of chutes so it's time to learn how to freefall, I thought as I opened my car door.

I reached for a smoke but they were gone.

Worse, the flask was empty.

Worse still, I'd left the nurse without a sob story.

I pulled out of the lot. A lime-colored Ford followed me. I

checked the rearview as I cruised and saw it about four car lengths back. I passed a couple of cars and took a few sudden turns but couldn't shake it. I kept on until I got into the city and then I sped up, made a sudden left, did a U-turn, pulled into a parking garage, circled a few times and parked. Had Jean taken a preemptive strike or was someone else after a pound of my mangy hide?

As I sat, I thought about my father. He had a talent for building things. He knew how to shape wood and steel and he made a fortune in construction. I didn't inherit anything from him but his shoe size. God knows I tried my hand at construction but everything I built turned to shit. Stubborn, I kept at it anyway until a retaining wall collapsed and snapped my left leg like a twig. Then I gave it a rest, went back to school, learned what I could do.

It was the art class final where it hit me like an overloaded semi. We had to produce a facsimile of a famous painting. I copied "American Gothic"; it's the one of the farmer holding the pitchfork, his wife and bleak house behind them. The art teacher about fell out of his chair when I brought it in, even the signature looked genuine. It wasn't long after that a guy approached me with an offer to make fake state IDs at fifty bucks a crack. After that it was legal documents, passports, and counterfeiting. I became a walking printing press.

A knock on the passenger window spiked the hair on the back of my neck.

"Hey, buddy, no sleeping in the garage. Wait for a hooker somewhere else, you sad sack a shit. Move it along," said a surly attendant with a hair lip and nicotine-stained teeth.

I told him to go fuck himself and, if he had a dog, to screw the pooch a few times too, then I fired up the engine and buried him in exhaust fumes as I peeled away.

It wasn't hard to find Jean. I shadowed her from her lawyer's office to her apartment downtown. I cornered her, told her all I needed were a few answers. I asked about the how's and the why's of what happened to the old man. I listened intently to her story. I nodded at all the right intervals and held her in my arms as she wept fake tears that rolled down her cheeks and stained her shirt. I played the dumb grieving college boy who didn't have a clue she'd played my old man like an overeager teenager at a fifty-cent carnival game.

I planned to kill her before she wiped the bullshit off her lips but it occurred to me that I could have some fun. And as I looked her over, I had to hand it to the old bastard; he knew how to pick them. She was a ripe one. My fingers itched to find out how ripe. I said fuck it and asked her to dinner. Told her we'd talk about the will the old man wrote the week before his accident. Jean went from grieving to greedy in less than a heartbeat.

"He didn't have one. What will?" she asked coldly.

Thought, Got your attention now, bitch.

Said: "This one," pulled it out of my pocket. "Here's a copy." She had one of those proportional bodies worthy of Greek sculpture. I undressed her several times in my mind as she fumbled to take in this new revelation and come up with an answer. It left me in control of the estate and gave her the pittance she deserved.

"It's . . . it's not possible," she stuttered. "Your father told me everything. We were very intimate. Where did this come from?" she asked, looking for somewhere to sit down.

"U.S. Mail a couple of days before he decided to take a high dive," I said pointing to the postmark on the envelope.

"Well, I am getting a little hungry," she said in a stunned tone.

"Me, too. I know a steak place down the block that knows how to serve it still mooing," I said, taking her arm in mine and moving her down the sidewalk.

I could tell by the way she fidgeted, Jean wanted to get me

out of her hair fast but I didn't let that happen. I ordered a few drinks and one by one she let her guard down. I invited her back to my hotel.

"What about your father? It's too soon," she said, looking for a reaction.

"Trust me, he doesn't mind."

"Yeah, the doctors said he should be dead."

"He'd be better off."

"How can you say that? He's your father."

Gorillas have better, I thought.

Said, "That's not living, it's letting death trickle in."

"It's a marvel."

More like an abomination, I thought.

Kept myself in check. Wanted to get laid. Let it go.

Said, "Don't let ventilators stand between us. See me tomorrow."

"Okay, pick me up at seven," she said as she turned and walked into the night.

It went on like that for a week or so. Then she thawed like a lake in spring. I could feel it at dinner that night. I wondered why but not hard enough.

I paid the bill in cash, then we took a cab to the hotel and then went up to my room. My heart raced a little when I glanced out the back window; I swore that the same car I'd seen outside the hospital was following us but when I looked again, it was gone.

The sex was better than good; it was the sex of two people with ulterior motives.

After, I pretended to fall into a deep sleep. She let a few minutes pass to make sure I was good and out and then she got out of bed. I watched her out of the corner of my eye as she crept around rummaging through my suitcase, my wallet, and my pants for some indication that she was being scammed. She came up with nothing but a handful of lint. Satisfied, she went to the can. Once I heard her lock the door, I crept to her purse and took out her ID. I scanned it quickly into my laptop, replaced it in her wallet, and crawled back into bed. I was asleep before she put on her shoes and walked out the door.

I called her the next day after noon to give her enough time to run the will I'd given her by her lawyers.

"I want to see you again," I said, honestly wanting to have her at least once more before the end.

"Last night was a mistake. Your father meant so much to me. I was confused, please forgive me."

"How could you call that confusion, baby? If so, that's sure as hell not what you shouted."

"It happened so quickly. First your father and now, now . . . I never anticipated this. I'm not sure about anything right now. I need time to breathe, to think."

"Would you like an order of fries with that?"

"Don't say it like that, don't make it cheap. Be serious for a minute."

"I'm serious when I say I want to ravage you again. Maybe right here over the coffee table?"

"I can't meet you right now."

"Got another hot date?"

"That's right. Why, jealous?" she purred.

"How 'bout in a couple hours?" If I could hold out that long.

"Okay, meet me at your father's at three. I need to pack a few things."

"Going somewhere?"

"No, I left some clothes and things there and I haven't been back since it happened." She said it with such sincerity that I almost believed for a second that the old man had taken a tumble on his own.

"Okay, princess, three it is," I said, hanging up.

I did some work and watched the clock. The hours lingered like bugs drowning in pinesap.

At two-thirty I drove out to meet her. I rapped on the front door with my knuckles and when no one answered I let myself in. I called her name but she didn't respond until I was halfway up the stairs. I followed her voice to the bathroom.

She was taking a bubble bath and invited me in.

"Fuck yes," I said. I stripped off my clothes and hopped in. She was drinking red wine from a crystal glass. She had a glass for me and I took a sip, kissed her, and downed the rest in one big swig. I moved closer, entered her, our bodies moved in unison, water spilled out and hit the floor. I was close so close, then I lost focus, the world wobbled, went gray, then black as a nun's habit. Lady Luck was no match for Mickey Finn.

I woke. Jackhammers bit into my skull. I tried to look around but I couldn't move much. Whoever tied the knots could shame a sailor. I went to work on them and managed to wrestle one hand free before the door flew open and a guy with big shoulders and fists like hams laid a solid left on my chin.

"We know you fudged the will."

"I don't know what you're talking about. Where the hell am I? Who are you?"

He didn't bother answering. Instead, with a flick of his hand he broke my nose. A river of red ran down the valley of my face and splattered onto the concrete floor like a Jackson Pollock knockoff. The room spun and I closed my eyes.

"It's too early to checkout, pal," he said punching me conscious.

"The room service needs improvement," I said, spitting blood.

"Bad move," he said, pulling something from his pocket as he grabbed my right hand. Pain shot across first my thumb, then the rest of my fingers, making the shotgun's blasts in my skull feel like a theme park ride. I was afraid to look down but he made me. And there I saw the tips of all five fingers on the floor.

"It could be worse. It could be your pecker. You're lucky she likes you. If it was me, I would have started there." Then the filthy bastard laughed and grabbed my balls. A rainbow of pain embraced me.

"Okay, okay," I gasped.

"Now that you admit it, you need to fix it. Jean, Jean, get down here! He's ready." Now it was my turn to laugh but lucky for me it came out as a gurgle or a croak.

It didn't take her long to float into the room. She looked in my eyes and said, "Say it. Say you're sorry, you son of a bitch."

"Okay, okay, I'm sorry. Jesus, is this really necessary? I figured we had a good thing."

"We're not stupid, pal. We do our research. We found out who you are. Mr. Counterfeiter. Mr. Fancy Pants."

"How do you know?"

"I listened at the bathroom door, opened it a crack and saw you sneak into my purse and scan my ID. I figured you were either a cop or something and . . ."

"Then we asked around," interrupted ham hands.

"You didn't hurt him permanently did you? You did as I instructed?"

"Yeah, nothing he won't live through. Can I make him bleed more for you?"

"No, you've done enough of that for one day. Now leave us."

"But, he can't be trusted."

"He's not going anywhere."

"Okay, if he gives you any trouble, I'll tear his throat out."

"He won't. Will you, dear?"

"Nope. No trouble."

"Good boy. I knew you were a quick one."

After the orangutan stomped off, my heart beat a little less quickly but maybe that was from the loss of blood.

She waited to make sure he was gone, then said, "I need your help. He's going to kill me."

"You gotta be kidding. You couldn't have found another way to ask?"

"Listen, I couldn't risk tipping him off. I wanted to ask you in the bathroom but he barged in and I had no choice."

"I should know better."

"Fortunately, you treated me very well."

"I suppose that's something. Quite the scam you got going. How many times have you done it?"

"I've done what I had to," she said with a touch of indignation in her voice.

"And big brother?"

"He's not my brother but he is handy when a less delicate approach is needed."

"Then what's his name? And what's your tie?"

"Jack's his name. Jack Turner. We met back home. He was a logger; I was a waitress at the Knotty Pine Diner. We went out a few times. He took it more seriously than he should have. When I left, he followed. I tried to lose him and start over but I couldn't get away, he followed me from place to place. I really tried with your father. I assumed I'd finally gotten rid of Jack but I was wrong."

"You had him follow me the whole time, eh?"

"No, it wasn't my idea; it was his. He's been watching you. He's jealous. He's the one who killed your father."

"Really?"

"Yeah, I had no need. I was set, but then he showed up and started causing problems."

"What kind of problems?"

"At first Jack said he wanted money but it was clear he wanted me. Jack threatened your father but your father laughed him off. I warned him but he said not to worry, that he'd take care of it and he went to meet Jack. I begged him not to go but he was stubborn, he said he was going to fix it once and for all. Honestly, when your father didn't come back and Jack showed up I surmised that was it, that he'd won and he'd drag me back to some hick town where he could keep me locked up like a favorite pet. But then you showed up."

"And got the stuffing knocked out of myself."

She gave a little smile.

"You did more than that, for the first time in weeks, you gave me hope. Come by tomorrow and drop off the will."

"What the hell's taking so long down there? Hurry it up or I'll carry him out in pieces," hollered Jack from the top of the stairs.

"Think of a plan. I know I can count on you," she whispered, her breath hot and urgent in my ear as she untied me.

I cleaned up in the sink. She gave me bandages and I taped up my fingers.

"He didn't go deep so they should heal up okay," she said.

"Easy for you to say."

"Don't be late."

"I won't."

"Can you drive?"

"Yes."

"I'll be waiting. And bring plenty of cash," she said as she led me up by my left hand out of the basement and onto the front porch where she kissed me. Despite everything that throbbed, I kissed her back.

As I drove, I thought I saw a glimpse of green behind me but when I looked again, nothing. I rummaged for the half-pack buried in the glove box. I lit up and inhaled deeply until I felt the smoke put a stranglehold on my lungs. It did wonders for my state of mind. I eased off the gas, pulled over, and picked up some heavy-duty painkillers from a buddy of mine, then kicked myself all the way back to the hotel. That's what I get for sleeping with my old man's old lady. I took a long shower and passed out on the bed. I slept deep like a wet hunting dog.

Searing pain reeled in the day. I stumbled out of bed, stretched, pissed blood, got dressed, went to a pawnshop, and bought supplies.

Firing on all three cylinders, I hobbled to the car and reviewed my plan. It consisted of a fairly untraceable .38, a hunting knife with a sharkskin handle, and a fistful of pills. The gun and the knife were for Jack. I hope he didn't mind; they weren't wrapped. The pills were for me and I downed them with whiskey on an empty stomach. They took the edge off; after a few minutes the sharp bursts of agony in my fingers dulled to a piercing series of throbs. I shifted into overdrive, headed downtown, and picked up a couple hundred grand of funny money from a lock box. On sight or on feel they wouldn't be able to tell the difference.

I was early. I parked out of sight and tucked the gun in back of my pants, strapped the knife to my left leg. I put the envelope containing the new will in with the bag of cash and held it in my fingertip-less hand. I kicked the front door a few times, adamant as a door-to-door Bible peddler. Jack finally lumbered over and opened the door. He had a giant smirk on his Cro-Magnon face.

"Are you gonna ask me out or are you gonna cut to the chase and take my dress off?" I asked.

His smirk receded like water from a punctured kiddy pool.

"Stay there and hand it over. No sudden moves, pal," he said eyeing the bag.

"Sure," I said and gave it to him.

His grin returned as he reached in and read the will to himself.

Then as he put the will down and focused on the stacks of green, I pulled out the .38 from my pants. When he looked up I had the gun leveled on him.

"I'm going to bleed you slow this time," he said and charged.

It was a bad move. He closed on me fast but not faster than the bullet closed on him. He flew backward as it hit him square in the chest. But the bastard got up, came at me. I fired again, his face went white but he was on his feet, breath heavy like a bull in heat as he ran at me with his head down. He latched on to my right leg and bit me. I knocked the gun butt against his jaw but he wouldn't let go, he clamped down harder and put all his weight into me. I went down on my ass and lost the gun. He let go of my leg and went after it. I rolled and unsheathed the knife. He lunged, turned away from me as he got his fingers around the grip and grinned. But he was too late. Before he could spin around I stabbed him in the throat. His hands flew to the wound and I stumbled, grabbed the gun, stuck it in his face and fired. That put him down for good. The fucker was like Rasputin. I was tempted to roll him in a carpet and throw him in a river to make sure he was dead but I left him be. I had a date with Jean. His exit wounds smoldered as I mounted the stairs.

"Honey, I'm home. I've got a special delivery for you," I called.

Jean rushed out to meet me. She had on see-through lingerie.

I didn't need any encouragement; I rushed forward.

"You did it, thank God. I'm free for the first time since I can remember."

She kissed me. She unzipped my pants and straddled me.

I didn't say no. I dropped the gun. It was over quicker than I'd like to admit but she didn't look displeased. I carried her to bed.

"What about Jack?"

"He'll keep for a few hours."

We made the bedsprings sing for a couple of hours, then I fell asleep.

Stupid bastard.

The phone rang and rang. Why wouldn't the idiot give it up already?

I jerked awake choking on smoke. I rolled off the bed, gasping for air. The place was an inferno. Jean was nowhere to be found. The bag of funny money was gone, too. But there was a note next to the will on the bedside table.

It read:

> *Don't follow me. You're more astute than I realized. I didn't think you'd get the best of Jack. What I said about your father's accident was true. I don't care about his money. You've given me all I really wanted.*
>
> *Goodbye,*
> *Jean.*

I hustled down the stairs and out the door.

I caught my breath, locked the door, and then kicked it in. The cops would write it off as a burglary gone sour. I didn't care if the place was insured or not. I watched it burn.

Sure, there were plenty of questions but in the end the cops did what came easiest, they ate the story in front of them and then lumbered off to the next trough.

After the heat cooled to mere scalding, I went to the hospital, signed the paperwork, and pulled the plug. I had him cremated and scattered his ashes in Crescent Creek where he took me fly fishing for trout as a boy.

Then I found the nurse and told her my sob story. She bought it enough to invite me home. She wanted a spanking and I obliged.

A few days later I caught the morning news. A woman

named Margaret Thomas was arrested for passing a large amount of counterfeit currency at a department store.

"Don't worry, Jean, I won't follow," I said as I sat and smoked and waited for the coffee to knock the crust out of my eyes.

The nurse woke up and asked if I wanted breakfast.

I said, "I'll have ass," and grabbed her.

She squealed.

After awhile, I did, too.

Murder Boy

Bryon Quertermous

"I need tacos," Posey King said. "And beer."

Posey was Dominick Meade's girlfriend. His rock. The fount of reality in Dominick's fantasy-laced world. She also looked hot in a skirt and shaved her pubic hair in the shape of a star.

"And maybe some weed," Dominick said.

"Weed makes you stupid. And sterile," Posey said. "Get a 40 of something cheap for energy and then we'll go do this thing."

"Do this thing? You think you're in some kind of mob movie? Or a heist flick or something?"

"You're a writer but you only quote in movies or TV shows," Posey said. "Don't you read books?"

She'd been giving him this same shit for two years. She thought he was smart but working below his potential. She thought he should be writing some kind of epic shit. Something with a cast of six hundred and a war or a plague.

He said murder and violence was a plague of modern society but she wouldn't buy it. He stayed with her because he loved her. And she swallowed.

"I forget you're smart," Dominick said.

"What was the last book you read?"

"I've been working on my thesis."

"You watch TV, don't you? You went to the movies last night."

"I don't need this from you, too. You're supposed to support and encourage me."

"I let you fuck me up the ass. In exchange I'm going to make you a better person."

Parker Farmington came inside his teaching assistant and then farted as he rolled off of her. He peeled the condom off his limp penis and tried to make it into the trashcan next to the bed but missed.

"Pick that up before you leave, it's gross to find those later," she said.

He couldn't remember her real name. He always called her Austen because that's who she wanted to be and Jane sounded old and stupid.

"One of these times I'll make it," Farmington said. "Do you want eggs?"

"Why can't we do this at your house? It feels so creepy doing it here."

"This is your house, how can it be creepy?"

"I rent here. There are six other girls living here and they all bring home frat boys and rock singers, and hairy chicks from Europe."

"Do you wish I had more hair?" Farmington asked.

"I want this to be an adult affair. You're an adult. You live in an adult house and I want to fuck in your adult bed sometime," she said, getting out of bed and dragging the sheet with her.

"I told you, that's not going to happen," he said.

"Put your underwear on and get the condom off my floor. I'll see you in the kitchen."

* * *

The shells were loaded with rubber slugs instead of buck-shot. This didn't really please Titus Wade but the business was no longer "dead or alive" captures. Blowing off heads was too much damn paperwork these days. So he used rubbers.

Susan was fucking the professor again and she needed to be punished. This guy was a prick and pissed Wade off more than the others. Susan knew that and did it to flaunt him. Why else would she be with a loser like that? He wouldn't even take her back to his fancy house on professor row.

One barrel, six shells, two pumps. Titus was ready to go.

Dominick passed the plate of nachos and a 20-ounce Diet Coke to Posey as he slid back into the car.

"I want to change the world with a book *and* have a gun fight in there, too."

Posey kissed him on the forehead and winked at him.

"I know, baby, you're going to do it all. Really," she said. "Now tell me about this plan of yours."

"The professor needs to be taught a lesson. He refuses to sign off on my thesis and it's due tomorrow morning. If I don't have a thesis, I don't have a degree. Then I lose my fellowship in New York and I'll probably end up on the midnight shift at a liquor store dying in a shootout with a stupid motherfucking 12-year-old."

"And the lesson?"

"Crime fiction is relevant in modern society. I'm going to show him the cause and effects of crime on individuals in this ghetto-ass city."

"And the bounty hunter?" Posey asked, picking up a business card from the ash tray.

"My sister's new boyfriend. He's going to help us with the cause and effects."

Posey smiled wide and Dominick patted her thigh, lacing his fingers through hers as they drove toward the meeting spot.

* * *

Parker Farmington noticed the pick-up truck as he walked out of Austen's dumpy apartment building. Sure it was Detroit—Truck Town, USA—but this was the college and cultural area near Wayne State University, the last bastion of foreign cars in the city. And the truck wasn't even a Ford.

Farmington tried not to look directly at the truck as he made his way to the Honda hybrid parked in front of the building. When he was in the car with the doors locked, he called Austen on his cell phone.

"Somebody's watching your building," he told her.

She didn't say anything, but after a second, Farmington saw the blinds on her front window shimmy and saw a hand stick out and pull them apart.

"Jesus, girl, don't let him see you watching him. Close the blinds."

"I bet there aren't creepy people waiting outside of your house," she said.

"Not now. Just keep an eye on this guy—on the sly—and let me know if he tries anything."

"On me, or anything at all?" she asked.

Farmington huffed and ended the call. He watched the truck for another minute or so longer before he pulled away, switching the station from country music to NPR.

Who the fuck drives a hybrid in Detroit? Wade thought. Even though current gas prices were driving the price of filling his tank to more than he paid in insurance for the truck, he wouldn't drive anything else. Not only did a big black truck send the imposing image needed in his field, the storage space was unmatched and the suspension could take even the city's worst roads at high speeds without hurting the truck or himself.

But Jesus, a hybrid? What did it run on? Gerbil shit?

He wanted to move in when the professor was gone. Susan would be alone in the house and that's when he liked to work, but he'd promised his new girlfriend he'd wait for her dumbass brother. It was a revenge thing and he was all about revenge. Especially if he could get paid for it.

The Tigers game was on the radio and that little spic Zamia was lighting up batter after batter on Chicago's roster. It made him smile. Revenge and Tigers baseball. That's life in Detroit.

Dominick knew this girl Susan from advanced fiction workshop because they shared a passion for Michael Chabon and Mystery Science Theater 3000. She was dating the professor and was pissed at him for something so she agreed to let him know when he was staying at her house because it would be easier than doing this at his gated home.

She lived in the student ghetto section of Detroit where large rambling houses, once the estates of auto barons, had been left to rot and then cut into studio apartments or invaded by twenty college students each paying twice what the entire house was worth in monthly rent.

There were no cars in the driveway or directly in front of the house as he pulled up, but it didn't really register with him. Not as much as the big black pick-up truck sitting across the street.

"What do you figure that truck's doing here?"

"Boyfriend I guess," she said.

"You haven't met the girls who live here. They date painters and writers and each other," Dominick said. "I was considered an outcast because I drive a Cavalier."

"When were you here?" she asked, tilting her head.

"Study group."

"You had study group for a writing workshop?"

"We had to work on these fucking multi-media projects in

groups of three. Susan was the only one who had a computer with a big enough monitor to work on. She's a graphic design student."

"Well, isn't that lovely," she said. "And what was she doing in a writing workshop?"

"This is bullshit, Posey and you know it. Focus on what we're here to do."

"Whatever."

Susan forgot about Dominick Meade until he pulled into her driveway. She recognized the Cavalier right away and then it clicked. Luckily, Parker answered his cell phone when she called and told him she needed him again. Once she'd dodged that bullet, she remembered the condom on the floor.

It was the last one in the box and she'd neglected to get anymore because she was preparing for a sexual boycott until Parker let her come to his house once in a while. It was too late to get more so she just hoped everything went down before Parker got his clothes off.

The Cavalier had to belong to the guy he was waiting for. It was the only thing that stuck out on this block as much as his truck. If he did any more business with students or professors he'd have to get something more foreign. Though the only thing worse than not driving a truck would be driving a foreign truck. Who drives a truck made by Toyota? He might as well wear dreadlocks and flip-flops and call himself Woody.

When he saw a tall white guy get out of the car with a curvy brunette in a ponytail he knew this was his guy. Wade grabbed the nylon equipment bag from his passenger's seat and climbed out of the truck and toward the couple. He stopped when he saw Susan coming down the front stairs waving her arms.

How the hell did she know he was here? Or was she trying

to say something to the new kid and his girl? He decided to go back to his truck and wait behind it to see what happened.

Posey was the first one to see Susan coming down the steps waving her arms like they were on fire.

"Is she talking to us?" Posey asked, tugging Dominick's attention toward the front door.

"Oh yeah, that's her. I'm still curious about that truck. I think somebody's—"

"You've got to move your car," Susan said.

She was now right in front of them.

"He'll know the Cavalier doesn't belong here and think something is up," she continued.

"Goddamit. Why do I get such shit for buying cheap cars because my dad works for GM?"

"Do you want your car to fuck with your little plan?" Posey asked.

He admitted that he did not and moved the car down a few blocks to the same side of the street as the truck. As he approached the house again, he heard someone calling his name. Even though he wasn't high, his head was still foggy and it took him a second to figure out the sound was coming from the truck. Well, from behind the truck.

"Meade," the voice behind the truck said. "Over here."

Dominick hesitated briefly before going around to the passenger side of the truck. He tensed when he saw the hulking man dressed all in black who was leaning against the truck, but relaxed a little when the man didn't shoot him with the shotgun he was holding.

"Who the fuck are you?" Dominick asked.

"I'm either the guy who's going to help you 'cause I know your sister, or you're the guy I'm going to kill because you're fucking *my* sister."

"Ohhhhhhhhhhh," Dominick said. "Your *sister* is fucking the professor. I thought she was part of your harem or something."

"You thought I was cheating on *your* sister?"

Dominick shrugged. "She's kind of a slut. Probably cheating on you," he said.

"You're a little twat. Do you have the money?"

"Can't my sister pay you with like sexual favors or something? I'm really tight on cash this month."

Titus raised the shotgun toward Dominick, but instead of shooting him, he smacked him in the back of the head with it.

"She's a fucking lady, your sister. Show some goddamn respect."

Dominick rubbed at the back of his head with one hand and pulled an envelope full of twenties out of his back pocket with the other.

"I had to get this through sexual favors with my girl," he said, handing the money to Titus. "I'm just saying . . ."

Parker Farmington was happy he was going to get some more action before he tried to work on his new writing project. Sex with Austen always cleared his head, but their argument after the last round had made him mad and disoriented. He would try to end things on a happier note this time.

Maybe he'd go down on her and try this new thing he'd read about on the Internet. If he was lucky, maybe she'd pass out with pleasure and he could leave without saying anything.

He reached into his backpack on the seat next to him and pulled out a new purple vibrator he'd bought the other day—with Austen's needs, doing it on his own could give him early arthritis—and a bottle of his heart medicine. Sex this much was nice but would screw up his heart if he wasn't careful. He also dropped a role of duct tape on the seat with everything else.

His wife had been begging him to fix the broken something or other in the basement and this was the only tool he knew how to use. It looked very odd next to the vibrator and pills.

The truck was still across from the house and Austen was walking into the house with another girl and a guy he thought he recognized. He pulled into the driveway and let the car continue to run while he thought about what to do.

Maybe she wanted them to have sex with the new couple. That would mean he'd get to have sex with two women but he wasn't too sure about the other guy being there. He wondered if he could maybe talk them into doing it in stages, starting with him and the two girls. He could slip out after that and not have to deal with the other guy.

But what if there was something else going on? Could something nefarious be going on? He knew Austen wasn't cheating on him because she's the one who called him back. But that could be a trap, too. Did this have anything to do with the black truck? He decided it wasn't worth the potential danger and started to back out of the driveway. The car only went about ten feet before the baseball bat came smashing through the back windshield.

Dominick finally came to trust Titus Wade and went back to Posey and the two of them went into the house with Susan while Titus grabbed the rest of his gear. Dominick thought he heard a car pull into the driveway as they made their way into the house but he didn't bother to turn around, he was too focused on the job ahead.

It didn't even dawn on him that it could be one of the roommates coming home early, which would totally fuck with the plan, or that it could be the professor. Dominick assumed Susan had done her job and the professor was already in the house. Maybe even tied to the bed or something.

But the professor wasn't in the house when they went in. Nobody was there but Susan. She had put out a plate of cookies and a group of bottled water and cans of soft drinks and some discount beer.

"I didn't have time for a proper hospitality plate," Susan said, nodding at the snack. "Parker never lets me entertain his friends but I figured you might want some alcohol for the job."

Awkward silence.

"What exactly is the job?" Susan asked.

Dominick looked to Posey who shrugged.

"I'm not exactly sure of the specifics myself," she said.

"He needs to be taught a lesson," Dominick said.

Susan nodded along without yelling, so he continued.

"He refuses to sign off on my thesis. If I don't have a thesis, I don't have a degree. And then I lose my fellowship position in New York and I'll probably end up on the midnight shift at a liquor store dying in a shootout with a stupid motherfucking 12-year-old."

"And the lesson . . . ?" Posey asked.

"Crime fiction is relevant in modern society. I'm going to show him the cause and effects of crime on individuals in this ghetto-ass city."

"And the bounty hunter?"

"There's a bounty hunter?" This was Susan. "Oh shit, tell me you didn't."

Before Dominick could tell her he did, they heard the smashing glass and then the screaming.

Titus got pissed when he saw what the professor had in his hands. He didn't originally plan on dragging the condescending little asshole out into the street but when he saw the duct tape and the vibrator he lost it.

"It's not all for her," Farmington squealed and the glass from the window sliced his skin as he was dragged out through the window. "The tape's for—"

Titus punched him in the face and smacked both items out of his hands.

"I don't want to hear your sick plans for my sister."

Farmington tried to scurry away while Titus picked the vibrator and tape up from the driveway, but he didn't make it very far before he was grabbed by the neck and hauled to his feet. Titus crammed the purple vibrator into Farmington's mouth and down his throat then wrapped several layers of duct tape around his head, sealing the toy in Farmington's mouth.

"You keep your mouth shut or I'll turn that on, you hear?"

Farmington nodded eagerly and hoped the wet spot in his pants didn't show.

Susan saw the professor first. Dominick noticed that Titus's shotgun was on the ground with a roll of duct tape, and Posey was pretty sure the same kind of vibrator she owned was taped to the professor's mouth.

"Your plan's kind of kinky," she whispered to Dominick.

"This is not my fucking plan."

"Titus, get away from him," Susan yelled.

Titus shoved his sister out of the way as she ran into him and tried to pull him away.

"I'll deal with you later," he said.

Susan fell backward but caught herself before she hit the ground. She picked up the shotgun and pointed it at Titus.

"Fuck you, big brother," she said. "I wanted to shake him up but I think you're getting carried away. Just let him go and we'll deal with this ourselves."

"It's not your deal to call," Titus said, then he pointed to Dominick. "It's his cash, so it's his gig to call."

"Come on, Dominick," Susan said softly, "I'm sure we can all sit down and get your situation straightened out."

Dominick looked to Posey who had lost her smirk and was standing closer to him than she usually did.

"This probably isn't what you had in mind," she said.

"Kind of gives you a new outlook on crime fiction, doesn't it, Professor?" Dominick asked. "Adultery, betrayal, kinky sex, shotguns. Seems like it all has a pretty valid platform in *this* society, doesn't it?"

Farmington hung his head and struggled against Titus's grip on his wrists.

"Hold him for a sec, Titus," Dominick said. "Let me just go get my thesis form from my car. If he signs it you can let him go."

"And I keep the cash?" Titus asked.

Dominick nodded.

Parker Farmington struggled against the brute's grip, trying to get a hold of the heart pills sitting on the seat.

Now he knew who the kid was he'd seen going into the house with Austen. It was Dominick Meade, one of his graduate students. One of the more promising writers in the department, in fact. But hell bent on the course of commercial fiction which wouldn't get him anywhere in academia.

If Farmington signed that thesis form his reputation would be soiled by the manuscript it represented. Not only would his student become a pariah, so would Farmington. Once the book deal was finalized he'd be done with academics for good. But he needed to wait it out two more months so he could draw his full pension.

"Sign it," Dominick said, shoving a stapled set of papers at Farmington's head.

Farmington tried to say something, but even his mumbles

couldn't be heard through the tape. He squirmed his wrists against the big man's grip but couldn't get his hands free.

"If I let you go, you gonna sign the boy's paper?" the beast asked.

Farmington shook his head no. The beast flipped the switch on the vibrator and it started shimmying around in Farmington's head. The noise was unbearable and he felt like his teeth were going to explode from the pressure. He nodded his head vigorously until the beast finally shut the damn thing off. Dominick got in front of Farmington again and slapped the papers against his chest.

"Make my future bright," Dominick said.

But it was all too much for Farmington's heart. The stress and the vibrations had punched the last ticket on his heart attack card and when the papers hit his chest everything went to hell.

Titus was about to let Farmington's hands go when he took a dive at Dominick. Before Titus could do anything, Farmington was on top of Dominick flailing his hands at the boy's face and throat. Dominick struggled to get the professor off of him but fighting weight is hard to move so Titus lent him a hand by grabbing the professor by the neck and yanking him away from Dominick.

"Don't hurt him," Susan yelled out.

"He doesn't look right," Posey said.

Dominick scrambled out from underneath Farmington as Titus flung his still flailing body against the hood of the hybrid.

"Of course I don't look good," Dominick said. "The asshole sucker punched me."

Titus slapped at Farmington a few times and then slid him across the hood and heaved him back upright so Dominick could have a shot at him.

"I said leave him alone," Susan said, firing a slug at Titus's head.

She only wanted to pump the gun so it would make that intimidating clacking sound. Who knew a shotgun had such a touchy trigger? Leave it to her hyped-up asshole of a brother to have a hair-trigger.

"Oh shit," she said, as the rubber slug plowed into Titus's left eye.

"It's only rubber," she said, dropping the gun and running to her brother. "He only uses rubber. It's only rubber. My God. Why's he bleeding?"

"Rubber my ass," Dominick said. "I felt that shit burn past my face. You almost took me out, bitch."

"Hey, settle down, Dom," Posey said, getting in front of him before he could do anything to Susan. "It was an accident. And it is just rubber, you can see the slug next to his head."

"Oh my God, his heart pills. Parker needs his heart pills," Susan was now chanting.

She stood at the hood of the car spinning between the limp bodies of her brother and her lover. Posey reached into Farmington's car for an orange prescription bottle on the seat while Dominick kicked at the smoking pink slug rolling on the driveway near Titus Wade's head.

"Rubber or not, this shit's not supposed to hit you in the fucking eyeball," he said. "I think you fucking killed him, Suzy."

"He wasn't fighting you, Dom, he was having a heart attack," Posey said, shaking the pill bottle. "Check for his pulse."

Dominick ran two fingers along Titus's neck and couldn't feel anything.

"I don't even think he's breathing," he said.

"I was talking about the professor," Posey said. "But shit, I think they might both be gone."

"*OmigodomigodomigodwhathaveIdoneomigoditwas-
justrubberomigod*," Susan chattered.

"It was an accident. Nobody meant for this to happen. It's
nobody's fault, sweetie."

Posey gave Susan a hug while Dominick continued to feel
around for a pulse on Titus.

"Oh fuck," he said, when he rolled Titus onto his stomach.
"The forms."

"Now is *not* the time, Dominick," Posey said, patting
Susan's head and keeping her ear pressed against Posey's chest.
"You can deal with this in the morning."

"You don't understand," Dominick said. "If Professor
Farmington is dead, that puts my whole fucking thesis in
limbo. They'll tie me up in red tape so long I'll be paying for
my Ph.D. with Social Security."

"My God, Dominick, it was an accident. They'll understand."

"You don't get it, baby. They don't understand. They *feed*.
They will eat this shit up. No, they have to believe he's just
gone away for a while until my paperwork clears."

"I can keep them here," Susan said. "We have a cellar."

"You're not going to keep two corpses in the cellar of a
rental house," Posey said. "That's even fucked up in Detroit.
We've got to do something now. Like call the cops."

"Oh hell no," Dominick said. "You think academics rush to
conclusions? There's no way in hell we're explaining this one."

"There's no bullets. This one died of a heart attack and that
one, well it's not a bullet. That's got to mean something."

"And the bruises on the professor's hands? And the tape
marks on his mouth. And his fucking girlfriend's fingerprints
on the shotgun?"

"He has a wife," Susan said, peeking out from Posey's
bosom. "Someone should tell her."

"You think she's going to believe this was an accident if *you*
tell her?" Dominick asked, pointing to Susan. "*Ha.*"

"I think this has all gone to your head and you need to cool off and think for a while," Posey said. "Let's get these guys into the house and cleaned up and figure out what to do from there."

"If we clean up this scene, they're going to think we're hiding something," Dominick said. "So no cops. I know people. We can get rid of them later."

"But he's my brother," Susan cried. "My mom is going to want to bury him with Pop. Can't we just send him home or something?"

"Hold on, hold on," Posey said, rubbing her temples with the insides of her hands. "All you need is a signature right?"

Dominick nodded and said, "From a dead man."

Posey looked at Susan.

"Did the professor ever do any school business at your house? Might he have left any paperwork here or anything with his signature on it?"

Susan thought about that for a second. Dominick's hopes bloomed, her eyes flittered. And then she shook her head.

"He never wanted to burden me with his school work. It always frustrated him how bad most of his students were."

Dominick didn't bother sticking up for himself because he was too busy being disappointed.

"But wait," she said. "There might be something else."

The tease.

"He did a lot of his writing here. It always seemed to make him feel like a big man for me to see him signing all the paperwork for his book deals and such."

Without finishing the thought, Susan turned back toward the house and ran inside.

"I think he gave me a copy of his new contract to keep safe here," Susan said, when Dominick and Posey finally caught up to her in her third-floor bedroom.

She was digging through the bottom drawer of a small metal filing cabinet in her closet. Susan almost smacked her head on the low ceiling out of excitement when she snapped her hand up in the air holding a thick stack of folded paper.

"Aha," she said.

Dominick grabbed the papers from her and rifled to the back looking for the signature pages. Before he found it though, he found something else much more interesting.

"I know these guys, this publisher," he said. "They publish mystery novels."

Posey grabbed the papers from him and looked through for herself.

"He was going to be paid very well for it," Susan said.

"You knew about this?" Dominick asked. "You knew the asshole was publishing a mystery novel at the same time he was telling me not to?"

"He didn't want it to affect his pension," Susan said. "This was going to be good for him."

"Well, I'm sure he'd appreciate the irony," Dominick said. "That's one thing he always said I did well.

After a few tries on scrap paper, Dominick had Farmington's signature down enough to scrawl it in the three required places on the thesis form and then initial before signing his own name.

"You don't think they'll mind the blood?" Posey asked, trying to smear some of it off of the pages of the paperwork and onto her jeans.

"Hell, they probably expect it."

Eden's Bodyguard

David Bareford

It's not like I have to explain who Eden is. After four gold records, one double-platinum, a Grammy, and that movie with Tom Cruise, she's so well-known she stopped using her last name five years back. Every blink of her baby blues is tracked by tabloids, biz mags, e-channels, and hundreds of web sites. Any American not living under a rock can recognize her face on sight . . . try saying *that* about the Vice-President or the Secretary of State.

She's loaded, too. Private chauffeur, mansion in Beverly Hills, the works. Money attracts people the way a stink does flies, although most of them just buzz around begging for autographs or gushing about how her music changed their lives. Every so often, there's a wasp among those dungflies, though, and I step in like a two-legged can of Raid.

I'm Eden's bodyguard.

So why I am parked in a broken-down beater across the street from her mansion at five-thirty in the morning? Shouldn't I stand outside her bedroom door with sunglasses and a Glock, maybe wearing one of those earpieces that spiral into my gray tailored suit? Grow up, for Chrissake. This isn't a James Bond movie. I'm a professional. I stay close but apart, like her guardian angel. When I'm out here, those paparazzi pukes don't notice me and splash my picture across the supermarket rags. When I'm out here, the wackos think Eden's unguarded and they get careless, which makes them easy to spot. And to deal with.

Case in point: that bum over there.

He Dumpster-dives down the alley behind her compound, pushing a shopping cart loaded four feet high with bulging garbage sacks and topped with an American flag tacked on a yardstick. Her trash bin should be locked, but he's lifting the lid. Her dumbass Cuban maid must've left the chain off again. As he peeks inside, the bum goes up on tiptoe to get a better look, and I notice his shoes: black leather Versace.

I start the car and throw it in gear; he pulls a garbage bag from the Dumpster and looks back for more, holding up the heavy steel lid with one hand. As my Taurus cuts across the boulevard and launches into the alley, he looks up with owlish eyes and a slack jaw. I smash his cart and send it skittering and pinwheeling along the asphalt, spraying old clothes, empty cans, and lumpy plastic bags as it goes. The bum is so surprised he lets the lid drop and the heavy steel plate *whangs* across the fingers of his other hand, which still clutch the Dumpster's rim. He howls and hops around in a weird sort of dance, cradling his injured fingers.

Sometimes a little drama is good, so I bust out of the car like L.A. Vice and he lurches into a ridiculous, shuffling jog. I could catch him easy, but the point has been made.

"Homeless don't wear Versace, moron," I call after him.

I secure the Dumpster with the chain, making a mental note to tell Eden to get a new maid. The garbage bag I toss in the backseat: I'll go through it later to see what he was after.

* * *

The next few hours are uneventful, the way I like them. I eat my two-granola-bar breakfast and listen to Eden's first album, *White Roses.* Before I started working for her, I never listened to her music. Now it never leaves my tape deck. Her voice is a handful of gravel tossed in a pint of cream, and it makes me feel like she's right there in the seat beside me. I find myself toying with the silver hoop earring that dangles from the cigarette lighter.

I've only met Eden face-to-face once, the first and only time I've been backstage at a concert. A local radio station had a call-in contest to promote the *White Roses* tour, and I was lucky number thirty-seven. Caller Sixteen from the day before was also there, a ditsy teenage redhead with googly eyes and an "I Heart Eden" shirt. She kept eyeing the muscle-bound security guys in the waiting area like they were going to jump her. She should be so lucky.

After a second encore, Eden ran offstage, wearing a sheen of perspiration and a silver-spangled halter top. She dazzled the room with her smile. She shook Sixteen's hand, saw her nervous glances at the "bodyguards," and told her not to worry.

"They're just for show," she said. She was looking right at me.

She asked my name, and for a heart-stopping moment, I couldn't remember. She looked up at me through long lashes, waiting, her breathing still a little heavy from her performance. Her delicate pink tongue touched her upper lip. Her hand brushed a damp lock of hair from her face.

"It's Raymond. Ray," I said, as if dredging up an ancient memory.

"Thanks for coming to the show, Ray," she said. "It's great to have you here." But there was something else . . .

It suddenly clicked. She was asking for my help, asking for my protection. She had bodyguards, but *they're just for show. It's great to have* YOU *here.* Eden was privately offering me a job in the middle of a public conversation! I was amazed a rock star could be so subtle, so savvy. I made my decision on the spot.

"I'll be around for all your shows," I said, holding out my hand.

"Fantastic," she said. When she shook my hand, she pressed it with her left hand, too, sealing the deal.

She smiled and started to leave, then stopped. She pushed back her hair and took off the silver hoop earrings she was wearing. With one in each palm, she offered them to the girl and me.

"You guys want a souvenir?"

Sixteen nearly wet herself, but I managed to display a calm reserve I didn't feel. She pressed the earring into my hand, gave me a knowing smile, and was gone. A year and thirty-seven concerts later, I've kept my promise. I haven't missed a single concert (though I buy a general-seating ticket to keep a low profile) and no loony has ever gotten through to Eden on my watch.

It's nine-thirty when the action starts at her compound. The wrought-iron gate swings silently inward and her car pulls out. It's not a limousine—she's not that pretentious, no matter what *Variety* says. She rides in a black Cadillac Escalade with tinted windows and a driver named Johan. I happen to know the middle seats have been turned to face the third row so it feels like a limo inside.

I follow them down to Rodeo Drive, and they stop at a boutique called Chez Marcel. Johan starts to walk around, but she is out before he can open her door. Like I said, she's not pretentious. In public, she wears a baseball cap, sunglasses, and jeans and looks like any other girl trolling the Drive.

The Escalade leaves and I get out my digital camera and take a shot of the store. At some point I'll give the place a shakedown to check its security. Fans will go to any lengths to get a star's measurements, clothes they've tried on, anything. People are crazy, and I can't be too careful.

Forty minutes later, Eden emerges with several bags and makes a call on her cell, probably to Johan. A man in a gray blazer (he's got to be sweating in that, given the heat of the morning) approaches her and starts talking, and she chats back. It makes me crazy when she does this, but she likes "connecting with her fans." The guy seems sane enough: he's not mobbing her or anything, but I snap a few pictures of him anyway, zooming in on his face. After a moment, she shakes his hand and he walks away.

As her car glides up, Eden pulls off her sunglasses, biting the end of an earpiece. From across the street, our eyes meet, lock. Her lips purse around the earpiece as if she is about to blow me a kiss. *Careful,* I silently mouth to her. She quickly looks away and climbs into the car.

I follow her home and continue on two blocks to my temporary apartment. Eden won't go out again today, so I can relax a little. My place is on the fourth floor, above a liquor store and two levels of empty offices. It's not much more than an attic: tiny, dusty, and *sans* central air, but it's home for now. I rented it because it's two stories higher than the building next to it and has a window with the view I need. Its only decoration is a poster on the wall, an enlargement from the cover of the *White Lies* album.

I haul up the garbage bag stolen by the vagrant-*cum*-loony and drop it on the unfinished wood floor, then do a quick check out the window. The Escalade is in the driveway and there's no activity by the pool, so I crack a bottle of Cuervo and pour myself a double. This isn't the regular stuff, it's the Family Reserve, seventy-nine bucks a bottle, and the first sip reminds me why I buy the best.

Using orange latex kitchen gloves, I open the trash bag.

These checks I do monitor how conscientious her staff is about security; loonies can learn too much by going through unguarded trash. Nearby is a pad of paper and a pen for notes.

Among the food scraps and old newspapers are crumpled bags from Coco Chanel and Boulmiche. She should cut off the store names and burn them so fans won't know where she shops, but she tends to forget this. I make a note of it on the pad. There is an empty bottle of Cuervo *Reserva de la Familia*. It's an odd but endearing coincidence that we drink the same tequila, although she mixes it in margaritas and I take it straight. The rest of the trash seems to be the straightforward detritus of American life. Then I notice a few crumpled papers.

They are pre-printed with music tablature, but they've been marked up with several handwritten bars of notes . . . clearly an original song in progress. This is what that morning snoop was after. Spies like him plague the music business: why do you think so many radio songs sound the same? Of course, those young, no-talent "musicians" couldn't match Eden's voice even *with* her music, but some wooden-eared fans might not care. This is a serious breach of security, and I write ALWAYS BURN OLD MUSIC in block letters on the notepad.

Stripping off the gloves, I stroll with my glass to the window. Eden is lounging by the pool now, wearing a light blue bikini. Near the window stands a spotting scope on a tripod, and I peer through it to check on my charge. She seems to be in a relaxed frame of mind, so the fan at the boutique didn't bother her. Good.

It would be too easy to be distracted by her perfect body, so I return my gaze to the apartment. Eden smiles at me from the *White Lies* poster. It shows her from behind, looking sexily over her shoulder at the camera. Her right hand rests in the small of her back, and her index and middle fingers are crossed.

I didn't realize the significance of that hand until halfway through the *White Lies* tour. At a bus stop, a deaf man was bumming change in exchange for little cards printed with the sign language alphabet. I always help the less fortunate, so I gave him some change and looked over the card as I waited for the 93 Express. Then I saw it. That hand gesture, the crossed fingers? It's the American Sign Language symbol for "R."

For *Ray*.

That was when I realized that Eden is in love with me. Millions of men would kill to say that, but believe me, it's pure torture. Imagine waking up to a face like hers, with a voice like that in your ear! Such an exquisite temptation, dangling at my fingertips, yet I can't pluck the fruit. Like I said, I'm a professional. Whitney Houston may do the horizontal tango with her bodyguard, but I won't fall into that trap with Eden. I won't put my feelings ahead of her safety.

It hurts her though, I can tell. She still sends me messages, sneaks hints now and then ("Unrequited Love" on the *White Knights* album was basically written for me), but despite our mutual torment, I make her keep her distance. It's better that way, for now.

I drain my glass and gather the scattered trash off my floor when I notice a wadded ball of paper I hadn't seen. It turns out to be a letter from Sidney, her manager.

Eden, it says, *I think I've found a way to handle that guy that's been bothering you. I'll take care of it, don't worry.*

Anger simmers in my gut. If there's some loony on the make for Eden, he should have come to *me*. Sidney's a dickweed. Why do these amateurs always think they can handle things themselves?

I dash back to the window and scope the compound. Eden is still sunbathing, drinking a margarita and reading *Variety*. The boulevard is sleepy in the noon heat, the only traffic a lone rollerblader cruising by. Perimeter clear.

Wait.

A car, a convertible, idles down the alley behind the compound's wall, then turns left onto the boulevard. Just when I think it's nothing, it stops directly across from the front gate and the driver kills the engine. He is alone in the car; beside him on the front seat is a folded suit jacket. After a bit, he reaches for it and digs through the pockets for something. Sunlight glints off metal.

I zoom in. As he fishes out a pack of Camels, I can see a pistol on the seat under the jacket. A semi-automatic, stuck in a leather shoulder holster. The man lights up, and I recognize his face at the same instant I recognize his jacket: a gray blazer.

I recoil, horrified that I haven't noticed him around before. Just to be sure, I grab my camera and review today's shots on its built-in screen. Sure enough, it's Gray Blazer man from Chez Marcel. I take several more pictures of him and his car, cursing that I haven't bought that super-telephoto lens I've been wanting.

Movement attracts my eye. The front gate opens and Eden's manager emerges. Gray Blazer gets out of the car and meets him near the tall brick gateposts. They talk a moment, Sidney hands him a manila envelope, and the two shake hands and separate. I'm crazy to know what they said.

Gray Blazer returns to his car, still watching the front gate. He opens the envelope, pulls out a stack of cash and fans it. I can't quite see the denominations, but there are at least twenty bills in his fist.

"Dammit, Sidney!" I shout to the air, "You can't pay off these loonies, don't you know that?"

For the rest of the day, my face is glued to the scope, even though I develop a splitting headache behind my right eye. Not much happens: Eden returns inside, Sidney's Mercedes drives away, and Gray Blazer sits in the convertible. He doesn't even have the good grace to try to hide his presence.

As the sun sets behind the western palms and streetlights flicker on, the loony reaches for the jacket. He pulls the gun from its hiding place and slips the shoulder rig across his back, then dons the blazer. He starts the car and pulls a small device from a pocket, keying it toward the compound. The gate opens and he pulls in. Where on earth did he get a remote?

My heart leaps as I realize: Sidney *wasn't* paying off a loony. He was *hiring* him. Her own manager has contracted a crazy to kidnap her, kill her, rape her or worse, and I'm her last line of defense. Her White Knight.

I bolt away from the window and don't even shut my door as I dash out. By the time I pound down four flights of stairs to the street, I'm panting like a dog, but I press on and sprint the intervening blocks.

As I turn up the boulevard, I see the front gate is closed again, but I'm headed for the back anyway. A few weeks back, that dumbass maid (bless her little Cuban heart) broke the key off in the rear gate and then threw away the pieces. I had a new key made to replace it, but I keep forgetting to give it to Eden. It's still in my pocket, praise every god and his mother.

The key twists. The gate opens. I run by the pool, swatting aside low-hanging palm fronds and dodging the dim shapes of lounge chairs that crouch in the gathering gloom. There is a glass patio door leading to a darkened room, and I tug on the handle, expecting it to be locked. It slides open effortlessly, soundlessly. I enter.

Thick carpet absorbs my footfalls and I ease the door closed. The room is split-level, with a massive pool table in the lower section and a bar with several padded chairs on the upper. The air is still, chilled, and smells faintly of coconut oil; the only illumination is a soft ambient glow through a doorway on the far wall.

I hear a noise. Footsteps, close by, dress shoes on tile. It could be him, he with the Gray Blazer and the loaded pistol. I have charged into the dragon's cave without armor or a sword.

I suddenly feel very defenseless, and I cast about for some kind of weapon. A pool cue lies on the table, a three-piece job, designed to come apart for traveling. I unscrew the smallest section, leaving a wooden truncheon about three feet long. It'll have to do.

The doorway leads to an entry floored in green marble, lit by a brass wall sconce. A curved stone staircase sweeps up, railed with an iron banister.

He is already halfway up the stairs.

I wait until he reaches the upper landing and disappears from sight, then I kick off my sandals and whisper across the stone, climbing the stairs and brandishing the pool cue like a sword. My heart thuds in my ears and my breath comes quick and shallow, though from fear or exertion I cannot tell. A furtive peek around the wall reveals a short hallway with three doors on the right side, and a nearby table topped with some kind of African statue. The last door is just closing.

I move into the hallway, fixated on the third door, gripping the wooden cue until my knuckles blanch. Suddenly, the second door snaps open, trapping and blinding me in light. The doorway frames Eden, beautiful even when startled. She lets out a small shriek as she sees me—who can blame her?

"Stay calm," I tell her. "There's a man inside the house. He—"

—is barreling out the third door at me, the gun lifting to find its aim. My mind registers a thousand details. The spicy smell of Eden's perfume. The man, gray blazer gone, face twisted in anger. The sweat stains under the arms of his shirt. I leap past Eden, throwing myself between the assassin and my charge, and I bring down the pool cue with both hands. It cracks across his right forearm and snaps. He grunts and drops the gun, which discharges as it hits the floor. The bullet *whaps* past my left ear and sprays plaster from the wall. Eden screams.

He charges through the powder smoke and I grab him, wrestling to keep him away from her. My ears are ringing, my breath is short, and the man's strength is prodigious, but I bulldog him down the hall toward the stairs. We smash through the table with the African idol and he slams me into a wall. I dimly register my head shattering the glass of some painting.

I gather my strength, shoving forward and leveraging off the wall. He overbalances and topples back, dragging me with him at the last moment. Together we bounce and crunch down the marble stairs, careening into the iron baluster, slamming into stone risers, and ending in a heap at the bottom. A tangled pile of pain.

One of my eyes is swelling up and there is a slick wet feeling down the back of my neck. I try to rise, but pain stabs through my left leg and I collapse again. Gray Blazer tries to grab me, but one of his hands flops sickeningly and a splinter of red-smeared bone pierces the skin of his wrist. He screams in anguish, but still manages to latch onto my throat with his good hand.

"Who are you?" he shouts with a hoarse voice.

I slash a hand at his arm, striking the compound fracture with my fist. He screams again and falls back, and I heave myself on top of him, jamming my forearm into his trachea. I can taste blood in my mouth, the bitter taste of rust.

"STOP IT!"

Eden is halfway down the stairs, screaming through tears. Both hands clutch the pistol, aiming for Gray Blazer although her hands wobble and if she fires I can't be certain who she'll hit. I turn back to the loony, managing a gory smile.

"The name's Ray. I'm her bodyguard. Her White Knight."

Eden's face has gone strangely cold. I have never seen this side of her. She stands, swaying, and it's probably just the parallax from the stairs, but the gun seems to be pointing at me. She speaks in a voice as cold as space.

"*He's* my bodyguard, you stalker son of a bitch."

A thousand details. Hard-set baby blues. A muzzle flash. A spent casing spinning in the air, and the beginning of a deafening report—cut short by a mule kick to the head.

Then only the whiteness.

The Milfinators

Charlie Stella

"The fuck is a milf?" Tommy Burns asked Paul Costa.

He was holding a DVD cover titled *Milf Me in the Morning*. The body of the man he'd just shot in the back of the head lay across a glass coffee table. Burns stepped around the dead man's legs and accidentally knocked over a stack of DVDs.

"Jesus Christ," he said, then crossed himself.

"The hell was that?" Costa said. He was a big man with thick curly hair and heavy beard stubble.

"What was what?"

Costa imitated the sign of the cross. "That mean bunt or steal?"

"Not funny," Burns said.

"Are you kidding me?"

"It's personal. Let's not get into it."

Burns had recently been diagnosed with emphysema. He rediscovered religion during his recovery, which included a two-year hiatus from his former profession as a hired mob assassin. A few days after receiving his first call for a piece of work since his self-imposed retirement, the FBI showed up at his trailer home with an arrest warrant and a proposition. Burns assumed his second chance had come from God.

Now he was still confused about the DVD cover he was staring at. "What's a milf?" he asked Costa again.

"Mother I'd Love to Fuck."

Burns took a moment, then said, "What?"

Costa had already stepped into the kitchen and opened the refrigerator door. He spotted a half sandwich wrapped in plastic and grabbed it.

Burns was looking at the titles of some of the DVDs he had knocked over. "*Milfamania*," he read aloud. "*Any Milf'll Do.*"

"They're mostly older woman who bang young studs," Costa said when he returned to the den. He unwrapped the sandwich and took a bite. He spoke with his mouth full. "Some a' them are very old. Some outright geezers."

Burns was a short, thin man and had just turned sixty. He had gray hair and piercing blue eyes. Because of his illness, he was rationing cigarettes. He pulled a pack from his jacket pocket from habit, then put it back.

"Geezers?" he said. "What do you mean, like old ladies?"

"Some of them, yeah," Costa said. He swallowed what he'd been chewing. "The kind you ever saw without their clothes, you'd upchuck your last six meals."

Burns had another DVD in his hands, *Milf Maids 9*. He shook his head in disgust. "The modern world," he said. "You can keep it."

Costa took another bite of the sandwich.

"So, what, this is all porn stuff?" Burns asked.

"It's what the guy you just whacked did for a living. He was a porn producer. He filmed older broads with young guys, some of them kids. Apparently it's a big market."

Burns was incredulous at the mention of kids. "For who?"

he asked. "Who the fuck wants to see some old bag getting plowed? Who wants to see some kid doing the plowing?"

Costa finished the sandwich. He belched into a fist. "Excuse," he said. "Somebody does or they wouldn't make the movies. You go online, the Internet, it's a big business. I don't know where they get the old broads to do it, or the guys to fuck them for that matter, but there's a lot of them out there."

"And the broad living here with this jamoke, she did this shit, too? She made these movies?"

Costa nodded. "She's not a geezer, though. She's fifty-two, something like that, but, yeah, it's what we're here for. She made a couple movies got back to her son, some drug dealer doing his time in San Quentin. He's the one put out the bid. Wanted this clown and his mother whacked."

Burns was looking at the women on the back cover of a DVD. "Imagine your mother doing this shit?"

"No thanks," Costa said. "My mother weighed more'n me."

"Huh?" Burns said. "Oh."

"Anyway, that's how it was told to me, about the son wanting the old lady whacked. The guy, too, he was the priority, he's the one flipped on the kid, but she's supposed to go, too."

"Somebody's mother doing this shit. Unbelievable."

"Hey, it's no worse than priests sucking little boys' dicks, right?"

Burns shot Costa a hard look.

"Don't get mad at me," Costa said.

Burns let it go. "What were they doing out here?" he asked.

"Witness Protection."

"She rat on her kid?"

"No, I already said, was the guy," Costa said. "He cut a deal with the government. The son was supplying the drugs for the old bags our dead friend here was putting to work. Probably the guys in the films, too, and whoever else he could make a few bucks hawking the stuff to. The dead fella knew the kid from the neighborhood. Maybe he met the mother picking up his stash one day."

The FBI hadn't bothered telling Burns the details behind the contract Costa had approached him with. All he knew was the government was giving him a chance to keep from dying in jail. The more Costa went on about California porn and the drug dealing son looking to kill his mother and her boyfriend, the more bizarre it all seemed. Burns was finding it interesting.

"So this dead degenerate fuck, what, he charmed the pants off the kid's mother?" he asked.

"Must've, or maybe she was auditioning for the movies," Costa said. "Who knows? There was something about it in the local news in L.A., the kid getting busted and all and then the mother being involved in the movies and whatnot, but it came down to this guy giving up the son, why we're here. The kid's doing twenty-five to life, I remember right."

Burns was looking at the back of another DVD. He cringed at a picture of a naked elderly woman and the wrinkled cellulite on her legs. "Fucking people," he said. "It's a mortal sin."

"Way I heard it, some federal agent on the west coast sold our friend here off," Costa said. "Or maybe they cut a deal with the son and getting to our dead friend and momma was the kid's price. I wouldn't doubt it. Not anymore. Government does more work 'n you and me these days. Probably at a better price, too."

Only if they don't stiff me, Burns was thinking.

"I'm not even talking about the obvious shit," Costa continued. "Never mind Whitey Bulger up in Boston or that thing in New York with the Colombo people and federal agent there. I'm talking out-and-out hits."

Burns ignored the irony. He tossed the DVDs he was holding on a couch. "I guess the kid ordered this never heard of honor thy mother and father," he said.

"Don't get me wrong," Costa said. "It was my mother, I'd

want her dead, too. Especially I'm in the joint. The guy inside, his playmates there ever find out about his mother doing this shit, he might as well hang himself."

Burns had always avoided killing women except for the time a friend moving up in the New York mob had asked for a favor. Even then, Burns insisted on putting a hood over Rosemary Valentine's head before shooting her twice behind the left ear. A few days after her disappearance he saw her picture in the newspaper and had suffered periodic nightmares ever since.

He shuddered thinking about her now.

"Hey, you alright?" Costa asked.

"Yeah, yeah, I'm fine," Burns said. He waved the DVD he was holding. "It's just this here stuff. I don't understand what makes people do this shit?"

"Same as what makes us do what we're doing, my friend. Mean green."

Burns felt his face tighten. "So, what, this is about the kid's embarrassed for his mother or he's just looking to protect his ass inside the joint?"

"Survival is what I'm thinking," Costa said, "The guy needs to save face. The fact she's with this jamoke makes it twice as easy. Think about the kid's rep inside once word gets around. Guy puts a hit on his own mother?"

"Makes it hard to figure out which one is worse, you ask me."

"Maybe, but only one of them is paying us to do the work so he wins."

"Milfs," said Burns, shaking his head in disgust.

Costa smiled.

"What?" Burns said.

"That makes us milfinators."

"The fuck you talking about?"

"Like Arnold in *The Terminator*."

"Huh?"

Costa waited for Burns to figure it out. When he saw Burns wouldn't get it, the big man waved it off. "Forget it," he said.

Burns opened a closet door and saw another three stacks of DVDs on the floor. "He ship this shit from here?"

"He was living in Van Nuys before the feds moved him out here," Costa said. "Probably brought his entire stock with him. Was a producer. Probably made a thousand movies in his day."

"*Milf Maid Matinee*," Burns read off a DVD cover. "Mother I'd love to fuck. Who wants to see this shit?"

Costa belched into a fist. "We should probably head over to the diner," he said. "She gets off at seven."

"Why not wait here 'til she gets back?"

Costa glanced at his watch. "It's only five now," he said. "We'll be spending too much time in one place. Could be somebody stops over. Maybe they use a safety check the feds gave them. She might not come in the house he doesn't respond to something or other."

Burns tossed the DVDs he was holding back inside the closet. "Not a single Johnny Cash CD in the house," he said.

"Johnny Cash?"

"Guy was a god," Burns said. He had to call a phone number the agents had given him and needed an excuse to be alone. He stepped over the dead man on his way to the bathroom. "I gotta piss," he said.

Costa used the extra time to search the kitchen cabinets. He found a DVD with a picture of the woman they were looking for in a red bra and panties. The cover read: *Allison Robles, Bedside Manner: Diary of a Milf Night Nurse*. He jammed the DVD inside his coat pocket. He found a Snickers bar in a drawer and stashed it inside a pants pocket. He went through another cabinet and found a small bag of Doritos. He ripped the bag open, grabbed a handful of the corn chips and stuffed some inside his mouth. The rest fell from his hand to the kitchen linoleum.

Costa finished more than half the bag before Burns was finished in the bathroom. The two men left through the back door of the ranch home. They walked the length of the driveway to a gravel road where Costa had parked behind a wall of trees facing the main road.

The car started on the first try. Costa turned up the heat, but the vents blew cold air until the engine was warm.

"Imagine living here year round?" Burns said.

"I was through here once with the family," Costa said. "Took the kids down to Teddy Roosevelt National Park, must'a been twenty-five, thirty years ago. My boys got a kick out of it, the cowboy and Indian shit. The wife wasn't too happy, though. She wanted to go down to Florida visit her mother. I hate Florida. Don't know how you stand it, by the way, all that humidity."

"Air conditioning," Burns said. "The summers, I don't go outside unless I have to. It's not so bad in the winter. I listen to Johnny Cash and study the Racing Form."

"Johnny Cash, huh?" Costa said. "You becoming a hick down there the sunshine state?"

Burns spotted headlights through the trees and nudged Costa with an elbow. They both watched as a large pickup drove past the main road.

"What if our girl leaves with somebody?" Burns asked.

"I guess it'd be their unlucky day," Costa said.

He put the car into gear, then backed out into the driveway. He moved up to the main road and turned east heading toward Highway 52.

"What if somebody discovers the producer back there before we get to the broad?" Burns asked.

"We're fucked," Costa said.

"I don't know I like that."

"Look, it was tough enough convincing my people it was a two-man job," Costa said. "The way things are, I was lucky they paid for a second gun. This isn't knocking off the Pope here. It's some guy already inna joint paying to whack a couple of losers involved in the porn business. The only other way of doing this with more security'n we got is for each of us to take a target and trust the other we get it done, but that wouldn't really be security. I like you enough, Tommy. I know you from the old days as a square shooter and a standup guy, but going that route, going after different targets in different directions, that wouldn't be smart for either one of us. Not to mention we wouldn't have security of our own we go to pick up the balance on this."

"Fair enough," Burns said. "Although if we had the back end money, it wouldn't be such a bad idea, taking off in different directions."

"What?"

Burns smiled. "I'm pulling your pud," he said. "I already whacked the one guy, right? We're halfway home."

"Thank you," Costa said.

"Was a joke," Burns said. "Anyway, I wasn't so sure I'd come out of retirement after the emphysema, so I appreciate the work."

"The hell you do down there anyway in Florida?" Costa said. "Me, I got the grandchildren now, four of them, but without them around, I go nuts just hanging around the house. I tend bar the VFW Saturday nights just to stay sane."

"I look after my niece's kid," Burns said. "My sister's daughter. My sister passed last year and I'm looking out for my grandniece, I guess she is. Good kids, my niece and her kid. The one is struggling raising her daughter because of a deadbeat father, but she's going to school nights to be a nurse. It isn't easy for her. I watch the kid nights she's at school and help around the house when I can."

"Sounds pretty fucking boring to me."

"I don't mind the peace and quiet so much as trying to stretch what I put on the side, which is never enough. There's days I'd like to hop a plane to the islands there and blow a wad in the casino, get a couple broads up the room and so on, but that won't happen without a score so I try not to kid myself. Mostly I don't mind it, taking it easy."

"So it wasn't just the need for excitement you took this on?"

"Yeah, that and the twenny grand," Burns said.

"So, what, I coulda told you ten grand, you still would'a done it?"

"Coulda told me five, but you didn't. You told me twenny and twenny it is."

"I'm too generous," Costa said.

"Yeah," Burns said, "me, too. I got the same problem."

Costa drove eight miles to a truck stop diner off North Dakota Highway 52. He parked in the rear of the lot and left the car running for heat. The wind outside howled east to west. Gusts occasionally rocked the car.

Burns read the temperature off the digital display in the dashboard. "Six below," he said. "Makes my balls hurt to say it."

He was wondering if the call he'd made from the bathroom had been received on the other end. The agents had told him to dial the number he'd memorized and wait for the ring. He was to hang up after hearing it, but now he wasn't sure if something had gone wrong. Maybe he'd dialed the wrong number.

Costa produced the DVD he had taken from the house while Burns had used the bathroom. "I'll bet she's still making these," Costa said. He handed Burns the DVD. Burns read the cover aloud, *"Allison Robles, Bedside Manner: Diary of a Milf*

Night Nurse." He stared at the picture of the woman posing in red lingerie. "She's not half bad," he added.

"For fifty-two, what she's supposed to be, she's not bad at all."

Burns flipped the DVD over and looked at the collage of pictures on the back. "She was into it, yeah, she's probably still posing for the freaks buy this shit."

"It's how she was paying her bills before the feds moved them out here," Costa said. "What'd stop her now?"

"Getting caught, for one thing. Sooner or later there's exposure in making this shit. Somebody found out she was doing it inna first place, no? Her son, right?"

"She's probably not concerned about him since his conviction. There are black markets for this shit, too, now. They could've been hawking it up north in Canada or overseas someplace. No reason the guy had to ship it domestic. They could be doing private movies for guys with deep pockets. There's a lot of that shit goes on in the porn business."

Burns was looking at a picture of the star holding a long black penis with both hands. Her mouth was opened wide. "A broad gets this desperate, she should go out on the street," he said. "This is crazy, this shit. Putting yourself on camera for the whole world to see? It's nuts."

"Except she probably made more with that film in a couple hours than she does slinging hash in the diner for a month," Costa said. "Probably more'n she'd make on the street in two weeks."

Burns handed the DVD back to Costa. "Nice souvenir," he said. "I hope the law doesn't find it under your couch some day."

Costa stashed the DVD under his front seat. "I'll burn it after I watch it a couple times, but don't tell me you're not curious."

"What's to be curious about? Look at the pictures onna back there. Woman's a pig."

"You just said she wasn't half bad two seconds ago."

"I don't care she's Sophia Loren," Burns said. "She's doing that shit with kids half her age, black guys no less, she's a pig."

Costa chuckled. "Anyway, looking at the pictures is not the same thing as watching it. No way."

"It's still sick."

"Maybe, except if we had this shit when we were kids, I'm not sure I wouldn't've pulled it off, my dick. I thought it might fall off from yanking to Playtex bra ads in the Sunday news."

A middle-aged woman wearing a ski jacket stepped outside the kitchen door at the rear of the diner. She turned her back to the wind as she cupped her hands to light a cigarette. Burns noted the time to himself. He wasn't sure how much longer he could put up with Paul Costa or his conversation.

"I used to think you only got so many squirts," Costa said. "I thought you got like a thousand or two thousand or whatever, and then you went dry, you couldn't unload anymore. Like I'd run out some day. Once we had the class there, high school, health and hygiene, whatever they called it, I learned about the sperm and all that, I thought I'd never be a father from all the jerking off I did."

Burns was guessing it was already too late to make the eight o'clock flight out of Jamestown, North Dakota. If the call he'd made hadn't gone through to the agents supposedly waiting nearby, he wasn't sure what it might mean. At the least he'd be stuck there until the woman got off from work. Then anything could happen.

He started to feel anxious and pulled his inhaler out of a jacket pocket. He took a long draw on it.

"You okay?" Costa asked.

Burns held up his free hand while he took a quick second hit off the inhaler. He took a few breaths on his own, put the inhaler away, then pointed at the woman on the platform. She was shuffling from foot to foot.

Costa pointed to Burns's jacket pocket. "That from the smoking?"

Burns nodded.

"Fucking cigarettes," Costa said. "Why I quit, what you're going through now. I seen it happen too many times."

Burns had started to relax. He pointed to the woman. "That our girl?"

"Could be," Costa said. He motioned with his head toward a white Ford Taurus parked across the lot. "She gets in the white car over there, answers to either Allison or Betty, she's our girl."

"That the name the feds give her? Betty?"

"Allison is her real name, but I doubt she goes by that anymore. Bernsdorf's the last name now. Nordic name, I think. To blend in, I guess. That's what most of them around here are, Nordics. Swedish and so on. German, too."

Burns was squinting to see the woman.

Costa noticed and said, "You sure you're okay?"

"Yeah, I'm alright. I'm going on sixty-four and I still don't unnerstand this world. Mother I'd love to fuck . . ."

"How 'bout the guys they get to fuck the mothers?"

"Fuckin degenerates, I'm sure," Burns said. "But most guys'll fuck a snake. Not that I'm excusing them, guys involved in this sick shit, fucking old ladies. I can unnerstand a guy doing this shit a lot easier than I can some fifty-year-old broad, never mind the seventy-year-olds."

"The younger the guys the better, because the ones on the pictures onna back of the DVD all looked like they're in their twenties."

"They're all degenerates, porn guys. Big-dicked degenerates."

The woman on the platform tossed her cigarette away before heading back inside the kitchen. A short man carrying a large plastic bag filled with garbage stepped out onto the platform. He walked the plastic bag down the platform ramp to a metal Dumpster. He tossed the bag inside the Dumpster and ran back up the ramp to the kitchen.

Burns fingered a cigarette from the open pack in his shirt pocket. "The hell does a broad do in this situation?" he said. "How's she make the transition?"

Costa fished the Snickers bar he'd taken from the house out of his pants pocket and peeled the wrapper off. "What do you mean?"

Burns played with the cigarette before putting it back inside the open pack. "For entertainment," he said. "To do something. Anything. The rest of her life, I mean. You don't shed your stripes because you cut a deal. She can't be enjoying this shit, waiting tables in the middle of nowhere. She was living it up in California, what she do here now besides this shit?"

"You mean for cock?"

"For entertainment, I'm saying. That, too, I guess, yeah. What's she do she wants to get laid around here?"

"Samples the local talent, she wants. Or the guy you whacked back at the house. Maybe he gave her what she needed. They hooked up in the first place, right? Maybe they did it for each other."

"That guy hadda be sixty-five at least," Burns said. "She's fifty-two and not a bad looker, at least on that cover she wasn't, there's no way she was content with that old fuck. Especially she's making movies fucking kids. No way."

Costa was chewing a bite of the candy bar. "What are you a marriage counselor now?"

"I'm just saying. A broad isn't half bad, she wants her steady action, not some old geezer can barely get it up."

"How do you know the guy wasn't Jack-fuckin-LaLane,

barely get it up? He might've been a retired John Holmes, that guy."

"Who the fuck's John Holmes?" Burns said.

"Never mind," Costa said. "You're taking it too personal. Who cares what she does for fun and entertainment, who she screws or whatever? She lives out here because she was with the guy we just whacked. We gotta whack her now because of her son, because he's paying the freight."

Burns mumbled to himself.

"Hey, if it's the cigarettes, light up already," Costa said. "Don't take it out on me."

Burns fingered a cigarette from the open pack again. This time he lit it. "It's been four hours," he said. "I'm half an hour overdue."

"'Least that explains the rag you're on."

The two men stared at each other until headlights entering the parking lot caught their attention. Burns noted the time again as a black Dodge Ram pulled into the spot directly behind the platform leading to the diner kitchen. A tall man wearing army fatigues and a baseball cap got out. He headed up the ramp to the kitchen door, opened it and went inside.

Burns cracked open his window enough to let his cigarette smoke escape.

"You'd think emphysema might scare you into quitting," Costa said. He swallowed the last of his Snickers bar.

"You see me light one yet today?"

"No, come to think of it. Good for you."

"I haven't had one since you picked me up the airport."

"How many you down to?"

"Half a pack a day. Sometimes less. Took me two years, though."

"Ever get the chemo?"

Burns was watching the kitchen door for the tall man. "I

been warned," he said. "I been warned the last twenny years. I got enough to worry about without the chemo. I'm down the Glades there less than a year and I come out one morning, I hear the dog I just bought yelping, and what do I see but some fucking alligator the size of a small Buick's got the thing in its mouth. I took how many, must'a been twenny shots at the gator before it stopped moving, but the dog was dead already anyway. I don't need to worry about chemo while I got dinosaurs my back yard."

"That's another thing about Florida," Costa said. "Alligators. Nasty looking things. You should move north where it's too cold for monsters like that."

Burns was anxious to get the day over with. He was hoping the tall man would come back out, get in the pick-up and flash his lights before pulling out. Then he could whack Paul Costa and be on his way.

"I'm up in Michigan just over two years now," Costa continued. "It gets just as cold there as here, little more snow in fact, but the summers are just right. I want warm weather I hop a flight to the islands."

Burns opened his window enough to toss out what was left of his cigarette. "Everybody from New York goes to Florida," he said. "My sister had a place there so it was easy."

"I'm not sure I could handle retirement," Costa said. "Not fully."

Burns could give a fuck. He was tired and grumpy and sick of the cold weather and of sitting in a car most of the day. He was sure he'd have to drive to South Dakota and spend the night in some dumpy motel before catching a flight out of Sioux Falls in the morning. His chance of catching the eight o'clock out of Jamestown was just about over.

"Hey, you with me?" Costa said.

"What's that?"

"I said I'm not sure I could handle retirement," Costa repeated.

Burns shrugged. "Yeah, well, like I said, I appreciate the work. It was getting on my nerves doing nothing all day."

"No problem," Costa said. "Truth be told, people in our line of work, either they never have enough to stay retired or what you said, they can't stand the sitting around doing nothing. I remember what happened with you, that thing in New York, so I figured the retirement wasn't really your choice anyway."

"You're right about that. Guy I knew most my life, did time with when we was young punks, he was wearing a wire. Nobody knew until after some broad he was banging shot him, but I was more than lucky to get out from under that rock."

"Wiseguys are bigger problems nowadays than the law," Costa said. "Flip before they get the cuffs on. Seems nobody can handle going away anymore."

Burns smirked from the hypocrisy. The way the agents had explained it, Costa had cut a deal two years earlier that had gone sour when the Detroit mob boss the federal government was pursuing died in his sleep eight days ago. Costa had become an instant liability, which was why Burns was there to kill him today.

"They show the prison documentaries on the television and it scares the shit out of people," Costa continued. "That HBO thing, whatever it was called, the one with all the shines wearing socks on their heads. It was all bullshit, but people see that stuff, even street guys, and they shit their pants. They were whacking two guys a week on that show and people bought it like it was real."

"Huh?" Burns said.

"Not that I'm not anxious to find out," Costa continued. "I only went away once and those were the two longest years of my life. That was at Walpole twenty years ago and there were more than enough brothers in the joint then. I can't imagine what it's like today."

"It ain't a picnic," Burns said.

"Not for guys our age, that's for sure. Prison is a young man's game. I have a choice between going away and shooting it out, I'll take the bullet every time. They come and cuff me, that's another thing. That's when I look for a good piece of string and do the work myself."

Burns chuckled.

"What's funny?" Costa said.

Burns pointed to the tall man standing in the kitchen doorway again. The tall man stepped outside and then the woman was there, too.

"Think they're together?" Costa asked.

"Looks like it."

"That's not good."

The couple was talking on the platform. The woman lit up another cigarette.

Burns reached for another one of his own.

"She's got her own car," Costa said. "Unless she's gonna leave it behind for the night."

Burns could see the woman was listening to the tall man.

"Thing of it is," Costa said, "we whack this guy, whoever he is, the law will do a full court press."

The tall man had jammed his hands inside his front pants pockets. The woman's arms were folded across her chest. The cigarette remained in her mouth.

"Let's just hope he's not the law," Costa said. "He could be stalling until backup arrives. Maybe they already found the one back at the house."

The woman took a long drag on her cigarette before tossing it off the ramp. The wind got hold of it and bounced it along the asphalt creating tiny sparks until it was snuffed in a small puddle. The tall man headed back down the ramp toward his pickup. He got in, started the engine and flashed the headlights twice before backing out of the space. The woman disappeared inside the kitchen as the pickup pulled out of the lot. It turned west onto Highway 52.

"Boyfriend or acquaintance?" Costa said.

"Boyfriend," said Burns as she reached inside his jacket. "Definitely boyfriend."

"They didn't kiss."

"But he did all the talking," Burns said. He had hold of the Walther. He nonchalantly pulled the gun out of its shoulder harness. "He was an acquaintance, she would've been the one doing the yapping, like every other broad I ever knew."

Costa wasn't paying attention. "I'm still looking forward to seeing her in action," he said. "In fact I can't wait."

"That's because you're another fuckin degenerate," Burns said.

"Yeah, I guess," said Costa as he turned to smile at Burns. He lost his smile when he saw the Walther.

"The feds gave you my name, you should've thought why," Burns said.

Costa swallowed hard. His Smith and Wesson .380 was in an ankle holster strapped to the bottom of his right leg. There was no way he could get to it before Burns killed him.

"The hell is this, Tommy?" he stammered.

"Things change," Burns said. "In most cases not for the better."

"Wait a second," Costa pleaded. "Who you with on this? Who you working for?"

Burns fired two shots. The first went through Costa's left hand into his stomach. The second put a bullet through the big man's heart.

"Fuck's the difference?" Burns said.

He got up on his knees to reach across the dead man to flash the headlights twice. Then he leaned over to grab the DVD off the floor near the gas pedal. He wiped the cover clean before setting it back down at the dead man's feet. Burns got out of the car and waited less than a minute before the Dodge Ram pulled up in front of the Buick. The tall man nodded before opening the window to hand down a set of car keys.

"White Ford," the tall man said. "In the glove compartment."

Burns waited until the tall man pulled out of the lot before crossing the lot to the white Ford Taurus. He got in, started the engine, turned up the heat, then checked the glove compartment for his cash. He found two stacks of hundred dollar bills he hoped totaled twenty thousand dollars. He'd count it later.

He drove half an hour south before pulling off the highway to park behind the cover of an abandoned barn. He removed the North Dakota license plates and put on a South Dakota set, then counted his money. It was exactly twenty thousand dollars.

Two hours later, Burns was heading south on U.S. Route 83 when he lit his fourth cigarette of the day. The smoke felt good going down. He held it in his lungs a long while before finally releasing it with a series of coughs.

When he finished the cigarette, Burns tossed the tiny butt out the window. He turned on the radio and learned that a body had been found in a car behind a truck stop parking lot. The North Dakota state police were asking for anyone who might've seen what had happened to please call an emergency number.

Burns saw a road sign for Rice Lake. He looked off at both sides of the road but it was too dark to see water. He wondered if the lake was frozen and if that was one of the things people did around there, ice fishing, because there didn't seem to be anything else to do.

A few minutes later he saw a sign for a town called Hague. It had been a long day and he was getting tired. Burns considered taking his first break, but knew he needed to get rid of the Ford before he could sleep. He opened the window to wake himself up. The cold air was a shock to his skin. He quickly brought the window back up.

He turned on a country western station and caught Johnny Cash's *When the Man Comes Around* as Route 83 South led him closer toward Sioux Falls, South Dakota.

"There's a man goin' 'round takin' names."

Burns was familiar with the melody, but wasn't sure of the words. He bobbed his head as he listened.

"Hear the trumpets, hear the pipers . . . One hundred million angels singin' . . . Multitudes are marching to the big kettle drum . . . Voices callin', voices cryin' . . . Some are born an' some are dyin' . . . It's Alpha's and Omega's Kingdom come."

Burns stopped to yawn again. He saw a hotel billboard for lodging, gas stations, and food ten miles ahead in Herreid, South Dakota.

"Why not?" he said, then yawned one more time before trying his best to sing along with the radio.

"Whoever is unjust, let him be . . . still. Whoever is 'iteous . . . be righteous still. Whoever is . . . let him be filthy still. 'isten to the words long written down . . . the man comes around."

About the Authors

Stephen Allan—Stephen Allan is a crime writer who has published in *Spinetingler Magazine, Thuglit* and *Flashing in the Gutters*. He is currently working on a crime novel. Steve lives in Maine with his wife and two children. His wife tells him he owes all of his success to her. He agrees.

David Bareford—David Bareford hails from Chi-town, where he hands his paycheck straight to three dames: a wife, a 6-month old baby girl, and a daughter who is already a tall, cool blonde at age 3. His hobbies include oiling his .45, sharpening his straight razor, and waiting for the boys that will one day show up at his door.

Jeffrey Bangkok—Jeffrey Bangkok (a.k.a. Kuczmarski) received his MFA from the Art Institute of Chicago in 1998. His work has appeared in *The Briar Cliff Review, Cimarron Review, Karamu, The Ledge, The Mid-America Poetry Review, New Delta Review, Paper Street, Plainsongs, Rosebud*, the anthologies *Danger City, Danger City 2* (Contemporary Press) and, the best place for a stiletto in the eye on the web, Thuglit.com. And in 2006 he slashed the throats of nearly 19,000 other poets to earn an honorable mention for rhyming poetry in the *75th Writer's Digest Writing Competition*.

Ken Bruen—is the author of 20 books, has a Ph.D. in metaphysics, lives in Galway and loves New York.

Sean Chercover—Formerly a private investigator in Chicago and New Orleans, Sean Chercover now writes full time and generally stays out of trouble. Gravedigger Peace, the main character in *A Sleep Not Unlike Death*, first appeared as a sidekick to Chicago P.I. Ray Dudgeon in Sean's debut novel, *BIG CITY, BAD BLOOD*. Visit Sean at www.chercover.com.

Sam Edwards—Truly, other digests deserve recognition on bios. Instead, nasty Sam offers nothing . . .

Bill Fitzhugh—Bill Fitzhugh is the award-winning author of seven satiric crime novels. *The New York Times* called Fitzhugh "a strange and deadly amalgam of screenwriter and comic novelist. His facility, wit, and his taste for the perverse put him in a league with Carl Hiaasen and Elmore Leonard." His novels *Pest Control* and *Cross Dressing* are in development at Warner Brothers and Universal Studios respectively. The late Texas governor Ann Richards, commenting on *Heart Seizure*, said "Fitzhugh can skewer a politician better than just about anyone I know." Reviewing his latest, *Highway 61 Resurfaced*, *Time* magazine said, "Fitzhugh's dialogue is as cool as a pitcher of iced tea, and his characters are just over the top, like a Carl Hiaasen cast plucked from the Everglades and planted, as Dylan would put it, out on Highway 61."

After publication of *Radio Activity*, Fitzhugh was invited to write, produce, and host a weekly show on XM Satellite Radio's Deep Tracks channel called "Fitzhugh's All Hand Mixed Vinyl." He is one of only two outside hosts on Deep Tracks. The other: Bob Dylan. Fitzhugh has just finished *The Exterminators*, the sequel to *Pest Control* and he is currently working on a book with country superstars, Brooks and Dunn, called *The Adventures of Slim and Howdy*. Fitzhugh's books have been translated into German, Japanese, and Italian. He lives in Los Angeles with his wife, three dogs, and a cat named Crusty Boogers.

Victor Gischler—Victor Gischler is the author of four hard-boiled crime novels, the first of which, *GUN MONKEYS*, was nominated for the Edgar Award. His work has been translated into French, Japanese, Italian, and Spanish. He lives in Baton Rouge with his wife Jackie and his son Emery. He loves cold beer, hot wings, and black black coffee.

Jordan Harper—Jordan Harper was born and educated in Missouri. He currently lives in Brooklyn, and is completing *Poser*, a novel about sex, drugs, murder, and high school.

Vincent Kovar—Vincent Kovar lives in Seattle, where he works as a marketing consultant and as adjunct faculty at the University of Phoenix. He received his Masters in Teaching from Seattle University and a bachelors or two from the University of Washington. His work has appeared in *The Oregon Literary Review, Ellipsis Magazine, Thuglit,* and *The Blithe House Quarterly*.

Hana K. Lee—Hana K. Lee writes short and flash stories of violence and revenge. Her tales have appeared in *Thuglit, Out of the Gutter magazine, DZ Allen's Muzzle Flash, Flashes of Speculation, Hell's Hangmen,* and *Diabolic Tales 1*. She is also a deputy editor for *Out of the Gutter* magazine.

Mike MacLean—Mike MacLean owes Todd Robinson and his thugs a round of beers. Originally published in the third issue of *Thuglit*, "McHenry's Gift" went on to appear in *The Best American Mystery Stories*, alongside tales by Mike's literary heroes, Elmore Leonard and James Lee Burke. From there, it gained the attention of independent film legend Roger Corman whose production company hired Mike to pen a screenplay. A teacher of America's youth, Mike lives in Tempe, Arizona with his wife Bobbie, their daughter Chloe, and three lazy dogs. He holds a black belt in Ja-Shin-Do and watches far too many violent movies. Visit Mike on the web at www.mikemac lean.net.

Donovan Arch Montierth—Donovan Arch Montierth lives next door to his twin brother in Phoenix, Arizona. In his spare time he watches movies back to back to the annoyance of his wife. He has written for several websites such as bookflash.com and nightsandweekends.com. He has also found time to write several full-length screenplays and short scripts. Many of his short scripts have been made into short films and have toured the film festival circuit. "Reveille," which he produced and directed with his brother, starring David Huddleston (*The Big Lebowski* and *Blazing Saddles*), went to twenty film festivals around the country and won ten awards. They are working on producing two feature films this year; a family film based on "Reveille" titled *Capture the Flag* and a thriller called *Suicide Club*. You can view his web site by going to www.brothers ink.com.

Ryan Oakley—Ryan Oakley writes science fiction and ultra-violence. He's been published in all sorts of places that no one has ever heard of, reviews books for *BlogTO* and keeps his own blog at *The Grumpy Owl*. Although he used to wake up to a Gibson and go to bed in strange places like jail, he has quit drinking. Now he attends wine tastings just to spit out mouthfuls of expensive booze, thus showing his utter disdain for the weaklings and cowards at Alcoholics Anonymous.

Vinnie Penn—Vinnie Penn has been a fixture on Connecticut radio for years. He is known for his morning show on KC101 (which began in 1997, alongside CNN's Glenn Beck) and for his guest shots with Howard Stern (Penn made broadcasting history by being on with Stern on September 11). Nowadays Vinnie can be heard on Sirius Satellite's all-comedy *Raw Dog* channel. In addition to his stand-up being in rotation, he is a recurring guest on The Wiseguy Show, which features castmates from *The Sopranos*, and is regularly featured on Getting Late. And, yes, he can still be heard on Howard from time to time. Originally a music journalist, his own column ran for seven years in the *Connecticut Post*. He also "penned" a humor column, which ran for five in the *New Haven Register*. In 2000 he had a joke book published, *The Mother Load* (Great Quotations Publishing), which went on to become one of the publisher's top sellers, and last year he contributed the short story "Diary of a Superhero" to the Contemporary Press anthology *Danger City*. Vinnie's work has appeared in national music magazines such as *Hit Parader* and *Circus*. Most recently, his comedy writing has appeared in the new *Cracked* magazine and *Maxim*. www.vinniepenn.net

Bryon Quertermous—Bryon Quertermous's first play was a shameless rip-off of *The Maltese Falcon* and was produced when he was 19. He's been shortlisted for the Crime Writers Association Debut Dagger and his fiction has appeared in *Shots, Noir Originals, Crimespree, Crime Scene Scotland, Thuglit*, and *Hardluck Stories*, among others. He is the editor and publisher of *Demolition* magazine in a debt of literary karma.

B.H. Shepherd—B.H. Shepherd currently resides in his native Texas, where he is a bartender, bouncer, DJ, and occasionally, a writer. "Sweet Benny and the Sanchez Penitentiary Band" is an excerpt from his novel in progress.

J.D. Smith—J.D. Smith's crime fiction has appeared in *Thuglit, Demolition magazine,* and *Out of the Gutter.* In his non-thug life, his humor has been anthologized in Volumes 5 and 6 of the *Mammoth Book of Best New Erotica.* He was awarded a 2007 Fellowship in Poetry from the National Endowment for the Arts, and his children's book *The Best Mariachi in the World* will be published in 2008. Visit his web site at www.jdsmith writer.com.

Charlie Stella—Charlie Stella is the author of five critically acclaimed crime novels. Tommy Burns, one of the characters in "The Milfinators," has appeared in two other published short stories and Charlie's fourth novel, *Cheapskates.* Charlie's newest novel, *Mafiya,* deals with the Russian mob in New York.

Duane Swierczynski—Duane Swierczynski is the author of *Severance Package* and *The Blonde,* among other crime thrillers. He lives in Philadelphia, which in recent years has become the murder capital of the East Coast. Swierczynski does not take responsibility for this.

Patty Templeton—Patty Templeton enjoys hot tea, mad scientists, and high fives. She has a BA in Fiction Writing from Columbia College Chicago which enables her to work for www.thebookworks.com and also www.darkbutshining.com. Recently, she has quit grad school and now has a plethora of time. Contact her by emailing the quite obvious pattytemple ton@gmail.com.

Mike Toomey—Mike Toomey lives outside Boston with his wife. He thinks this is the Red Sox's year (no matter when you are reading this). He thought his life was more interesting before he wrote this. And he saw a blimp once.

Tim Wohlforth—Tim Wohlforth's story "Jesus Christ is Dead!" made the Distinguished Mystery Stories list in Otto Penzler's *Best American Mystery Stories 2005*. A story of his was chosen for inclusion in the Mystery Writers of America's *Death Do Us Part*, edited by Harlan Coben. Dennis McMillan has published a Crip and Henrietta story as part of his *Plots With Guns* anthology.

He is a 2003 Pushcart Prize Nominee and has received a Certificate of Excellence from the Dana Literary Society. Wohlforth has had seventy-two short stories accepted for publication in print magazines, e-zines, and 12 anthologies.

A contemporary noir novel, *No Time To Mourn*, was published by Quiet Storm. He co-authored the non-fiction book, *On The Edge: Political Cults Right and Left*, published by M.E. Sharpe.

Lee Child has called Wohlforth, "an exciting new voice." www.timwohlforth.com and tim@timwohlforth.com

Frank Zafiro—Frank served in U.S. Army Intelligence as a Czech linguist during the waning moments of the Cold War. From Augsburg, Germany, he watched the Berlin Wall tumble and the Velvet Revolution take place in then-Czechoslovakia. It was a fine time for freedom.

He became a police officer in 1993. This (and his over-active, dark imagination) is what he draws upon when populating the mean streets of River City. His first River City novel, *Under A Raging Moon*, was published in 2006. The second book in the series, *Heroes Often Fail*, was published in September 2007. Dozens of his short stories (most set in River City) have been published in print and online magazines such as *Thuglit*, as well as several anthologies like this one.

Besides writing, Frank enjoys reading, good movies, and hockey—something he both watches and plays. Because he is a goaltender, many people have rightfully questioned his sanity.

As soon as they discover he is also a writer, they become even more suspicious. Once anyone reads his work, that cinches the deal.

You can keep up with the action in River City (including his blog) at: http://frankzafiro.com.

Raise Your Glasses . . .

. . . to our year one editors, John Moore (Johnny Kneecaps), Robert S.P. Lee (Caesar Black), and Allison Glasgow (Lady Detroit). Without their tireless efforts, infinite patience, and impeccable taste, *Thuglit* wouldn't exist.

. . . to the boys of New York's finest crime-fiction writing institution, Write Club—and for asking a little too loudly in an uppity SoHo coffee shop: "Is cheesedick hyphenated?" (I still say no.)

. . . to Adam Chromy of Artists & Artisans and Michaela Hamilton of Kensington Books—the only two industry peeps who had the brass balls to put the work of our amazing writers into book form.

And finally—to all of the aforementioned amazing writers . . .

You are the blood that fills the veins and beats the heart of the beast that is *Thuglit.*

We couldn't put every story in this collection, but I'll be damned if you don't get a mention and our heartfelt thanks for having the guts and faith to send us your words.

Pete Hogenson—Bill Salfelder—Stephen D. Rogers—Anthony Neil Smith—Matt Casey—Greg Lathem—Pat Lamb—Carl Moore—James R. Winter—A. Glenorchy Campbell—James M. McGowan—J. Vandersteen—Nathan Crowder—Mary V. Kolar—

Colin C. Conway—Jason Paltanovich—Eric Boermeester—
Rob Rosen—Jason Gantenberg—Justin Porter—Tony Bur-
ton—D.Z. Allen—Eric M. Witchey—Christopher Freisen—
Max Callahan—Ron Klosterman—Ed Lynskey—Justin Gus-
tainis—Barbara Stanley—Johnny Bassoff—Rodolphe Cuzon—
Alejandro Pena—John Stickney—A.B. Gorrell—Brian W.
Alaspa—Marcus J. Guillory—Hugh Lessig—A.T. Mango—
Richard T. Lynch—Patricia Abbott—Albert Tucher—A.E.
Roman—Keith Gilman—Valerie Maczak—Craig McDonald—
Brad DiPietro—Tim McLean

You all put the bad in badass. As for the ass . . .